W9-AUN-641

PRAISE FOR *SLAYER*

"Will get *Buffy* fans up in their feels . . . A tale solidly set in the world *Buffy* stans love—and filled with all the demons, vampires, and shady folks they love to hate." —*Entertainment Weekly*

"White's new addition to the world of *Buffy the Vampire Slayer* is refreshing and hits the tone of the series at its best. . . . Slay on, Nina. Slay on." —*Culturess*

"Full of great characters, interesting plots, complex dynamics, and stakes about as high as they come." —*Hypable*

★ "Epic . . . Resplendent with quirky, endearing characters and imagination-sparking details, this novel feeds the soul of *Buffy* devotees, keeping the *Buffy* spirit alive." —*Publishers Weekly*, starred review

"White . . . taps into the ethos of the original series, mining its complicated ethics for new veins of moral dilemmas, betrayals, hidden identities, funky demons, and romance. . . . Readers familiar with the Buffyverse will find themselves delighted to be home again." —*BCCB*

"Exciting and well-plotted." —*SLJ*

"Fans of high stakes (apocalypse high), monster madness, and serious girl power will line up for this one." —*Booklist*

Also by
KIERSTEN WHITE

Chosen

SLAYER

KIERSTEN WHITE

SIMON PULSE

NEW YORK   LONDON   TORONTO   SYDNEY   NEW DELHI

This book is a work of fiction. Any references to historical events, real people,
or real places are used fictitiously. Other names, characters, places, and events are
products of the author's imagination, and any resemblance to actual events
or places or persons, living or dead, is entirely coincidental.

SIMON PULSE

An imprint of Simon & Schuster Children's Publishing Division

1230 Avenue of the Americas, New York, New York 10020

First Simon Pulse paperback edition January 2020

Buffy the Vampire Slayer TM & © 2019 by Twentieth Century Fox Film Corporation. All rights reserved.

Text by Kiersten Brazier

Jacket illustration by Talexi

Title logo by Craig Howell

Also available in a Simon Pulse hardcover edition.

All rights reserved, including the right of reproduction in whole or in part in any form.

SIMON PULSE and colophon are registered trademarks of Simon & Schuster, Inc.

For information about special discounts for bulk purchases, please contact

Simon & Schuster Special Sales at 1-866-506-1949 or business@simonandschuster.com.

The Simon & Schuster Speakers Bureau can bring authors to your live event.

For more information or to book an event contact the Simon & Schuster Speakers Bureau

at 1-866-248-3049 or visit our website at www.simonspeakers.com.

Cover designed by Sarah Creech

Interior designed by Mike Rosamilia

The text of this book was set in Perpetua.

Manufactured in the United States of America

2 4 6 8 10 9 7 5 3 1

The Library of Congress has cataloged the hardcover edition as follows:

Names: White, Kiersten, author.

Title: Slayer / by Kiersten White.

Other titles: Buffy the vampire slayer (Television program)

Description: First Simon Pulse hardcover edition. | New York : Simon Pulse, 2019.

Identifiers: LCCN 2018000122 (print) | LCCN 2018009503 (eBook) |

ISBN 9781534404953 (hc) | ISBN 9781534404977 (eBook)

Classification: LCC PZ7.W583764 (eBook) | LCC PZ7.W583764 Sl 2019 (print) |

DDC [Fic]— dc23

LC record available at https://lccn.loc.gov/2018000122

ISBN 9781534404960 (pbk)

To everyone who was never chosen,
but who chooses themselves

They, of all people, should have known better than to be in a cemetery as the sun set and night claimed the world.

The hunter watched the mother, straight as a lightning rod jammed into the earth, channeling her grief into the grave where her heart had been buried. On either side of her stood a little girl in pink cowboy boots. They were both skinny and pale, their red curls now leached of color in the darkness.

Darkness was the great equalizer. Everyone was the same in the dark. Colorless. Featureless.

Powerless.

The hunter would keep them that way. It was her job, after all. She turned to the vampire beside her. They were both invisible in the black recess of a mausoleum. "The woman lives. The children are yours."

Technically only one of the girls needed to die, but it was better to avoid any prophetic loopholes. The vampire strolled out toward the grieving family. He didn't hide or prowl. He didn't need to.

One of the girls tugged frantically on her mother's hand. "Mama. Mama!"

The woman turned wearily, without enough time to be surprised before the vampire threw her. She flew back, hitting her husband's granite headstone and falling unconscious to the soft ground over him. MERRICK JAMISON-SMYTHE: HUSBAND, FATHER, WATCHER loomed above her in classically carved letters. The hunter wished she could take a photo. It was perfect staging.

"Hello, girls." The vampire's glee was audible. The hunter checked her watch. She should have picked a hellhound, or perhaps the Order of Taraka. But they were outside her price range and, frankly, overkill. Two children needed a very minimal amount of kill. And she liked the symmetry of using a vampire.

He held out his arms, as though inviting the children in for an embrace. "You can run if you'd like. I don't mind chasing. Works up an appetite."

The two girls, who the hunter had expected to be screaming by now, looked at each other solemnly. Perhaps standing on the grave of their father, who was dead because of a vampire, they felt the truth: This was always their fate.

One of the girls nodded. The other threw herself at the vampire's legs with such startling speed and fury that the vampire fell backward, tangled up. Before he could kick the girl off, the other one jumped on his chest.

And then the vampire was gone. Both girls stood, brushing dust from their neat black dresses. The second little girl tucked the stake back into her flowery cowboy boot. They hurried over to their mother and patted her cheeks until she stirred.

At least their mother had the sense to be panicked. The hunter sighed, annoyed, as the mother pulled the girls to herself. Now they were all watching the night. Alert. The hunter had hoped to avoid the confrontation of revealing herself, but it had to be done. She pulled out her crossbow.

Her beeper chimed. She looked down at it out of habit, and when she looked back up, the family was gone.

She swore. She should never have used a vampire. That was what she got for trying a bit of poetic tragedy. She had orders to keep their mother alive if possible, and she had wanted their mother to live, alone, *having lost everything to the same pathetic half-breed of monster. Punishment for thinking she could hide from prophecy. Punishment for risking the entire world for her own selfish desires.*

Well. The hunter would find them again. She flipped up her hood and strode to the nearest gas station. A pay phone waited in an anemic pool of light. She picked it up and dialed the number on her beeper.

"Is it done?"

"No," the hunter replied.

"I'm disappointed in you."

"So ground me." She hung up, scowling, and then went inside the gas station. She had failed to avert the apocalypse, for now.

She needed candy.

1

OF ALL THE AWFUL THINGS DEMONS DO,
keeping Latin alive when it deserves to be a dead language might
be the worst.

To say nothing of ancient Sumerian. And ancient Sumerian
translated into Latin? Diabolic. My tongue trips over pronunci-
ation as I painstakingly work through the page in front of me.
I used to love my time in the library, surrounded by the work
of generations of previous Watchers. But ever since the most
recent time the world almost ended—sixty-two days ago, to be
exact—I can barely sit still. I fidget. Tap my pencil. Bounce my
toes against the floor. I want to go for a run. I don't know why
the anxiety has hit me differently this time, after all the horror
and tragedy I've seen before. There *is* one possible reason that
tugs at my brain, but . . .

"That can't be right." I peer at my own writing. "The shad-
owed one will rise and the world will tickle before him?"

"I do hate being tickled," Rhys says, leaning back and
stretching. His curly brown hair has once again defied its strict

part. It flops over his forehead, softening the hard line of his eyebrows, which are perpetually drawn close to his glasses in thought or concern. After we finish this morning's lessons, I'll tidy up my small medical center, and Rhys will train for combat with Artemis.

I shake out my hands, needing to move *something*. Maybe I really will go for a run. No one would miss me. Or maybe I'll ask if I can join combat training. They've never let me, but I haven't asked in years. I really want to hit something, and I don't know why, and it scares me.

It could be the demonic prophecies of doom I've been reading all morning, though. I scratch out my botched translation. "As far as apocalypses go, tickling's not the worst way to die."

Imogen clears her throat, but her indulgent smile softens the severity. "Can we get back to your translation, Nina? And, Rhys, I want a full report on half-human, half-demon taxonomy."

Rhys ducks his head, blushing. He's the only one here who's in line to be a full Watcher, which means he can join the Council one day. Someday he'll be in charge, part of the governing body of the Council. He wears that weight in everything he does. He's the first one in the library and the last one out, and he trains almost as much as Artemis.

Watchers were meant to guide Slayers—the Chosen Ones specially endowed to fight demons—but over the centuries we evolved to be more hands-on. Watchers have to make the hard decisions, and sometimes the hard decisions include weapons. Swords. Spells. Knives.

Guns, in my father's case.

Not all of us train, though. We all take our education seriously, but there's slightly less pressure for me. I'm just the castle medic, which doesn't rate high on the importance scale. Learning how to take lives beats knowing how to save them.

But being the medic doesn't get me out of Prophecies of Doom 101. I push away the Latin Sumerian Tickle Apocalypse. "Imogen," I whine, "can I get something a little less difficult? Please?"

She gives me a long-suffering sigh. Imogen wasn't supposed to be a teacher. But she's all we've got now, on account of the regular teachers being blown up. She teaches for a few hours every morning, and the rest of her time is spent managing the Littles.

Her blond ponytail swings limply as she stands and searches the far bookshelf. I hold back a triumphant smile. Imogen is always nicer to me than to anyone else. Actually, everyone here is. I try not to take advantage, but if they're going to treat me like the castle pet just because I'm not all with the stabby stab, at least I should get some perks.

The shelf Imogen is searching is technically off-limits, but since Buffy—the Slayer who single-handedly destroyed almost our entire organization—broke all magic on earth a couple months ago, it doesn't matter anymore. The books that used to pose threats such as demonic possession or summoning ancient hellgods or giving you, like, a *really* bad paper cut are now as benign as any other book.

But that doesn't make them any easier to translate.

"Magic *is* still broken, right?" I ask as Imogen runs her fingers down the spine of a book that once killed an entire roomful of Watchers in the fifteenth century. It's been two months without a drop of magical energy. For an organization that was built on magic, it hasn't been an easy adjustment. I wasn't taught to use magic, but I have a very healthy respect-for-slash-terror-of it. So it's creepy seeing Imogen treat that particular tome like anything else on the shelf.

"Fresh out of batteries and no one can find the right size." Rhys scowls at his text as though insulted by the demon he's reading about. "When Buffy breaks something, she breaks it good. Personally, I think that if confronted with the Seed of Wonder—the source of all magic on earth, a genuine mystical miracle—I might opt to, say, study it. Research. Really think through my options. There had to be another way to avert that particular apocalypse."

"Buffy sees, Buffy destroys," I mutter. Her name feels almost like a swear word on my tongue. We don't say it aloud in my family. Then again, we don't say much in my family at all, besides "Have you seen my best dagger?" and "Where are our stake-carving supplies?" and "Hello, my twin daughters, it is I, your mother, and I love one of you better than the other and chose to save the good twin first when a fire was about to kill you both."

Okay, not that last one. Because again: We don't talk much. Living under the same roof isn't as cozy as it sounds when that roof covers a massive castle.

"Think of all we could have learned," Rhys says mournfully, "if I had had even an hour with the Seed of Wonder. . . ."

"In her defense, the world was ending," Imogen says.

"In her not defense, she was the reason the world was ending," I counter. "And now magic is dead."

Imogen shrugs. "No more hellmouths or portals. No more demons popping in for vacations and sightseeing."

I snort. "Foodie tours of Planet Human are canceled. Sorry, demonic dimensions. Of course, it also means no current tourists can get back to their home-sweet-hellholes."

Rhys scowls, pulling off his glasses and polishing them. "You're joking about the disruption and destruction of all the research we've compiled on demonic traveling, portals, dimensions, gateways, and hellmouths. None of it is current anymore. Even if I wanted to understand how things have changed, I couldn't."

"See? Buffy hurts everyone. Poor Rhys. No books on this subject." I pat his head.

Imogen tosses a huge volume on the table. "And yet your homework still isn't done. Try this one." A poof of dust blows outward from the book; I flinch away and cover my nose.

She grimaces. "Sorry."

"No, it's fine. I actually haven't had an asthma attack in a while." It's fine that my asthma mysteriously disappeared the same day Buffy destroyed magic, the world almost ended, and I got showered in interdimensional demonic goo. Totally fine. Has nothing to do with the demon. Neither does the fact that I'm desperate to go running or start training or do anything with my body besides snuggle up and read, which used to be its primary occupation.

I pull down my sweater sleeve over my hand and carefully wipe the leather cover. "'The Apocalypses of . . . Arcturius the Farsighted'? Sounds like the dude just needed a better prescription for glasses."

Rhys leans close, peering curiously. "I haven't read that volume." He sounds jealous.

Notes have been scrawled in the margins, the handwriting changing as it moves through the centuries. On the last few pages there are orange fingerprints, like someone was reading while eating Cheetos. The Watchers before me have made their own notes, commenting and filling in details. Seeing their work overwhelms me with a sense of responsibility. It's not every sixteen-year-old girl who can trace her family's calling back through the centuries of helping Slayers, fighting demons, and otherwise saving the world.

I find a good entry. "Did you know that in 1910, one of the Merryweathers prevented an octopus uprising? A leviathan demon gave them sentience and they were going to overthrow us! Merryweather doesn't give many details. It appears they defeated them with . . ." I squint. "Lemon. And butter. I think this is a recipe."

Imogen taps on the book. "Just translate the last ten prophecies, how about?"

I get to work. Rhys occasionally asks Imogen questions, and by the time our class period is almost over, he has what looks like half the extensive shelves piled on our groaning table. In years past, Rhys and I wouldn't have studied together. He'd have been in classes with the other future Council hopefuls. But there are so few of us now, we've had to relax some of the structure and tradition. Not all of it, though. Without tradition, what would we be? Just a bunch of weirdos hiding in a castle studying the things that no one else wants to know about. Which I guess is what we are *with* tradition too. But knowing I'm part of a millennia-long battle against the forces of evil (and apparently octopuses) makes it much more meaningful.

Buffy and the Slayers might have turned their backs on the Watchers, rejecting our guidance and counsel, but we haven't turned our backs on the world. Normal people can go on living, oblivious and happy, because of *our* hard work. And I'm proud of that. Even when it means I have to translate dumb prophecies, and even if I've wondered more and more the last few years if the *way* the Watchers and Slayers fight evil isn't always right.

The library door slams open and my twin sister, Artemis, walks in. She takes a deep breath and scowls, crossing past me and tugging open the ancient window. It groans in protest, but, as with all things, Artemis accomplishes her goal. She pulls out one of my inhalers from her pocket and sets it on the table beside me. Everything in this castle runs because of Artemis. She is a force of nature. An angry but efficient force of nature.

"Hello to you, too," I say with a smile.

She tugs my hair. We both have red waves, though hers are always pulled back into a brutal ponytail. I have a lot more time for moisturizing than she does. Her face is like looking in a mirror—if that mirror were a prophecy of who I'd be in another life. Her freckles are darker from spending so much time outside. Her gray eyes more intense, her jawline somehow stronger. Her shoulders are straighter, her arms are more defined, and her posture is less snuggly and more I-will-destroy-you-if-it-comes-to-that.

In short, Artemis is the strong twin. The powerful twin. The chosen twin. And I am . . .

The one who got left behind.

I don't just mean the fire, either. The moment when my mother was forced to choose to save one of us from the terrifying flames—and chose Artemis—was definitely life changing. But even after that, even after I managed to survive, my mother kept choosing her. Artemis was chosen for testing and training. Artemis was given responsibilities and duties and a vital role in Watcher society. And I was left behind on the fringes. I only sort of matter now because so many of us are dead. Artemis always would have mattered. And the truth is, I get it.

I was born into Watcher society, but Artemis *deserves* to be here.

She sits next to me, pulling out her notebook and opening it to today's to-do list. It's in microscopic handwriting and goes past the first page and onto at least one more. No one in this castle does more than Artemis. "Listen," she says, "I might have hurt Jade."

I look up from where I'm almost finished with this book. Every other prophecy had margin notes detailing how that particular apocalypse was averted. I idly wonder what it means that this is the last prophecy. Did Arcturius the Farsighted finally get glasses, or was this apocalypse so apocalypse-y that he couldn't see past it? It also has no Watcher notes. And Watchers are meticulous. If it doesn't have notes, that means it hasn't been averted yet.

But my own castle emergencies are far more pressing. "And by 'might have hurt Jade,' you mean . . ."

Artemis shrugs. "Definitely did."

On cue, Jade limps in. She picks up her tirade midargument. "—and just because magic is broken, doesn't mean that I should be Artemis's punching bag! I know my father worked in special ops, but I don't want to. I was good at magic! I am not good at this!"

"No one is, next to Artemis," Rhys says. His voice is quiet and without judgment, but we all freeze. It's one of the things we don't talk about. How Artemis is inarguably the best, and yet she's the assistant and Rhys is the official golden boy.

Watchers excel at research, record keeping, and not talking about things. The entire organization is ever-so-British. Though technically Artemis and I are American. We lived in California and then Arizona before coming here. Rhys, Jade, and Imogen— who all grew up in London—still laugh when I treat rain like a novelty. It's been eight years in England and Ireland, but I *adore* rain and green and all things nondesert.

Jade flops down on the other side of me, hauling her ankle up onto my lap. I rotate it for range of movement.

"That one translates as 'Slayer,'" Artemis says, peering over my shoulder. She crosses out where I had mistranslated a word as "killer." Same difference.

Jade yelps. "Ouch!"

"Sorry. Nothing is broken, but it's swelling already. I think it's a mild sprain." I glance at Artemis and she looks away, guessing my thoughts as she so often can. She knows I'm going to tell her there is no reason to train this hard. To hurt each other. Instead of rehashing our usual debate, I point to my translation. "What about this word?"

"Protector," Artemis says.

"That's cheating," Imogen trills from where she's reshelving. "It doesn't count as cheating. We're practically the same person!" No one calls me on the lie. Artemis shouldn't have to do my homework on top of everything else, but she helps without being asked. It's how we work.

"Any word from Mom?" I ask as casually as I can manage, probing around the topic even more gently than I'm probing Jade's ankle.

"Nothing new since Tuesday. She should finish up South America in the next few days, though." Artemis planned our mother's whole scouting mission. I haven't heard so much as a word from her since she left seven weeks ago, but Artemis merits regular updates.

"Can you focus?" Jade snaps. She was on assignment in Scotland keeping tabs on Buffy and her Slayer army antics. It didn't do us much good. Buffy still managed to trigger an almost-apocalypse. Now that Jade's back at the castle without any magic, she's not happy about it, and she lets us know.

Frequently.

"Rhys," I say, mindful that Artemis would do it in a heartbeat, but her to-do list is already super full and I don't want to add to it, "can you go to my clinic and get my sprain pack?"

Rhys stands. He shouldn't have to run my errands. He ranks far above me in pecking order, but he puts friendship before hierarchy. He's my favorite in the castle besides Artemis. Not that there's a tremendous amount of competition. Rhys, Jade, and Artemis are the only other teens. Imogen is in her early twenties. The three Littles are still preschoolers. And the Council—all four of them—aren't exactly BFF material. "Where is it?" he asks.

"It's right next to the stitches pack, behind the concussions pack."

"I'll be right back."

He saunters away. The medical clinic is actually a large supply closet in the opposite wing that I've claimed as my own. The training room is amazing, naturally. We prioritize hitting, not healing. While we're waiting for Rhys, I elevate Jade's ankle by propping it on top of books that used to contain the blackest spells imaginable but now are used as paperweights.

George Smythe, the youngest of the Littles, bursts into the library. He buries his face in Imogen's skirt and tugs on her long sleeves. "Imo. Come play."

Imogen puts him on her hip. During teaching hours, Ruth Zabuto is in charge of the Littles, but she is as old as sin and far less pleasant. I don't blame George for preferring Imogen.

"Are you done?" she asks me.

I hold up my paper triumphantly. "Got it!"

Child of Slayer
Child of Watcher
The two become one
The one becomes two
Girls of fire
Protector and Hunter
One to mend the world
And one to tear it asunder

"There's a postscript, like Arcturius can't help but comment on his own creepy-ass prophecy. 'When all else ends, when hope perishes alongside wonder, her darkness shall rise and all shall be eaten.'"

Imogen snorts. "Devoured. Not eaten."

"In my defense, I'm hungry. Did I get the rest?"

She nods. "With help."

"Well, even with Artemis's help, it doesn't make sense. And it doesn't have any calamari recipes." I tuck my papers back into the book.

Rhys returns with the supplies just as the other two Littles break into the library and swarm Imogen. She's the busiest person in the castle, other than Artemis, who has already left to prepare lunch for everyone. Sometimes I wish my sister belonged as much to me as she does to everyone else.

Rhys strides toward me with the sprain pack. Little George runs at his legs, and Rhys trips just before he gets to me. The pack flies out of his hands. Without thinking I lunge and save the kit in midair with one hand, the whole motion feeling surprisingly effortless for my usually uncoordinated self.

"Good catch," Rhys says. I'd be offended by his surprise if I weren't experiencing another ripple of anxiety. It *was* a good catch. Way too good for me.

"Yeah, lucky," I say, letting out an awkward laugh. I break the ice pack and wrap it into place around Jade's ankle. "Twenty minutes on, an hour off. I'll rewrap you when the ice comes off. That will help with the swelling. And rest it as much as possible."

"Not a problem." Jade leans back with her eyes closed. She's substituted all the time she used to spend on magic with sleeping.

I know it's been rough on her—it's been rough on everyone, having the entire world change yet again. But we do what Watchers do: We keep going.

My phone beeps. We avoid contact with the outside world.

Paranoia is a permanent result of having all your friends and family blown up. But one person has this number and he's the highlight of our tenure here in the forest outside a sleepy Irish coastal town. "Cillian's almost here with the supplies."

Rhys perks up. "Do you need help?"

"Yes. I don't know how I'd manage without you. It's absolutely essential that you come out with me and flirt with your boyfriend while I check over the boxes."

The great hall of the castle, always chilly, is lit with the late-afternoon sun. The stained-glass windows project squares of blue, red, and green. I fondly pat the massive oak door as I step out into the crisp autumn air. The castle is drafty, with questionable plumbing and dire electrical problems. Most of the windows don't open, and those that do leak. Half of the rooms are in disrepair, the entire dorm wing is more a repository for junk than a living space, and we can't even go in the section where the tower used to be because it isn't safe.

But this castle saved our lives and preserved what few of us are left. And so I love it.

Out in the meadow—which has finally recovered from having a castle magically dropped into the middle of it two years ago—old Bradford Smythe, my great-uncle, is sword fighting with horrible Wanda Wyndam-Pryce. Though sword *bickering* would be more accurate, since they pause between each block and strike to debate proper stance. The mystery of the Littles escaping is solved. Ruth Zabuto is dead asleep.

I watch her across the meadow to make sure her chest is moving and she's only dead asleep, not *dead* dead. She lets out a snore loud enough for me to hear from this distance. Reassured, I

follow Rhys to the path outside the castle grounds. I can still hear
Wanda and Bradford arguing.

Cillian is on a scooter, boxes strapped to either side. He lifts
a hand and waves brightly. His mom used to run the sole magic
store in the whole area. Most people have no idea that magic
is—was—a real thing. But his mom was a decently talented and
knowledgeable witch. And, best of all, one who could keep her
mouth shut. Cillian and his mother are the only people alive who
know there are still Watchers in existence. That we didn't all die
when we were supposed to.

We haven't told them much about who we are or what we do.
It's safest that way. And they've never asked questions, because
we were also their best customers until Buffy killed magic. But
even now, Cillian still makes all our nonmagical supply deliver-
ies. Weirdly, online retailers don't accept "Hidden Castle in the
Middle of the Woods Outside Shancoom, Ireland" as a proper
address.

Cillian stops his scooter in front of us. "What's the story?"

"I—"

There's a flash of movement behind Cillian. A snarl rips apart
the air as darkness leaps toward him.

My brain turns off.

My body reacts.

I jump, meeting it midair. We slam into each other. The
ground meets us, hard, and we roll. I grab jaws straining for my
throat, hot saliva burning where it falls on me.

Then I twist and snap, and the thing falls silent, still, a dead
weight on top of me.

I shove it aside and scramble to my feet. My heart is racing, eyes scanning for any other threats, legs ready to leap back into action.

That's when I hear the screaming. It sounds so far away. Maybe it was happening the whole time? I shake my head, trying to force the world back into focus. And I realize there's a creature—a dead creature, a creature I somehow killed—at my feet. I stagger backward, using my shirt to rub away the hot sticky mess of its drool still on my neck.

"Artemis!" Bradford Smythe runs up. "Artemis, are you all right?" He hurries past me, bending down to examine the thing. It looks like hell's version of a dog, which is accurate, because I'm almost certain it's a hellhound. Black, mottled skin. Patchy fur more like moldy growths. Fangs and claws and single-minded, deadly intentions.

But not anymore. Because I killed it.

I *killed* it?

Demon, a voice in my head whispers. And it's not talking about the hellhound.

"Nina," Rhys says, in as much shock as me.

Bradford Smythe looks up in confusion. "What?"

"Not Artemis. That was Nina. . . . Nina killed it."

Everyone stares at me like I, too, have sprouted fangs and claws. I don't know what just happened. How it happened. Why it happened. I've never done anything like that before.

I feel sick and also—elated? That can't be right. My hands are trembling, but I don't feel like I need to lie down. I feel like I could run ten miles. Like I could jump straight over the castle. Like I could fight a hundred more—

"I think I need to throw up," I say, blinking at the dead thing.

I'm not a killer. I'm a healer. I fix things. That's what I do.

"That was impossible." Rhys studies me like I'm one of his textbooks, like he can't translate what he's seeing.

He's right. I can't do what I just did.

Bradford Smythe seems less surprised. His shoulders slump as he pulls off his glasses and polishes them with resignation. Why isn't he shocked, now that he knows it wasn't Artemis? The look he gives me is one of pity and regret. "We need to call your mother."

2

"HOW COULD THERE BE A HELLHOUND in Shancoom?" Wanda Wyndam-Pryce's tone, along with her pinched and furious expression, seems to indicate that it was my fault. Like I signed up to provide doggy day care and accidentally checked the "Unholy Hellbeast" column.

I can't stop staring at it, there, on the ground, dead.

Dead.

How did I do that?

Bradford Smythe smooths his walrus mustache. "It is troubling. Shancoom has always had natural mystical protections. It's part of why we picked this location."

"No mystical protection left." Ruth Zabuto retreats further into her cocoon of scarves and shawls. "Can't you feel it? Everything is gone. Only evil is left."

"What are you all doing?" Artemis demands, hurrying up to us. She takes in the hellhound and, before we can explain, throws herself between me and the dead demon. Her first instinct is always to protect me. "Lockdown! Everyone into the castle. Go!"

Rhys startles, and the older Watchers—three-fourths of what's left of the once illustrious and powerful Council—have the sense to look scared. If there's one threat, there might be more. They should have known that. Artemis didn't have to think about it. Rhys grabs Cillian and pulls him along.

Cillian frowns. "The castle's off-limits to me, innit? What was that thing?"

"Go!" Artemis jogs backward, scanning the trees for more threats. Sticking close to me. She's the one with training. The one who can handle this sort of thing.

Crack went its neck.

I hurry along the path to the castle doors. I should be terrified that there are more of those things out there, but it doesn't *feel* like there are. Which worries me. How would I know that?

Once we're inside, Artemis bars the door, barking out orders. "Jade and Imogen will guard the Littles in the dorm wing. Bradford, go tell them. Rhys, take Cillian and Nina. Barricade yourselves in the library. There's a secret room behind the far shelf with a window for escape if we lose the castle."

"There's a secret room?" I ask, at the same time Rhys says, with genuine hurt, "There are more books I didn't know about?"

Cillian steps toward the door. "Barricade? Losing the castle? Bloody hell, what is this?"

Artemis holds up an arm to block his way out. It's not lost on me that Rhys was assigned to protect Cillian, the innocent civilian, *and* me. She has no idea I killed the hellhound myself, and I don't know how to tell her. It feels like it happened to someone else. I'm . . . embarrassed. And terrified. Because if it felt like something else took over, that means all the weirdness in my body I've been ignoring the last couple months is definitely, super, for-sure real.

Artemis opens a dusty old chest beside the door and passes out weapons. Wanda Wyndam-Pryce recoils from a large crossbow. Artemis glares up at her. "Would you prefer a wooden switch?"

"Watch your tone," Wanda snaps. I don't understand the exchange, but Wanda takes the crossbow and hurries away. Rhys gets a sword. Bradford Smythe takes another crossbow. Ancient Ruth Zabuto pulls a wicked-looking knife from a sheath on her thigh beneath her swirling, layered skirts.

"What about—" I start.

"Library!" Artemis barks. "Now!"

Bradford Smythe shoots me a heavy, mournful look. He seems like he has something to say. I half expect him to pull a hard candy out of his suit pocket and give it to me with a pat on the head. That's about the extent of our interactions over the last several years. There's never any reason for the Council to talk to me. After all, my mom is on the Council, and she never needs me. Why should any of the rest of them?

Rhys grabs Cillian's hand to tug him along, and I run after them to the library. Jade is gone, hopefully back to her room, where Bradford Smythe can find her easily. Rhys locates a lever on the far shelf and it swings open to reveal a cramped, dusty room. We shut ourselves in.

"Explanations," Cillian says, panting. "What was that thing? And why are we locked inside the castle? And am I finally allowed to ask how the hell you lot moved a castle here in the first place? Because I have been working mightily to pretend otherwise, but

I've lived in Shancoom my entire life, and I'm certain if we had always had a castle in the forest, I would have known about it. And, Nina, what—what—*how* did you do that out there?"

His gaze on me is searching and incredulous. We've been friends since before he and Rhys started dating. He's more freaked out about what I *did* to the hellhound than the fact that there was a hellhound. I stare at the well-worn floor planks, polished by generations of my people walking here, learning here, planning here. Resting here.

The castle was never our main headquarters. It used to be a retreat for Watchers. But two years ago, way before the Seed of Wonder fiasco, the old Council and nearly every member of the Watcher society got blown up by fanatic followers of an ancient entity known as the First Evil. And it all happened because Buffy threw the balance of good and evil so out of whack that it left an opening for the First to wriggle through.

The First sent out its acolytes to murder everyone who could fight it. That meant all the potential future Slayers it could find—girls who were born with the possibility to someday take up the mantle of Slayer when the previous one died. It also meant all the Watchers. Even after Buffy rejected us, the First knew we were a threat. Buffy ended up defeating it and saving the world.

But she didn't save a single Watcher.

Those of us who survived were either out on assignment in deep cover—only Bradford Smythe and Wanda Wyndam-Pryce's daughter, Honora—or here on a field trip. Rhys Zabuto, Jade Weatherby, Artemis, Imogen Post, the Littles, and myself. My mother, Ruth Zabuto, and Wanda Wyndam-Pryce brought us to see what we could look forward to someday, to get some fresh air, and to undergo a few ritual cleansings to prepare for magical training.

I wasn't going to do those. No magical training for me, just like no physical training. I was supposed to watch the Littles while Imogen went through it. Back in those days she took care of them part-time. They wouldn't let Imogen train to be a full Watcher, because her mother, Gwendolyn Post, had betrayed the Watchers and tricked the Slayers into giving her a weapon of unimaginable power. It had always nagged at me that Imogen was held accountable for something she hadn't even done. We were here because of our parents, sure, but that didn't mean we *were* them—or even who they wanted us to be. I knew that better than anyone.

But Ruth bent the rules for Imogen because she wanted everyone who could to have basic spell training, and the best place for it was our seat of ancient power. So our heritage saved our lives. The castle protected us from being blown up along with the rest of our people.

"We should be out there with them." I place my hand against the shelf sealing us in. I don't say what I really mean, which is that *Rhys* should be out there with them. He's the one who got picked to train as a future Council member. But we both know why Artemis is running the defense and Rhys is hiding here with us.

First, Artemis is more skilled than he is. She always has been.

And second, Artemis put Rhys in here to protect me. Bradford Smythe had called me Artemis out there. He assumed that I was her. Because *I* couldn't do something like I did. It's impossible. I've never trained, never fought.

Never been allowed to and never wanted to.

Rhys stares at me as if I were a stranger. "The way you moved out there. What you did. You looked like a . . ."

Cillian interrupts us. "Again, what the hell? Would someone please explain this to me? What was that thing out there?"

I lean against the shelves, grateful to have to explain things to Cillian so I don't have to think too hard about what I did. What Rhys might have been about to say. "It was a demon."

"A what now?" Cillian rubs his hair, buzzed close to the scalp. His mother is British-Nigerian, and his father grew up in Shancoom. Cillian is the first person since Leo Silvera I've had a crush on, and it lasted all of three minutes before I realized he was not and could never be into me. Lucky Rhys.

But still better than my last crush, which ended in such a humiliating disaster that I haven't managed to work up another viable candidate in the last three years. Maybe in another three years I'll finally get over my Leo Silvera mortification.

But I doubt it. Of all the trauma in my life—and I've had plenty—hearing my lovesick poetry read aloud to my crush remains among the worst. Gods, the *least* Honora Wyndam-Pryce could have done was also kill me on the spot. But she has zero capacity for mercy.

No one knows if Leo Silvera and his mother are still alive, as they haven't been heard from in years. In Watcher society, that means they're more than likely dead. The Giles line is gone now, along with most of the Zabuto, Crowley, Travers, Sirk, and Post. Causes of death, respectively: neck broken by former ally, demon, demon, exploded, exploded, and arm-cut-off-while-being-struck-by-lightning. That last one was Imogen's mom. Poor Imogen. I'm glad she's here to give me perspective. My mom actually *could* be worse.

Regardless, there are so few of us left. I hope that, somewhere out there, the Silveras are still alive.

Just as fervently as I hope I never have to see them again.

I don't know why all this terror has made me think of Leo. Wait. No. It makes perfect sense that heightened, terrible emotions trigger my memories of him.

"A demon," I repeat, trying to refocus. "There are a lot of different types. Some of them are transplants from hell dimensions. Some of them are part demon, part human. True demons don't usually exist on this plane, but sometimes they can infect people. Like vampires."

"Vampires?" Cillian squeaks as he turns to Rhys. "Those are real. Vampires are real. I thought——I knew about magic, obviously, but I thought you were just some divvy cult. You never mentioned *vampires*. That seems like pretty critical information you could have given me sometime in the year we've been dating. 'Hey, Cillian, you've got nice lips and also did you know there are demons and vampires in the world?'"

Rhys barricades the bookshelf door with a table. He looks mildly abashed. "I didn't want to talk business with you. I like that you aren't part of this. And I kind of assumed you knew, what with your mother being a witch and all."

"That was crystals and chanting and shite! Some light levitation! None of this. Exactly how many demons are there in the world?"

"Too many to count? Thousands. Maybe tens of thousands. And it depends on how you classify them."

Cillian leans back so abruptly in his chair he tips over, landing roughly on the ground. "Tens of thousands? Why isn't the government doing anything about it?"

"Which government?"

"Ours! Nina's! Anyone's! Surely someone is taking initiative."

"Sometimes they do. But demons are good at being secret." I move to tug on my hair but freeze. I grabbed a hellhound's jaws with these hands, snapped its life away. Shuddering, I tuck them into my pockets and let Rhys fill in the rest. Demons have been around forever. Portals, hellmouths, and magic allow them to hop in for visits from their dimensions. Hard to track. Hard to fight.

"That's where we come in," Rhys says. "Our group has been working since the darkest of dark ages to help protect humanity. We know all the prophecies, the demons, the looming apocalypses. But even from the start, we couldn't do it alone. We— they—imbued a girl with demonic powers so she'd become the Slayer and hunt demons."

Cillian raises an eyebrow. "So these ancient blokes thought, hey, let's pick just *one* girl to keep humanity safe? What kind of stook plan was that?"

"Those are our ancient ancestors you're criticizing," Rhys says, mildly hurt.

But I've gotta admit, I'm with Cillian on this one. Except that's why there were Watchers, too. We didn't give Slayers that responsibility and then abandon them.

They abandoned *us*. Buffy led the charge, as always. She was the first Slayer in our entire history who rejected our guidance. Our knowledge. Our help. Like we were holding her back instead of supporting her.

My head is spinning. I keep feeling the crack of the neck. "But then Buffy, the most recent Slayer—"

Rhys interrupts me. "The most recent-ish. All Slayers started out as Potentials. When the current Slayer died, the next one was called. So there was only ever one. Most Potentials never became Slayers. Anyway, Buffy died once—"

"Twice," I correct.

"Irrelevant to the current explanation," Rhys huffs. "She died, so another Slayer, Kendra, was called, but then Buffy was resuscitated, so there were two Slayers, but then Kendra died, and the Slayer after her was—"

"Give me the Wikipedia version, for God's sake," Cillian says.

While Rhys tells the story, I climb up on a chair in front of the high window and peer out at the trees. I don't want to listen to what Rhys is saying. I already know it. Two years ago when Buffy was fighting the First Evil, she was going to lose. So she did what she always does: She broke something. This time it was the binding of the Slayer power. The rules that had been in place, that had worked since the beginning of time, were eliminated.

Suddenly every girl with the potential to become a Slayer *did* become a Slayer, or would become a Slayer when she was old enough.

She let the Watchers die, and then she flooded the earth with almost two thousand new Slayers. And then she got around a thousand of them killed in battle, because of course she did. There's a reason there was only supposed to be one Slayer and a whole organization of Watchers. And having all those new Slayers didn't tip the balance in favor of good. It did the opposite. Demons content to slurk through the night, doing their demon-y things? Suddenly felt threatened. The more Buffy pushes, the more the darkness pushes back. And it pushed back so hard, the world almost ended.

I give up on the window. There's nothing out there. I don't know how I know, but I do. And I feel sick with dread at what all these new abilities and senses might mean. For sixty-freaking-two days I've been able to ignore them. But I can't anymore.

Rhys has caught up to Buffy's most recent terrible exploits in his explanation. "Do you remember a couple months back when the world almost ended?"

"The world almost *ended*?" Cillian asks, aghast.

"Oh, right." Rhys rubs his forehead. Maybe this is the real reason we don't talk about this stuff to anyone who isn't a Watcher. It's *complicated*. "The world almost ended because another dimension was taking over ours."

"Sixty-two days ago," I whisper. And we had to sit here in our castle, watching it unfold, because if we revealed ourselves, odds were we'd die in the crossfire. I hated it. Artemis about went mad. But what bothers me the most is, even without our help, it worked out. Sort of. "In order to prevent the end of the world, Buffy destroyed the Seed of Wonder that fed all magic on earth."

Cillian whistles low and soft. "I thought it was just . . . one of those things. Like we lost the magic Wi-Fi signal or something."

"Didn't you notice that day the sky burst open and there were earthquakes and tsunamis and stuff?" I ask.

He shrugs. "Global warming."

Rhys has gotten lost in the spines on the bookshelves. It's hard for him to focus, looking at all these books he didn't know we had. So I continue. "Right. Global warming, and also transdimensional global threat. And all of this—the broken magic, the new Slayers, the almost end of the world—it's all because of Buffy."

Cillian snorts. "Sorry, I just. I can't get over her name. *Buffy*."

I fold my arms, glaring. "What, she has a girly name, so she can't destroy the world?"

Cillian holds up his hands defensively. "That's not what I'm saying."

"She was a cheerleader before she became a Slayer," Rhys says.

Cillian bursts out laughing.

I don't want to defend Buffy—ever—but I'm annoyed anyway. "Have you seen a cheerleading competition? Each and every one of those girls could take you, even without mystical Slayer powers."

"Is that how you killed the demon thingy out there, then? You've trained as a cheerleader?"

I feel the crack all over again. "That's not the point. I don't even like Buffy. All she ever does is react. She never thinks through the consequences, and my family keeps paying the price." I take a deep breath to steady myself. "And the whole world too. Because this last time, she also broke it. No more magic. No more connections to other worlds. And no more new Slayers. Ever. She blew the door wide open, and then she slammed it shut."

"She needs to make up her mind," Cillian says. "Make more Slayers! End the Slayers. Break the world! Save the world."

Rhys takes over my chair at the high window, looking out. "To be fair, a lot of people have tried to destroy the world over the years. It's a whole thing."

"Huh. Who knew?"

"We did," Rhys says.

"Fair enough." Cillian grabs my hand and makes me sit next to him. "So, what's your story, Nina? This Buffy. It's personal, innit?"

I close my eyes, words that have been drilled into my brain since birth swimming into focus. *Into every generation a Slayer is born: one girl in all the world, a Chosen One. She alone will wield the strength and skill to fight the vampires, demons, and forces of darkness; to stop the spread of their evil and the swell of their number. She is the Slayer.*

There's a painful lump in my throat when I speak. "Every Slayer used to get a Watcher. And Buffy got the best." I open my eyes and smile. "My dad was her first Watcher."

When Merrick Jamison-Smythe found her, she had no idea who she was or what was coming for her. My dad had worked his whole life training Slayers, teaching them, helping them. And he watched those he trained before her die. So when faced with a choice between allowing himself to be used against Buffy or dying, he chose the Chosen One.

He saved her. And we lost him. Rupert Giles took over, becoming the Watcher everyone remembers. Their relationship—his indulgent refusal to follow rules or establish needed structure, his rejection of his own heritage—was the beginning of the end of everything. And still when anyone thinks of Buffy's Watcher, they think of Giles. Not my father.

"So who is your Slayer now?" Cillian asks, deftly changing the subject. But he puts his hand on my shoulder, a light, reassuring pressure. He understands dead dads.

"We don't have one." Rhys climbs down from the chair at the window.

"Shouldn't you have, like, a bunch, since there are so many?"

"After most of us got—" Rhys pauses. *Blown up*, I think. He chooses the more tactful "With so few of us left, we've been trying to determine our best course of action."

We don't know how Slayers would react to being contacted by us. How Buffy would react if she found out there was still an active group of Watchers. I honestly don't know if we'll ever fix the rift Buffy created between Slayers and Watchers. But in the meantime. . . . "Trying to determine our best course of action" feels like Watcherspeak for hiding. Doing nothing. I get that it was in our best interests to lie low and pretend the Watchers Council was gone for good. Disbanding for real was never a question. We are still Watchers—protectors—no matter what. But now that the world is filled with Slayers (Buffy's fault), magic is dead (Buffy's fault), and all the interdimensional portals are dead (Buffy's fault), things have changed yet again. That's what my mom is out there doing. Making sure we understand how everything has changed, what the new threats are.

I'm not sure what the Council's long-term plan is after my mom's scouting work is finished. Still, if we don't check that every hellmouth and portal is *actually* closed, who will?

That's why it's so important that the Watchers remain. In a world remade again and again, where the rules keep changing, where a Chosen One becomes Chosen Many, where magic disappears, where the old ways are broken, we are the one constant.

We still keep watch.

It's not enough, though. The Council hasn't been able to decide what to do. Because there are so few of us now and so many of them. How do we pick one Slayer with so many options?

And how do we risk our own lives, knowing what Slayers inevitably bring? Their gift is *death*.

And that's my struggle, the truth of my life among the Watchers, growing up and aiding a society that exists because of Slayers: I hate them. What they are, what they do.

And I hate none of them as much as I hate Buffy.

3

"ALL CLEAR," JADE SHOUTS FROM THE other side of the bookshelves. "And they've called a meeting." When we open the hidden door, she's waiting there, cringing in pain. Her ice pack is gone, her ankle poorly wrapped.

I kneel to fix it. The meeting will be Rhys, Bradford Smythe, Ruth Zabuto, and Wanda Wyndam-Pryce. Artemis will be there to take notes. And my mom would be there, if she were here, which I'm glad she's not. As castle medic, I don't merit a spot. Usually this bugs me—one more way in which healing isn't valued. Today I'm relieved.

"I'll walk Cillian back to his scooter when I'm done with your ankle," I say nonchalantly, hoping that with all the chaos, no one will ask me questions. Hoping they'll be so focused on the hellhound they'll conveniently overlook the fact that I was the one who killed it. They've ignored me for years. Surely they can keep doing it.

"Cillian can wait." Jade pops her gum, brushing her choppy brown hair from her eyes. "You gotta go. They're holding the meeting about *you*."

Fear twists me in its grip. I *can't* go to that meeting. I've known something was wrong with me for two months. Now everyone else knows it too. And Watchers don't exactly have a good track record of being gentle with demons or those corrupted by them.

"That's okay," I blurt, fastening the sprain wrap and then hurrying past her. "I don't need to go."

We may have gotten the all clear, but I feel pursued. I hurry toward my bedroom. Those of us who are not on the Council share the dormitory wing of the castle. Once, these rooms were packed with young Watchers-in-training, competing and studying and vying to be given the ultimate calling: a seat on the Council.

Most of the Council had some experience working with Slayers, though their knowledge tended to be more academic than practical. With one Slayer and a full Council, most Watchers never worked directly with the Chosen One. Watchers who were actually assigned Slayers had . . . reputations. For being too close to the darkness. For lacking the level of professional detachment and farsightedness required to make difficult decisions. That's why my father and mother were such a good team. He was on the ground; she was up next for the Council.

Still, there were so many Council hopefuls who tested high enough that people like me—people who would never be an active Watcher or qualify for the Council—wouldn't have been allowed in the dorms. Legacy Watcher family members like Jade, Imogen, and me would have been shuffled to soulless office buildings to do accounting, far-flung outposts to study magic, or, if we were lucky, assigned as support staff for the Council or special ops. We were never destined for this castle. Then Buffy took destiny and pummeled it to bloody, broken pieces. And here we are.

Dorm rooms for younger trainees were once lined with bunk beds. We cleared all those out two years ago, quietly and without ceremony. Now the Littles are bunked together with Imogen in a suite. The rest of us have our own rooms, except for Artemis and me. Not because there isn't space—if there's anything in the Watcher ranks now, it's space—but because Artemis didn't want to be far from me, even while sleeping.

I *hate* sleeping.

Every night in my dreams, I'd be left behind in the flames. And it was Artemis who woke me up from the nightmares. Though lately I've been having a hard time falling asleep. As soon as the world darkens, my body begins buzzing with adrenaline and nerves. And when I do sleep, my dreams are not so often about being left behind. Usually they're not about me at all.

I've been hiding in our room for only a few minutes before Artemis finds me. She slips in and hugs me so fiercely I can feel her trembling. It stuns me. We haven't hugged in years. She shows her love for me in the most Artemis ways possible. Monitoring my diet to be certain I'm getting the correct nutrition. Making sure my inhalers are always filled. Sleeping close in case I need help.

Physically affectionate Artemis makes alarm bells go off. If she's hugging me, I'm right. Something is seriously wrong.

"I had no idea what actually happened," she says, pulling back and inspecting me, searching my face to confirm I'm okay. "When I saw the dead hellhound outside, I assumed Rhys killed it. God, Nina. I should have been there."

"You couldn't have known. None of us could have."

"How did you kill it?"

I swallow the rising panic. There's so much I've kept locked away inside, unwilling to confront it myself. So much I couldn't say aloud, because that would make it real. The dam finally opens. "It was like—like I wasn't me anymore," I admit. "Artemis, I'm scared." My eyes fill with tears.

"The closet?" Artemis's tone is gentler than I've heard in a long time.

Suddenly she's not Castle Artemis. She's *my* Artemis—my twin sister, who I can trust with anything. We climb into the closet and sit shoulder to shoulder. We used to do this in our old house, hide in our closet when we were little and did something naughty. Later, it was where she'd take me when the nightmares were too bad and I was too scared to sleep. It's our place for telling secrets.

And I've never had a bigger one.

I scoot so that my back is against the wall, smashing the hanging clothes. Mine are all bright, rainbow colors, pieces that make me happy when I need it. Artemis's are all black, utilitarian. If she ever needs cheering, she doesn't have time to look for it in what she wears.

She mimics my posture. "Tell me."

I take a deep breath. "I didn't know what I was doing when the hellhound attacked. It was like instinct. My body took over completely and I killed that thing without even thinking."

She doesn't respond.

The thing I'm most scared of, the thing I've been ignoring, comes to the surface like a demon crawling from the blackest depths. I should have told her the day I first felt it. But what if Artemis can't fix this? Artemis fixes everything, but this might be too much for even her. What will that do to her, if she can't help? What will it do to me?

"I've . . . I've been feeling weird. For a couple of months now."

The timing is not lost on her. "A couple of months generally, or a couple of months *precisely*?"

"Do you remember the day with the big transdimensional demons?"

Artemis chokes out a laugh. "I do, in fact, remember that day."

We had been outside, on one of Artemis's rare breaks.

I shifted on the blanket and squinted up at the sky. "What does that cloud look like to you?"

Artemis didn't look up from her sandwich. "Water vapor."

I elbowed her in the side. "Come on. Use your imagination."

"I can't. My imagination died a long, agonizing death due to inhaling too much weapon polish."

I shifted onto my side to face her. "You don't have to do all the grunt work, you know."

Artemis rolled her eyes. Sometimes I watched her face and wondered if mine looked the same when I made those expressions. We had mirror features, but mine didn't work like hers. Everything she did was pointed, precise, powerful. Everything I did was . . .

Not.

I shooed away a fat black fly buzzing close to my face. "You're smarter than all those stuffy old layabouts, anyway. You should be doing the research and writing while they do the polishing."

"I didn't pass the test, so this is my role. And it's not like there's anyone else to do it."

Rhys collapsed onto the blanket next to me. He and Artemis had been training since they were children. As soon as we rejoined the Watchers, Artemis was put straight into full potential Council training. Our mother insisted on it. She never even let me try. But why couldn't we have Council members who were focused on healing? Who viewed the world—both natural and supernatural—as something to be fixed, not fought?

"What does that cloud look like to you?" I asked, pointing.

Rhys's voice sounded like a scowl. "Do you know how hard it is to get rid of bodies? I just spent four hours testing different chemicals to try and dissolve an Abarimon skeleton, only to be informed by Wanda Wyndam-Pryce that in the case of those types of remains, they just drop the bodies in the ocean."

I clucked sympathetically. "Makes vampires look considerate, what with the poofing and all. No cleanup."

"Least they can do. Anyhow, they made me leave. The Council's freaking out over something." He yawned. "Above my ranking, apparently."

"They kicked me out too," Artemis said.

I didn't mind the company. "If you all need something to do later, I'm cataloging inventory in my clinic."

Artemis's hand rested on my forehead. "Have you been taking your vitamins? You look pale."

"So do you."

"It's almost like you're twins," Rhys said.

Artemis ignored him. "Have you eaten yet? I can make you something."

"*I* can make *you* something. Your cooking is awful." I stuck my tongue out at her so she would know I was teasing her. Though Artemis cooked breakfast and lunch, we all took turns with supper. No one liked it when it was my week. Half the time when I arrived in the kitchen, Artemis had already prepared everything for me. I couldn't decide if I loved her for it or wished she would just give herself a break and let everyone deal with one night of my overcooked spaghetti with canned sauce.

She closed her eyes, relaxing. It was rare to see her face at peace. Rhys, too, was trying to catch a nap. A skill I far surpassed both of them in. Probably the only one.

I looked back up at the sky, enjoying that for these few minutes, Rhys and Artemis were shuffled to the side like I always had been. The clouds really were putting on a show. They pushed together faster now, swirling and billowing. And growing. And behaving decidedly uncloudlike.

Then the first tentacle appeared.

"Um. Guys?"

"Mm." Artemis shifted so her head was closer to my shoulder. She froze, listening to my breathing grow strained. She pushed herself to sitting, looking only at my face. "What's wrong?"

I pointed upward. "Is it just me, or does that cloud look like a giant demon emerging through a tear in the sky?"

"Oh," Rhys said. "Oh. Yes. I don't know what classification that one is."

A brief, silent moment passed, and then—

"Weapons!" Artemis shouted. Rhys snapped out of his stupor and tore across the courtyard to an outbuilding. He returned with crossbows, pikes, and as many swords as he could carry.

He had a nasty-looking rifle as well, already loaded with darts I knew could knock out even the biggest demons.

But this was bigger than the biggest demons. This was a monstrosity, a behemoth. Most demons we saw were hybrids or vessels for true demons in another dimension.

The thing coming from the sky didn't look like it belonged *in* this world. It looked like a world killer.

I heard chanting and turned to find Imogen and Ruth Zabuto gesturing, the charmed boundaries of the castle activated by their words. The air shimmered like a dome over us, marking the edges of the protection. Artemis gave instructions to Rhys. And I sat on the blanket.

Doing nothing.

Because all I had been trained to do was heal people. Fix them. And right then, I doubted any of us would have enough left for me to fix when this was over.

After the fire, maybe because of my nightmares, my mom had always insisted I couldn't handle stress. I was supposed to avoid intense situations. But a giant demon with one eye and teeth-covered tentacles descending from what had been empty sky only moments before? Pretty impossible to avoid.

We were dead.

Everyone was dead.

The demon settled over the magical boundary. The scent of burning flesh made my stomach turn, my throat feel ragged. The demon didn't pause. Pustules along its underbelly burst, coating the barrier in steaming, sizzling orange putrescence. Tentacles encompassed the entire shining dome. The demon was as big as the castle itself.

Ruth Zabuto's voice was trembling. Imogen ran back into the castle, presumably to find and protect the Littles. My mother burst out, but she didn't come to us. She stayed at Ruth's side, adding her fierce voice to the older woman's. I wanted her with me, but, as always, she chose to protect someone else.

I looked over at Artemis. She looked at me. This time our mother was choosing the Watchers over both of us.

"I'm getting Nina out!" Artemis grabbed my arm, hauling me to my feet. My heart pounded so hard in my chest that it hurt. My vision was narrowing, the world blurring around me.

"Help them," I said, barely able to push out the words. Something was wrong with my body. Every nerve was on fire, everything exploding.

"The barrier won't last much longer. We need to run while it's distracted." She dragged me toward the forest, where a stone archway was unaffected by the magical barrier. It was the only way out. As we passed through, I glanced behind us.

The last Zabutos. The last Smythes. The last of all of us. My mother turned toward us, the same expression on her face I had seen once before when she chose to save Artemis and leave me behind. Now Artemis had chosen to save me, and we had left my mother behind. My mother lifted a hand in farewell.

But the Littles were still in the castle.

I stopped, Artemis stumbling with the loss of momentum. "Nina, we have to go!" She took a few steps, waiting for me to follow.

I tried to squeeze out the words to tell her I couldn't leave them behind. And then I looked up and saw a single tentacle, gray and green with fangs instead of suction cups, swinging through the air. Right toward my sister.

The world narrowed to a single point: Artemis. I threw myself at her, and as we collided, three things happened at once.

The magical barrier disappeared as though it had never existed.

A pulse of energy like I had stuck my finger in a socket hit me so hard I flew off Artemis and rolled into the trees.

And the demon exploded.

Later we'd learn that the demon exploded when Buffy destroyed the Seed of Wonder and cut off magic and our connections to other dimensions. But that day all we knew was we were going to die, and then we weren't.

And I was absolutely drenched in interdimensional demon goo.

"So you're saying," Artemis says, "that you felt changed at the precise moment the Seed of Wonder was destroyed? The last possible second before magic left the world forever?"

I pick up one of her boots and fiddle with the laces. "Yeah."

"This happened months ago, Nina. Why didn't you tell me?" Castle Artemis is back—the softness is gone, and there's a chiding edge to her tone and expression. I half expect her to pull out an "Is Nina a Demon?" checklist.

"I was scared. I mean . . . I was worried that I had been infected: demonic power transference. There's precedence. I kept waiting to grow tentacles. When that didn't happen . . . I don't know. I didn't know how to tell you." *Because you aren't the same you. And we aren't the same we. And now I'm not even the same me.* "I hoped it would go away," I say aloud. "And nothing has been different. Not really." Except the way I feel, all the time. And my sleeping habits. And the nightmares.

Artemis has not failed to catalog this information. "You haven't been sleeping nearly as well. And your nightmares are different. Fewer about the fire, more about . . . monsters."

"But look at what we do! Of course I dream about bad things. I spend half of every morning researching doomsday prophecies and demon family trees."

Artemis leaves our closet and sits on the edge of her bed. I follow. We stare at her quilt. Mine is handmade from all the T-shirts we grew out of. Hers is so blank and scratchy it looks like it belongs on a hospital bed.

"If you felt this change right before magic was destroyed, then there's a chance that you could be a——" She pauses. Revulsion and anger flicker over her face.

Demon, I think.

She says something even worse. "Slayer."

Slayer.

I burst to my feet, wanting to run from the word. It's as abhorrent to me as what I did to that hellhound. I am *not* a Slayer. I'm a Watcher. Besides, there's no way the seers we used to employ would have missed a Potential Slayer in our own ranks.

I pace in tight circles. "I *can't* be. There aren't any more being activated. The magic ended along with everything else. No more Slayers. Besides, does it make any sense that *I* would be a Slayer?"

"No!" Artemis says, and the force of her exclamation is a little insulting. She didn't have to agree quite so quickly. It confirms what I'm saying, though. None of us would want to be a Slayer, but if any of us were going to be, I'd be the least obvious choice.

She stands, perfectly still. Her eyebrows are drawn together, her expression troubled. "But I think . . . we know latent Slayer abilities are triggered by a big moment of fear or bravery, which you've never had to face since the fire because I kept you so safe—I've always kept you so safe!" She takes a deep breath and rubs her forehead. "It seems impossible. And wrong. But this doesn't sound like demonic transference. And the timing works. What if you were changed into a Slayer at the last possible second before the Slayer line was ended forever?"

"No," a voice snaps, as cold and dark as the castle cellar. We look up to see our mother standing in our doorway. Just when I thought this day couldn't get any worse.

4

WE HAD THREE MOTHERS, EACH WITH A
distinct time period.

The first: dream mother.

In my memory, she smells like snickerdoodles.

She sang to us. Read books with pictures of happy things
instead of scaly demons. Laughed. I think she laughed, anyway.
Whenever I try to picture it, I can't quite manage to match up
sound with image. It's like watching a silent movie. And the end of
the movie is my dad, with his graying mustache and his kind eyes,
kneeling to give each of us a hug.

Mom says something to him—what does she say?—then
kisses him. We wave as he walks out the door. Mom looks
proud and sad all at once and shoos us into the kitchen for
cookies.

My dad never came back, and that mom—snickerdoodle
mom—was gone too. In a way, Buffy took both of them from
me. I never met the Slayer. I don't even know if she knew we
existed. But when my dad died for her, dream mother died too.

The second: ghost mother.

After that night we were attacked in the cemetery, Mom was always there, but . . . she wasn't. We moved constantly. I can't remember her working or doing anything.

There were no cookies. There was only the two of us and our mother, hovering. Haunting and haunted. Standing by the window with the curtains drawn, peering out the crack where they didn't quite meet. We had lost our father, and we lost our mother too. She was a shell of herself. We looked to her for comfort and found only fear. So Artemis and I whispered, played quieter. Hid our stakes in less obvious places so she'd stop taking them away. Figured out how to care for each other so we wouldn't disrupt her vigil. It wasn't ideal, but it was okay.

And then everything burned down.

The third: not mother.

After the fire, she stopped being our mother and started being a Watcher. I didn't realize how odd it was that we had been raised apart from them until we rejoined them in London and I saw how Watcher society functioned. We didn't even live together as a family anymore. Artemis and I went to the dorms, and my mother had her own apartment in the Council's wing.

It felt like she was rejecting me again. But maybe part of her decision to switch from being a mother to being a Watcher was so that she didn't *have* to face me. We never once talked about why she picked Artemis first. I sometimes thought about forcing it, but in the end, I preferred not knowing. It couldn't be any worse than what her actual explanation would be for why she left me behind.

I hadn't died that night, but sometimes, when I was with my mother, it felt like I had. Like I was as missing from her world as my dad was.

With our mother standing in the doorway, illuminated with rage, I feel very, *very* seen.

"Mom," Artemis starts, but our mother raises a hand like a sword, cutting off her words.

"Nina is not a Slayer." She isn't confused or even worried. Why did she move straight to anger? It doesn't make any sense.

I want to agree with her—I don't even *want* to be a Slayer!—but the way she dismisses it triggers my latent teen rebelliousness. Like me, it hasn't had any opportunity to flex its muscles, but its reflexes are superb.

"How do you know?" My voice raises an octave. "You haven't even been here." We haven't seen her in two months. This entire time I've felt different, afraid I was infected by demon or worse. Slayer counts as worse.

Would she have noticed? I doubt it. But now she's back, and she's telling me how I feel instead of asking me. Just like she told me I wasn't right for full Watcher training. Just like she told Artemis that she was. How much of our life has been controlled and determined by her?

She doesn't even ask about the hellhound. It's like she doesn't care. And maybe she doesn't, since I'm the one at the center of it. She likes me to be invisible.

Artemis faces our mother. Her back is to me, blocking me out of the conversation. "She killed a hellhound! If you're so sure she's not a Slayer, then there's something else, and we need to take care of it."

"I'm disappointed in you, Artemis. Nina never should have been put in this position. She never should have come in contact with a demon in the first place."

"I was twenty feet from the castle!" I throw my hands up in the air. They're talking about me like I'm not even here. "What, should Artemis walk me around on a leash? She can't protect me all the time! And apparently she doesn't need to."

Artemis flinches. I didn't mean to hurt her. I know how much she defines herself as my protector. And I've let her take that role without question. Maybe that was a mistake for both of us. I reach out to place a hand on her arm, but she crosses her arms tightly instead. "Regardless," she says. "Slayer or something else. We have to figure it out."

Our mother stares at the space above my head. Her face is tight and pinched with anger. Her own soft, auburn hair is pulled back into a severe ponytail, her gray eyes beginning to wrinkle in hard lines. What right does she have to be angry with us? None of this is my fault. Or is she mad that this means she has to actually interact with us? Then I realize she has . . . tears pooling in the bottoms of her eyes?

Oh gods. Buffy. The Slayer. My mom lost everything because of a Slayer. If it's hard for me to think about Buffy, how much harder is it for my mother?

"Mom," I choke out.

She turns away on one sharp heel, cutting me off. "I have to go speak with the Council. There's no need for you to come. We're still on lockdown, so don't leave."

Artemis and I look at each other in confusion. It's not that I'm surprised to be ignored by our mother. But for her to refuse to even talk about something so obviously dire?

My sister quickly shifts from confused to *pissed*. "That's it? She comes home to the news that the castle has been breached by a hellhound that *you* killed, and we get dismissed?" Her jaw sets in determination. "Let's go to the meeting."

"I think it's pretty clear we're not invited now that Mom's here."

"We can go if she doesn't know we're there." Artemis stands, her face as cold and hard as the stones of our walls. She storms out of our room; I follow more warily. But she turns in the opposite direction of the Council chambers, sideways across the dormitories. We're in the rear of the castle, a confusing warren of hallways connecting a tangle of mostly unused rooms.

Imogen pokes her head out of her suite. I go in there only to do well-child checkups. Measure their growth, listen to their heartbeats, deliver lollipops. Whenever I do, I'm reminded with a pang of kindly Nurse Abrams. She taught me back at the old headquarters. She used to wear an apron with the front pockets filled with lollipops, even though she mostly worked on adults. "Even Watchers need sweetness," she told me once. "Especially them, I think."

We lost so much more than our headquarters to the First. We lost our heart, too.

"What's going on?" Imogen always looks exhausted, but there's a new and frantic layer of fear on top of it. "Has there been another attack? Your mother walked by. She's never in the dorms."

"No new attacks," I say. "Our mom was just . . . saying hi after her trip."

Imogen doesn't believe me, and I don't blame her. But she has enough grace to pretend like my mother stopping by for a friendly maternal visit is something that might have happened. Imogen glances over her shoulder at the door cracked open, the Littles gathered around a table and playing with clay. "They don't know we're on lockdown." She pauses, then juts out her chin as though daring us to challenge her. "We're not telling them. They've had enough things to be scared of in their lives. If it gets dangerous, I'm loading them in a car and I'm not looking back."

I wonder why we didn't do that in the first place. But if we lose the Littles, we lose the next generation of Watchers. The last one, quite possibly. And they would never know their heritage or what their parents died for.

"Rhys's on patrol with Jade." Artemis pats a sleek walkie-talkie hooked onto her belt. I hadn't noticed it before, and I'm instantly jealous. Of course they've never given one to me. All I have is the castle cell phone with its terrible reception. Half the time it doesn't even send texts. But I've never mattered like Artemis. Do I matter now? Do I want to, if it means being a—?

I shudder. It's hard to even think the word.

Imogen nods curtly. "Let me know if there are any updates on the hellhound." We all know the Council won't bother to tell her. I might be walkie-talkie-less, but the Council never loops in Imogen, either. She's the only person more sidelined than I am. Selfishly, I've always been grateful that she's lower on the rungs, even if it is completely unfair. Otherwise I might have gotten stuck with nanny duty, and while I like the Littles, I definitely do not like them that much.

Artemis leads to me to a section of the castle that's closed down. Various relics of bygone eras—a grimy toolbox, a moldering wall hanging, a mushroom-print shirt crumpled in a corner, and a stuffed rabbit with cotton spilling out like guts—litter the floor. Artemis moves past it all to a splintering door and tugs it open. The interior is pitch-black. I can already feel the spiderwebs clinging to my skin, and I haven't even walked in yet. I just *know* it's a spider closet.

"Come on," she calls. I step in, holding out my hands, but I don't bump into Artemis. A tiny point of light waves and I see a hand sticking out of a person-size hole at the bottom of the wall. I would never have thought to look down there.

The penlight jerks impatiently. "Come on," Artemis repeats. I get onto my knees and crawl through. There are no spiderwebs. So either there are no spiders, or this particular secret crawl space is frequently used. I suspect the latter. Which means Artemis has never told me about it.

I'm hurt. We might not be finish-each-other's-sentences twins, but we don't keep secrets about our different lives here at the castle.

Except, of course, I did keep something from her. Something so much bigger than a secret passageway. I can't help asking anyway, "Why didn't you tell me about this?"

She shrugs. "I was worried it would trigger your asthma."

I've had mild asthma since the fire. But she could have at least told me. It's yet another reminder that this castle holds more than I'll ever have access to. I scramble through, finally able to stand. The space is narrow and frigid, and other than Artemis's tiny penlight, it's completely dark.

"This way," she whispers. I follow her as the passage twists and turns. Sometimes the black gapes to either side, hinting at other passages.

"How many rooms does this go to?" I whisper.

"A lot."

"What have you used it for?"

"Spying."

"Really?"

"I'm not invited to every meeting, but everything they decide impacts me. So I invite myself. Also, sometimes I don't want to be found by Wanda Wyndam-Pryce and her endless list of things she can't be bothered to do by herself. So I hide in here."

I imagine Artemis sitting alone in this black space just so she can have a moment to herself, and my resentment snuffs out as Artemis turns off the penlight. That's why she never shared it. It wasn't a happy secret. It was a tired, cold, dark secret, and she's always tried to shield me from things like that. Being on the inside isn't always a privilege.

"Not far now," she says. I place my hand on her back and follow as she confidently navigates a turn. Another void opens up beside us, and suddenly a figure lunges toward me.

I grab their arm, spinning the person and slamming them into the wall.

Rhys gasps. "It's me!"

I have him pinned, my forearm against his throat. I release him, embarrassment burning my cheeks. What is wrong with me that my first reaction to everything today is attack-injure-kill?

Slayer, my mind hisses.

"Thanks a lot, Artemis," Rhys whispers.

"Yeah, that was Nina." Artemis sounds annoyed.

"Sorry?" I reach out blindly and pat Rhys's shoulder. "I honestly didn't mean to." I've never hit a person before, never attacked anything, and—

A memory forms. A cemetery. A stake.

But I can never recall the details of that memory. It's so far from who I became. Maybe I remember it wrong. Surely Artemis was the one with the stake, not me. I should ask her. It feels important all of a sudden. But we don't talk much about our childhood, what with the giant fire right smack in the middle. Neither of us wants to reminisce about that.

Artemis pulls me next to her. Rhys takes a spot on my other side. Their faces are pressed against the wall. Several tiny holes have been drilled into the stone, pinpricks of light. They're so small you wouldn't notice them unless you put your eye right up against them. Which is what I do.

It's the Council's room. Our view is behind the Council members, their backs to us. But I don't give them a second glance once I see what—or rather, who—the meeting is about.

I desperately wish all the hellmouths hadn't closed, because I'd like nothing more than for one to swallow me up. Any hell dimension would be preferable to this new reality.

Because standing in front of the table is Eve Silvera.

And her son, Leo.

The first time I met Leo Silvera, I almost died.

We weren't supposed to be outside. Artemis and I had just turned twelve. It was our last night together—Artemis, Rhys, Jade, and me. The next day Rhys would move to the dorms to begin his

immersive training for the top levels. I was sad and jealous and . . .
excited. Because I would have Artemis all to myself. I wouldn't
have to share her with her books and training. She'd still have work
to do as they determined where to place her, but it wasn't the same
as being in full Watcher training. It was being on the sidelines. Like
me. Like Jade, too, who had failed the test. No one was surprised
when that happened, but when Artemis failed . . . none of us knew
how to react. Me least of all. Artemis didn't fail at anything. Somehow only Rhys had been chosen to progress as a Watcher destined
for active duty and eventually the Council. It didn't make sense.
Rhys was smart, but Artemis was too. And she beat him in magic
and in physical combat skills across the board.

How had she failed?

"Hurry up, slowpokes," Jade said. She walked fast, and I
didn't bother trying to catch up. We were all heading for the
same ice cream, anyway.

Rhys stayed back with us, silent and distracted. Ever since
the test, he wouldn't quite meet our eyes. I assumed he felt bad
that he had made it and Artemis hadn't.

Artemis had been even more affected by the test. When she had
come back, she'd looked . . . haunted. "I don't want to be a Watcher,"
she had said. But being a Watcher was what she had *always* wanted. I
couldn't wrap my head around her not being on the Council someday in the distant future. In my mind, she already was.

When I tried to talk to her about the test, she refused. For the
last four years she had been there for me, but I didn't know how to
offer her the same support, so I pretended like nothing was different. She let me. It was easiest for both of us.

I hated myself for it, but a part of me was glad. My mother

never let me train, so I never had a shot at being a full Watcher. I
had always been jealous that, once again, Artemis had been chosen. And now she wasn't. I didn't talk to her about it because I
didn't know how to make it better and because I didn't *want* it
to be better. We'd be sidelined together. Working Watcher support together. I wouldn't lose her to the field like our father, or,
worse, to the Council like our mother.

The air outside smelled like freedom. The dorms smelled
like burning dust from the ancient heating system. It made my
nose and lungs tickle and gave me bad dreams. Anything that
smelled like smoke did. Next to the dorms was the building
where the Council members were housed. It had been converted
from a cathedral, and it was beautiful—the spires pointing to the
sky like a warning to creatures of the night.

The other benefit of its conversion was that it was positively
unwelcoming to vampires. Unlike the dark, wild grounds we
slinked across to get to the nearest street.

None of us should have been surprised when a vampire
stepped out from behind a tree. Of course there was a vampire.
Of course it had been watching the Watchers' compound, waiting for someone to be alone or vulnerable. We weren't alone, but
we were definitely vulnerable.

Or I was, at least.

"Down!" Artemis shoved me to the ground as the vampire
lunged. She twirled to the side, drawing it away. I knew I should
run for help, but I couldn't move. Fear and panic paralyzed me.
A vampire had killed my father. One had attacked us after we
buried him. Had we survived just to be killed by one today?

"Jade!" Rhys shouted. I heard the sound of a fist connecting with flesh, and then somebody landed heavily next to me. Rhys. He was unconscious.

"No!" Artemis jumped on the vampire's back. He spun in circles, trying to get her off.

And he was *laughing*. He was having fun.

After making sure Rhys was still breathing, I reached into the interior pocket of my jacket. My trembling fingers almost dropped the vial of holy water, but I managed to uncap it.

The vampire got ahold of Artemis and tore her off his back. "You wanted to protect her?" He dragged her toward me with his hand around her neck. "The weak one? She would have slowed me down. You could have saved yourself. Now you'll have to watch her die, and then die yourself."

Artemis answered, but her tortured voice addressed me— not the vampire. "I'll never leave you behind again."

The vampire loomed. Artemis's eyes were filled with tears, and fear. But they were not a mirror to mine. Because they also contained a fury more frightening to me than the monster that held her. The vampire smiled. He held Artemis over me, so close I could hear every strained breath.

I threw the holy water. The vampire barely flinched. "I want you to be close enough to hear the life leaving her body," he said to Artemis. She closed her eyes. She refused to watch me die. I didn't want her to, but I felt so much more alone, not having her to witness it.

The briefest flash of surprise crossed the vampire's face, and then he disappeared in a shower of dust. I lay on the ground, coughing and gagging on his remains. Artemis crawled to my side, but I could only see our savior.

He was older than us but still young. A teenager. He had dark hair that curled almost to his shoulders, dark eyebrows, full lips. He was beautiful. And he had saved me. He reached for my hand, his long fingers soft and cool against my own. We weren't going to die. And it was all because of this boy.

"I'm Leo Silvera," he said, like we were meeting in the cafeteria. "I'm going to help train Rhys."

"I'm Athena," I gasped, my asthma mildly triggered. I didn't know why I introduced myself that way. No one here used my real name. But I wanted to sound older, more confident than I felt. Which was difficult, since I was struggling for air.

"Everyone calls her Nina," Artemis said from where she was checking Rhys's head. I should have done that, but I was too focused on my own breathing. Jade ran up. She had come back either too late or just in time.

Leo ignored Artemis, focusing only on me. "Just breathe. In and out, in and out. You're going to be okay."

"Promise?" I whispered.

"I promise, Athena." His smile was softer and darker than the night around us. It was a smile I wanted to curl into; I wanted to live forever in the way it made me feel. "Now, where were we going?"

"For ice cream."

"Fantastic. I love ice cream." With Leo leading us, the night held no terror. He bought me a double scoop of mint chocolate chip, and by the end of the hour, he had us all laughing about an encounter with a chaos demon who had taken over a dry cleaner's just to try and keep its clothes clean from its own secretions. We had forgotten how close we had all come to dying.

When my mom found out, I was grounded and restricted to the dorms for the next six months, but I didn't mind. Any time a vampire reared up in my nightmares, Leo appeared behind it to save me.

With a start like that, was it any wonder that I developed an agonizing crush on him?

And was it any wonder that it ended in disaster?

5

"OF COURSE WE LOOKED FOR YOU," EVE
Silvera is saying. "But the castle was missing from where it had stood
for centuries. We assumed it had been destroyed along with everything else. Imagine our shock when Helen found us in Costa Rica!
We thought we were the only ones left."

It feels weird to hear my mom casually called Helen. Like
she's a real person.

I had forgotten what Eve Silvera looked like. We didn't
interact much. I only took notice of her because she was the
mother of my crush. She's tall, and there's something powerful
in the way she holds herself. Her body offers no apologies for its
presence in the world. She wears a red blazer over crisp black
pants, and her heels manage to be elegantly aggressive. Combined with her red lips and her black hair, she is everything I
aspire to be (and probably never will). Her voice has a quality
that makes it sound as though she might break into laughter at
any moment. It softens her, makes her human.

I didn't remember any of that. In my memories, she was just . . . tall.

Leo, unfortunately, is exactly as I remember him. His hair falls in waves to his shoulders. Black eyebrows frame his large, dark eyes. I spent countless hours in contemplation of those eyes. Imagining them turning to me. Widening as he realized that we were meant to be together.

I didn't think about his lips once. Because I literally never *stopped* thinking about them. They were the subject of one of the poems Honora read aloud.

Your lips are a promise
I'd love to keep
They haunt me when waking
And tease when asleep

His poetic lips part as he answers a question about Costa Rica. I'm annoyed with them for taking up time. Shouldn't the Council be talking about the hellhound? And me? Even when I do something that should have been impossible, actual trained Watchers take precedence. Typical.

Leo *has* changed, though. It's been years, after all. He's taller. He was always lean, but what had been youthful skinniness has filled out into muscles, much like his face has settled into the best version of itself. If anything, he's handsomer than ever.

What an absolute *butthead.*

His jerk mouth opens and his jerk voice answers another question about his time in South America. "Yes, sir. I continued my training. We had to be flexible, of course, lacking the resources of the Council. My Watcher project was more of a practical examination than a scholarly presentation. I studied the habits of a parasitic demon in Venezuela and determined a magical inoculation that prevented it from feeding on the people there, killing it."

"What have you been doing here?" Eve Silvera asks the Council. She seems so nice that I feel bad resenting her. But I want them *gone*. I can't imagine they'll stay here long. Leo will probably do what Honora did—she's out hunting demons, her ear to the ground so we'll know if anything big is coming. After all, what's a Watcher without—

"Slayers?" Eve asks, finishing my thought for me. "You mean to tell me you haven't brought in any of the new Slayers? What have you been doing all this time?"

"There were the children to think about." Bradford Smythe's voice is so low it sounds growly even when he's being cheerful, which he isn't right now.

"Yes, but there have always been children. We're all that's left of the Watchers. We have a responsibility to do our jobs, and our jobs don't exist without a Slayer."

My mother answers. I don't remember her having a British accent when we were little, but now her words are clipped, efficient. Vowels are wrangled into perfect order. Even her voice changed when we rejoined the Watchers. "Safety was the first priority. We couldn't risk revealing our location after the attack. With so many new Slayers, they couldn't be properly vetted. And then the world changed yet again with the destruction of magic."

"But you were looking for Slayers," Eve says. "That's where we found you. Outside that poor girl's village. We were all too late."

My mother's words grow even more deliberate, as though each is chosen for its utter lack of meaning. "I was conducting Slayer-related field observations in conjunction with confirming the closing of all hell-dimension access points."

Artemis shifts beside me. We both know what it sounds like when our mother gives a nonanswer in order to avoid a lie. Why would she tell us that she was checking hellmouths if she was actually searching for Slayers?

Ruth Zabuto's voice trembles. "Do *you* have any magic, Eve?"

Eve shakes her head, gentle and apologetic. "Since Buffy destroyed the Seed of Wonder, we have not seen any evidence of magic. And all the portals are gone. We've been traveling too, checking them to make certain nothing remained that we were unaware of."

"I'm surprised we didn't find each other sooner." Once again my mother's tone is so careful I suspect there's more meaning to her statement.

Wanda Wyndam-Pryce clears her throat. "Best to be thorough with our checks. Well done." She acts like she assigned the Silveras to do it. She has a way of saying things that makes it sound like everyone works for her, all the time. "I expect you'll have a written report for us soon."

I'm still annoyed this is taking precedence over today's hellhound attack, but there *are* hundreds of semipermanent portal sites across the globe. My mom has covered only the UK and North, Central, and South America. So there's still work to be done. A goal. A goal that will take the Silveras away from here before I ever have to look in Leo's eyes again.

After all, his eyes are like *two pools of blackness, so dark and deep, when I look at him, I cannot breathe.* Oh, I hate him. Or I hate poor thirteen-year-old me.

"Between Helen's information and ours, we can officially declare all hellmouths and demonic portals inactive. Now that we're reunited, it's time to move forward. To become Watchers again. It's time," Eve says, my hopes for their swift exit sinking, "to get a Slayer."

"We already have one," Ruth Zabuto says with a dismissive wave of her hand.

Bradford Smythe reflexively coughs.

My mother speaks first, her tone no longer passive. "*No*, we do *not*."

Wanda Wyndam-Pryce pounces. She's always hated my mother. The Wyndam-Pryces were once considered the most prestigious Watcher family, but then their golden boy, Wesley Wyndam-Pryce—they have a thing for alliteration *and* for feeling superior—was so staggeringly inept that he was fired from the Council. Wanda has never gotten over her disappointment that my father's tenure as a Watcher is held in esteem while the Wyndam-Pryces' only actively assigned Watcher ended up as a private investigator in Los Angeles—working for a *vampire*.

So Wanda is gleeful as she senses my mother's anger. "Oh yes! We have reason to suspect that our very own Nina is a Slayer."

Leo startles. His eyes widen at his mother, but she ignores him. He's definitely upset by this news, but I can barely register it because Rhys gasps and turns toward me. I don't know what to say, so I don't say anything. I keep my eyes on the room.

"Imagine," Wanda continues, "being her mother and never realizing she might be a Potential Slayer. And the change had to have happened at least two full months ago. How odd that you didn't notice something so dramatic, Helen."

My mother refuses to be baited. But her stillness is as much a tell as someone else wringing their hands. She is freaking out. A small, mean part of me feels smug. She didn't want to talk with us about it, but she can't avoid talking to the Council. "Nonsense. Nina would have been identified by our seers. Besides, she only killed a hellhound. Every member of our community should be able to do the same. It doesn't mean anything."

Hearing her say it so dismissively triggers that rebellious feeling again. Because she knows I was never trained. She didn't let me. And she knows how I feel about violence. The *way* I killed the hellhound can't be ignored. It was like something had awakened inside me that had been sleeping there for a long time, just waiting for an opportunity. Something awful and powerful and terrifying. Something I had no control over.

Bradford Smythe shifts, turning his head so I can see his profile. His lips are pursed so tightly beneath his mustache that they disappear. He sighs. "I'm sorry, Helen."

"Don't," she says. I flinch from her tone, but Bradford doesn't react.

"It's too late now." He pauses. My heart is beating so loudly, I wonder how they can't hear it through the wall. Then he tugs on his mustache and speaks. "We were always aware that Nina was a Potential Slayer."

Rhys gasps even louder this time. Artemis swears. The walls are thick and the Council is making their own variations of shocked noises, covering ours. I stagger back, losing my view of the room. It can't be true.

It *can't*.

They would have told me. It doesn't make sense why they wouldn't. I'm a Watcher! Wouldn't they have been all over the opportunity to raise a Potential Slayer in their midst?

And my mother went so far out of her way to keep me from being trained. She insisted I wasn't suited to it. Prevented me from getting even the basic Watcher fighting instruction and pushed me into healing. Artemis received the physical training.

Bradford Smythe starts talking again, and I struggle to focus on his words over the pounding of my heart and my own racing thoughts. "It's part of why the kids were here when our head-quarters were attacked. We heard rumblings of the threats to Potentials, so Helen took all the younger students with her to avoid anyone narrowing in on Nina."

So it wasn't mere luck that we were away during the attack. They were protecting me. But why go so far to protect me if they weren't ever going to train me or tell me the truth?

"After magic was destroyed and the Slayer line ended," Bradford continues, "we assumed that her potential wasn't triggered in time and that she would never become a Slayer. It appears we were wrong."

Artemis and Rhys haven't moved. I feel them in the dark-ness, staring at me instead of the room. Suspecting I was a Slayer is nothing compared to knowing. And finding out that this infor-mation was always here, deliberately withheld from me—and most of the Council as well? It's not just a shock. It's a betrayal.

"You failed to inform the Council that your own daughter

was a Potential?" Wanda Wyndam-Pryce doesn't sound angry so much as smug. "This calls for a full censure and a review of your position here on the Council. Yours too, Bradford, for being part of the conspiracy."

"What *Council*?" Ruth Zabuto snorts. "What, are we going to banish Helen? Demote Bradford? For doing what? It's foolish enough that you haven't let dear Artemis be a full Watcher. The test shouldn't count against her now that there are so few of us. You and your rules can go sit on a pin, Wanda." She pulls out her knitting and gets to work, shaking her head.

Wanda Wyndam-Pryce huffs. "Well, I for one will not let this egregious betrayal of our standards go without repercussions. We are nothing without our rules. They still mean something."

"The girl is alive because of the secrecy." Bradford Smythe's voice is soft but clear. "I think that alone justifies Helen's decisions. I support her now as I did then."

"And it means we have a Slayer." Eve's eyes are alight with emotion. She puts her hands to her mouth, and I swear she's on the verge of tears. "Right here. One of ours."

My mother stands, slamming her chair backward. "She is not *ours*. She is mine. There are a thousand other girls out there. If you want a Slayer, go find a real one." With that, she stalks from the room.

I feel a gentle hand on my shoulder. I want to shake it off. Want to pretend like my mom's words—and these revelations— don't mean anything.

But if I suspected there were tears in Eve's eyes, I know there are tears in mine.

"Nina," Artemis says.

"You must—" Rhys starts, but I cut him off.

"I can't talk about this right now." Literally. I don't even know how to feel, much less how to form everything into words. I'm scared and I'm confused and I'm *furious*. My entire life has been a lie. "I need to be alone."

I stumble back through the dark. I'm half certain I'm lost and will die in these walls, but eventually I bump into a dead end and see a hint of light from the crawl space.

Back in my room, I throw myself onto my bed and stare up through my tears at the metal ceiling fan. It was the biggest expense my mother ever approved. Artemis and I sharpened its blades to razor's edges. It wasn't the only modification we made to our room. Several snow globes decorate various surfaces, all filled with holy water, acid, and flame accelerant. The desk legs are easily removable and sharpened to stake points. Artemis and I have systematically stocked every room we ever lived in with weapons. We did it so I could feel safe. So that we would have weapons even I could use without training.

But what if *I'm* the weapon now?

Not only has my whole life changed, but my whole history, too. Everything is different now. My mother knew—*always* knew. And she still chose Artemis. She still pushed Artemis to train, to be the better of the two of us. Did she think—hope— that the seer misidentified, and Artemis would be the Slayer, not me? Or did she know it was me and hate me because of it?

My phone buzzes on my nightstand. I wipe my eyes and pick it up to see a series of frantic messages from Cillian. Usually he only texts me to pass notes along to Rhys or if there's a shipment of supplies he's going to deliver.

But this one is for me.

Nina emergency please come to my house

Right now

God nina please

Come alone

Can't explain just please begging you come right now

My adrenaline kicks back into gear. I grab my shoes and run.

6

IT'S JUST PAST MIDNIGHT. THE ONLY light is from the almost full moon. Everything is pale illumination and blackest shadows. Beneath my cable-knit sweater, I'm itching from the inside out—buzzing as I sprint through the trees, spooking at every crack of a twig or rustle of dying leaves. Cillian's panicked texts have me feeling like I'm going to jump out of my own skin.

There is, in fact, a demon that can jump out of its own skin, which is where the saying comes from. When surprised or in danger, the demon *literally* jumps out of its skin and leaves it behind, much like some lizards can detach their tails. I saw an illustration of it once, and firmly hope to never see it in real life.

I started out tentatively—my mom always insists I never exert myself, so all my trips to town are accomplished at a leisurely walking pace—but now I'm running faster, and faster, and faster. Running away from who she told me I was. The girl who shouldn't be exposed to stress or panic. The girl who shouldn't push herself.

I stumble as the truth slides into place like a knife into a sheath. *She was trying to keep my Slayer potential from being activated.* I had believed that she didn't want me exposed to stressful situations because she was trying to make up for the fire. But Potentials become Slayers when they hit physical maturity and encounter a moment that requires something of them. She tried to make certain I never had that moment. It took an interdimensional demon to get past the coddled, safe box she placed me in. Otherwise I never would have become a Slayer at all.

And I don't know which option is worse—never knowing what she hid from me or having to be a Slayer.

I run so fast the forest blurs dizzily around me. For the first time in my life, I have no idea what my own physical limits are. I don't want to push, because pushing, running as fast as I can, or enjoying any of this makes the fact that I'm a Slayer—*I'm a Slayer*—real. And I don't want it to be.

Cillian's waiting for me as I skid to a stop outside his house. He looks as shaken up as I feel.

"What's wrong?" I search him for wounds, but he seems fine, physically.

"I, uh, have a problem. I need to show you what's in my yard."

Cillian's house is a cottage built on the edge of Shancoom, abutting the forest. His backyard is a small space with a sturdy shed against the fence. In the two years since we dropped a castle inside the trees, no one in the village has accidentally found it. We used to have magical wards to deter them, but it turns out people are just super uncurious about the woods.

I've been to Cillian's only a few times, but I like it. It's an actual home. And as much as I rationally know that living inside a castle is cool, whenever I walk into Cillian's house I'm hit with a sense of familiarity and comfort. A cozy, curated space, shared with people you love. A building that functions only to take care of you.

Of course, Cillian's house has been emptier of late. His mom hasn't been back in six weeks. I try not to ask for details—it's none of my business, and I can see in the soft way Rhys approaches the subject that it's a tender one.

Which reminds me.

"Why didn't you want Rhys to come?"

Cillian bounces nervously on the balls of his feet as he looks through the open front door of the dimly lit house and toward the dark, fenced-in backyard. "Um. You need to see it. Then you'll understand."

I follow Cillian through his house to the back door, my curiosity warring with trepidation. He flips on the backyard floodlights. Something must really be troubling him if—

I throw an arm out in front of Cillian, every muscle on high alert, every nerve in my body screaming fight or *fight*, having left flight entirely out of the equation.

There's a demon.

Collapsed unconscious on the grass is a lanky thing in a Coldplay T-shirt and skinny jeans. It has acid-yellow skin, black horns, and black lips to match. The demon's face is bruised and swollen, one scaly cheek sliced down to the bone. Peeking out from its clothes are a lot more wounds. One arm is at an angle I'm pretty sure no arm should ever be at, even when attached to a demon.

That makes two demons within twenty-four hours. Threatening my family. My home. My friends. A pulse of blinding rage fills me, and I take a step toward the demon.

"It's a demon, right?" Cillian's voice snaps me out of my enraged stupor. I blink, trying to shake off some of the kill-kill-kill roaring through me. It feels foreign, like my brain playing a song I don't know. Once, when we still lived in London, Artemis and Jade snuck me into a concert. The bass was so powerful I could feel it inside, competing with and overtaking my heart. This is similar. Like my heart isn't mine anymore. The beat is a foreign entity.

Slayer, something whispers deep inside. I shove it further down.

Cillian is wigging out. His eyes are open so wide they practically glow in the darkness of the house. He hasn't crossed the threshold into the yard. "I know you guys told me about demons, but I didn't really believe it. That thing earlier could have been some crazy, sick dog or wolf or hyena. In Ireland. But this? I believe you now."

"Did you do something?" I turn to him. "Summon them? How?" Summoning shouldn't work anymore. All the portals are gone, any magic used to lure the demons broken.

"No! God, no. Why would I want this? I didn't realize that thing was out here until an hour ago. I couldn't sleep and went to get the rubbish bins for collection before I forgot."

Though I can't discount the connection that both demons have been found around Cillian, I still believe him. Cillian has never been anything but helpful. If he wanted to hurt us, if he had some sinister ulterior motive, he could have done something ages ago. And I know he loves Rhys. The way they look at each other is so sweet it practically gives me a sugar rush.

"Right. So. There's a demon in your backyard." I tug nervously on my hair. "Why did you ask *me* to come? Did you ask because I killed——because of what I did to that other one?"

Is that already my role? Stabby-stabby-kill girl?

Or breaky-breaky-neck girl, really, since I don't have any weapons. I'll need weapons if demons are going to start popping up everywhere. I usually have a stake on me——like a comfort blanket that can kill things——but stakes aren't a one-size-fits-all demon-slaying tool.

Cillian shakes his head. "No, that's not why. I mean, maybe a little. I don't want anyone to get hurt. But we don't know anything about it."

"We know it's a demon."

"Right, but it's wearing a fecking Coldplay shirt. How evil can something wearing a Coldplay shirt be?"

He has a point. "So why did you ask *me*?"

"Because you fix people. You're always watching those horrible first aid tutorials. And all the medical supplies you have me order? You know how to help people. I thought——" Cillian shrugs, suddenly sheepish as we both look at the radioactively yellow demon. "I thought it might need help."

Relief and gratitude wash over me. Cillian didn't ask me here to kill something. He asked me here to *help* something. I want to hug him for being my friend, for thinking of me the way I think of myself: as a healer. I'm the girl who patches things up. Not the one who breaks them.

My initial instinct to attack nags at me, filling me with guilt.

I want to at least give Coldplay there a chance. Being a Slayer doesn't mean I have to kill everything that moves.

Actually, I have no idea what being a Slayer means. And *I don't care*. I'm a Watcher, so I'll deal with the demon our way. Study first, reach an informed conclusion, and then decide on a course of action. True Watcher procedure at its best, like I've tried telling Artemis for years. Our role was never supposed to be the violent one.

I nod toward the shed. "Got anything in there we can use to restrain it?"

Cillian squinches up his face, then snaps his fingers. "Yeah, actually. Could you help me get it in?" While he unlocks the shed door, I cross the yard and grab the demon's arms.

"Eew!" I shriek, pulling back my hands as though burned. Cillian whips around, terrified. "It's sticky. Oh, gross, it's sticky." Shuddering, I try to touch only the clothed parts of its body. I start to lift the demon, and I nearly toss it up into the air. It's so much easier than I expected it to be. But I don't feel elated over this surging new strength. It's another reminder of how my body is something *other* than what I've always known.

"How? How are you doing that? Is the demon bloke filled with helium or something?"

The grossness of what I'm holding comes over me again. "Open the shed—oh gods, the stickiness is seeping through my shirt. It's my favorite shirt. I'm going to have to burn it. And also my skin. And everything. Just—hurry!"

As soon as Cillian opens the door, I push past him and drop the demon unceremoniously on the floor.

Cillian is possibly more freaked out by me than by the demon.

"You carried that—that thing like it's a bag of . . . things that don't weigh much. And that's after you went Terminator on the hellhound. You've never been like this. Did something happen when you killed that dog thing?"

"By *thing*, you mean demon. Just like this discolored horny thing."

"Could we say 'horned,' not 'horny'? Because I am already creeped out enough."

Cillian pulls a chain hanging down from a bare bulb, which throws everything into yellow-tinged relief. His mother's shed is as cluttered as Rhys's bookshelves, holding what appears to be the detritus of at least a dozen different lives. Dream catchers, Buddhas, crystals and incense, a stack of Bibles along with what looks like a Book of Mormon and a whole pile of L. Ron Hubbard novels, several statues of gods and goddesses of various traditions and religions, and an entire bin of ghost-hunting and medium shows.

"Welcome to the shed of cultural appropriation." Cillian sweeps his arms around with a bleak expression. "At least now my mum's with ascetic monks, so she won't bring back souvenirs. We're already jammers with junk."

In the middle of the chaos, the only item that is clean and dust free is a framed photo of Cillian's dad. I've never seen him before. I pick it up to take a closer look.

"Twelve years he's been gone," Cillian says. "And she's still trying to find some way to reconnect with him. With magic offline, she's desperate for anything else."

"I can't blame her. He's handsome. He looks a little like Orlando Bloom."

"Dammit, Nina! Orlando Bloom?" Cillian snatches the photo away from me. "I can't unsee that! My feelings about my dead dad were already complicated; now I have to worry that I'm oedipal, or whatever the guy-crushing-on-his-own-dad equivalent is. I swear to God if you so much as *breathe* about more handsome men in connection to anyone I'm related to, I will never speak to you again."

"You're not messed up! I'm sorry. He looks nothing like Orlando Bloom. Or any other person you've ever had a crush on."

"Just shut it and let me find the handcuffs."

I turn away from Cillian's definitely Orlando Bloom–look-alike father and wait, keeping a wary eye on the demon.

"Here they are!" Cillian holds up a pair of handcuffs triumphantly. He's been rooting through a box labeled with his father's name. There's a stack of photos, what I guess is a 3-D metal puzzle made up of interlocking triangles, a heavy ring, and some loose photos. I wonder how many times Cillian has gone through the box that he knew the handcuffs were in there.

Artemis and I don't have anything of our father's. That's part of why I love the library so much. At least I know he studied those same books, looked at those same pages.

I take the handcuffs, tugging lightly on the metal, afraid I might break it if I really try. "Do I want to know why there are handcuffs in here?"

"Stop creepifying my parents!"

"I'm sorry! I'm sorry. It's been a confusing day." I pause. "Seriously, though, why do they have handcuffs?"

"My father was a volunteer with the local police. I used to play with those, so I know they're real."

"Good." There's an exposed section of support beam in the back of the shed. I pull on it experimentally, and it barely budges. So unless the demon is stronger than I am—in which case we are in trouble, regardless—it should be enough.

I drag the demon closer, then cuff its wrist to the beam before tying its ankles together with some rope I find on one of the shelves, figuring it can't hurt to double up. I pause over its wrists, where lingering bruises and sores indicate I'm not the first person to bind it.

It's unnerving. I don't want to cause any more damage. I need Rhys. He's a freaking encyclopedia of demonic variations. I've done my homework—all of it, always—but the Council gives Rhys information I'm not important enough to have. Besides, my focus has always been on human bodies. For all I know, this demon can light things on fire with its mind, and as soon as it wakes up, we're dead.

I brush the demon's wrists, and it whimpers in pain. The sound is soft and vulnerable. I feel it on a level I can't quite explain. I know what it is to be hurt, to need help. In that moment, my mind is made up. I can't get Rhys because he'd alert the Council, and so soon after the hellhound scare, they're bound to be in kill-first-ask-questions-later mode. I don't want anything else dead because of me.

Cillian moves a stack of gilded religious books off a table and sits. I lean as close as I dare to the demon. The wound on its face doesn't look good. Black ichor oozes onto the cement floor. I glance around for a first aid kit, but the shed is a dumping ground, containing nothing useful. Unless I want to learn the *Seven Secrets of Successful Spirit Summoners*. Secret one: Live in a world where magic isn't dead.

"Do you have a medical kit? I don't know if demons can get infections, but I'd like to clean out this cut and close it. And I'll try to fix its arm, too. I think it's out of the joint. If it's broken, there's not much I can do here."

Cillian nods, obviously relieved to have a task. He hurries from the shed. I shouldn't fix the demon. But it nags at me, seeing something hurt and helpless. Knowing how easily—how willingly—I could have been the one to hurt it. Besides, if the demon dies of shock or infection, I can't very well get information out of it. I need to know why it's here. Why the hellhound was here. Who, if anyone, is behind it. And whether there's another threat to the castle or if it's all some big, sucky, sticky coincidence. It doesn't seem likely, but a girl can hope. I might feel compassion for the demon, but I'm not dumb. It's still a demon.

I examine what's visible of the rest of the demon's body— unwilling to undress it, because my sympathy definitely does not extend that far. There are some other cuts, some more bruising, and the dislocated arm.

Before I have time to rethink anything, Cillian's back with supplies.

"Okay." I shake out my hands to steady them. "If it wakes up, I need you to be ready to hit it on the head with something heavy."

"So you're going to try to fix the damage, and if it works, we're going to hurt it again?"

"I don't know!" I pour rubbing alcohol on my hands. "I guess only if it tries to attack. This is all new to me too."

"Fine." Cillian picks up a large metal clamp. "Before you assume anything disgusting, this is from my mum's quilting phase."

I pour some of the alcohol onto a strip of gauze, then, figuring I might as well get it over with, pour it directly into the wound. The demon flinches—Cillian raises the clamp—but it doesn't wake up. I carefully pull the wound shut and tape the skin in place.

The demon's left arm is definitely not the same as the right arm, in a bad way. "Does this look dislocated to you?"

"I don't know!"

"Crap on a stake," I moan. I'll have to take a million showers to get the sensation of its skin off mine. Putting a hand against the demon's shoulder, I hold on to its arm and pull. I feel the pop as it slides back into place. The demon shudders. Its eyes flutter open for a second, and I swear it whispers, "Thank you," before going limp and unconscious again.

I can't be sure, though. I'm too distracted by the way its shoulder popped. It reminds me of the hellhound's neck. One pop to fix something broken, one pop to break something forever.

"I'm going to lose my supper," Cillian says.

I feel the same.

Cillian sets down the clamp out of reach of the demon. "Does that mean the demon will be in fighting shape when it wakes up?"

"It's secured. We'll be fine." I hope. I rub at an itch on my ear with my shoulder. I don't want to touch any part of myself with my demon-goo hands. What if it's contagious? Sometimes demons can infect people with abilities or curses or other demony things. That's why I was so paranoid about feeling different after the demon apocalypse day. And why I missed the huge, obvious truth that I, of all people, should have guessed. Though I don't like "Slayer" any better than "demon infection." It's not even that different.

"Sooo," Cillian says, drawing out the word. "When are you going to admit you're a Slayer?" I flinch, and he grins. "Knew it. I mean, like, for the last ten minutes I knew it. Been thinking about it all day, and your strength tonight confirmed it. That's brilliant, though, right? Slayers are the whole reason you lot do your job. Multitasking now."

I hesitate, then blurt, "Can I tell you a secret?"

"Besides the massive number of secrets you've dumped on me in the last twenty-four hours? By all means."

I don't know what anyone expects of me now. What it will actually mean to be a Slayer among the Watchers. If they'll expect a lot from me. Or if, being me, they'll continue to expect nothing. Artemis seems upset, my mom is livid, and Rhys and most of the Watchers are confused. But I know how *I* feel. "I hate Slayers. I don't want them to exist, much less be one."

Cillian surprises me by folding me into a hug. In all the Slayer talk, no one had asked me how I felt about it. Artemis wanted to fix it. Rhys couldn't believe it. Eve and the Council thought it was great. My mom denied it. But in this moment I know exactly what I want, what I've needed all day:

Someone to just *be* there for me.

Cillian's expression is gravely sincere. "You've lost a lot, and that always leaves a mark. It's okay to feel that way. You have my permission to freak the hell out."

I snort, and he pats my back.

"I'm glad we're both sharing things, though. You're sharing your new scary Slayer status. And I'm sharing the demon in my shed. Do you think it'll wake up?"

Its skin is textured like a drought-stricken riverbed, all

cracked and flaking, with the black sections between cracks shining with ooze. I don't know if that means it's unhealthy or if that's standard. The horns are black, as are the fingernails and, I suspect, the teeth. Its ears are pierced with delicate gold hoops, and its Coldplay shirt has a cheerful rainbow on it.

"I don't know. We have lots of books on demons, but they all revolve around, like, how to summon, control, and destroy. None of them talk about how to administer first aid."

"You did your best. Hopefully the demon takes that into account when it wakes up and eats us."

"Most demons don't eat humans. Or at least, not the whole human. Certain organs, for sure. Hearts. Sometimes brains. Or just your blood. There's an entire subspecies of demon that survives on eating human teeth, which is actually where the tooth fairy mythology came from! But they don't take them from underneath your pillow. They take them from—"

My story is cut short by my phone chirping in my pocket. I pull it out to see the castle's main line. Busted. Someone knows I'm gone. I don't answer, because I don't want to lie.

"I gotta go. I can't have them come looking for me, not until we figure out what this thing's deal is." I pause. "I don't want to ask you to keep secrets from Rhys, but . . ." But the Council has kept secrets from me. And I feel so out of control right now, like everything is spinning away from me. For once in my life as a Watcher, I want to be in charge.

I know it's irrational to protect a demon. But it also feels like a rebellion against my Slayer calling, and I'm all about the rebellion lately. I'll tell Artemis, though. She'll know what to do. She can handle anything.

"Text me if it wakes up," I say. "I'll come back later to secure it with more chains. Until then, stay out of this building. You should sleep in the shop."

I see Cillian safely there and hurry back to the castle. I run faster but feel slower, weighted by so many unanswered questions.

It took her too long to find them again.

Their mother knew what she was doing. She disappeared. And not only did she disappear from conventional means of tracking, she used magical wards and shields to prevent mystical tracking as well. But the hunter was patient and had plenty of resources. Eventually the mother would make a mistake, and then the hunter could finish the job.

A little more than a year after the vampire's failure, her opportunity came. Watchers were creatures of habit, and even in hiding, the mother responded when a Council member asked to meet. The hunter knew the date and time of the meeting.

She stood outside a nondescript house in a Phoenix subdivision. Everything here was beige. The landscape. The houses. The auras. It was the least magical place she had ever encountered. It might have been the opposite of a hellmouth—a demonic dead spot. Even hell was preferable to Arizona.

That was probably why the mother had chosen it. With the heat of the day still radiating from the pebble-strewn excuse for a yard, the hunter crouched low and watched the house. The lights were on. She waited until she saw one flash of red curls. Then two. They were inside.

Evening slipped into night. She imagined the mundane tasks that were happening inside. Baths. Were the girls old enough for showers now? Brushing teeth. Perhaps a story, one where monsters were defeated and then the book ends.

But monsters never respected endings in real life. They just kept coming and coming and coming. They never stopped needing to be defeated.

The bedroom light went off. And then, as promised, the mother stepped out of the house. Her movements were furtive, suspicious. She climbed in her car and drove away to her clandestine meeting.

The mother should have known better.

The hunter popped a piece of bubble gum into her mouth. She had the just-released video of Titanic *at home waiting for her as a reward for finally finishing this task. "I'll never let go, Jack," she whispered to herself as she cut her hand and began activating the runes that would end the prophecy once and for all.*

7

THE CASTLE LOOMS OVER ME IN THE night. It's not a fairy-tale castle, made of spun sugar and happily-ever-after dreams. It's not even a nightmare castle filled with spikes and creeping darkness. It's the castle equivalent of an urgent care clinic. Its job is to keep you alive. That's it.

The windows are mainly narrow slots, left over from the days of arrows and crossbows. To be fair, we still use crossbows a lot. A few of the windows have been expanded in the living quarters, but those were done artlessly, like the wrong eyeglasses for a face shape. The only tower crumbled before my great-grandparents were alive, so the entire building is a squat rectangle. The outer wall is gone, along with matching outbuildings, left behind when Ruth Zabuto and my mom transported the castle here. Instead, we have several cheap sheds. There's one long garage that was converted from a preexisting abandoned stable. The entire thing is as grouchy as Bradford Smythe and as unpleasant as Wanda Wyndam-Pryce. *And* as lacking in magic as Ruth Zabuto.

Still, it's home.

Which means it's full of people I can't risk running into right now. I half suspect that if I bumped into someone from the Council, I'd blurt out everything. It's a huge tenet of Watcher society that you listen to the Council. You obey them. And, less explicit but more of an unspoken tenet, you don't hide demons in your friends' sheds without telling them about it.

So instead of going in through the front, I circle around to the back and locate what I'm pretty sure is my window. It's on the second story. The whole first story of the castle is off-limits. They shut it down when they moved the castle here. There's a light in my window, like a beacon. If I can get to my room, I'll be able to tell Artemis what happened, and she'll know what we should do. She always has a plan.

I mentally calculate. It's about fifteen feet up. There's a wide stone ledge; the walls are a foot and a half thick, and the window is set toward the inside.

If I can run super fast now, then maybe . . .

I crouch low and jump. With my arms straight up, I manage to catch the ledge with the tips of my fingers. I expect to fall, but they hold. I pull myself up, laughing, and haul my whole body into the space in front of my window, folded and crammed up against it.

That's when I remember it's locked—and it swings *out* when it opens, not in. I might have Slayer strength, but it didn't improve my ability to think plans out thoroughly in advance. Maybe that's why Buffy always reacts instead of planning. When your body can do amazing things, it's easy to try first, regret later.

A face pops into view and I scream, almost falling backward. My scream has a mirror image in Artemis. Then she scrunches up her face and shouts.

"What the hell are you thinking?"

"Obviously I wasn't!"

She gestures at the window hinges. I'm blocking its ability to swing outward.

"Give me a sec." I lean out, trying not to think about the empty air below me. The stone above the window cavity is rough enough that I manage to find finger holds. I climb a few feet up the wall, holding myself above the ledge.

"Come on!" Artemis says. Her voice is no longer blocked by the glass.

I swing myself down and through, landing in a crouch on our rug.

"Did you forget we have a door?" she says, unamused. "What's wrong with you? You could have been hurt!"

"But I wasn't. I handled it."

"Because I was here to open the window! What would you have done if I wasn't here?"

"I would have—"

She waves a hand, cutting me off. "You have no idea what you would have done. Because I'm always here. You can't act like things are different now. They're not."

I match her glare. "They are. Everything's different."

"Nothing is different! Nothing is ever different. If you keep pretending like you're a superhero, you're going to get hurt. You're the one who was always talking about how violence isn't a gift or even a tool—it's a crutch. How Slayers get so focused on killing that they never think things through, like it's possible to talk things out with demons or something."

"I never said——"

She cuts me off again. "And then there's your lectures about how *we* need to be smart and cautious. Prioritize other solutions, like my fight training was somehow something to be ashamed of. But as soon as you get some strength, all that flies out the window, just like you!"

Her words sting. "Technically I jumped into the window, not out."

She doesn't smile at the joke. "Don't you get it, Nina? You *never* trained. You're like a loaded weapon in a child's hands. Dangerous to everyone, most especially you. You should have run from the hellhound, not attacked. How am I supposed to protect you from yourself?"

My plan to tell her about the demon slinks away. When presented with a demonic problem, I decided to come straight back to Artemis and dump it on her. I don't want to prove her right. I've depended on her for so many years. But how much of it was me actually needing her, and how much of it was just doing what we've always done?

Besides, she definitely would think I'm an idiot for waiting for this demon to wake up so we can talk it out, exactly like she said. I can't trust her not to hurt the demon before we have more info. Not when she's already so worked up about protecting me.

I'm not telling her. A few months ago, living with secrets from her would have been unfathomable. But after the last two months of having to hide my constant fear of the changes inside me, this almost feels natural.

I unlace my sneakers, trying to act like I'm not hiding anything. Trying to act like her words didn't hurt. "I came in through
the window because I didn't want to see anyone. If you hadn't
opened it, I would have jumped back down and gone around to
the front. It's not a big deal."

"Why did you leave in the first place? I called you."

Thank goodness it was her and not someone else. "I couldn't
deal after what we heard the Council talking about. And I didn't
want to take your hiding spot in the passages, so I went outside."

She softens ever so slightly, then flips her ponytail away from
her shoulder. "Next time you decide to bolt, tell me first. I didn't
know where you were. Also, this was under our door when I got
back." She holds out a thick cream-colored note. Artemis has
already broken the seal, even though my name is on the front.
Someone has elegantly written the following:

> Nina.
> Please meet at 5 a.m. in the training center. Due to certain Council
> politics, discretion is necessary. Until then, sleep well and remember
> the power of your dreams.

It's such precise cursive it looks like someone old wrote
it. It must be from Bradford Smythe. He has answers. He's the
one who knew I was a Potential to begin with. And, unlike my
mother, he'll talk to me about it. I want to ask Artemis why she
opened my note, but I don't want any more tension between us. I
try to lighten the mood instead. "'Remember the power of your
dreams'? That's the dumbest aphorism I've ever heard. Is it supposed to be inspiring?"

"I think it's supposed to be literal." Artemis sits cross-legged on her bed with her back against the wall. "Slayer dreams. You know. Tapping into the power connects the whole line of Slayers."

"Right. Yeah. Slayer dreams." I say it with so much false enthusiasm that Artemis immediately knows I'm lying. Her eyes narrow. I flop onto my bed and pull my pillow over my face. "I don't know what those are. I didn't take advanced Slayer classes, remember?" I only ever studied the basics. Maybe my mother was worried the teachers would figure out what I was really destined to be. Maybe she was worried *I* would figure it out.

If I weren't a Potential, would I have been pushed into full Watcher training like Artemis? A different life opens up before me. One where I mattered in Watcher society. One where I would have been given the ear of the Council, able to have voice and influence.

But if I weren't a Potential, we wouldn't have been taken away to be protected, and we would have been blown up alongside everyone else.

Gods, I can't even hate being a Slayer without it getting complicated.

"Slayers are always important to study," Artemis lectures, unaware of my internal strife. She's annoyed with me again. "Sometimes their dreams are prophetic. The original Slayer communicates through them, and dreams used to link each former Slayer to the next. Ruth Zabuto has theorized that, with so many Slayers now, there might even be direct dream-to-dream connections, like everyone in a big group chat. You need to read up on it."

"Great. Now I have even more homework." Homework I won't do. I don't want to be a Slayer, much less delve into Slayer theory. Besides, the dreaded Buffy hasn't shown up in any of my dreams in the last two months. I doubt she's going to make an appearance now.

Unless knowing I can do this makes it possible for me to do it. . . . Great. Another thing to worry about.

"You should take this seriously!" Artemis says.

I yank my pillow away. "You just told me nothing is different and I shouldn't act like a superhero!"

Artemis turns off her lamp and nighttime engulfs the room, separating us. "Whatever. Do whatever you want. I can't help you be a Slayer." It's such an un-Artemis thing to say. Never in our lives has she told me to do whatever I want. She's told me to do whatever she thinks is best for me. So either she no longer cares what's best for me or she doesn't know. And she's pissed at *me* for it.

Being a Slayer is literally the last thing I would have asked for. Doesn't she get how much this is killing me?

The realization that Buffy has, yet again, changed my entire life without my permission hits me so hard that I finally feel winded. Because if I'm a Slayer, it's Buffy's fault. I never would have been the Chosen One under the old one-at-a-time system. I would have forever remained an invisible Potential. And I never would have known. As furious as it makes me, it also seems preferable to this. Maybe my mom was right to keep it hidden.

Buffy cost me my father and, in a way, my mother. I won't let her ruin my relationship with Artemis, too. She's always taken care of me. Maybe she needs to feel like she still can.

Or maybe now it's my turn to take care of her.

I didn't understand the language coming out of my mouth, but I knew what I was saying as I directed my people to light spears on fire, to gather the children in the center of our village, and to do whatever they could to slow down the demon hordes descending on us.

I would not let the darkness claim my people.

I fought in a fury of blood and blades, slashing and hacking through everything that moved. Behind me, my people were screaming their own battles. Dying. If I took out the queen of the horde, her demons would scatter. I just had to live that long.

Claws raked across my back. Something caught my forehead and blood streamed into my eyes. I fought on pure instinct, a machine of death.

And then I was faced with the queen. She towered over me, seven feet of muscle, claw, exoskeleton, and death. Her scream pierced my eardrums, leaving the world a silent, throbbing mystery. I was blind and deaf. But I was not dead.

Her claws, poisonous, pierced my sides as she lifted me overhead. Just as I had hoped. Smiling, I threw my arms in the air to give the signal. Burning arrows slammed into me, and my gas-soaked clothes immediately caught. The queen screamed, trying to remove her claws from me, but I threw my own arms around her, embracing her in fire and death.

My people were safe.

My people were—

Red, and then black, but a soft black. The black of sleep. The black of a struggle over and a rest well-earned.

A thousand voices sighed in unison. I smiled. I felt it all. The pain and the fear and the fury. And now I feel the pride and peace of her death.

The darkness rips away from me. It isn't mine. Not yet. I

roll onto the floor, choking. Smoke is everywhere. I know if I open my eyes, I'll see flames so dark and purple it hurts to look at them, the colors wrong, the flames wrong. And I'll see my mother holding Artemis.

I can't breathe. Shouting pulls me from the dream, and I claw my way to consciousness to find my blanket wrapped around my head. Someone's shaking me.

"Nina!" The blanket is yanked away.

My hand covers my racing heart. "Who was screaming?"

Artemis sighs as she lies down beside me. "You were. The fire again?"

I don't need to answer her. "And something new. Let's never talk about Slayers before bed again." But weirdly, that first dream—filled with demons and blood and death—wasn't disturbing. I felt energized. Proud, even. Then the fire came and ruined everything, as always.

Artemis stays, which I'm grateful for. She hasn't slept in my bed for a long time. But even when we fight, no one makes me feel as safe as she does. She quickly falls back asleep.

I don't want to sleep. Not now. Not ever.

My body disagrees, and I slip right back under. The only dream I have is of a woman—petite with blond pigtail buns— sitting on the edge of a roof overlooking the Golden Gate Bridge. Though the scene is quiet, I feel the pulsing presence of others around me. Unlike the darkness that had claimed the girl fighting the demon horde, there's no peace here. We all watch, and we all feel the same thing, feeding off each other into a frenzy.

Rage. Focused on her.

Buffy sighs, her shoulders slumping. "I'm sorry," she whispers.

I have never been part of something so big, so overwhelming. Surrounded, I lose myself in it. I surrender. I *want* to. The rage swells, a swarm of invisible violence focused on her. We are angry, we are multitudes, and we are buzzing.

And beeping.

Beeping.

Beeping.

I awake with a start, grabbing my clock. It's 4:50 a.m. I turn off the alarm.

Whoever is waiting for me, they had better have coffee. And doughnuts. And a puppy.

"What?" Artemis asks, her voice muffled by the pillow.

"I have that meeting with Bradford Smythe." I want to stay in bed, pretend nothing ever changed, that none of this ever happened. Anxiety seizes me as I consider the unknown future.

But I've been kept in the dark my whole life. I need answers before I decide what happens next. And I'm positive I just had Slayer dreams, which means that simply by knowing about a power, I was able to tap into it. What else can I do if I understand myself better?

"Yeah." Artemis checks the clock and groans. She gets up at five forty-five every morning. I hate depriving her of these last precious minutes of sleep. "Let me get ready."

"Why?"

She glares blearily at me. "I'm coming."

"Oh. Okay." I didn't realize until this moment that I don't want her there. Which is new for me. I'm nervous, but it'll be worse if she comes. I'm worried that she'll take over and I'll let her, because it's easier.

Her face hardens. "Fine. If you don't need me to."

"I didn't say that! I *don't* need you to, though. It's just a meeting. I'm sure you'll hear all about it. You hear everything."

"Except about you being a Potential, apparently."

"That's not fair! I didn't hear that either, and it was about *me*."

Artemis sighs and sits up. Her face reluctantly resettles from angry to understanding. "I know."

Some of the tightness in my chest loosens. We're going to talk about it. Really talk about it. Cillian's hug was what I needed yesterday, and Artemis's open ear is what I need now. "Who do you think will be at the meeting?" I ask, working myself up to the big things.

"Obviously they're trying to hide this meeting from Mom; otherwise they would have called you to the regular Council room at a normal time."

"Do you think I should do it? If the whole Council doesn't approve?" Maybe I'm hoping she'll say I shouldn't. That she'll give me an out.

She rubs her face, then tugs her hair back into a ponytail. "It's not like you have a choice. You're already a Slayer. Ignoring it won't make it go away."

It stings. "I know that. Obviously. But that doesn't make it suck less that I don't have any choices here."

Artemis stands, turning her back on me as she pulls clothes out of the closet for herself. She's going to the meeting even though I told her not to. Her voice is soft when she finally speaks again. "When have we ever had choices?"

I stand to go to her, but she turns and tosses her clothing selection onto her bed, avoiding my eyes. "I can train you. Besides, we don't even know what they're going to say at the meeting. One step at a time."

"Thanks." I mean it. I feel better with her on my side, because she's *always* been on my side. She's the one who got them to approve my castle clinic and the funds to stock it, after all. Even when she doesn't care about the same things I do, she cares about me. I start to rethink my decision to hide the demon from her. "Listen, last night—"

There's a knock on our door. "Artemis?"

It's our mom.

We share a look of fear. I throw myself back into bed, feigning sleep. Artemis opens the door softly. "What?" she whispers.

"Good, you're up. I need your help checking the perimeters to see if we can determine where the hellhound came from."

"Give me a second to change."

The door closes. Our mom never visits us at this hour. I half suspect she was using the hellhound as an excuse to make sure I was here. I don't peek my eyes open, just in case, as Artemis gets dressed and then slips out. I sit up, annoyed. I don't even get a conversation, let alone a request to help, even though it was me who killed the hellhound. Artemis is still the one our mother chooses. Even when I'm a Chosen One.

And now I'm going to be late. I pad silently through the castle's dark halls, careful that I don't bump into my mother. The training center is located in the old throne room, which was converted to a gym. Another room I never had a place in. But I know where it is.

I duck inside just in time to see a knife flying through the air, right at my face.

8

I STARE UP AT THE KNIFE, EMBEDDED and still quivering in the door where my head had been a split second before. I'm on my back on the floor. My body knew how to avoid the danger, even if my brain didn't.

"In situations such as this," Bradford Smythe says, sounding like he's delivering a well-rehearsed lecture on geometry, "you're supposed to *catch* the knife. That way you avoid being stabbed and take control of the weapon for your own use."

"I'll remember that the next time someone throws a knife at my head!" I stand, furious, and then freeze. Because it isn't just Bradford "Good Morning, Here's a Knife" Smythe in the training room. It's also Eve Silvera.

And Leo.

I am suddenly aware—with more panicked urgency than the knife had induced—that I rolled out of bed and came straight here. My hair is wild on one side and flat on the other. My face probably still has pillow creases. And I'm wearing a long-sleeved flannel shirt three sizes too big . . . with shorts underneath so short it looks like I'm *only* wearing the shirt. I was so bleary from my whacked-out dreams that I didn't even bother changing into appropriate clothes for knife dodging. Which I would have had to borrow from Artemis in the first place. But I thought this was a *talking* meeting, not one that would threaten my life.

"Hello, Athena," Leo says.

I had forgotten. He's the only person around here who calls me by my real name. When I was little I was always Athena, but after the fire and my brief hospital stay, somehow it turned into Nina. I became someone to be taken care of and got pet-named right out of the Greek pantheon. The way Leo said my name used to flutter my stomach, because I thought it meant he *saw* me or respected me or wanted to marry me once we were both older so we could be the ultimate Watcher couple and save the world together while also maybe riding horses under a rainbow along a beach.

(There was a poem about that too. I've never been so prolific about anything in my life as I was during my Leo Poetry phase.)

I tug my shirt down, which makes the neck slip over one of my shoulders. Oh, sweet hellmouths, *I'm not even wearing a bra.* When I imagined meeting Leo again—which wasn't often, because I was pretty sure he was dead and it was easier to not imagine him at all—it had always been in some really cool way. Like he was horribly injured and my quick thinking stopped the bleeding and saved his life. Or . . . well, actually, all my scenarios involved him being horribly injured. It was comforting. And it meant he would be the one embarrassed, not me.

None of them involved him standing professionally beside his mother while I was in my pajamas.

Gods, I hate him.

"Nina?" Eve asks.

I hastily do the top two buttons of my shirt and focus on her instead. She's dressed as formally as she was during the meeting we spied on, but now her blazer is a deep plum. Her lipstick matches it again. I remember I'm not supposed to have been listening to the meeting, so I should be shocked they're here. "Hi! Wow, you're back."

Her lips twist in an amused smile. "I am well aware of the secrets of this castle. Namely that it *has* no secrets. You don't have to pretend like you didn't know."

I hurry to change the subject, not wanting to reveal the secret passageways. "I'm glad you guys aren't dead!" Oh gods, let me stop talking. "I mean, we thought you were. Dead. And we were all really sad!" It comes out sounding cringingly insincere, which makes me feel awful—despite my never wanting to see Leo again, it was terrible believing the Silveras were dead. "It's, uh, nice for someone to be alive for once. Usually it's the opposite. Hey, does anyone have another knife they want to throw at me?"

Bradford Smythe lets out a phlegmy laugh. Then he gets serious, his bushy eyebrows half covering his eyes, like Spanish moss hanging on a tree. "Nina, my child, you're a Slayer."

I don't have it in me to pretend to be shocked. I shrug. It sums up my feelings pretty adequately.

He continues. "Now that you have been Chosen, you have a responsibility. The life of a Slayer is never easy—that hasn't changed even now that there are more. It is our duty to train you, to prepare you for what your future holds. Of course, the training will be a challenge. This is most irregular."

He clasps his hands behind his back and paces, looking thoughtfully at the walls. They're lined with pads, practice weapons, real weapons. I brace myself as he pauses in front of a wicked-looking mace and chain. "We can't very well do the Tento di Cruciamentum when you turn eighteen. You were raised by us, so you'll know all about the muscle relaxers and adrenal suppressants we secretly inject so the incapacitated Slayer has to face a vampire without her abilities."

"Right." I hope my eyes aren't as wide as they feel. "Right, I know *all* about that, so there's no reason to do it when I turn eighteen, which is still not for two years. So, yeah, that trial's out. No point in even scheduling. And since we're talking about it, I never technically agreed to be a Slayer? Or said I'd train as one. We should stop and think if this is really the best option for everyone." *For me.* "I mean, we've never even tried to find any of the other Slayers. Maybe we should do that before jumping on the yay-Nina-kills-things-now bandwagon, which is a pretty bad bandwagon as far as bandwagons go."

Leo looks engaged for the first time this whole conversation. Before, his face had been blank. Now he looks anxious. Eager, even. "Athena has a point. There are so many Slayers now. We can't ask her to do something she doesn't want to—"

"We aren't asking her," Eve says, interrupting him. "And we're not commanding you either, Nina. But training or not, you *are* a Slayer. And that is something wonderful and I'm sure more than a little overwhelming and terrifying. But you can't change it by ignoring it. To do so would be irresponsible. Dangerous, even."

I flinch, remembering Artemis's comment about a loaded gun in the hands of a child. Leo is staring at me. He gives me an almost imperceptible shake of his head. It's clear he disagrees with his mother. Which makes me want to listen to her more.

Eve closes the distance between us, putting her hands on my shoulders. "You've always had so much to offer the Watchers, but you've never truly been utilized here, never truly had a place among us. This is a tremendous opportunity for *us* to learn from *you*. It's time to take your rightful spot alongside the Council. Where your father would have wanted you."

I still don't want to be a Slayer, but the way Eve is looking at me with hope and warmth melts away some of my fear. *Would* my father have wanted this? "I guess—I guess we could try."

Eve beams. "That's our girl." Then she releases my shoulders to take stock of what the room has to offer. "I assume you've had basic combat training?" Her assumption hurts, but it's nice of her to give me the benefit of the doubt.

"I wasn't allowed to. My mom said no. But I've read most of the manuals! And I, uh, know a lot of first aid. I've been working as the Watcher medic. I'm really good with stitches. And ice packs. Expert ice packer."

She smiles, and there's genuine delight there. No judgment or mockery. I'm so glad it's her here instead of stupid Wanda Wyndam-Pryce. "That's wonderful. I love that you have experience outside of the narrow focus a Potential would have been given. How is your demon lore?"

"The lore-iest! Super up on demon lore. Name a demon, I know the lore." Actually, Rhys is the resident demon expert, but he likes to talk and I don't mind listening. Most of my studies have been human oriented, but I do know more than the average Slayer. And I definitely know more than Buffy, who was notorious for being unwilling to do research or study on her own.

Rupert Giles always babied her. Now he's dead too, just like my father. It's usually *Watchers* who bury more than one *Slayer*. Buffy never did like the status quo, though.

"Tell me about D'Hoffryn," Eve says. "What do you know about him?"

"Oh! I know this one!" I clap my hands, excited. I usually don't get pumped about demony stuff, but Eve has this way about her that makes me yearn for her approval. Maybe because I feel like she actually cares, like she's rooting for me. Leo's eyes have moved from me to the door, and his hands are clasped behind his back. "D'Hoffryn is a true demon—not a hybrid. He has the ability to corrupt humans into vengeance demons. He has no known weaknesses. He comes to this plane only when summoned by a vengeance demon or drawn to a new candidate." I pause, thinking. "But . . . with portals to and from demon dimensions closed, can he keep creating vengeance demons? I'm guessing he can't! So that's good. Score one for no magic."

"Do you know whether he was on earth when the portals closed?"

I shrug, wishing I could impress her. "No idea."

Bradford Smythe answers. "I believe he is trapped here. He'll still have his basic demonic abilities but will be considerably handicapped by the lack of magic."

"Didn't anyone think this might be a good time to go after demons like D'Hoffryn?" Eve asks, forehead creased.

"We don't have the resources." Bradford doesn't sound offended. Just wistful. "What you see here is what we have, my dear."

Eve smiles at me, and the furrow leaves her brow. I find myself standing straighter. "What I see here is all the start we need."

I know I'm blushing, and I don't care. Being looked at with pride and hope by such a remarkable Watcher is a feeling I never realized how much I needed. No one ever congratulated me for learning a new splinting technique or complimented my ability to time a pulse. But Eve not only believes I'm a Slayer . . . she's *glad* I am. She might be the only one.

And the way she looks at me makes me feel like I might actually be able to do this. She might even be the person I can trust with Cillian's demon. I'll have to feel her out and wait until Bradford Smythe isn't here, but I'm already relieved at the anticipation of shifting the burden onto someone more capable.

"Helen can't know." Bradford sighs. "She means well, but it is . . . complicated."

Eve nods. "Families always are." She turns back to me, and her head tilts to the side. "I do have a question about the timing. When, exactly, did you feel the change? It had to have happened before the Seed of Wonder was destroyed."

"I think it happened exactly then. It's why I didn't tell anyone I felt weird. There was a big demon and a sort of magical aftershock wave, and we were splattered in demon goo. That's when I felt like I was—it's hard to describe . . . being unmade? Like everything in my body shifted so I wasn't me, but I was more me than I had ever been. I was afraid it was a demon thing, so I ignored it. Until the hellhound attacked, and my body just reacted."

Eve's face shifts with amazement. "Nina, if you changed from

Potential to Slayer at the very moment the magic was destroyed, that means you are the last Slayer. Ever. The end of the line stretching back to the very first one."

The weight of that settles on my shoulders. I don't want this mantle. I never asked for it. But one part makes sense: I got picked last. Some things never change.

Eve squeezes my shoulder again, then looks around the room as though imagining what I'll do. "We'll train you in secret. Bradford's right: Your mother can't know. And frankly, I don't care for Wanda's politics. Ruth probably won't have an opinion one way or the other."

I still don't know how I feel about training, but she's so supportive, I don't want to take that for granted. And training doesn't mean becoming Action Girl Slayer. It just means figuring out how I've changed, which is a good thing. I hope.

"Can Rhys be involved?" It feels traitorous not wanting Artemis—who already offered to train me—but Rhys is so much easier to be around. I'd feel better with my friend at my side. If anyone is going to help Eve, I want it to be Rhys, not Leo. He's practically radiating coldness. Ever since he got shot down for agreeing that I shouldn't jump right into training, it's like he's not even in there anymore.

Eve shakes her head. "Rhys has his own studies to complete. And we don't want to force him to lie to your mother. It's best to keep this contained. No Rhys, no Imogen or Jade. As far as the Council is concerned, only Bradford and I will know."

"Artemis already knows."

"That's fine. But your closest relationship should be with your Watcher."

She thinks I need a Watcher. It's such a funny concept to me. Like being a member of a race-car-driving family, and then learning you need your own driver. Bradford is too old—I hope. It's going to be Eve. I regret all the fantasies I entertained of her being horribly injured so that Leo would fall at my feet, weeping with gratitude that I saved his mother, after which I would calmly and coolly reject him.

I might not have wanted to be a Slayer, but with Eve as my Watcher, I feel like maybe I can do this. Like maybe I can be *great* at this. I'll show my mom how wrong she was to keep me sidelined. I'll show Artemis that she doesn't have to worry about me anymore. And hell, maybe I can show Buffy what a Slayer *should* be. The things I hate about her, the struggles Watchers have had with Slayers over the centuries—I can avoid them. There has to be a better way to keep our world safe, a way that doesn't rely so heavily on pure violence. I'll find it.

"It won't be hard keeping it a secret from my mother," I say. "She never notices me anyway."

"Be patient with her," Bradford says. "She's lost so much. She's very protective of you. But I believe it's more dangerous not to train you."

I don't think he knows my mother very well. "Protective" doesn't describe her. Cold. Unyielding. Even manipulative, now that I know the truth she's hidden from us. And "protective" isn't a word I'd use for a woman who left me behind in a fire. No, the only reason I can imagine she's so against me being a Slayer is because she hates Slayers.

The thing I hated too. But maybe I only hate the way Buffy is a Slayer. The Slayer from the village in my dream last night—she was amazing. If she'd had someone to help her plan, she probably could have avoided dying, even. I want to be a Slayer and a Watcher in one.

"My sister said she'd help train me," I say. If Rhys is off the table, Artemis will have to do.

Eve shakes her head. "It's fine if she knows, as long as she can keep a secret from your mother. But Artemis doesn't have the skill or experience to train you."

"That's not true, she—"

"Artemis is exceptional. But she hasn't been fully trained. She's been an assistant rather than in line for the Council. We have to give you the absolute best, Nina. You're too important."

My ego balloons, and I don't even care. I have never been important in this castle, never been valued more than Artemis. Ever.

So I nod.

"Excellent," Eve says. I lean forward, expecting a hug. Wanting one. But Eve holds out her hand toward Leo, gazing upon him with pure maternal pride. "I'm sure you and your new Watcher will be a perfect match."

9

AS SOON AS EVE SILVERA AND BRADFORD
Smythe leave, Leo's rigid stance relaxes, and he grins at me. Like
he didn't fall all over himself to agree I shouldn't train and then go
dead silent when they decided I should. Like now that he's been
assigned as my Watcher, we should both forget that happened.

"I can't tell you what a relief it was when we found your
mum and she told us you were all okay. It's amazing to see
you—it's like old times." He stares at me for a moment, and I
could swear I see a hint of a blush. "You've changed. A lot. You
grew up."

"Yeah, that happens. And it isn't exactly like old times.
Those days I was on the balcony watching, not on the training
floor. Ever."

He flinches, then tucks his hair behind an ear in a nervous
gesture. So he hasn't forgotten either. Good. I mean, bad. I
wish he had. But then again, if he had managed to forget the
most humiliating moment of my life, I'd probably be even
more offended.

"Of course things are different," he says. "You're a Slayer now. I'm not surprised."

I raise an eyebrow. He didn't want me to train as one, and now he's saying he's not surprised? "Really? Everyone else was surprised."

"I always knew you were special. I'll admit I didn't assume that meant *Slayer*, but it does settle an old bet." His face shifts into a sly smile. "I wagered Honora fifty quid that you would be able to take any of us in a fight one day."

The mention of Honora is the last straw. "I don't want to *take* anyone in a fight. Fighting is pointless. Your being able to throw a punch then didn't make any of you better than me, just like being a Slayer now doesn't make me any better than I was before."

He cringes. "Right. I know that. I'm just—I think we got started on the wrong note."

"You mean when you immediately agreed I shouldn't train and we should look for other Slayers instead?"

The confusion on his face is deeply satisfying. He takes a hesitant step forward, and then one back. The small, mean parts of me exult in throwing him so off balance. Leo was always precise in everything he did. Right now? He's a mess. And I made him that way.

He shakes his head. "I thought someone should offer alternatives to training as a Slayer. It seemed like you didn't want to. You shouldn't have to do anything you aren't comfortable with or ready for."

I can't blame him for picking up on the truth. Be that as it may, his speed to dismiss me was telling. He's acting like it was about what I wanted, but I suspect it's more about him still seeing me as a pathetic child. "All Watchers have to do things we might not be ready for. Artemis always had to. I shouldn't be an exception. If this is what the Council wants, then it's my responsibility." I might be fronting a tad. But I refuse to have the same power dynamic here that I always have—mainly that everyone *else* has all the power.

Leo's voice is firm again, all hesitation gone. "The Council shouldn't count more than you. Ever. That's my first piece of advice."

"As my Watcher?"

"As your friend."

"I'm going to change my clothes," I snap. "And then we can train as Watcher and Slayer. Not friends." His face falls as I leave the room. For a moment I feel guilty, especially since he really was picking up on how I was feeling. And it does mean something— however small—that he believed I was strong even back when no one else had any reason to. But I steel myself. I don't want anything from Leo Silvera. If he has to be my Watcher, fine. But he'll never be my friend again. I owe that much to my past self.

Leo and Honora were sixteen. Artemis, Rhys, and I were thirteen. Unlike Artemis, Rhys had passed his Watcher trials the year before.

Those in line for active Watcher (and future Council) status faced a series of tests, both practical and mystical, to determine whether they'd be approved for training. There were loads of different positions within the Watcher society, but all of them— special ops, mystical consultants, nurses, librarians—were subordinate to full Watchers. Being an active Watcher was the goal.

When she didn't pass the test, Artemis became an errand girl. An understudy of sorts. I wanted her to join me in my medic and first aid studies, but our mother had sent a note that it would be "a waste of her abilities," even though it apparently wasn't a waste of mine.

Rhys was already stressing out about his Watcher project, an in-depth study presented to the Council. Most famously, Wesley Wyndam-Pryce had done a genealogy tracing the sirings of vampires all the way back to the original demon that created them. It took seventeen days to present. Rhys always spoke of it with a wistful, dreamy look, as though he wished he had been old enough to attend.

Another Watcher had done a study of a vampire named William the Bloody. I tried to read it once, but Artemis took it from me, saying it was *inappropriate*. Even though she was the same age and had obviously read it. She wasn't fully a Watcher-in-training, but she still had access to information I didn't.

Leo and Honora had passed their trials three years before. They were well into the training, nearly ready to accomplish their final tests and be granted full Watcher status. It would be years before they'd be able to apply for Council positions, but they were both on their way.

Part of their responsibilities was overseeing the magical and physical training of Rhys. Artemis mostly worked alongside Rhys, the idea being that she'd eventually be his assistant.

She was still lucky, in a way. Close to the things that mattered. Jade had been shuffled off to magical special ops. Imogen, like me, wasn't even allowed to test.

We sat together sometimes, when Imogen wasn't on nanny

duty. We'd climb up to the balcony overlooking the training room. With our legs stuck through the bannister rails, we'd lean our foreheads against it and watch those lucky enough to train for things we'd never get to do.

"Aren't you mad?" I asked her once.

She shrugged. "It was nice of them to let me stay. I don't have anywhere else to go. And I'm not like my mother. I don't want power. I want to help. So if me taking care of the Littles while their parents do important things helps? I'm glad I can do it."

I liked Imogen, but I didn't understand her. I would have been pissed. I *was* pissed. I watched my sister training with a body that should have been identical to mine, and I envied her. I wanted that same level of ease in my skin. For our thirteenth birthday, my mother had given Artemis weapons. She'd given me DVD collections of *ER* and *Chicago Hope*.

At first it felt disappointing, but then portentous. I *could* do something. I could have a role. That was when I gave up my previous hobby and started learning all the ways human bodies could be broken—and all the ways I could fix them. It was just as important as, if not more important than, knowing how to hurt things.

Unfortunately, my previous hobby had been poetry. And it had all been focused on the crush I had nurtured since the year before, when Leo had shown up, saved me, and made my body realize that not only were boys super cute, he was the super cutest of *all* boys. Every part of me felt electrocuted around him. I filled notebook after notebook with doodles of his name and poetry dedicated to him. I didn't interact with Leo much, but whenever I did, he was so nice, it left me floating for days. Sometimes we'd eat lunch in the dorm cafeteria on the same day. Once, six months before, he had been given two oatmeal-chocolate-chip cookies. Any day with chocolate instead of raisins was a treat. When he walked by, he slipped the extra one onto my tray. I saved that cookie until it crumbled.

There weren't too many of us, even back then. Rhys, Artemis, Jade, and me. Imogen. Leo and Honora. A few trainees a year or two older than them. And then a gap until the Littles. But whenever Leo noticed me, I felt *special*. That was real magic.

One day I was quietly studying alone on the balcony when Artemis dumped a stack of spell books on the training room's floor. I glanced over, uninterested. They didn't know I was up there. I wasn't supposed to be in the room when they did magic practice. But I'd often stay, quiet, trying to sneak peeks into the aspects of our world that were hidden from me.

"I found every book I could that wasn't in the library," Artemis said. "We had some boxed up in our rooms. Maybe my dad's old books."

"Ooh." Honora sat down next to Artemis. "This could be good! They're so restrictive in what they'll even let us look at."

I hated Honora Wyndam-Pryce. Artemis idolized her. Honora was wickedly clever, her tongue as sharp as the knives she specialized in. She was smart and deadly, and when Artemis wasn't around, she called me Wheezy on account of my asthma. She acted like it was a pet name. But I already *had* a pet name. I didn't need one that felt mean.

Plus, she was a Wyndam-Pryce. The whole family was insufferable.

I chose to ignore Honora, focusing instead on Leo. He was

sword training with Rhys. His movements were fluid and graceful. He made me feel like I was having an asthma attack in my heart.

"I'll go grab our lunches," Artemis said. She walked back out, and I returned to my paramedic manuals. My dad had died from a bullet to the brain. I couldn't have fixed that. But there were a lot of things I *could* fix, if I knew how. And I'd learn them all. Except the magical ways, of course, because my mom still kept those off-limits.

That's why I didn't see when Honora picked up a book that should not have been there.

Honora started laughing. "Oh gods. These are the greatest spells I've ever heard. Would you like to hear them?"

I was only half listening until I recognized the words. And then I froze.

"'Your lips are a promise / I'd love to keep / They haunt me when waking / And tease when asleep.'"

No. No no *no*.

A few months before, I had run out of notebooks and found a dusty old magic book that was mostly empty. So I filled it with the best of my poetry, enamored that my love was written like spells in a leather-bound book. Whenever I wrote one in there, I pretended like it was an actual love spell that would make Leo see we were meant to be.

Rhys paused in his training. "What is this?"

I crawled to the balcony and watched, numbing with horror, as Honora read poem after poem, each more embarrassing than the last. But maybe she wouldn't say who they were about. His name was written only in a few of them.

Honora was in performance mode, standing on a bench in

front of Leo and Rhys and reciting each poem with the relish
of a Shakespearean performer. She wouldn't say his name. She
wouldn't. But then she looked up—right at me—and winked.

She knew I was up there. She had the whole time.

"This one," she said, "is the best. It's an acrostic. Please
imagine the letters going down the side, starting each sentence."
She cleared her throat. "'And when / The days are too / Hard /
Endless in knowing I will / Never be / Anyone important—'"

She paused. "That's ATHENA, for those of you too dumb to
spell on the go." She lifted an eyebrow at Rhys. I wanted to run
or scream at her to stop. My body wouldn't do either.

"'Looking at you gives me / Optimism / Very real and true /
Everything will be okay / Someday.'" Honora smiled, baring her
perfect white teeth. "Rhys, what did that one spell?"

Rhys looked at the floor. "You shouldn't be reading those."

"Give it here." Leo held out his hand, but she lifted it out of
his reach.

"It spelled 'loves,'" she said. "And here's the grand finale:
'Love is / Everything I feel *when I think of you* . . . / Orgasmically.'"

"That's not what it says!" I squeaked. Everyone looked up
at me, my face pressed against the balcony railing bars, tears
streaming down my face. What I had written was "Love is /
Everything I feel / Over the fear." She had not only taken the
most embarrassing thing possible—she had made it worse. So
much worse.

A door banged open. "Okay, today we have— Nina? Nina,
are you okay?" Artemis set down her trays and ran up the stairs
to me. Honora slammed the book shut, her face bright red from
laughing.

Leo raised his sword at Rhys. "Second and fourth forms," he said, as though nothing had happened. As though Honora hadn't just read my entire heart out loud in front of him. As if I weren't suffocating from shame and panic. He didn't even care.

After that I pretended I was sick and didn't get out of bed for a week. One of the mornings, someone left an oatmeal-chocolate-chip cookie outside my door.

I ground it into crumbs.

Leo had gone right back to practice, shrugging off the worst moment of my life. He wouldn't fix it by offering me a *cookie*.

I finally worked up the courage to leave my room when I heard that Leo and his mother had been shipped off to an assignment in South America. Not long after, Honora graduated to full Watcher status and was assigned fieldwork monitoring demon activity in Ireland.

Rhys never pushed the subject. When Artemis asked why I was so upset that day, I asked her why she failed the test. Neither of us answered, and we never spoke of it again. I prayed Leo was gone forever and tore up every scrap of paper I had ever desecrated with my stupid crush.

Our history trails from me like smoke as I stomp back to my room. So Leo's back. Whatever. I refuse to care. That's another problem Buffy had. She always made her relationships with her Watchers so personal. I can treat Leo as a coworker. Calm. Cool. Collected.

Except I'm none of the three. And I can't afford to be calm, not with everything going on, not the least of which is the demon I left in my friend's shed. Once I start training it will be harder to sneak away. Forget changing—I need to check on the demon.

My room is fortunately empty. Artemis must still be out with our mother. I try not to be bitter about this. I know it's weird to be jealous of having to patrol with our mother, but I've always envied how *needed* Artemis is. My days are filled with empty spaces between studying and doing my chores around the castle.

But I guess that will change now too. At least in secret.

There is one way Artemis could have helped out today. I could have begged her to go back to the training room in my place. Leo would think she was me, be so impressed that he'd decide I don't need training, and then he'd leave. Walk away. Walk off a cliff, preferably.

I sneak out of the castle. The light is lovely and soft in the dawn glow. There's a storage shed where we keep the weapons and tools that aren't in regular rotation. It waits for me under the shadow of forest trees yearning to reclaim our land. I consider the heavy padlock securing it.

Then I twist it until the metal snaps.

"Cool," I whisper to myself. I still don't want to like anything about being a Slayer, but I have to admit it does have perks. Inside the shed, boxes and shelves are neatly labeled in Artemis's handwriting. She organized chains by size and material, as well as by whether or not they're magically charmed. The last option doesn't matter anymore, but I appreciate her thoroughness. I pick a medium-weight chain set that has ankle shackles.

The demon's wrists are in my mind like gunk on the bottom of my shoe, sticking and tugging with every step. The old bruising around its wrists tells a story of captivity long before Cillian's shed. I don't know what it means, but I don't want to layer injury on top of injury. Not until we know whether the demon has to be killed.

I accept that it might need to be. Watchers never flinch from what needs to be done. But I don't have to be cruel in the meantime, and I certainly don't have to rush to assume this will end in more death. Anticipating violence always seems to create it.

I sling the chains over my shoulder and sprint for Cillian's. I don't think even the ATVs we keep in the garage are faster. When I get there, I jump the fence right into the yard and snag the padlock key from under the rock where Cillian hid it. Cringing at each metallic click, I unlock the door and open it, fully expecting the demon to be standing, waiting to devour me.

It's still slumped on the floor. I hide the key under a bowl of crystals on a table out of reach and tiptoe forward, anticipating attack. Then another fear strikes me. I crouch, peering closely— the demon is still breathing. Not sure whether I should be relieved or disappointed, I secure the chains to the beam and shackle the demon's ankles, noting the handcuffs still in place on its wrists. Since it hasn't moved, I do a quick check. Its facial wound is closing nicely. I did good work there. I want to move its arm to make certain it has full range of motion, but even I know that's going too far.

I linger for a few minutes, but the demon is out. Maybe forever. I know I shouldn't, but I feel a twinge of sadness at the thought. My years of studying medicine taught me to value all life, and apparently that extends to even demons. Reading about demons in gruesomely illustrated books isn't the same as seeing them in real life. This one is less terrifying and more pathetic. I know they're not all that way—the hellhound certainly wasn't, and neither was the giant interdimensional monstrosity—but it does make me feel better about not alerting the Council.

I lock the shed again, then hop the fence and jog through town to the shop to update Cillian. I want to check on him too. Make sure he's okay. Plus, I wouldn't mind some sugary comfort. With magic a bust, Cillian has shifted the shop away from spell supplies and toward soda of all types. Though I'd prefer hot chocolate this morning. I wrap my arms around myself, shivering, and jog faster.

I love the tiny village. Gray rocks, thatched roofs, and cobbled streets wind through the village straight to an ocean seemingly designed to complement the weather. There's something natural about Shancoom—as though it were simply a feature of the landscape. Even the way it's laid out feels organic, with its homes clustered around a meandering central street. So many cities in America exist in defiance of the land they were built on. But Shancoom *belongs*.

The early morning fog lingers, drifting through the streets like the ghost of a long-dead river. I imagine it flowing over the cobblestones, straight to the cliffs, and spilling in a slow-motion waterfall to the ocean.

The fog plays tricks on my eyes. I see movement where there is none. I jog faster, feeling hunted.

Then a low growl makes me realize: I *am* being hunted.

I stop dead outside the soda shop. I can see Cillian inside, asleep on the floor beneath the counter. The door is locked up tight. He's safe.

For now.

I crouch, using the fog to obscure myself too as I slip past the soda shop and loop back around to try to get behind whatever is following me. The fog parts enough to reveal frenzied eyes and sick-looking patches of skin with tufts of fur growing like fungus.

Another hellhound. Where are they coming from? How did it find me? It sniffs the air and then cuts straight through the fog toward me.

My first instinct is an overwhelming compulsion:

Attack.

My muscles strain, heartbeat soars, blood pounds in my head.

I take a deep breath. Send cooling thoughts into my veins, use that same Slayer strength to restrain my own limbs. Force myself to think like a Watcher, to look at the bigger picture. To think, think, think, not move.

It's not about me. What is the common link between the two hellhound sightings? The first one was following Cillian. And now this one is here in town, not at the castle. So the first one might not have been looking for us at all. It might have been looking for something else. Something linked to Shancoom, and to Cillian.

And then I realize: the Coldplay demon.

I didn't wash my hands after securing its chains just now. The hellhound might not be hunting *me* at all. And the first hellhound was right behind Cillian, who had come from his house, where the injured demon was probably already hiding. Whether friends or foes of the Coldplay demon, the hellhounds are looking for it. And I'm not going to let them succeed. Because whatever side the hellhounds are on, I'm on the opposite one.

Shancoom will wake up soon, though. Hellhounds fixate on their prey with unshakable intensity, but that doesn't mean they won't rip apart anything they encounter along the way. Done hiding, I stand and whistle. "Hey, doggy! Here, doggy, doggy!"

The hellhound freezes, cocking its head in confusion. Then it growls and leaps into motion. I turn and sprint, pushing myself as fast as I can run. Hellhounds are fast, but I'm faster. I let out one involuntary whoop of sheer adrenaline-fueled joy.

I am faster than a demon.

Only just, though. I race through the woods, branches clawing at me. I leap logs and duck obstacles. I hear the hellhound in pursuit. When the castle comes into sight, I put on a burst of speed, praying no one is outside yet. My luck holds. I yank open the door to the storage building, then jump up and catch the door frame, pulling my legs under me right as the hellhound leaps for them. It overshoots, smashing into the shelves.

I drop and slam the door shut, trapping the hellhound inside. Chest heaving, I consider my options. I've trapped a hellhound right outside my own home. In the building with all the weapons and chains I could have used to subdue it.

Stake me. Why couldn't my brain run as fast as my legs?

I can get weapons in the training room. I don't want to think about what I'll have to do when I let the hellhound out. I'll figure it out when I get to that point. I have my very own Watcher now, but he's the last person I want help from. I could ask Artemis, but—

I turn around and scream. My mother is standing right behind me. Interesting that she could make me scream in terror, while the hellhound, not so much. But only one of them is a mortal threat to me right now.

"Nina," she says, "we need to talk about yesterday."

Now she wants to talk? There's a crash from the shed. It sounds like a shelf being torn down. My mother frowns, looking over my shoulder.

I grab her arm, turning her away. "I was reorganizing. Knocked one of the shelves loose. Sorry! I'll fix it. Let's go talk in the castle."

The hellhound slams itself against the door. The entire building shudders from the impact.

"What do you have in there?" My mother steps toward the shed.

I hold out my arms. "Nothing! Just, let's go inside. Okay? Please?"

"Open the door, Nina."

Normally, the voice she uses would have me shrinking into myself like a tortoise. She's been more Council member than mother since we rejoined the Watchers. And I always obeyed the Council. Maybe it's part of my new Slayer powers. I'm compelled to kill demons *and* I'm compelled to defy the Watchers. But I can't do what she tells me to. Not this time. "Don't open it. Please trust me. I'll take care of it."

The door shudders again. There's a cracking noise. I'm worried it'll break before I can decide what to do. And then it does just that.

The hellhound bursts free, claws and fangs ready. I push my mom out of the way and drop to my back, using my momentum and legs to propel the hellhound over my body. It slams into a tree. I jump to my feet and spin to face it again, fists raised. I'm hyperfocused on the hellhound. But part of me still manages to feel exultant that my mother is here. She'll see what I can do.

She'll see that even if she didn't bother saving me all those years ago, *I* can save *her*.

Maybe my mom could ignore me when I was the Watcher medic, but there's no way she can ignore me as a Slayer.

The hellhound charges toward me again. I dig my feet in, ready for the impact—

Three loud pops. The hellhound drops to the ground, motionless.

My ears are ringing. I turn to find my mother holding a gun. Her expression is as hard and cold as the metal death machine in her hand. The shock and violence of it leaves me stunned.

My father might have died because of a vampire, but it was a gun that killed him. How could she use one? How could she stand to even hold it?

Then an even worse thought seizes me: What if it's my father's gun?

My mother calmly unloads the rest of the clip into the hellhound's head. I look away, sick to my stomach at how the demon's body twitches with the force of the bullets.

She holsters the gun in a leather brace I've never noticed. No wonder she always wears those bulky blazers. How long has she been hiding a gun there? Each word she speaks is as shaped and piercing as her bullets. "The world doesn't need Slayers anymore. Whatever you *think* you are, it isn't your calling. You're not the Chosen One."

Then she walks away from me. Just like that night. As if I didn't already know—hadn't known for years—that in her eyes, I'm not the one she would choose.

10

THE FIRE WAS PURPLE.

But not normal purple. Black-light purple, purple that felt wrong, that made my eyes want to slide away from it because they couldn't quite make sense of it. Was it purple, or was it black, or was it *nothing*?

Whatever it was, it was hot, blistering and cracking my skin even at a distance. The smoke attacked my lungs, ripping me out of sleep and throwing me, coughing, onto the floor of the bedroom I shared with Artemis.

"Athena?" Artemis cried out. I slid across the floor to her, pulling her out of bed and down to me. The fire was, inexplicably, over the window. A solid sheet of flames blocked our exit. There was no way outside. I grabbed a book and threw it at the window. It disintegrated in the flames before ever reaching the glass.

I crawled to the door. The doorknob burned my hand and left a shiny pink scar that I would never lose.

"Stay down." I ripped a sheet off my bed and gave it to

Artemis, gesturing for her to breathe through it. I didn't know if it would filter out the smoke, but maybe it would help. I was only eight, but I knew enough of the world to know this wasn't a normal fire. It was magic. The bad kind. The kind my mother knew how to fight.

She would come. She would save us.

Why wasn't she here yet?

We huddled together, the flames eating past the window and onto the wall. But the window didn't break. It stayed perfectly intact, still a solid flame that I couldn't see how to get past. Maybe everything outside was on fire too. Maybe the whole world was on fire.

Finally the door burst open. The flames ringed it, impassable, but in the center stood our mother. She glowed clean white, some sort of magical aura allowing her to stand in the flames without being burned. I tried to run to her, but it was too hot. She looked at us, her face far worse than the horrible flames. Nothing is more terrifying than seeing your mother afraid.

She glanced over her shoulder. The whole house was consumed. She was the only safe harbor. After one more moment of hesitation, she rushed into our room and scooped up Artemis.

I stared at her, uncomprehending. In that instant, my mother's fear slid away, and her eyes went hard in the same way they did when she reprimanded us for not looking both ways before crossing the street.

"I can only take one at a time," she said. "Be strong."

Then she ran through the fire, her shield extending to the daughter she had chosen to take with her first.

I was left behind.

The flames spread. The smoke got worse. I waited, the room so hot that my tears felt cool on my face. And then everything went black.

The paramedics resuscitated me. She had come back for me, but by then it was almost too late. She could have carried us both. I know she could have. She picked Artemis first, and I almost died. She was willing to lose me over Artemis. And none of us have ever forgotten it.

I hastily wipe away new tears. Am I crying or just remembering the smoke? At least the tears blur the body of the hellhound. I wonder if my mother will put the castle back on lockdown. I could have explained to her where it came from, what it was actually hunting, if she had given me a second to speak. But she never does.

I drag the hellhound into the trees and tuck it against some roots. That way at least none of the Littles will stumble across it if they go outside to play. And if my mom asks where it is, I'll tell her.

She won't ask.

Corpse removal accomplished, I want to hide in my room. Maybe forever. I thought I was finally in control. Finally able to do things to make a difference. My mom showed me otherwise.

I send Cillian a text to stay away from his house. He didn't touch the demon, so any other hellhound on the hunt shouldn't zero in on him personally. Unless my mom is going to hang out there with her *gun*, Cillian isn't safe at home.

At that thought, I hurry into the castle after my mother. She might not talk to me about it, but I can talk to her. "Hey!" I shout at her back. She stops but doesn't turn around. "Don't you want to know where it came from?"

"I can determine that on my own. You aren't needed for this, Nina. I thought that was apparent outside."

"I can—"

She finally turns around. There's a smile pasted onto her face. It's almost as repellent as the gun—just as cold and metallic. "Sweetheart, take the day off. It's been a confusing time for you. Go read or paint your nails. Or you must have some chores to handle in your clinic."

"You've *never* cared about my clinic."

"That's absurd. I'm the one who suggested that course of study in the first place."

"Why did you, if you knew I was a Potential? You sabotaged me!"

"Sabotaged?" She has the audacity to look hurt, and for a second, she almost—*almost*—meets my eye. But right as she comes close, a shadow passes over her face and she lifts her chin. "I am a member of the Council and your mother. Everything I do is for the good of the Watchers. Don't question my decisions." And then she walks away. Again.

I stare after her, trembling with emotion. Then I lift my middle finger at her back.

"Um. Hey."

Leo is standing in the door to the training room. Which is where my mother and I had our entire conversation, in perfect hearing range. His hands are shoved in his pockets as he leans against the door frame. "She's jet-lagged," he says. "It was a long trip back."

"Don't make excuses for her." I hastily wipe under my eyes. I cannot handle another humiliation. And tears in front of Leo—the star of my greatest humiliation ever? Not happening. I won't let him see what my mother obviously sees: That I'm weak. That I don't deserve to be a Slayer. That no one needs me to be one.

When she first assigned me to the medical branch of study, I was proud. It felt like she noticed I'd be good at it, and I worked so hard in order to prove her right. But she was really just putting me out of sight, out of mind. Where no one would ever see my potential.

Including me.

I stomp past him into the room. I barely got any sleep last night, but I'm as buzzed as if I'd had four cups of tea. I want to hit something. "I'm ready."

He follows, taking his time. "Watcher mums are . . . hard. Even the good ones."

"You're lucky you have a good one."

"I meant your mum."

I snort. "Well, you obviously don't know her."

"No, I don't, I guess. But I've been alone with mine for three years. It was—" His face darkens, then he shakes it off. "I'm just saying . . . what I was trying to say earlier. That I'm glad to be back. I feel lucky to be back here with you. With all of you. The happiest times of my life were when I was training."

Ugh, I do not want to soften toward him. But I think about what he said, and I wonder what he's been through in the last few years, out there on his own with Eve. He's probably lived through trauma I can't begin to imagine.

"Well, some of us didn't get to train. So let's make up for that now." I gesture meaningfully to the walls. I still wish that none of this were happening—that I didn't have this simmering, powerful force inside me. It doesn't escape my notice that I should be exhausted and instead my body feels . . . *disappointed* that I didn't get to fight.

My mother took control away from me again with the hellhound. I don't want that to happen anymore. I can use my power to be who I want to be.

And now a part of me wants to turn into the baddest, most kick-assingest Slayer ever. Then I can rub my prowess in my mother's face.

So: priorities. Change this disaster into something okayish by training so I can take full advantage of whatever I am. And prove my mom wrong by doing so.

Leo positions himself in the center of a wide mat that takes up most of the floor. There's a hint of stubble along his narrow jaw. His cheeks hide the dimples I know are there, lurking beneath the surface. The dark circles under his eyes are new, though. He gives me a gentle smile.

I want to hit him. Hard. I should have asked Artemis how she sprained Jade's ankle.

I hate the violence coursing through my veins. But I still remember the way it felt that horrible poetry day, seeing Leo return to practice as though nothing had happened. I can't reject his help, though. No matter how much I want to. So I steel myself and pretend like I'm not the kid crying on the balcony anymore. Because I'm not.

I'm a *Slayer*.

Leo finally clues in to my body language and stops smiling.

"Your natural instincts and strength are already there. We can't teach you those—and we don't have to. But what we can teach you is technique. Drill into you the best ways to react, the best ways to hit, so that, combined with your inherent Slayer abilities, you'll be as efficient and capable a fighter as possible. We'll also focus on weapon training."

Weapon training. Ugh, of course. I avoid them all except stakes. I guess that has to change now. As long as I'm going against my nature, I might as well choose the last thing I'd ever decide to pick up. I grab a wickedly heavy-looking set of nunchucks. "Sounds good." I spin them experimentally, then faster. They blur in the air. I'm going to show Leo I'm not the innocent, weak little girl he remembers.

The last thing I see is one of the wooden clubs coming right for my face before everything goes black.

11

A GIRL PACES THE CRACKED LINOLEUM floor of a tiny apartment. Her blue hair shimmers like it's underwater, and I can't hear what she's saying, but I feel it—bright red pulses of anger, with an undercurrent of darkest black seething fear. There's a picture of the Golden Gate Bridge stuck to the wall with a long, sharp knife.

"Buffy," we whisper at the same time.

Then the girl's in a warehouse, everything black except a light hanging over her head. She's bound to a chair, her face bleeding. A woman licks the blood, smiling as her true face is revealed. Vampire.

"Dublin is ours, Cosmina," she says, petting the girl's head. "You know that." She hits the light and it waves wildly, revealing a faded sign for O'Hannigan Ironworks, then swinging back to illuminate the girl's blue hair.

The flash of blue turns into a blinding blue light that revolves into red, then blue again. A girl who looks impossibly strong and powerful—every muscle full, her core like a barrel of gunpowder—

is handcuffed and put into the back of a police car. The police hold out a bag, puzzled by the stakes inside.

Red and blue and red, red, red; the Slayer's anger flashes with the lights.

"Buffy," we say together.

A flash of red makes me close my eyes, and when I open them, I see a figure sitting on the edge of a building rooftop. She's small, like me, blond hair done in two buns on top of her head. Cute. Sweet. Maybe to combat all the things she's done.

I can't see her face, but I can see in her body—she's sad. Exhausted.

And all around her, pulsing with my own heartbeat, I feel the fury of a thousand Slayers just like me. It licks the air, caressing me, swirling me closer and stoking the flame inside me higher and higher until I can't understand how she can breathe, much less sit there without feeling it.

"Buffy," we breathe in unison.

She looks up.

Before I can break away from the collective rage to tell her how I feel—how I hate her, how she ruined my life, how she's selfish and doesn't deserve anything she has, anything that was sacrificed for her—I'm pulled away. Walrus-faced Smythe lies snoring in bed. The darkness around him swirls, then takes form and settles, a blacker black, on top of his chest. He smiles, and his face is filled with longing so intense I feel icky just witnessing it. His breathing becomes labored. His eyes behind the lids roll wildly, but he doesn't open them, doesn't move.

"You're so stale," a voice like shadows croons. And then it pauses, slowly turning toward me. I open my mouth to scream, and—

"I don't know!" Artemis shouts. "Nina's the one who knows everything about concussions."

"Uneven pupils," I groan. I try to sit up but can't. Why am I on the floor? "Unconsciousness. Dizziness. Confusion. Are you okay? How did you get a concussion?"

Rhys shoves his face right in front of mine. "Well, that makes three out of four. Let me see your pupils."

"No!" I jerk my head away, which makes it swim. "They're mine! Did anyone check on Cosmina?"

"Athena," Leo says, and I freeze. Oh no. No no no. The nunchucks.

"I'm fine! I remember what happened." Unfortunately. I allow Rhys to stare at my eyeballs until he's satisfied they're the same dilation. "You aren't supposed to be here," I say.

"Leo ran out for help. I was the first person he saw. So I guess I know you're training now." Rhys grins at me. I'm relieved he knows. We can trust him, and I don't want any extra secrets right now. The ones I have are plenty. Artemis presses an ice pack to my forehead. I'm annoyed, because that means she rifled through my things in the clinic. That is *my* place. I'm also annoyed that Eve has joined us. She's watching everything with a concerned eye, but at least she's not fussing. I'd be even more embarrassed if she were.

"So maybe we'll start with something more basic and practical than nunchucks." Leo holds out a hand to help me up, but I use Artemis's instead.

"Who is Cosmina?" Eve asks.

"Blue hair. Kidnapped by vampires." I pause, frowning. "We don't know anyone named Cosmina, do we?"

Concerned, Artemis leans in to examine my pupils too. "No, we don't."

I gently push her away. "Just weird dreams. They seemed so real. Have you seen Bradford Smythe around?"

"I saw him at breakfast," Artemis says.

"And he looked . . . fine?"

"Well, as fine as the crusty old man ever looks. Why?"

"No reason." So that rules out prophetic dreams. Though I'm not sure if he was actually threatened or not. He seemed to be enjoying—whatever was happening. I shudder.

Artemis frowns thoughtfully. "Although, now that you mention it, he was a bit paler than usual. I think all this stress with you turning out to be a Slayer and the hellhound may be starting to get to him—"

"Bradford has weathered worse," Eve interjects. "It's his job to handle this stress and far more. Let's stay on target. Time may be of the essence here." She purses her dark-stained lips. "This Cosmina—you say she's been kidnapped? Do you think it may have been a Slayer dream?"

I tenderly probe the borders of the goose egg on my forehead. It'll be nice to be reminded of this newest embarrassment every time I look in the mirror. If being a Slayer does nothing else for me, please let it heal this bruise in record time.

"Umm, maybe? There was a lot happening. Flashes of things I couldn't quite understand with vampires, and Buffy, and a—" I grimace, my thoughts suddenly back to Bradford Smythe. That one I'll chalk right up to the head injury. "Part of it definitely wasn't."

"So this Cosmina, do you think she was a Slayer?"

I grasp for the remnants of the dream. The picture on her wall. Mentioning Buffy. And the vampires . . . "She could have been? Yeah. Probably a Slayer. And if that part's true, then maybe the rest was. She needs help." I know it in a way I can't explain.

Fortunately, judging by the look on Eve's face, I don't have to. "How can we find her?" she asks. Leo shuffles his feet, something shutting off in his face. He must be deferring to her. So even though he's my Watcher, she's still in charge of him. I like that. I trust Eve. *And* I've never written a single poem about her.

"Do we need to find her?" Artemis bites her lip, clearly debating something internally. I don't need twin instincts to tell me she has information she wishes she didn't.

"I don't think I would have dreamed about her if she didn't need help." I remember the other dream I had, the one with the Slayer and the demon horde. "The last time I dreamed about a Slayer, she died. In the dream. But Cosmina wasn't dead yet. Maybe that means she can still be saved." I say it thinking Eve and Artemis will do the saving. My mouth goes dry as I realize it was my dream. My responsibility. I'm not ready to be super-saving girl.

"So it's life-or-death," Artemis says.

"I mean, I can't be positive. But it felt life-or-death." I want Artemis to believe in me. I *need* her to. She's always been the one who's there for me, the one who has my back. I've never had the chance to have hers, not in any meaningful way. And I know she's worried I'm not ready to be a Slayer, but if I can save

Cosmina—if I can prove that I can be a good Slayer by *helping* people instead of just hurting them—maybe she'll feel better about it. Maybe I will too.

Artemis sighs. "I know how we can find her. There's a . . . database. Of Slayers."

"What?" Eve does not look pleased. "Why wasn't I told?"

Rhys and I share equally puzzled looks. "Since when?" I ask.

Artemis pulls out her ponytail, redoes it even tighter. "Mom has one. She said it was classified and I was never to mention it. So I think the rest of the Council doesn't know."

I try not to show how hurt I am that, yet again, Artemis has been keeping secrets from me—and this time it's worse, since it's a secret she has with our mom. When it comes to Mom, I always thought Artemis and I were a team. Us against her. But I guess that's not the case. "Why would she have a Slayer database? Mom is the one who's always been opposed to getting new Slayers to work with. She said it was a security threat."

"She set it up not long after we moved the castle here. I only know about it because I had to teach her how to use all the programs. The Watchers Council isn't exactly known for being tech savvy." Artemis glances sheepishly at Eve, who laughs.

"That's true. Perhaps if any of them had a cell phone, I could have found you all two years ago. But I'm intrigued by this information. And if it can help us save Cosmina, then we're obligated to use it. Slayers are vulnerable out there, alone. It's our duty to protect them. I don't know why Helen didn't share this or make Slayers a priority. It's concerning." She picks up the nunchucks and returns them to their place on the wall. "She's been keeping too many secrets from the Council. I respect your mother, tremendously, but I can't understand her decisions. What if we ask her for the database and she refuses?"

"We don't ask," I say, still angry with my mother from this morning. And, well, from forever. "We just take it." Then, thinking about the events of the morning, I remember a complication. "Are we on lockdown again?" If we are, there's no way we'll save Cosmina in time, even if we can find her info.

"Why would we be?" Eve asks.

So my mother didn't tell them about the hellhound. That's odd and a bit troubling. But I won't be the one to admit I drew another hellhound right to our front door—and that my mom killed it, not me. I wonder why she didn't think it merited lockdown. She doesn't know what I suspect, that the hellhound was looking for the demon and had no purpose at the castle other than chasing me. Is it possible she doesn't want everyone to know how bad I messed up in bringing the hellhound here? If so, it would be almost kind of her. I can't imagine that's why, but I can't think of why else.

"No reason," I say. I'm not sure if I'm covering for my mother or she's covering for me.

Eve promises us an hour. We give her a head start to get my mother out of her rooms. Then Artemis, Rhys, Leo, and I hurry to the Council members' residence wing. They're on the south end, which stays cooler during the summer and warmer during the winter. Our wing was originally servants' quarters. The rooms are claustrophobic, the hallways mazes. But this wing housed the important people both historically and now. The hallways are wide enough for all of us to walk side by side, and the rugs are plush beneath our feet. The windows here were more carefully updated, and though they're still narrow, the glass actually fits.

Leo guards the entrance to the wing. He'll warn us if my mother is on her way, but hopefully this won't take long. Her rooms are at the very end of the wing. I wonder which door hides Ruth Zabuto, muttering over dead relics and useless crystals. We pass a door that's been fussily surrounded with vases. I'm positive it's Wanda Wyndam-Pryce's, and I want to stop and key it. Wanda sometimes pretends like she can't remember my name. You can count the teens in the castle *on one hand*. She does it to make me feel small.

Instead, we go straight to our target. I've been in my mother's rooms only a handful of times. She comes to ours if she needs us, or we meet in one of the common areas. The last time we were here, it was because we had baked a cake for her birthday. The cake wasn't good, and neither was the surprise celebration. She tried to pretend like she was enjoying it, but we couldn't even manage a conversation. It was awful.

This castle was supposed to function as a boarding school. I wish it really were. It would be easier if my mom never saw us because she didn't live here instead of because she just . . . never saw us. At least Artemis can say that our mother actually needs her sometimes, like when she asked for Artemis's help on this database.

What would that feel like?

Artemis picks the lock faster than she should be able to. I raise my eyebrows. She shrugs. "Just one of the many skills I thought would be useful if I were an active-duty Watcher." Her voice is so determinedly unemotional that I feel a pang, and for the thousandth time, I wonder about the test that determined infinitely capable Artemis wasn't full Watcher material.

My mother's suite hasn't changed. There's a sterile sitting room—a stiff sofa, a high-backed armchair, a practical ottoman. A metal table with one chair where she must take her meals. Something about the lack of a second chair makes me lonely. At least I have Artemis, even if we haven't been seeing eye to eye lately. She's still *there*. Does my mom see the lack of my dad every time she faces the emptiness across the table? Artemis and I trade our memories of him back and forth like gifts. They're fuzzy and worn around the edges, shared so many times I don't remember which are hers and which are mine. Who does my mother share anything with now? Why can't she *talk* to us, give us new memories of him to treasure?

A door to our right leads to her bedroom, which is as impersonal as a hotel room. The bedspread is plain white, the nightstand empty except for one item.

I walk over to it, drawn like a magnet. It's a photo of our family—our *whole* family—the last one we ever took. My father has his arm around my mother. Artemis and I stand in front of them, beaming with gap-toothed grins. Our hair is in matching pigtail braids. I should stare at my father, but I find myself unable to look away from my mother.

Dream mother wasn't a fantasy I made up after all. Her smile is *dazzling*. She looks utterly vibrant, more happiness captured in a single frame than I've seen from her in years.

I pick it up, running my finger over the family I once had.

"I can't believe it." Artemis groans.

I set the photo down. I hadn't even noticed the laptop on a utilitarian desk in the corner. Artemis has it open, but the screen is asking for a password. "What's wrong?" I ask.

"She changed the password! I don't know how she even knew how to do it." Artemis rifles through drawers and stacks of papers. "Maybe she wrote it down."

Rhys helps her search while I stand there, dazed and useless. I know my mother sleeps here, lives here. But it feels so *empty*. Idly, I check out the nightstand drawer. In it are two leather-bound journals. I instantly recoil, remembering my own journal being read aloud.

But these are Watcher diaries covered in dust. My mother hasn't looked at them in a long time, but they must be here for a reason. I want to show them to Artemis, but I'm worried she'll tell me to leave them. I don't want to. My mother never gives me anything—so I'll force her to. I tuck them into my waistband at my back, pulling my loose shirt out to cover them.

"Got it!" Artemis triumphantly holds up a piece of paper and types in the password. Once the laptop loads, Artemis quickly taps through, then she swears. "It's gone. Deleted. And I can't find the files anywhere. Even the trash folder is emptied. She wrote down her password, but she emptied her trash folder?"

"Does that worry you?" I ask. "She not only had a secret database, she also wiped it?"

Artemis twists her lips and stares at the laptop as though it will reveal our mother's mysteries. As with all things maternal in our lives, she's disappointed. "I don't know. Maybe it was an accident. Or maybe the database never worked out. We can't jump to conclusions."

"We better get out of here." I can't help imagining my mother alone in here every night. Where does she keep her gun? Is that why the nightstand is nearly bare? Or does she put it under her pillow?

We hurry out, remembering to lock the door behind us. We're passing Wanda Wyndam-Pryce's room when Leo rushes toward us. He motions for us to turn around and walk with him. Then he laughs. "And that's how we saved an entire birthday party from vampires. I'll never look at piñata sticks the same! Neither will those poor kids."

"Nina? Artemis?"

I spin around and feign surprise. My mother walks toward us, frowning in suspicion.

"Oh, hey, Mom." I pray that she didn't notice the bulge of stolen books under my shirt.

"What are you all doing here?"

"Hello, Mrs. Jamison-Smythe." Leo looks like one of those stock photos that comes in the empty frames as he smiles at her. Utterly harmless and handsome. It strikes me that I haven't seen a genuine expression from him, even in front of his own mother. Everything is carefully posed, deliberate. Fake. Some part of me knows that the last few years weren't as easy for him and Eve as she's made it sound, but what made him so closed off?

I remember the painful awkwardness of this morning, his vulnerability in saying how happy he was to see me again. Maybe I caught a glimpse of the real Leo. And then I was *curt and dismissive*. Ugh, I hate that I feel bad now. I shouldn't ever have to feel bad about Leo.

"We're going to look at my DVD collection," he says. "We

thought we'd have a movie night tonight. I think everyone needs
to decompress a little."

To my surprise, my mom looks at me. Really looks at me.
One of her hands twitches as though she wants to reach out to
me. Then she frowns. "What happened to your forehead?"

I lift my hand to the bruise. "Oh, I—"

"I opened our bedroom door right as she was about to grab
the doorknob." Artemis grimaces apologetically. "I got her hard."

I think our mom buys it. I'm torn between feeling triumphant—*we* finally have secrets from *her*!—and hurt at how easily
she buys our lame excuses. She doesn't want to push deeper. She
pulls a few pound notes from her pocket and holds them out. I
take them, numbly. Why is she giving me money?

"We don't have a good television here. It will be nice to get
away from this castle. Go see a film in a theater. You can pick
up that helpful boyfriend of yours, Rhys. Leo, you have your
license?"

Leo nods. "Yes, ma'am."

"Good. Go be teenagers." Her smile is as tight as Artemis's
ponytail. "Try it out. You might like it." She's clearly trying to get
rid of us, even though she and I both know there was a hellhound
sniffing around this morning.

But I can't call her on her shifty behavior without revealing
my own secrets—including the demon in Cillian's shed. So we
walk stiffly past her. She doesn't tell us to invite Jade and Imogen,
so apparently only we have this free pass from being Watchers.

We never get outings. My mom is too paranoid, and Artemis
and Rhys are too busy. The most we ever have is an occasional
afternoon in Shancoom. Which doesn't have a movie theater, so

we'll have to range out at least an hour if we're going to follow her instructions. I dart to my room under the excuse of changing my shirt and grabbing a coat. I also hide the stolen books under my mattress.

I meet the others out at the garage. The autumn sun slants toward late afternoon, which surprises me. I lost a lot of time to head trauma.

Leo picks the sleek black Range Rover left over from the days when the Watchers had a whole fleet of vehicles. Back then we also had boats, helicopters, and a private jet. Now we have one golf cart, three cars, a motorcycle, and two ATVs. Plus scooters and tricycles for the Littles.

"Are we really going to a movie?" Artemis sits beside me in the back seat. She sounds dubious but a little excited. She only gets one afternoon a week off, and this isn't her day, so she's hit the jackpot. Normally, I'd love to see a movie—with Artemis and Rhys, at least. Not Leo. But today . . .

"Cosmina was still alive in my dream," I say, "but I don't know how long that will stay true. Not that I have any idea how to find her, since Mom's database was a bust. Still, we can't go sit in a movie theater if there's a chance she needs our help, right?"

Leo drives carefully out of the garage. "Speaking of your mother . . ."

Sure enough, our mother's standing at the castle door, watching us leave. I wouldn't put it past her to have the car tracked too.

She told us to pick up Cillian. And even though we're ignoring the rest of her plan, it's a good idea. I need to make sure he understands not to go home. And I want him with us as much as possible so we can keep him safe in case there are more hellhounds. I call him as Leo navigates the bumpy unpaved road. We maintain it enough to be usable, but if you didn't know it was here, it'd be hard to find.

Cillian answers after the first ring. "Nina? Do you have any more info about—"

I cut him off, unsure if his voice is loud enough for the others to hear. "Hey! I'm in a car with Artemis, Rhys, and Leo, my, uh, new Watcher. We're coming to get you."

"You have a Watcher? You *are* a Watcher. And why are you coming to get me?"

"It's complicated. All of it. But allegedly we're going to a movie."

"Allegedly?"

"We *were* trying to break into my mom's computer to get information on a Slayer we think might be in trouble, and while we were leaving, we got caught and shooed out of the castle." I pause to ask the others. "Where *are* we going?"

"If there's a Slayer in danger, we'll do whatever we have to in order to find her." Leo speaks so matter-of-factly, it sounds like he's reading it straight from the Watchers' guide.

"Wait," Cillian says. "Who's the Slayer and why is she in danger?"

"I'm not really sure. Like I said, we didn't get the information we needed." The Range Rover hits an aggressive pothole and I bounce, almost dropping the phone. "I dreamed she was being held hostage by a vampire. Not much to go on. Blue hair. I think she's in Dublin. Her name's Cosmina."

There's a pause, and I wonder if I accidentally hung up on him. Then he says, "Got her."

"What?"

"Cosmina Enescu. Nineteen, single, blue hair. Lives in a crappy flat in a not-nice area of Dublin. She's quite fit, though."

"You *found* her!" I shout. "*How* did you find her? Are you a hacker or something?"

"Love, it's called Facebook. I'll make you a profile if you want. No one has to be a hacker these days. Cosmina is an unusual enough name, so there weren't many options. And blue hair? Only one."

My heart is pounding. We found her. And that means we can save her. Assuming she needs saving, and I wasn't just dreaming of some random girl in Dublin. I don't know whether I'm more relieved that she's findable or terrified that now I really do have to chase her down and try to help. And as a Slayer, not as a Watcher or medic.

But in the last couple of days I've faced two hellhounds and a demon, not to mention my long-lost crush. The dream came to me. That has to mean my inherent Slayerness thought I needed it or could handle it. Doesn't it? I close my eyes, thinking of any other details. "Is there a building, maybe abandoned, called . . ." The light swinging. Cosmina's blue hair, and . . . "O'Hannigan Ironworks?"

"Give me a sec."

I wait, holding my breath. I hope he finds it. And I hope in equal parts it doesn't exist.

"Got it. Also in Dublin."

That's that, then. Slayering I go. "Thanks, Cillian. We'll be there in five minutes." I hang up, trying not to tremble.

Artemis looks concerned. "Why are we bringing Cillian? It could be dangerous."

So could leaving him here. I scramble for an excuse. "He's got the address and a better phone, and he's better at finding information than we are. We'll make him stay in the car."

Leo drives to the soda shop, and Cillian comes out with a basket of Cokes and snacks. He always special orders root beer for me because no one else here likes it. It's one of many things I miss from my childhood. Along with water parks, air-conditioned malls, dads who aren't dead, and houses that haven't been burned down in lung-searing terror. Oh, and also tacos.

"Who's switching up front?" Rhys asks, ready to climb in the back so he can sit beside Cillian. I freeze. I already have to spend all this time with Leo now. I don't want to have to sit next to him for the whole drive. Then I might have to feel bad about more things, and I don't want to feel bad when it comes to Leo. I only want to feel angry.

Artemis, in a rare move of emotional sensitivity, picks up on my tension. "I got shotgun." She meets my eyes in the rearview mirror. I mouth *thank you*. I never told her about my crush on Leo, though it was probably obvious. But since I didn't tell her about the Honora Poetry Incident, she doesn't know why I'm uncomfortable around Leo, only that I am. And I've never been more grateful for her protective instinct than I am in this moment.

When everyone's settled, we leave Shancoom for a date with a vampire and the hopefully still-living Cosmina. It's time for me to be a Slayer.

But if I'm being totally honest?

I'd rather go to a movie. At least I know how to do that.

The hunter had made another mistake.

She had to leave before the fire reached its inevitable conclusion. Even she could do only so much to avoid being arrested or questioned by the clueless police officers who would arrive on the scene. So once the trap had been set, confident that the girls could not escape, she had walked away.

Did some part of her not want to see them die? Was she really that weak? She would sabotage the mission for her own tender sensibilities?

She should have stood in the yard and watched them burn. Killing them was the right thing to do. She didn't question that. She never had.

She listened, numb, as the voice on the other end of the line berated her. On the TV, Jack died a frozen death, yet again. No matter how many times she watched Titanic, *Jack always died and Rose always lived. Because that's how it was written. Who could change what was written?*

She drew on her arm with her ballpoint pen, pressing so hard she raised welts beneath the thin black lines. She wrote their names. And then she crossed them out with such a vicious slash, she drew blood.

She could change it. She would.

But not right now. The girls' mother had made the only choice possible, fleeing back into the Watchers' arms. It was less than ideal for the hunter. The things that needed to be done couldn't be done in their headquarters. The mother had allies too high up, ones who refused to see the truth.

The girls were protected. Watched. But the hunter could watch too. She could be patient. She had time. Unlike the girls, who had only a countdown—either to their destruction or to everyone else's. And the hunter would not let the world down. Even if it kept letting her down.

12

AUTUMN IS CLAIMING THE EMERALD
Isle, shifting greens into golds, yellows, and oranges. I love wrapping myself in the same colors, my burnished hair reflecting the brilliant foliage. My coat is a bright marigold peacoat. I pull it against me tighter, seeking comfort, and then realize it's wrong for what we're doing. I should be wearing black. Something inconspicuous. Like Artemis.

We haven't even left the car, and I've already made a bad decision. In the castle, I could wear whatever I wanted. No one cared what the medic looked like.

And medics don't need to sneak around in the shadows.

What have I gotten myself into? Will the others expect me to jump into the lead? Take command? Fight? I don't know how to do any of this. I still don't know if I even want to. Being strong enough to help people is one thing, but tapping into those violent Slayer instincts again is quite another. In my dream the vampire wasn't killing Cosmina. Maybe there's still time for reasoning. For strategy. Maybe the kidnapping hasn't even happened yet!

"Do you need to wee?" Cillian asks.

My discomfort must be obvious. And embarrassingly mis-interpreted. I stop squirming and slouch further into my seat, avoiding Leo's questioning gaze. "No! I'm fine."

At last we hit the outskirts of Dublin. It had taken longer than planned—we had to stop at a petrol station, the Range Rover surprisingly gas guzzling. And even though I did need to pee, I wasn't about to go inside after Cillian's awkward question. By the time we entered the city, afternoon was rushing toward evening, the slanting sun lighting the buildings gold.

"So, we're expecting vampires?" Cillian asks. We've filled him in on the basics. "Exciting, innit? I mean, Dracula and so forth."

Rhys clears his throat, knowing how heavily Artemis's and my history is hanging in the car. "Not exactly. Vampires are demons that walk around wearing the bodies of people you loved. People with families. They kill those people, and when the soul is gone, they take the remaining shell and use it to kill. Demons exist to prey on humanity. They aren't native to this ecosystem."

Cillian makes a *yikes* face. "Sort of like cats in Australia."

I take another root beer from him, pressing the cool bottle against my face. "If the cats also sucked out people's souls or ate them or disemboweled them or occasionally tried to trigger the apocalypse to bring about an all-cat dimension on earth, then yeah."

"I know that should be scary," Cillian says, "but an all-cat dimension still sounds kind of snuggly. And no one can convince me that cats don't actually suck out people's souls."

"Fair points." I stare at the neighborhoods of Dublin passing by us. I suddenly wish we *were* here for fun, to see the city, to be *normal*. Like a normal group date with my friend, his boyfriend, my sister, and the boy I never wanted to see again and would prefer still lived on the opposite side of the world. It's truly a testament to what we're facing that hanging out with Leo sounds more pleasant in comparison.

Dublin is only two hours from Shancoom, but somehow, I've never been. Watchers aren't big on sightseeing or vacations. They used to regularly visit hellmouths and demon portal hot spots, but those trips were less about relaxation and more about decapitation.

I close my eyes. *Don't* think about decapitation or disembowelment. I have to focus, to prove that I can do this. I'm a Jamison-Smythe. Fighting demons is my heritage. The Watchers need me—which is a thrilling and terrifying new sensation. All I've ever wanted was to make people's lives better. And if being a Slayer will help me protect humanity from—

"Pizza!" Cillian shouts.

Pizza! We never have pizza. We can't exactly call for delivery to a hidden castle. But Leo shakes his head. "Demons first. We don't know how Athena's dream compares to reality. It could have already happened or might not happen for another few days."

"Who the hell is Athena?" Cillian asks.

I raise my hand.

"Oh, that makes so much more sense. I had questioned your mother's intelligence, naming one of you Artemis and the other Nina. The whole point to having twins is to give them matching names."

"Yes," Artemis deadpans. "That's why our parents had us."

Artemis was the goddess of the hunt; a protector. It fits my sister perfectly. Athena was the goddess of wisdom and war. It's never escaped my notice that everyone thought Nina fit me better than my real name.

Everyone except Leo.

"If we have twins someday," Rhys says, "we'll give them matching names."

Cillian nods in agreement, then claps his hands together. "Little Sonny and Cher will be so adorable."

"Jane and Austen," Rhys says.

"Meryl and Streep," Leo offers without looking back.

"That's the one!" Rhys shouts.

"You can be their godfather." Cillian beams. Artemis rolls her eyes so hard I can almost hear it. Cillian refocuses. "Right, then. Looking for vampire evidence. Perhaps one of them left a business card? Or a punch card. 'Drain ten humans and the eleventh goes free' or something."

I appreciate his attempts at humor, but I can't manage a smile. Does every Slayer feel like this when they start out? I know so much more than most new Slayers would. I can't tell if that makes it better or worse.

Buffy's first threat was in Los Angeles, pre-Sunnydale. An ancient, powerful vampire named Lothos was hunting her specifically. I've never thought how terrifying that must have been for her. A whole new life dropped onto her, complete with instant mortal peril. I've only thought about how her calling devastated *me*. How would I feel if my first days as a Slayer were spent being stalked by unspeakable evil?

At least I'm doing this on purpose. I'm helping, not being

hunted. We might not know what, exactly, we're heading into, but my dream showed only one vampire, and there are five of us. We can handle a vampire. Hell, we can probably scare her off.

I remember the snap of the hellhound's neck and flinch. *Just one vampire*, I think to myself. *Just one.* They're already dead. Killing them shouldn't bother me.

I know it still will.

We enter a district where the charm of Dublin has been consumed by the cement monotony of industry. Leo stops the car in front of a block of buildings. The outsides are dingy, in the utterly soulless way of everything built in the eighties. What happened during that decade that caused architects to hate themselves and the rest of the world so very, very much?

"My sleuthing says we're in the right place." But Cillian looks as dubious as I feel. We all sit, unmoving, staring out at the twilight. There's not a soul in sight. "Kind of . . . dead around here, innit? You could almost say it was *undead*."

"No," Rhys says. "You could not. We are done punning tonight."

"Fine. But aren't you a wee bit bothered?" Cillian gestures around. There are no lights. No people. Only a couple of cars parked, but they look like they haven't been moved in months.

"It's an industrial district," Leo says. "Everyone is probably home for the night."

"So how come we haven't gotten out of the car yet?"

My finger is pressed against the lock button so hard it's gone bloodless and white. I slowly release it. "Just assessing the situation." I unlock the car, and the click sounds far louder and more ominous than it should have. That's when I realize I have no weapons. What kind of Slayer goes into potential battle without weapons?

Oh, right. The dead kind. Or the dud kind. Probably both, in my case.

Artemis slings her bag over her shoulder, and it clinks. She remembered weapons. Of course she did. I open my mouth to ask for one, but her comment about me being a loaded weapon in a child's hand comes roaring back. I'm proving her right already.

Leo pops the trunk and removes a duffel bag filled with supplies. He holds out a stake to me, catches my relieved expression, and grins. A pang I thought I had long since smothered catches me by surprise. Suddenly he's the guy who passed me an extra cookie just because he knew it would make me happy. And back are those dimples I had hoped to never see again. The one on the left is deeper than the one on the right. I hate that I still notice that.

"I'm a Watcher," he says. "It's my job to prepare you. It's your job to slay."

Ah, right. He's not thinking of *me* me. He's thinking of Slayer me. And we're all about to be disappointed, because I *know* I'm not prepared for this. Artemis has straight up told me as much, and soon Leo and Rhys will know it too. They probably already do. After all, the most damage Leo has seen me do is to my own head. I wish he had seen me kill the first hellhound.

Ugh. That's a terrible way to think. *I wish he had seen me kill something because then he might think I'm not a screwup!* As if it takes murder to prove your worth.

Although in our world, it kind of does. It's why no one has ever taken me seriously before. And why I'm afraid killing things is the only way to get them to believe in me now.

"Wait in the car," Leo says to Cillian as he climbs out.

"Right, because I want to be the scene in the horror movie where you run back to the car, flooded with relief that I'm at the wheel, until you put your hand on my shoulder and I fall over, and you scream, but I can't scream because I'm dead, and the monster is already behind you and I can't warn you because, again, *I'm already dead*."

"No one is going to die," Rhys says, "and no one is going to scream, because—"

A high-pitched scream tears through the night.

Instinct takes over, and I run toward it. I can hear Leo and Artemis behind me. I turn into an alley two down from where we parked and spot a girl slumped on the ground. At the far end of the alley, a shadow disappears. I crouch beside the victim. She's breathing. But her neck is bleeding and she's glassy-eyed with shock.

"Which way?" Artemis demands.

I point. Artemis sprints away, followed by Leo.

"She bit me," the girl says. She's maybe eighteen, twenty tops. Curls that put anyone's to shame framing a sweet face. A face that's going alarmingly pale. I gently remove her hand from her neck. I know what I'm doing. I've studied for this exact scenario. I can do this. I *can*.

"Someone get me a clean cloth," I say, peering at the wound. It's bleeding, but the flow is steady, not pulsing or spurting. "There are no air bubbles. That's good. That means your esophagus wasn't punctured. Your breathing won't be affected. You're still getting plenty of air, so let's focus on steady breaths. Deep, steady breaths. Do you do yoga?"

"A little bit," she says.

"Good! Good for you. Think about your breathing. Focus on that. We're going to put pressure on this wound." I hold out my hand for the requested cloth. Rhys hands me his outer flannel shirt. I fold it and press it against the girl's neck. "You're doing great. Breathe in, two three four, out, two three four."

A light hand on my shoulder tells me Cillian is here too. "Cillian, call emergency services. We don't know how much blood she's already lost. Tell them to hurry." I look at the ground, knowing I won't see anything helpful. And sure enough, there's no pool of blood.

Vampires are efficient, I have to give them that.

"You're doing great," I say. "What's your name?"

"Sarah," she whispers, locked onto my eyes like I'm the only thing anchoring her to consciousness. I probably am.

"Sarah! I love that name. Just try to take nice, deep breaths. I'm going to keep pressure on the wound, and soon the para-medics will be here to get you to a hospital." I keep my tone low and soothing, the way I would want to be talked to. The way Artemis used to talk to me when I woke up from nightmares insensible with terror.

"I don't see anything," Artemis shouts. "Are you sure?"

"Kind of busy!" I shout back. Sarah tries to look in Artemis's direction. "Hold your head still for me, okay? That's good."

Artemis runs back to us. "Your attacker. Did she make you drink blood?"

I glare at her in exasperation. Sarah needs to relax right now, though I get why Artemis is asking. If the vampire had forced Sarah to drink its blood and then she died, she'd come back as a vampire. But she isn't nearly so far gone, which Artemis would understand if she knew as much about human bodies as she does about vampire attacks. Or if she had asked me.

Sarah keeps her focus on me. "No. We met online. She seemed nice. Said there was a cool club hidden back here. And then she— God, do you think she was rabid?"

"It might be good to get checked out." That's probably a less horrifying scenario than reality. Poor Sarah.

"Nina," Artemis says, "we're losing time."

I take Sarah's wrist with my free hand. Her pulse is weak but steady. The vampire didn't take too much if Sarah's still coherent enough to talk. She must have heard us coming and run.

Leo rejoins us, shaking his head. "Nothing."

"Did you call emergency services?" I ask Cillian, ignoring Leo.

"Yes. They're on their way."

Leo speaks again. "We need to go."

"She won't come back," I say. "Not with all of us here." Surely Sarah is safe now, and I don't want to risk moving her.

"No." Leo's voice is as slow and careful as my own, as though I were the one bleeding out on the ground. "I mean we need to go find Sarah's *friend*. She probably needs attention too. You should be good at finding this type of *person*."

"*Should* be," Artemis says, emphasizing the first word.

My face burns with shame. My instincts are all wrong. I've been thinking about keeping Sarah stable rather than chasing after the monster that hurt her in the first place—a monster that could end up hurting so many others if we don't take it down. I'm thinking small. Like a medic.

Not like a Slayer.

"Rhys and I will stay with her," Cillian says.

Rhys eases his hand under mine. "You go do what you need to. We've got this."

I press to show him the right amount of pressure. "Keep talking to her. If she passes out, note the time so you can tell the paramedics how long she's been unconscious."

"I want her to stay!" Sarah says, eyes getting wider. "I want you to stay, please."

"*Nina,*" Artemis says.

"I'm sorry," I say, avoiding Sarah's desperate gaze. "You're going to be fine. I promise." Everything in me knows it's wrong to leave her. This is what I want to do, how I want to help. But it's not my calling.

I take off for the darkest end of the alley, where the vampire disappeared and where, according to Cillian's map, we'll find the warehouse. Running by my side, Leo passes me the stake I had left behind on the ground. It feels like a promise that I'm not sure I want to keep.

13

ARTEMIS PAUSES AT THE ALLEY'S END.
Buildings stretch in either direction, their facades as blank and
unhelpful as a dead cell phone. "We wasted too much time back
there."

Anger flares, but Leo speaks before I can. "Athena saved that
girl's life."

It sounds like he's talking about someone else. Maybe that's
what I liked about him when I was thirteen—it felt like he saw
someone else when he looked at me. But now I worry he still
sees someone else: Someone capable. Someone who can do
this. Someone like Artemis, not me. Because I did save Sarah.
But what if the vampire kills someone else before we stake her?
That's on me.

Artemis looks from side to side, checking for threats. "Which
way is the warehouse?"

I'm disoriented too. Most of the lamps are broken. The
buildings back here are derelict. It's almost totally dark now, the
full moon obscured by clouds.

I look to the left and see nothing. I look to the right and see nothing either, but there's a sick twist of my stomach and a spike of adrenaline that make me suddenly sure I do *not* want to go that way. Not for anything in the world.

Artemis turns and stalks to the left.

"Down here, I think." I point to the right.

"How do you know?" Artemis asks.

She's the one who wanted me to chase the vampire, and now she's questioning my instincts? "Because I'm terrified and I also feel like I could lift a car over my head." Slayer feelings are no joke. It's like little jolts of electricity are shooting through my body, pumping my blood closer to the surface of my skin. I'm attuned to every physical sensation inside, and every emotion and potential in the air outside of me. I feel myself being *pulled* in the direction of danger.

Artemis grits her teeth but nods. "Behind me," she says, prowling forward.

I should be the one taking the lead since I'm technically the strongest, but as soon as that thought pops up, it disappears. I may be the strongest, but Artemis is the most competent. And even with my new powers, I don't see that changing.

My shoes sound loud, though not as loud as the pounding of my heart. Up ahead there's a building with the windows boarded up. Every window, in fact. Most of these buildings have the windows smashed out, with nothing replacing them. Why board up these? Unless there's something inside that has a personal reason to avoid sunlight.

I stumble, my body tensing with remembered trauma. Leo's not going to save me from a vampire tonight. Now it's *my* job to save people. And I know this is our building as surely as I know I'm not ready to go in.

"There," I say.

Artemis stares up at the building, hands on her hips. "There has to be a way in. Leo and I will scout. Nina, you stay by the door and alert us if anyone is coming."

"Shouldn't Athena—"

Artemis cuts Leo off. "We're the ones with training. We're not putting her in harm's way any more than we have to."

Part of me is glad she's taking charge. But part of me is annoyed. It's my Slayerness, my dreams, that brought us here. I shouldn't be on lookout duty. Except I don't want fighting duty either.

The closest door is boarded up from the outside. Huge new planks have been nailed in place. Why did the vampire do it from the outside, instead of the inside? It looks more Keep In rather than Keep Out.

There's a ladder halfway up the building's brick wall, rusted iron from the looks of it. It's hard to tell in the dark if it goes all the way to the roof, but my guess is it does. And if there's a ladder leading up, that means there's probably a way to get in from the roof.

It's too high to reach, though, thank goodness.

Then I cringe. It *is* too high for a normal human. Artemis won't approve. She wants me outside, safe. But I have to believe that I have these powers for a reason. I crouch and then jump with all my might. I overshoot, sailing up past the last rung and scrambling for a hold somewhere in the middle. The ladder groans in metallic protest, but it holds. Unfortunately.

"Dammit, Nina!" Artemis stomps her foot. "We can't get up that way!"

"Go around and find a door."

"No. Come back down. Now."

There's a popping noise. I climb up as fast as I can, the ladder pulling free from the wall. I jump the last few feet, hanging on to the roof's edge as the ladder swings drunkenly away from the building. No one else is coming up that way.

"Nina!" Artemis hisses.

"I'm fine! Go around the back. I'll look for a way in from up here."

She curses. "Don't you dare go in without us."

I hear them running and pull myself up all the way onto the roof, rolling to the flat surface and lying on my back. For a second I'm tempted to obey Artemis—to wait for her and Leo to find another way in. But that's not what a Slayer would do. My sister may have more experience hunting vampires, but I have Slayer powers, and it's not safe to let her go in first. Even if she is treating me like I need a babysitter.

Propelled by anger, I jump to my feet and scour the roof's landscape in the dark. There are a few bulky metal boxes that look like air circulation units. And there's one square set low against the roof. I hurry over to it and find a hatch door.

I don't have a sword. Or a flamethrower. Or an Uzi. I close my eyes, take a deep breath, and whisper, "I can do this."

It was only one vampire in the alley and in my dream. I have holy water in my pocket and a stake. I can scare off a vampire. And I don't even know if the vampire's in there. Like Leo said, Slayer dreams don't exactly come with a time stamp. I open the hatch and peer inside, trying to make out any forms, but the room is dark. I climb through and drop down, planning to land in a badass crouch. Instead I land on a metal structure. One of my legs falls straight between two bars. My stake slips out of my hand.

And then I look down to see half a dozen snarling creatures, every single blood-crazed eye trained on me.

14

WITH SIX HELLHOUNDS BENEATH ME, I
consider several things at once:

First, that my leg is stuck through the bars and it's within
their reach.

Second, that it's unfortunate they're named after hounds,
because it's really souring me on the idea of ever getting a dog.

And third, the same as the first: My. Leg. Is. *Stuck*.

I tug with all my might and it pops free just as the nearest
hellhound leaps. The hound smashes against the roof of the cage,
jaws closing around one of the bars.

"Bad doggy!" I shout.

A snarling behind me signals the presence of more than hellhounds. I leap down from the cage, fists up, but I don't need to
bother. Everything in here is caged. And though the room is almost
pitch-dark, barely lit by some emergency lights blinking above us, I
can see there are a *lot* of cages. My Slayer instincts are going haywire.
I force myself to inspect the room even though my body is screaming
at me to *do* something. I *really* hope my dream hasn't happened yet.

Because I'm pretty sure this is the room Cosmina was in. And if she was already in here, she certainly isn't anymore. . . .

I creep closer to the next cage, expecting more hellhounds. In the corner of the cage are ragged human clothes, ripped to shreds. I gasp in horror. Something throws itself at the bars in front of me, bouncing off and growling.

It's a werewolf. The clothes belong to it, not some victim. But my relief is short-lived, because it's a *werewolf*, and the moon is full. I do a quick sweep of the cavernous space. My six hellhound buddies in one cage with dividers, six werewolves in separate cages, and six . . .

I take a step back. Inside the last cage, divided like the hellhounds, are six monsters. I've never seen anything like them. They're wearing human clothes, and they look almost like vampires—but *wrong*. Which is saying something, because vampires are already wrong. These creatures are a perversion on top of a perversion. Gone is any semblance of humanity. I thought that was the worst thing about vampires—the way they look and talk like humans but have no souls. However, seeing these mindless, deformed, still human-shaped but now possessed things as they snap at the bars and stretch their clawed fingers for me makes me want to vomit.

Demons are demons. Vampires are corruptions of humans. These? I don't know. I dart back into a dark corner, cursing my yellow coat as a door opens and someone new walks in.

"Hello, pets!" a woman sings. "Look at you all, already frenzied. You know we have something special for you tonight, don't you?" She pauses to coo at the hellhounds. But when she passes the cage of unknown creatures, she spits at them. "Abominations," she mutters, checking a few levers on the outsides of the cages. She's the vampire from my dream. I'm almost positive, even in the dark.

I should stake the vampire. I know I should.

My body knows it should.

But my brain has enough control now that the thought of retrieving the fallen stake, creeping up to her, plunging it into her back, watching as she disappears . . .

It's not the right move. I need more information. Maybe there's someone waiting for her, someone who would raise an alarm if she didn't return. Or maybe she'd hear me trying to find the stake and let the monsters loose on me.

I'm making excuses. I know what Artemis would do. What Buffy would do, even. Yet I still can't bring myself to take a step toward the vampire.

Exhausted from fighting my instincts, disappointed in myself, and confused about what the right choice is, I use the cover of the loud creepy creatures and darkness to slide along the room's perimeter. I debate finding a way outside to meet back up with Artemis and Leo. But the door the vampire came from is calling to me. There's more going on here than I expected, and a good Watcher would figure out what it is. A good Slayer would too. I have to be both brains and muscle in this scenario. I'll stake the vampire as soon as I know more.

The door leads to a damp stairwell, the stairs rusted and noisy. I do my best to creep down them. Another door waits for me at the bottom. I take a moment to calm myself, sure that after the previous room, I'm ready for anything. Then I open the door.

Okay, I wasn't ready for this.

The room is packed with people. They mill about, drinks in their hands, the whole room buzzing with conversation and excitement. It looks like a sporting event. I straighten, sauntering in like I belong there. Fortunately for me, it's still quite dark, the main lights focused brilliantly in the center of the space. A closer look reveals a pit flooded with light. It's twenty feet deep and about the same in length and width. The floor is packed dirt. The pit's walls, however, are lined with bright shining barbed wire. I suspect it's at least tipped with silver. There's a hum in the air that doesn't seem like it's coming from the floodlights. That's when I notice two generators hooked up to cables that lead to the barbed wire. Electrified wire.

Whatever is going to happen in that pit, it's not good. I squint upward, trying to see past the lights. The ceiling has big square hatches in it. If I'm calculating it right, they're all placed directly beneath the cages.

Something wet splashes on my coat sleeve. I whip around, terrified that I've been caught. A demon with brilliant red, symbol-carved skin grimaces. "Sorry. So bloody dark in here. And now I need a new beer." He raises one scar-where-an-eyebrow-should-be, grinning hopefully at me. "Can I get you one too?"

"You're not my type," I blurt. Then I cringe. Pissing off a demon in the middle of enemy territory is not a good idea. "Girls!" I say. "I like girls!"

He laughs. "Me too." Winking, he wanders away. Here's hoping all my demon encounters this night are so easily solved.

He reminds me to take better stock of the crowd, though. It's mostly human, but there are a few demons like my would-be suitor scattered throughout. There's one line to buy drinks, and another where people are exchanging money for slips of paper. Maybe I did make the right call in not killing the vampire. If this group knew there was a threat, I definitely couldn't take them all out. And I shouldn't, either, with so many humans.

A large glowing board behind the exchange table flickers to life, and an amplified voice echoes through the room.

"Good evening, ladies, gentlemen, and those who are not quite so categorizable!" A demon next to me rolls its eyes. All seven of them. "Welcome to tonight's event!"

A man in a sleek suit with an equally sleek ponytail is standing on a raised platform holding a microphone. Next to him is a woman wearing head-to-toe dull gray leather. I can't see her face in the shadows, but she's not the vampire from the room upstairs.

Where is Cosmina? How do I find her? If Artemis were here, she'd know what to do.

I steel myself. It was my dream. My instincts. Cosmina needs *me*, not Artemis.

"We have something special for you during tonight's dog-fight." The announcer pauses, mugging in the spotlight. "I kid. We would never actually hurt dogs. What kind of monsters would do that? No, we're here to make Dublin a safer place! Because this is *our* city, innit?"

The crowd roars, lifting their drinks in the air.

"And if we're entertained and make some money in the process, well, good on us." The announcer gestures to the board. "We have all the usual categories. Time in the pit, which breed will last longest or have the most survivors, you know the drill. But tonight, my friends—tonight we have a wild card." He pauses, savoring the anticipatory silence. "Tonight, we have . . . a Slayer!"

My heart seizes. I spin in a circle, ready for attack. I can see the exits. If I run fast enough . . .

The room erupts into noise as everyone shouts. I duck, covering my head, but they all shove past me to place more bets. No one is coming for me. A few of the more demonic types slip free of the crowd and disappear. I want to follow their lead and get out. But a good Watcher would stay and learn all she could.

What would a good Slayer do? I have no idea. Probably start punching things. I try to look inconspicuous. They said they had a Slayer. It's obviously not me. Oh *no*. No no no. That means it's got to be—

A door in the center of the ceiling opens. Cosmina falls through, her hair a brilliant streak of blue. She lands hard in the middle of the pit. This is so much worse than one vampire.

I rush to the barricade around the perimeter of the pit. Cosmina stands, breaking the ropes that had bound her. She doesn't seem to be hurt from the fall, but her face is bruised. She squints up, shielding her eyes from the blinding lights. Then she lifts her index and middle fingers and flips off the crowd, British-style.

Gods. She's *cool*. If our situations were reversed, Cosmina would know how to help me. Would already have done it.

Now I have to save Cosmina in front of everyone. And the clock is ticking. Why didn't my dream fast-forward past the relatively easy vampire-only threat and give me a sneak preview of this much, *much* worse scenario? Whoever created this system was an idiot!

Oh. Right. My ancestors created it. Thanks a lot, jerks.

"No need to leave, my scalier mates," the announcer calls

as a few more demons book it out of the room. "I take it you've encountered our lovely Cosmina before. She's been drugged. It'll wear off quickly—we want a good show!—but she can't get out of that pit. Don't fret, though, little Slayer. You'll have company soon enough!"

The room settles some, and the board flashes with new betting options.

"Before we give odds, a vote on tonight's format: three at a time, or melee?"

There are a few bloodthirsty screams for melee. But the majority wants a longer show. Three at a time wins.

"Zompires and hellhounds and werewolves, oh my. What a night! Odds are on the board! Betting is open for the next two minutes, and then we begin!" The announcer sets down the microphone and wanders over to talk to the woman in leather. The vampire from upstairs has yet to reappear. Maybe I should have staked her after all. Or stayed up there. I could have saved Cosmina before she ever dropped into the pit. My instincts were wrong.

No, my instincts told me to kill the vampire. I could have killed her and found Cosmina. We'd already be out of here. But I hesitated. Made the wrong choice.

Now I have *two minutes*. I could attack the announcer, hold him hostage against Cosmina's freedom. But is he in charge? I don't know whether everyone—or even anyone—in here cares about his safety.

If I jump the barrier to get to Cosmina, a hundred sets of eyes will immediately be on me. And this is a crowd that has no problem killing Slayers.

I'm not so prideful I'll risk Cosmina's life to prove I can handle being a Slayer. I need Artemis. I'll run out and—

A bell dings and a buzzer sounds. Three doors open, raining a werewolf, a hellhound, and whatever the hell the other creature is down on Cosmina.

The werewolf and the hellhound immediately go after each other, jaws snapping and claws grappling. They're down in a frenzy of limbs. But the third thing—the announcer said "zompire," a term I've never heard—zeroes in on Cosmina, running at her with fangs bared. Cosmina ducks and rolls past it, jumping to her feet and kicking it in the back. It flies into the barbed wire with a shower of sparks. The crowd roars.

The zompire falls, twitching.

And then it crawls toward Cosmina.

Some sense alerts me. I spin, snatching an object out of the air before it hits me. A stake. On the edge of the crowd I see Leo, who looks . . . proud. I didn't duck this time. I caught the weapon so I could control it.

Leo and Artemis are here. I have help. But Cosmina needs it more than I do.

I whistle. The werewolf and the hellhound pause their fight, panting, and Cosmina looks up at me. I throw the stake to her.

The zompire lunges. Cosmina sinks the stake into its chest.

It poofs into dust like a vampire would. Which means it *is* a vampire. Sort of. But I don't have time to think about it, because the hellhound and the werewolf have stopped fighting each other and noticed Cosmina instead.

Another buzz. Three more creatures drop down.

"Whoops!" the announcer says. "My hand slipped. Only fair, since someone changed the odds."

Cosmina crouches, the stake gripped in her hand, as she waits for the next attack. But she isn't the only human down there. The werewolves are people too. I don't want to do this. I want to do anything *but* this.

But for the first time, I'm certain that this is what I *need* to do.

I leap the barrier, then jump out into the pit so I won't hit the barbed wire. I land hard, right next to Cosmina. This time I nail the badass crouch. It's short-lived as I duck the stake that comes swinging at me.

"I'm here to help!" I shout.

"Who the hell are you?" she demands. A hellhound lunges and I grab it, spinning and throwing it away from us.

"I'm a Watch—a Slayer!"

"Stay out of my way." She shifts to engage the newest zompire. I duck a huge paw swiping at me, then twist and kick a werewolf hard in the chest. It flies across the pit, hitting the electrified wire. It howls in pain, then falls, unconscious.

The next werewolf bounds toward me. I drop onto my back, then kick out with both legs, using its own momentum to fling it, too, into the wire.

That's two down. They're out, but they're not dead. My body knows exactly what to do, even when *I* have no clue. I scramble back onto my feet. Cosmina's dusted the zompire, and one of the hellhounds is tangled in the wire, slowly cooking to death. My stomach turns. It's a demon, but I don't want to watch it suffer.

Cosmina kicks the last hellhound right into me. I catch it, holding it in place.

"Well?" she shouts.

I give her an incredulous look. "Well, what? You have the stake!"

"Great. A newborn Slayer. Just my luck." She yanks the hellhound away from me and throws it as hard as she can straight up. It lands past the edge of the pit and scrambles away. There are shouts of fear and surprise, then several shots ring out. I assume the hellhound is dead.

"Very naughty, girls," the announcer chides. This isn't close to over. We've eliminated only two of each type. Which means there are four hellhounds, four werewolves, and four zompires left.

"This got interesting!" The announcer is more gleeful than worried. "We have two for the price of one on this Slayer deal! What do you say we even the odds?" A series of buzzers sounds, and two of each of the remaining creatures drop down into the pit.

At the same time, a sword flies in, landing on the ground next to me. I grip the hilt so tightly my hands ache.

"Do you know how to use that?" Cosmina demands.

"No!" I go back-to-back with her. She sounds like Artemis, and I'm *done* with it. "I'm doing okay so far!"

"No one asked you to—" She breaks off, dodging the zompire lunging for her. I have my own to deal with. It avoids my clumsy strike, hitting me hard in the side. I fly across the pit and fall just short of the electric wires and certain incapacitation—and therefore death. The monster races after me. I lift the sword and its momentum impales it.

It snarls, sliding farther down the blade toward me, fangs bared.

"*Stake* to the heart—a sword is useless that way!" Cosmina shouts. "Cut off the head!"

"Right!" I knew that; obviously I knew that. I brace both feet against the zompire and kick it free of the sword. Standing, I swing the sword like a baseball bat. It slices clean through the zompire's neck.

And then something that *was* becomes something that *isn't*, disappearing in a poof of dust. I feel a surge of adrenaline, my heart racing, blood singing in my veins. It's gone, and I'm *alive*. I have never been this alive. Power and strength suffuse me. With a scream, I swing the sword at my next attacker.

It cuts deep into the arm of a werewolf.

"No!" I pull the sword free. The werewolf howls in pain. As I stumble toward it to help, something slams into my back, knocking me to the ground. The sword skitters away. I roll, but a hellhound pins my shoulders. I'm face-to-face with my doom.

It yelps, collapsing onto me. The sword sticks out of its back. I shove the hellhound off, then wrench the sword free. Cosmina's on the other end of the pit. She must have thrown the blade. She's got the uninjured werewolf pinned, her arm around its throat. She's going to snap its neck the same way I snapped my first hell-hound's.

But that isn't a hellhound. It's a person.

"Stop!" I sprint to her, grab the werewolf, and throw it against the wire. It falls, unconscious.

"I had that one!" Cosmina snarls.

Slayers only kill *demons*. Not innocents. "They're people!"

"Not tonight, they aren't!"

The buzzer sounds once, twice, three times. They're dump-ing the rest on us.

I drop the sword and get on one knee, making my hands into

a cradle. Cosmina doesn't hesitate. She puts her foot in my hands and I throw upward with all my might. She sails through the air, landing just past the edge of the pit. And then she runs. Away from me.

What. The. Hell.

I'm alone.

No, I'm definitely *not* alone. I have nine new monsters surrounding me.

15

I PICK UP THE SWORD. MY LIMBS SHAKE. My vision tunnels. It's like the worst asthma attack ever, only I'm still breathing. But for how much longer?

One-on-one, I might have had a chance. But fighting nine monsters at once? I can't protect myself *and* the werewolves. I doubt I can even protect myself.

The first zompire lunges. I swing on pure instinct, taking off its head. A hellhound jumps at me and I slice into its stomach. The blood spurts, coating my hands in liquid so hot it burns. I want to puke. But that part of me is pushed aside by the kill-kill-kill running through my brain and body like an electric current.

I give myself over to it entirely.

The hellhound is dead. I swing up and take the arm off one of the other zompires. That doesn't even slow it. I spin, kicking high and catching it on the head. It stumbles into the wire, its clothes catching there.

The other two hellhounds tear at their dead packmate. I lower my head and run at one of the remaining werewolves, throwing it into the wire. The second werewolf grabs me, tossing me through the air. I land hard on my back but roll away from its pounce. The werewolf pins me. Then it yelps and goes limp, a deadweight on me. I shove it off. There's a dart in its shoulder.

With a whining yelp, the third active werewolf goes down, a dart in its chest. I pick up the sword as the hellhounds lose interest in their meal. They both leap at me at once. I slash one, spin, kick the other. It falls shy of the wires and scrambles to its feet. I lift the sword and jab. It goes in the hellhound's mouth, straight through the back of its skull. I try to pull the blade free.

It's stuck.

The other hellhound jumps. I yank the sword up, swinging the dead hellhound's body as a weapon. The impact sends both hellhounds—alive and dead—into the wire.

I stand in the center of the pit, panting. There are bodies all around me. Most are dead. The six werewolves are still alive. I'm so busy counting I don't notice movement until something falls to the ground behind me. A singed hellhound with a crossbow bolt in its back is dead inches from me.

Leo is standing on the edge of the pit, holding a crossbow. He looks determined. He also looks terrified. "Are you okay?" he shouts.

I lift a shaking, blood-covered hand to give him a thumbs-up. One of the barriers from the viewing area sails over the side and lands at the bottom, leaning against the barbed wire.

Artemis appears, leveraging another one so they form a ladder. "Wait until I cut the power!" she shouts.

Leo fires the crossbow at someone I can't see, then reloads. There's a crashing noise and the electric hum is gone. I can't stay in this pit a second longer, surrounded by the carnage. Soaked in the knowledge that I was pure Slayer and it still wouldn't have been enough without Leo and Artemis to help me. I run at the barrier ladder, climbing up as fast as I can. My clothes catch on the barbs. I tear free without pausing.

I rush out of the pit and into Leo. He catches me, his arms tightening around me.

"Thank God," he says. In that moment, I finally know I'm okay. I'm going to be okay. I saved Cosmina. None of the were-wolves died. That was me.

Leo releases me and I stumble a bit, feeling drunk on adrenaline and I don't know what else. Artemis joins us, and I grab her hands, my whole body still a live wire of sparks. "We did it!"

She raises one eyebrow. "Yeah." Her tone is more bruising than any hits I took in the pit. She turns away from me, her stance solid and ready for anything. But everyone who was here is gone or running. The platform is empty, the organizers vanished. The table that held the bets has been overturned. Money and strips of paper litter the ground.

There are also several bodies. They all look like demons, but in the darkness, I can't be sure. Who killed them? Artemis? Or . . .

"Where's Cosmina?" I ask.

My question is answered as the vampire from upstairs skids across the floor, sliding straight over the edge into the pit. Cosmina stalks past us.

"Come on, love," the vampire says, standing and dusting herself off. "We didn't mean any harm. I put a lot of money on you winning!"

Cosmina holds out her hand. "Give me the crossbow," she says.

Artemis looks like she's gearing up for an attack. I put a hand on her shoulder. I didn't save Cosmina just for Artemis to rip her limb from limb.

Leo's face is hard. "You left Athena in there alone."

Cosmina spins, hitting Leo across the jaw. Leo barely budges. Cosmina swears, cradling her hand. I flex my own fingers. I didn't notice pain down in the pit. That's as unnerving as anything else. Every part of my body accepted what it was doing. Embraced it, even.

"Fine," Cosmina says. She picks up one of the remaining wooden barriers and snaps it. Then she throws it like a javelin. The vampire doesn't have time to duck as the wood shears her head from her body.

Artemis sweeps an arm at the ruined venue. "What the hell was this?"

I'm stuck looking into the pit. The werewolf I hit with the sword is bleeding heavily. I do my best not to look at the hellhounds.

I left *corpses*. My revulsion is almost as strong as the rush of adrenaline I'd had. And that's what bothers me most: I was terrified, and it was awful, but . . . I also liked it. *Loved* it. The heady rush of battle. The iron tang of blood in the air. The way my body moved, a weapon in and of itself.

The power was intoxicating.

I'm a healer. I've dedicated my life to it. Fixing bodies is all I've ever wanted to do. But now? I have a body *count*.

Cosmina sounds indifferent as she answers Artemis's question. "I got caught eliminating their supply of zompires."

"Zompires?" Artemis asks.

If the term is new even to Artemis, that says something. I shake off all the thoughts about myself and what I did to focus on Cosmina's reply.

"Zombie vampire. It's what happens now when a vampire sires a new victim. With the hell connections cut off, any new vampire turns into those things. They form hives. I've got Dublin almost all clear. Didn't realize these assholes were keeping them for a reason." She stretches her neck, sighing. Then she starts gathering the money scattered on the floor, shoving it into her pockets. "They run this whole bloody town. Now I've got to fig-ure out how to make this up to them."

"Demons run Dublin?" Leo sounds surprised and concerned. We're only a couple of hours from Dublin. Does that make it our responsibility? And why weren't we already on top of it?

"Not demons. The people who organized this."

"And you let them?" Artemis asks.

Cosmina shrugs. "They're cleaning it up. They've made Dublin safer from supernatural beasties than it's been in decades. I tip them off when I find something too big to handle."

Artemis is rightfully aghast. "You *work* with these people? The ones that hold demon fights? That threw you in a pit to die?"

"There's a saying where I come from: Hold hands with the devil until you're both over the bridge. I haven't found the other side of the bridge yet."

"Come on," I say. I'm overwhelmed, but there's still a task that needs doing. I try to focus on it. "We have to help the were-wolves. Get them somewhere safe."

Cosmina scoffs. "You mean the things that tried to rip us limb from limb?"

"It's not their fault! And I cut that one. I didn't mean to. But I don't think werewolves heal supernaturally fast." I look to Leo and Artemis for confirmation, but neither responds. Rhys is the expert. I'm glad we left him and Cillian outside. They stayed safe, and they didn't see what I did. I wanted Artemis to see so she'd look at me differently.

Now I find I want my friends to look at me the same. Cillian's first instinct was to call me when a creature needed help. If he had seen this, he wouldn't have. I've lost so much in the last couple of days. So much of who I thought I was, who I thought I was going to be. I want to hold on to what I can.

Cosmina finishes gathering what she can of the scattered bank notes. "You want to help those things, you're on your own."

"*Excuse* me?" Artemis says. "My sister saved your sorry ass, and you didn't so much as turn around to help her. What kind of a Slayer are you?"

Cosmina whirls, her eyes narrowed sharper than my sword. "What kind of Slayer am I? I'm a living one, that's what kind."

"Well, today you're alive because of us!"

The Slayer closes the distance to Artemis, leaning close to my sister's face. Artemis doesn't flinch. Cosmina pulls her long blue hair aside, revealing a mangled ear and scarring that goes down her neck.

"Werewolf?" I wonder if that's where her animosity comes from.

"No, idiot. Another Slayer. So pardon me if I'm not interested in making friends. There's a reason there was only supposed to be a Chosen *One*. We're hunters. Killers. And we don't work well in packs." She pauses, studying me. "I *know* you. Dreams of a fire—purple flames—Mommy choosing to save someone else?"

Cosmina smiles cruelly at the horror written on my face. "Dreams go both ways. I hope you get killed soon. I'm tired of reliving your fire." She flips her hair back into place and stalks out.

The shock of the evening and everything that's happened—everything I've *done*—catches up to me. I came here to help because I saw her, because I thought we had a connection. That she needed me. But she's seen me too, and all she feels toward me is derision.

"You should have let her die," Artemis says after a beat.

I blink. *"What?"*

"She wasn't worth risking your life for. If you had waited a few minutes, Leo and I would have been here with weapons. We would have handled it. You can't jump into fights."

My heart starts pounding again and I struggle to stay calm. "Artemis, look at that pit. I did that. That was me." However much it bothers me, it's the truth. "I can handle myself."

"No, you can't! You would have been dead without the two of us here to help you."

I open my mouth to argue, but then stop. There's no point. I know she's trying to take care of me, but she's wrong. I shouldn't have waited. I chose to wait upstairs and it made everything a hundred times worse. No matter how much of a jerk Cosmina is, I had to help. She didn't ask me to rescue her, and she doesn't have to thank me. Helping was the right thing to do. And I'm going to do the right thing again.

I jump over the side of the pit, ignoring Artemis's shout. I can't leave the werewolf I hurt. The arm is cut almost down to the bone, but the bleeding is slow. Maybe a werewolf thing?

"Athena." Leo tosses me a first aid kit. I nod in gratitude, then patch up the werewolf's arm as best I can. It won't bleed to death, at least.

There's a flash of movement on the upper floor. I tense for attack, instantly ready. But it's Artemis. Walking away. My stomach sinks. We're moving further and further from each other, and I don't know how to stop it. I want my sister back. But maybe we've been playing roles for so long, we don't know how to be sisters now that things have changed.

"Come on," Leo says. "They'll be okay until morning. We'll leave the barriers here so they can climb up when they're back to human form."

I nod, numb. I'll worry about Artemis later. As for the werewolves, this is all we can do. I briefly consider hauling them each up myself, but then we run the risk of them waking up. And what would I do with them once I got them up? Put them back in the cages? Then I'd have to stay until morning to let them out again. And we—

Oh no. No no no.

"Oh my gods." I scramble up the makeshift ladders. "We're dead. We're *so* late."

Leo laughs, the surprise of my statement getting past his concern. My breath catches as his whole face changes. His eyes crinkle up until they're almost closed, his throat moves, his head tips back, and his mouth stretches wide in such a delighted expression I can't help but smile back. Leo is the only bright thing in this terrible room.

"You fought a pit full of monsters and protected the innocent while you were at it. And the most scared I've seen you all night is when you realized you're going to get in trouble with your mum. Athena Jamison-Smythe, you are a wonder."

Leo thinks I did a good job. He didn't criticize or question my choices, and he approved of what I was trying to do with the werewolves. He even helped by sedating them instead of killing them. He gets it. The smile still hasn't left my own lips. I bite them, trying to get it off, but it won't budge. *Oh gods, Nina.*

Not again.

Artemis checks the room for clues but comes up with nothing. Cillian and Rhys are outside without protection. Rhys can handle himself, but after what I've seen tonight, I'm more worried about the *people* than the monsters that might be out there with them. The werewolves will have to be okay until morning.

Relief washes over me to see Rhys and Cillian waiting at the car for us. Sarah had been safely transferred to the paramedics, who assured Cillian and Rhys she'd be fine. Artemis doesn't say anything. I want her to acknowledge that I did a good thing. But she's watching the night, tensed for attack.

Cillian eyes me in mute horror. My favorite marigold peacoat is splattered with gore. Shuddering, I tear it off and leave it on the sidewalk.

"You okay?" Cillian whispers. I lean against him. I don't answer, because I don't know what the answer is. Rhys takes my other side, putting his arm around me.

As Leo loads the gear into the car, he seems preoccupied too. He barely looks at me. Which is fine. Good, even. He performed admirably as a Watcher tonight, and that's all he is to me.

When Cillian and Rhys get in the car, I reach for Artemis's bag to pass to Leo. She snatches it away. "I got it."

"What's your problem?" I ask, stung by her dismissive tone.

She lets out a shocked, bitter laugh. "What's my *problem*? Do you have any idea what it felt like, running in and seeing you in the middle of an attack?"

"No, but do *you* have any idea what it felt like being in the middle of it? I was so scared, but—I wasn't, too. It's like, there's this thing inside me, coiled, waiting, and it's terrifying and exciting and *strong*. . . ." We stare at each other, both angry, both hurt. I relent first. "I'm sorry I scared you. I'm glad you were there."

Artemis turns to put her bag in the car, but some of the tension drains out of her shoulders. "Right. I'll always be there. Don't go thinking you don't need me." But it sounds less playful and more . . . sour. She grabs my arm as I climb in, her grip almost painful. It probably *would* have been painful two months ago. Not anymore.

"Promise me," she says, "you'll listen next time. You won't do something like this again."

Something like saving another Slayer? Like taking on monsters and winning? I did okay. I won. And her only acknowledgment is asking me to promise I won't fight to help someone again.

But . . . if I have to be a Slayer, this is exactly the kind of Slayer I want to be.

Artemis has no idea what it feels like. She's always been strong. And now that I am too, she wants me to hold back. She still sees me as the one who got left behind, the one who needs protection and help.

I might not know how to untangle my emotions, but I do know that I need to stop lying about them. And I *want* to talk to her, to tell her everything. She's been fighting these fights for so long. She really can help me.

"I can't promise that, Artemis. But—"

She recoils like I burned her. Without another word, she gets in the front seat and slams the door.

On the drive back to Shancoom, the night seals us in. Something tremendous has shifted. Artemis is closed off, staring out the window. Rhys and Cillian are curled up around each other, half asleep. I'm stewing, annoyed at Artemis for shutting me out just like our mother does.

I reach toward her seat but stop, horrified. My hands are still covered in blood.

I stare at them, and I know what's different. Why we all feel like strangers. I might have become a Slayer the day magic ended, but tonight was the first time I really *was* a Slayer. I was a creature of instinct and brutality, fighting monsters. And I *liked* it.

Now in the car, surrounded by my old life—my real life— that fact bothers me more than anything else.

I saw Cosmina. She was a Slayer. A real Slayer. A killer. But when I jumped in the pit, the only thought in my mind was about saving someone who needed me. It felt right. It felt *good*. Cosmina can hate me all she likes, because she's alive to do it. Six werewolves will wake up tomorrow morning, sore but breathing. Because of me.

I just need to figure out how I can be a Slayer without losing what makes me *Nina* in the process.

16

I SIT STRAIGHT UP IN BED, MY HEART racing.

What is *wrong* with my sleeping brain? Of all the things I could dream about, my subconscious settles on Bradford Smythe again? I would have taken being back in the pit fighting monsters, or even a dream about the fire.

I need therapy.

"You okay?" Artemis mumbles sleepily from across the room.

"Do you ever have weird dreams about the Council?"

"Every damn night. Ruth Zabuto uses my fingers for knitting needles, and Wanda . . ." She trails off, muttering something about spiders and switches, and then she goes quiet, her breathing even.

At least Cosmina didn't come hang out in my dreams. I'm more than happy never to see her again. And I don't trust my Slayer dreams. Not only did my dream about her fail to give me very pertinent information, it also sent me to her against her will.

I flop back on my bed. It's 4 a.m. and I've been asleep for only an hour.

My phone buzzes. I scramble to get it before Artemis stirs. The screen shows a text from Cillian.

It's awake

"Stake me with a million splinters," I whisper. I glance over at Artemis. I was going to tell her about the demon yesterday morning. Then everything spiraled so quickly. And she's been so mad. I don't know what she'd do with the demon.

My demon. I can handle this.

Do not engage, I text. I'm on my way.

Weapons, weapons, I need weapons. Only as a precaution. I pull on my slippers, throw a fuzzy robe over my pajamas, and sneak into the hall. I'm halfway through the dorm wing when the smell of cigarette smoke pulls me up short.

Imogen leans against a recess in the wall. Her eyes are heavy and tired. "Hey, Nina. Where are you off to?"

"Oh. Um. Getting some water."

"Here." She passes me the cigarette, then disappears into the Littles' suite. I hold the cigarette gingerly, like it might come alive and force its way into my lungs. Imogen always wears long sleeves, down almost to her fingers. Isn't she worried her sleeves will catch on fire?

She laughs quietly at my obvious horror when she comes back out. "Sorry. I didn't think. That was rude of me." She takes the cigarette, handing me a bottle of water and a juice box. "We have a lot of middle-of-the-night drink requests. I'm always fully stocked."

"Thanks." But now Imogen is between the weapons-stocked

gym and me. And I can't let anyone know what I'm doing.

She taps out the cigarette in a little dish on the floor. "Sorry about this. I never do it where the Littles can see. But some days." She shakes her head, her silky, thin blond hair curtaining her face. I've always liked her, but she doesn't really hang out with the rest of us. For one thing, she's older. Early twenties. But mostly Imogen exists to take care of the Littles. They're her priority, always.

I nod. "Some days."

"So, you're a Slayer, yeah?"

Oh gods. We forgot to tell her! Did we tell Jade? It's only a secret that I'm training, not that I'm a Slayer. I have so many secrets lately, I can't remember what is actually a secret or only sort of a secret. I shuffle my slippered feet. "Yeah. Surprised?"

Imogen shrugs. "Not really. Makes sense."

"It does?" I figured it was an unspoken sentiment that if anyone should be a Slayer, it should be Artemis. Maybe my mom even trained her hoping the Slayer abilities would settle on the right twin. Maybe . . . maybe Artemis wishes that too.

"Of course it does. You spent all these years learning the best ways to help and protect others. I think you'll be great." Her hazel eyes are dark brown in the dim hall lighting. They're tight with exhaustion, and it makes her look sad. "I can't wait to see what you'll do."

"Thanks." It feels inadequate to say, but I'm grateful she feels that way. And then I remember that Imogen doesn't know I'm training, because I'm not supposed to be training. Gods, the castle has gotten complicated. "I mean, I'm probably not going to do anything. Slayerish, that is. My mom doesn't want me to."

"Mums." Imogen's twisted smile is bleak.

I cringe. "Sorry. I'm going back to bed. Thanks for the drinks. And the vote of confidence."

With Imogen showing no signs of going back into her room, I head toward my room. Then I pass it, going deep into the dorm wing. I navigate the discarded furniture, everything menacing shapes in the near darkness, until I find Artemis's secret passageway closet. The Council room isn't far from the gym, and there's bound to be another exit somewhere.

I turn on my cell phone as a flashlight. Sweeping it from side to side, I see branching passages. I bet I could get to nearly every room here without ever being seen. I turn toward the gym. I hope. The passage here is narrow, the cold, damp walls brushing my shoulders. I angle myself so I'm walking sideways. My dim screen illuminates only a few feet in front of me. I pass several yawning exits.

The blackness moves in one of them.

I freeze. I slowly back up, my light bouncing as my hands shake. Then I sweep the light through the passageway where I had sensed the movement.

It's empty.

I had expected a zompire looming. More hellhounds. Something dark and bloodthirsty to take me into the darkness with it, where I belong.

Unable to shake the sensation of being watched, I scramble until I find a door. I don't care where it spits me out.

I slide it open, squeezing into a tiny space even more cramped than the passageways. There's a heavy wooden panel in front of me. I push. It gives, but only a little. I push harder. It scrapes open.

Books. So many books. I've found the secret library room! I walk to the only door. It, too, is hard to push. I can't imagine what people with non-Slayer strength must have to do to get it open. Maybe it's designed to be a two-person door, so no one can get in here alone with the dangerous books. I overshot the gym, though. The library is next to the Council residence wing.

I employ every ounce of Slayer stealth as I sneak past where my mother, Eve Silvera, Leo, and all the other Watchers are sleeping. Including Bradford Smythe. I shudder, remembering that stupid dream.

The gym is unlocked. I take a short black stick that delivers electric shocks—used by Watchers, not Slayers, but I'll make an exception for myself. I do *not* take the nunchucks.

Stupid nunchucks.

I'm still in my robe and slippers. I didn't think this through in my rush to get to Cillian. But if I get caught coming back, no one will suspect I was out with a demon. Who talks with demons while wearing rainbow-print pajamas?

"Who talks with demons while wearing rainbow-print pajamas?" Cillian hisses at me in the dark. He's in front of his house, arms crossed, stamping his feet impatiently. It's freezing, and I already took off my robe so it wouldn't hamper me if I needed to fight.

"I didn't have time to change! Is the demon loose?"

"No. I heard some movement in there and peeked in a window. It's awake. But still chained up."

I try to psych myself up. "That's good. This will be fine. It'll all be fine. I'm going to go in. If I'm not back in ten minutes, call Rhys and Artemis. Or the army."

"That's reassuring, innit?"

I walk straight through his house and into the yard. The shed lurks, waiting in the darkness to swallow me whole.

I grip the shock stick and run through worst-case scenarios. The demon is free and inside, waiting to kill me. The demon is free and not inside anymore, already killing people and it's my fault. The demon isn't free and is still inside and I'll have to figure out what to do with it, including potentially . . . killing it.

The last option bothers me the most. It's one thing to kill creatures while fighting for your life. It's another to have to actively choose to do so. Watchers have to make calls like this all the time. And Slayers don't even make the call. They just act.

Taking a deep breath, I unlock the door and stomp inside with my aggression slightly dampened by fuzzy slippers. I pull the chain for the light.

"Ack, give a guy a little warning." The demon squints up at me, its—his, I think—handcuffed-together hands lifted to shade his eyes. They're a shockingly normal brown. Next to his radioactively bright skin, it looks like a kid with a crayon box and no sense of color families designed him.

"Oh." His voice is cringe-inducingly discordant, filtered through materials not quite the same as human vocal cords and mouths. "Hey. Hi. Listen, you and I both know that I'm more valuable alive. But did you know my secretions are steadier and higher quality when I'm happy? So keep that in mind as you decide how to punish me." He lowers his hands, eyeing me with a puzzled expression. "You don't look like a bounty hunter."

"Thank you?" I don't move, and neither does he.

"Look, I'm sorry I ran away. But conditions were less than

ideal for me. If you get Sean on the phone, I'll apologize and we can figure out a compromise. Ideally one that involves less torture. I don't want to die, and you don't want me to die either. And he's going to kill me if things continue as they were."

I lean against a table, very aware of the length of the chains and how far he can reach should he surprise me by lunging. "I have no idea what you're talking about or who Sean is. We found you unconscious. There was also a hellhound."

He startles, panicked, as though perhaps a hellhound is hiding in the tiny shed. "Where is it?"

"I killed it."

He snorts skeptically. "You killed it."

I fold my arms, feeling defensive. "Yes."

"With what? Did you smother it with a teddy bear? Have a slumber party and braid its hair to death?"

I channel Artemis. "Do you *really* want to insult someone who killed a hellhound with her bare hands?"

He shifts with a jingle of chains. "Okay, okay, sure. I'm believing you. You killed the hellhound. Thanks for that."

"There were two, actually." I don't mention what happened to the second one. I want him to be impressed with me or scared of me. "Why were they here? Were they chasing you, or do you own them?"

"Bloody demon mutts. I wouldn't own one. They're as likely to kill you as they are their prey. And it's no picnic being their prey, either, let me tell you."

I feel a wash of relief. At least I didn't save the demon responsible for the hellhounds.

He shifts his weight with a clinking of chains. "Can I make

a suggestion, love?" He smiles, revealing double rows of blunt black teeth. "Let me go. Forget we ever met. Forget you ever saw me. I promise it'll be better for you that way."

"I can't let a demon go!"

"Fantastic." He leans his head back against the wall. "What are you, some sort of vigilante? I'm not a bad bloke. Really, I'm not."

"Why does this Sean want you, then?"

The demon holds out his hands. "You might have noticed I have a bit of a skin condition."

I wrinkle my nose. "Yeah, your skin condition got all over my shirt and my hair when I carried you in here."

He snorts a laugh, then quickly tries to cover it as a cough. "Wow. Sorry. My particular breed of *demon*, as you call me, secretes a substance that has a psychotropic effect on humans. 'Psychotropic' means—"

"I know what 'psychotropic' means." Every good medic studies drugs. "You secrete tranquilizers?"

"Depends. People react differently when they ingest it. For some it has a powerful antidepressant effect. Sometimes triggers euphoria. Sometimes puts people to sleep. And sometimes makes people hallucinate. But always in a happy way."

I must look horrified, because he shrugs. "Literally can't help it. I'm worth quite a bit on the black market, if you know the right people." He looks me up and down, lingering on my rainbow pajamas and slippers. "I *don't* think you know the right people. And Sean would find you the second you started making inquiries to sell me. So again, your best bet is to let me go."

"Why do you secrete that stuff? Let me guess: Your victims are so blissed out that they don't mind when you eat them."

He wrinkles his nose this time, the cracked skin bunching up. Then he grimaces and lifts his fingers to the cut I taped shut. "I happen to be vegetarian. Sort of."

"Sort of?"

"I eat emotions. That's what we do. We make you happy and then we breathe in all that bliss. And then we move on, because why keep eating the same happiness when you can experience something new every meal?"

"And your victims?"

"What victims? At most they have a mild headache when they come down. No lasting damage. They'll even have happy memories. I don't hurt anyone." He shakes one manacled ankle at me. "Unlike humans. You never saw a creature you didn't prey on."

"That's not true!"

"Innit, though?"

I open my mouth to argue, but . . . well, he has a point. We're a deeply predatory race. Look what being imbued with demonic power does to us, after all. We become Slayers—humans made solely to hunt and kill.

I shake my head, refocusing. "I have volumes and volumes on demons. I can look you up and find out whether you're telling the truth."

"Good. Go do that. And hope that Sean doesn't find you while you're reading. Because I won't hurt you, but Sean definitely will."

The demon's intensity makes me feel like he's telling the truth. And then I think of something. I've run into hellhounds twice in connection to this demon, and once somewhere else. "This Sean. Does he work in Dublin? Nice suit? Ponytail?"

All the open disdain in the demon's face shifts to wariness. "I thought you didn't know him."

"I don't. But I crashed one of his parties last night."

He pushes back like he'd burrow into the wall of the shed if he could. "You should let me go. And you should run too. You seem like a nice kid."

I tap the shock stick on the table. "I can handle myself." It's too many coincidences, though. The demon showing up here. My dream leading me to Cosmina, who was connected to the man the demon is connected to. "Why did you run *here*?"

"I made for the forest first. Hellhound was on my heels, so I kept going. Something about the shed seemed safe. It called to me, I suppose. I was trying to make it inside. Didn't get past collapsing over the fence, though."

"No, I mean Shancoom. This area specifically."

The demon looks away, shrugging. He rubs his shoulder, which must be sore, but it's working. I did a good job there too. "I like the seaside. Lovely little town."

"Were you looking for someone?" It can't be a coincidence that he ended up by our castle.

"You don't want to get mixed up with this. You might think you already are, but it goes so much deeper. Release me. I'll meet my contact and disappear and you'll never hear from me again. You fixed me up when you didn't have to. That was kind. I don't want to see you dead. Stay away from Dublin."

I shouldn't care, but I like that he thinks I'm kind. It heals some of my fears after what I did in the pit. I can make the right choices while fighting and while choosing not to fight. "Who is your contact?" I ask.

He shakes his head. "I'm not involving you, kid." Then he grimaces. "Can you at least try to feel happy? I'm starving, and you reek. Seriously, *how* do you smell so bad?"

"I do not smell bad!" I showered as soon as we got back to the castle, spending as long as possible scrubbing hellhound blood and zompire dust and guilt and adrenaline from my body.

"No, really. It's like . . ." He cocks his head. "There's this scent clinging to you like smoke. It's anger and despair and violent rage. So much more than one girl would ever have access to." He leans forward, suddenly interested. "Who are you?"

"Nobody," I squeak. Could he smell the Slayer in me? Maybe I should tell him. Maybe it would scare him into giving me more information. But I don't want to use it like a cudgel or a threat. And I don't want to go giving my identity to demons left and right, even if he does seem like he isn't much of a threat.

I can't let him see he's rattled me. I fold my arms and continue my best Artemis impression. Firm. Capable. In charge. "Until you tell me who your contact is and what's going on, you're not going anywhere."

The demon stretches his legs out as far as the chains allow. "Don't say I didn't warn you if Sean comes looking."

"I think I can handle him."

"Right. You'll slipper-kick him to death." He closes his eyes. "Bring me someone happy soon, though, or I'll starve. Or you can do us both a favor and lick my skin. Best day of your life, I promise."

"Yuck." I recoil from him, wanting to rinse my mouth with Listerine at the very thought of it.

"Yeah, you can totally handle Sean. He's not going to slit

your throat." The demon yawns. His teeth aren't teeth at all. They look more like sponges.

"Maybe I'll call him right now."

At this, genuine terror flashes across his face. "Please," he says, his voice soft. "Please don't. Keep me in here. Forever, if you have to. But please don't give me back to him."

My heart responds to his fear. I can't make promises to a demon, though. So I don't say anything. But his expression haunts me as I go to turn the light back off. I hesitate. "Do you want the light on or off?"

"On, please? I don't like the dark."

I nod. Me neither. I leave the shed with more questions than answers. And if I want to see if he's telling me anything that's true, I have only one course of action available to me:

Research.

17

I KNOCK ON RHYS'S DOOR AS SOON AS
it's a reasonable hour. He opens it and peers out. "Is something
wrong?"

"No, nothing! I kind of wanted to do . . . some research."

Rhys blinks in surprise. "Research? Really?" His eyes narrow
slightly. This is a request I've never made. I can't have him suspecting there's a very real reason behind it. I hate manipulating
him, but short of going to the Council, it's my only option.

"I just—after last night I want to feel normal. And what's
more normal than us hanging out in the library studying demons?"

Rhys smiles, genuine fondness in his face. I feel a deep twinge
of guilt over misleading him. I think he'd help—really help—
but then I'd have to ask him to keep secrets for me. I understand
now how wearing and awful secrets are. I don't want to burden
him with this.

"I would like nothing more," he says. "Did you have a specific
research goal? Or go wild and play bookshelf roulette?"

I laugh. "Focus on demons? There was a new kind last night.

Zompires. It made me realize how much I still don't know."

"Perfect! We'll bulk up on demonology. And you can give me all the zompire details, plus help me narrow down my ideas for my Watcher project. All my previous efforts were scrapped when Buffy tanked magic. I need something new. Something practical but also sensational."

Rhys and I walk to the library together. He breathes in deeply, rubbing his hands together. "Where to start?"

I trail my fingers along the shelves. It really is a beautiful room. The window slots provide abundant golden light that cuts the room in rays, illuminating the dust motes dancing languidly in the air. Most of the books are bound in leather, their spines faded. Illegible covers have neatly labeled cards beneath them. Artemis's handwriting. Yet another thankless chore she's done. Do I ever tell her how much all her work is appreciated? Does anyone?

But Artemis's labels don't tell me what type of demon I have in Cillian's shed or whether he's dangerous. "Is there anything that categorizes demons by . . . color?"

Rhys shakes his head. He's already pulling vampire books as well as several books whose titles begin with "necro-," which is a prefix I normally avoid if possible. "Is 'zompire' a technical name? It sounds like a nickname."

"I doubt you'll find them in any books. Cosmina said they popped up after the link to hell dimensions was cut off."

He sets down several of the books, his face falling. "So we'd need field reports. Which would be easy if we had more than Honora in the field. And if she *ever* checked in. Leo hasn't encountered them?"

"Not that he mentioned, but feel free to ask him." I need to redirect Rhys's excellent brain. Zompires are something new, which isn't good because it means no info, and we thrive on info. But the demon in the shed is more pressing than zompires in Dublin. "What about a book that organizes demons by type? A comprehensive reference. Like an encyclopedia of demons."

He scratches his head, looking around with a dazed expression. "No. Most of the books were written about specific demons. Areas of the world. Periods of history. But . . . *wow*. That's an amazing idea. If I could condense this information into an easily searchable reference guide . . ."

And I've lost him. I snap my fingers. "Okay. Let's narrow it down, then. I'm interested in hybrid demons. But I'm feeling a little squeamish. So how about hybrid demons that eat things other than people. Maybe ones that eat . . . emotions?" There's a sign as neon yellow as the demon flashing over my head saying NINA IS UP TO SOMETHING.

Fortunately, Rhys is in his element and doesn't notice my obvious guilt. "So empath types? Actual emotions, or emotional energy? Or just energy?" He starts pulling books at what looks like random. He knows these shelves so well he can grab books without looking. "This one has a section on fear demons. Nasty little blokes. Emphasis on 'little.' Oh, this has a good primer on incubus- and succubus-type demons, with several in-depth studies. A history of Pylea, that's useful. Hmm, these demons are psychic, but that might overlap with what you're studying. Do you want demons that only eat emotions? This one lives on emotions but also has a fondness for kittens."

"As pets?"

"As snacks."

I grimace. If my shed demon eats kittens, I've definitely been too nice to him. "I guess focus mainly on emotions, but outliers are okay."

Rhys sets down the books, along with a notebook and a pen. "As you're studying, note the demons in alphabetical order, categorize them by type, and also include a detailed bibliography so we can reference back to it."

"Homework?"

Rhys grins. "If you're doing this, do it right."

His excitement would be infectious if my research didn't have such a pressingly real time crunch behind it. He grabs three more books—easily thousands of pages worth of information—and adds them to the pile, patting them fondly. "This should get us started."

"Started?" I whimper.

"I'm going to make our demon reference book as my Watcher project! It's applicable even with the death of magic, and I can update the notes to reflect the change in the world! It will also give us a good starting point for determining which demons are earthbound and which are sealed away from us. We can also add new things, like zompires." His nose wrinkles in distaste. "I'll come up with a suitable Latin name for them. Anyhow. The whole demonic landscape has changed, and it's up to me to catalog it!" He hums to himself, going back to the bookshelves.

I get to work, but it doesn't go well. It turns out there are any number of demons that consume emotion. And emotion and energy are so closely linked, oftentimes the entries don't make any distinction. Plus, none of the frequently gruesome drawings look anything like my Coldplay demon.

I shake my head, snorting a laugh. "Oh my gods, *he was all yellow.*"

"Hmm?" Rhys looks up from his own book.

"Nothing."

We're interrupted when old Ruth Zabuto creaks in with Jade in tow. "Hello, dear ones," Ruth says.

"Hey, Grandma." Rhys barely looks up.

"Hey, Jade," I say. I want to mention that I'm a Slayer, because I feel guilty for not informing her and Imogen. But I don't know any nonawkward way to bring it up.

"Morning." She wrinkles her nose with distaste at both the word and the concept of mornings. She looks rough, like she's barely been sleeping. Which is odd. Jade sleeps all the time. "Shouldn't being a Slayer get you out of research duty? If I were a Slayer, I'd never set foot in the library again."

Of course she knows. It's a miracle I have the secrets I do, living in Castle Gossip. Although I'm relieved I don't have to tell her. "My mom doesn't want me to train. So I figured I'd be a new kind of Slayer. The smart, researchy kind. A Watcher-Slayer."

Jade looks disgusted. "What a waste."

Ruth Zabuto's voice is wobbly and her eyes brim with liquid. She looks worn down and pale and with even darker circles under her eyes than normal. "Jade, dear, pull all the books of magic we have extra copies of. Artemis marked their spines with chalk." Jade sighs and shuffles up and down the rows.

"What are you doing?" I slam my book shut on a gruesomely detailed drawing of a demon eating fear by inserting its needlelike tongue into an amygdala. I'd prefer the kitten snacker to that one.

Ruth's heavily lined face wrinkles further. "Have you heard of a thing called . . . E. Day?"

"eBay," Jade corrects.

"Yes. E. Bay." Ruth separates it into two distinct words. "Many of these books are antiques. And that's all they are." She runs her fingers along the cover of a gold-embossed book with a single eye in the middle. "Did you know, this was a real eye. It used to open and give you the angriest looks for daring to explore its magic." She jabs her finger into the eye, as though trying to get it to wake up. "Just a book now."

"Grandma!" Rhys stands. I've never seen him this angry. "You can't sell the books!"

"Only the magic books, dear. And only the ones we've already copied. We need money more than we need history books. We have to think of the Littles, their future. We don't have the resources we used to." She pats his hand and then continues down the row with Jade. Rhys slumps in his chair.

This is our history. Our heritage. This is all I have connecting me to my father. And it's yet another thing we're losing because of stupid Buffy. If she hadn't broken everything, we'd still have magic *and* money. If she hadn't messed up the Slayer powers so deeply, I wouldn't have become one. My life would have stayed simple.

Although, even as this familiar resentment runs through my mind, I have to admit to myself that I'm not entirely sure I *do* wish my life had stayed uncomplicated. The changes have thrown things into stark relief. The idea of going back to being the medic—ignored, discounted, letting Artemis be in charge of both the castle and my life . . . it's not appealing. It was unfair to both of us. And I see now that as a Watcher I was never going to shift anyone's way of thinking or working.

Becoming a Slayer was the last way I imagined my life changing for the better, but the universe has a perverse sense of humor. I wanted to change the Watchers? I had to become something else.

The door opens and my mother breezes in. "Ruth, don't tell Wanda what we're doing. She'll insist on a meeting and then demand to be in charge of new fund allocations, and we both know where the money will go if—" She stops midstride when she sees me. "What are you doing in here?"

"Rhys wants to make an encyclopedia of demons. And since I'm not busy," I say, leaning into the lie to prove just how much I'm not training as a Slayer or fighting hellbeasts or doing anything else that will get me in trouble, "I figured I'd help."

She frowns in thought. "That's a very good idea, Rhys. Practical." Her eyes dart to various shelves, never quite settling on me. "Are you feeling well, Nina?"

"I'm fine," I snap.

"Did you have fun at the movies?"

"The—" I cut myself off before I can ask what she's talking about. "Oh yes! Super fun. Didn't we have fun at the movies?" I ask Rhys.

"It was a little bloody for my taste," he deadpans.

"Good," my mother says. "Good. Well, let me know how your project goes, Rhys. Nina, may I speak to you for a moment in the hall?"

I'm surprised she didn't make me schedule an appointment through Artemis. I follow her out. Maybe she's going to talk to me about the second hellhound, the one she shot. Explain why she didn't bother telling everyone else about it or put us on lock-down again. Because the more I think about it, the weirder that is. Wasn't she worried there would be more? She doesn't know what their target was, so she has no idea that as long as the Coldplay demon's not here, we're safe.

"I have something for you." She hands me a pamphlet. I'm still thinking about her and the gun and the hellhound, so it takes me several seconds to process what I'm reading. And then it's several more before I can speak through my shock and confusion. "Boarding school?"

"You'd be starting late, but it will set you up nicely for university and your future medical studies."

"I— What? What do you mean? I'm already studying. Here."

For a second I glimpse that same vulnerability I thought I saw in her face yesterday. Like she's ready to talk *to* me for once instead of sending commands in my general direction. The look swiftly disappears behind her firm, no-nonsense expression. She's not my mother in that expression. She's a Council member. "The castle has never really been the right place for you."

The "castle," meaning the Watchers. She's implying that all the things I've done don't matter. That what I always suspected—I have no place or purpose here, among the people I love best and the organization I want to serve—is true.

"But I'm part of this." My voice is tight with pain. I want to be angry, but I'm so hurt I can't access those emotions. Being here, doing this work—it's what I do with Artemis. And it's my only connection to my dad. "I'm a Watcher."

"You're not." She doesn't say it meanly. It's a statement of fact.

And it's a true one. I'm not, and I never was going to be. Not fully. That was saved for Artemis. I *haven't* mattered much over the years. I don't doubt that my fellow Watchers care about me, but I also know that they've never needed me. Not the way they need Artemis or Rhys or Leo. A week ago my mother could have sent me away and it would have had almost no impact on the castle's functions.

But that was a week ago. I lift my chin defiantly. "So I'm not a Watcher. That's fine. I'm a Slayer." Each time I say it aloud, it feels a little more real, a little more right.

My mother flinches as though I've struck her. "That's not what you want."

"You've never asked me what I wanted!" I shove the pamphlet back at her. "Not once. And what about Artemis? She's going to leave all this behind and go to boarding school too?"

"Artemis needs to stay with me. It's best for everyone."

"No, it's not. I'll bet you've never asked Artemis what she wants either." For that matter, have I? Have I ever actually heard Artemis say she wants to be a Watcher? She was devastated when she failed the test, but was it about being a Watcher, or failing?

"I wish I could make my decisions based on what you want, Nina. But I can't. There are bigger things at play here than your feelings. One day you'll understand. Until then, you have to trust that I'm doing what's right for you. For both of you. I'm your mother."

"My mother?" I want to hurt her as much as she's hurt me.

"No. You're a Council member. And since, according to you, I'm neither a Watcher nor a Slayer, I don't have to follow your commands." I stalk back into the library. Jade sees my expression and opens her mouth to ask me something, but I grab my stack of books and carry them to the far shelf. I kick the secret door aside, then storm through the hidden room, through the tunnels, and finally out into the dorm wing.

I drop the books in my room. Then, keyed up and furious and more than a little worried my mom will show up for round two, I go for a run.

It doesn't clear my mind. I was never trained to know my body, to use it to its full ability. I used to be precisely aware of all my limitations. I have no idea what they are now.

My mother's latest attempt to get rid of me nips at my heels. I can't run fast enough to get away from it. The Council wouldn't let her. Bradford would probably go against her. Eve definitely would. And Leo—I'm positive Leo would fight for me to stay. It makes me feel a little better, knowing I have the Silveras. Though I'm a bit surprised by my absolute confidence that Leo is on my side. Maybe I should tell *him* about the demon in the shed. But it would be so humiliating to admit. And then I'd have to tell Eve, because I'm sure he doesn't have secrets from his mom. And she'll tell the rest of them, because she's on the Council.

Come to think of it, why hasn't Leo found me today? Is it because we need to lie low and pretend so my mom doesn't get suspicious? Or is he avoiding me after last night? Maybe he and his mother are talking about me, deciding what to do.

Everyone here is a Watcher before everything else. I need a

Slayer to talk to. Or at least someone who understands what I'm going through.

As I leap over logs and duck under branches, a detail I had forgotten in all the chaos strikes me. I have access to people who knew Slayers better than anyone. Or at least, I have access to their writing.

I stole two Watcher diaries from my mother's nightstand. It's time to find out what they knew.

Artemis is in our room when I get back. She doesn't hang around in the middle of the day—her work keeps her busy. And I still don't know where we stand after last night.

"It's Tuesday," she says. It sounds like an accusation.

Then it hits me. It's *Tuesday*.

Tuesday afternoon is Artemis's only time off. We spend it together. Doing manis and pedis, refilling the holy water supplies, and sharpening stakes while watching movies on our ancient laptop. We eat protein bars we keep stashed so she doesn't even have to go near the kitchen and dining hall. Normally, it's my favorite day of the week. I spend the six days before carefully curating a selection of movies and choosing nail polish colors. But this week, I haven't prepared at all.

"You forgot, didn't you?" Artemis's face is tight.

I did. But admitting it will hurt her even more. So again, I lie. "After what happened last night, I didn't know if you'd want to hang out."

The lie didn't work. She looks even more hurt. "Do you not want to?"

"Of course I want to! I always want to." I'm not in the

mood for movies, though. I'm in the mood to hit something. To run more. To do something, anything, with all this energy itching through me. I need to find Leo, to see if Eve has any additional insight about what we ran into last night. And the journals taunt me from their hiding place. Whose are they, that my mother kept them? What might they tell me about how to be a Slayer?

I sit on my bed. "I just don't know where we are right now. I didn't want to force you to do this."

She carefully lines up our bottles of polish. She always wears black, but she lets me paint her fingernails in bright rainbows. "Maybe this seems pointless now, with everything going on. But I want a normal afternoon with you. If you want."

She can't mask the hurt in her voice. I was always the one who counted down to these days. But maybe she needed them even more than I did.

Guilt washes over me. My changes have disrupted her life too. I've been mad at her—with good reason—but I can also be patient and understanding. The Watcher diaries aren't going anywhere. Neither is the Coldplay demon. "I want that too," I say quickly. "A normal afternoon. You pick the movie."

As she looks over our stacks of DVDs, it strikes me that Artemis is just a teenager. Like me. We're sixteen, but she never gets to act it except these few precious hours once a week. Thinking of how young we are reminds me of why I ran from the library. "So," I ask casually, "did Mom talk to you about boarding school?"

"What? No. What are you talking about?"

I take a deep, shaky breath. What if Artemis agrees with our mother's reasoning? It will break me. But I can't keep any more secrets. I can barely hold the ones I have. "She wants to send me away."

Artemis whips her head around and stares at me in shock. "Are you *kidding* me?"

"She had a pamphlet and everything."

Artemis's eyes flash with fury. "No. I won't let her do that. She's not separating us."

My relief is sudden and overwhelming. Whatever we might disagree on or fight about, Artemis is still on my side. She might do more with our mom, might be the one our mom wants to stay, but Artemis is *mine*. I plop down on the bed. Artemis sits beside me, and I lean my head against her shoulder.

Now that I know for sure it won't happen—Artemis won't let it—I can relax enough to actually think about it without being angry. "What if you came with me? Traded fight training for physical education. Demonology for geology. Latin for . . . well, Latin, I guess, but probably less creepy Latin."

Artemis snorts. "Can you imagine us in a normal school?"

I close my eyes. "I can, actually. And think: If it were an all-girls school, so many options for a babe like you."

Artemis laughs, but it's dark and a little sad. "I'm never getting out of here, Nina. Mom would never send me. And the Council wouldn't agree. Or pay for it. I don't know if they even could at this point. Besides, now you're a—"

I wait for her to say "Slayer." I want her to. As soon as she acknowledges it, maybe it will break this weirdness between us. I can tell her how confusing last night was for me. I can tell her all the things I'm feeling. And I can tell her about the demon in the shed.

But she doesn't finish the sentence. "Well, whatever is happening with you, we'll figure it out together. Mom's not sending you away from me."

It's not quite the validation I was hoping for. But I appreciate that she'll still fight for me. Out of the secrets piling up between us, I pick one truth to tell her. "I stole something from Mom's room."

She puts the laptop aside. "What?"

I slide off her bed and go to mine, where I retrieve the diaries. She sits on the floor across from me. I open the first one to the front page. It's Bradford Smythe's Watcher diary.

"Weird," Artemis says. "Why would Mom have that?"

"I didn't know he was ever an active Watcher. I can't imagine him in the field."

She grabs the other one, then makes a noise like a wounded animal and drops it to the floor. I pick it up.

The name engraved on the front cover—that I hadn't seen through the dust and in my hurry to hide the book—is Merrick Jamison-Smythe. I eagerly open it, but Artemis puts her hand on top of mine and gently closes it again. "No," she says.

"Why not? It's *Dad's*. Don't you want to know what he wrote?"

She looks haunted. "No. It's not Dad's. It belongs to the Watcher Merrick Jamison-Smythe. I want to remember him as Dad. Being a Watcher consumes every other aspect of my life. I just—I need to keep Dad as *Dad*, you know?"

I don't agree with her, but I do understand. And a private part of me is glad. My father knew I was a Potential, and his journal is about his time with Slayers. Now that I'm a Slayer too, I almost feel like he wrote this for me, and me only. I push it under my bed, promising to return to it when I'm alone.

Artemis picks up Bradford Smythe's diary and starts flipping through it. "Why would Mom have this one?"

"It was in her nightstand with Dad's. I don't get it either."

She settles on a page, skimming. "Oh, I see. He worked with a Potential. I don't recognize her name. This was decades ago."

I lean close to read over her shoulder. "What happens to Potentials who age out? Or, I guess, what happened? Past tense." They were the lucky ones. When only one Slayer was called at a time, if a Potential got too old, her odds of becoming the new Slayer dwindled and disappeared. I would have been a dwindler for sure.

"The ones who were identified and trained from childhood were absorbed into the Watchers. They knew too much at that point, and it provided new blood for the old families. Most never made full Watcher status, but that's how they staffed such a large operation. Back when it was large."

"So even though they didn't become Slayers, they still weren't off the hook?"

"Nope." Artemis pops the *p* on the end of the word. "Once a part of Watcher society, the only ways out are death, prison, or failure so complete you join Wesley Wyndam-Pryce in private investigation working for a vampire named Angel." She grins wickedly. "I can never get over how funny that one is. I try to bring it up whenever possible in front of Wanda. 'Sorry, are these boxes *private*? Can I *investigate* them? Isn't Imogen Post an *angel* with those children?'"

I cackle. *This* is my Artemis. This is the sister I know and love.

She smirks. "I have to figure out ways to make the days bearable. Sometimes I play tricks on Ruth Zabuto. I once switched out her focusing crystals with rock candy. She didn't notice. Ever. So when she complains about magic being gone, just know she wasn't good at it even when it was here."

"What do you do to Bradford?"

She shrugs. "He's like an old teddy bear. He only asks me to do things that matter and he always thanks me, so I don't mind. Though I do occasionally switch out his mustache gel for toothpaste. He smells extra minty-fresh those days."

"And Mom?"

Artemis's eyes lose their sparkle. "Nothing." She hands me the journal, pulling her knees up and resting her chin on them. "Nina, I know you're jealous. That I work with Mom. That I always know where she goes and what she does. But it doesn't make us closer. If anything, it makes us even less like mother and daughter. She watches me so carefully, and she's so strict. There are times when I'm jealous of you. Puttering around in your clinic, helping everyone."

"But I don't! Not really. Anyone can do what I do in there. You're going to help so many more people."

She turns so her cheek rests on her knee and she's looking at me. "You help people just by being you. You help me. Watchers all live with one foot in the darkness, but you . . . you always manage to bring the light. If I've been hard on you the last couple of days, it's because—I don't want you to lose that."

I want to tell her everything I've been feeling. And this is my chance. "Artemis, I—"

"It's okay." She shakes her head, cutting me off. My heart

sinks. She doesn't want to talk about me being a Slayer. It helps that I know at least part of why. But it means I still can't be honest with her.

She continues. "I can protect you from this darkness. Even if I'm not a real Watcher. If there even is such a thing as a real Watcher now. I've got you." She pokes at the book. "What else does the diary say?" Her abrupt subject change is not lost on me. But if Artemis needs to not talk about things, I'll respect that. She's helped me so much over the years. I'm still learning how to do the same for her.

"A lot of training procedure." I flip through pages of dietary schedules, tests, and techniques. I skip to the end, wondering how this particular Potential ended up. What did she get assigned to do? Did she become one of our accountants? A cook? Special ops? It took a lot of different jobs to keep us running when we were at full capacity. I wonder if any of the Slayers ever ended up as medics. Maybe I would have had something in common with one.

"Wait." I point to one of the last entries. "She *did* become the Slayer. And she had a baby. And then—oh, sad. She got killed by vampires. She was only Slayer for a few months. It looks like Bradford Smythe took the baby in." The name of the baby is at the end of the book.

"Helen," Artemis and I both read at the same time.

Helen. Our mother.

How many times can my past break and reform itself? Our mother wasn't born to be a Watcher. She was adopted into it. She was the daughter of a Slayer. A woman she never knew. A woman who died for a calling I now have. The same calling that killed my father.

I should be stunned that she would keep something so huge from us, but that's the least surprising part of this. My mother has been an opaque mystery to me for so long now. But this revelation answers one thing.

"No wonder Mom hates Slayers so much," I whisper. "It goes way beyond Buffy. Artemis, do you—do you think she hates that I *am* a Slayer, or does she hate *me* for being a Slayer?"

"Mom doesn't hate you."

"She's pushed me away all these years! She lied to everyone about me being a Potential. And gods, I get it now. It's not just about Dad. It's her whole life. I represent everything that's ever hurt her." I feel burdened by my mother's pain, irrationally angry with her for having a tragic history. I didn't ask for any of this. I don't want to feel sorry for her. I won't.

"The whole Slayer thing, it's not fair," Artemis says. I think she's talking about our mom, until she continues. "Why would it even happen to you? It makes no sense. I don't get it. It never should have been you."

"Who should it have been, then?" I ask, feeling defensive. I'm conflicted about being a Slayer, sure, but it's a mystical event. If I was Chosen, it's because I was supposed to be.

Artemis surprises me. "No one," she says, her voice harsh. "No one. They never should have forced this on anyone. Not since the very first Slayer. A bunch of weak, arrogant men decided what was *best* and saddled all the rest of us with the consequences." Artemis grabs the diary, slams it shut, and throws it in the corner of the room.

She climbs back on her bed. "Come on. I just want to watch a dumb movie and not think about anything."

Artemis is done with the conversation. And now that I'm seeing what a toll this life has taken on her, *I'm* determined to protect *her*, instead. So we put on a rom-com, and I paint her fingernails crimson, my hands steady, the paint perfect. She does mine, but her fingers tremble and leave my cuticles looking as bloody as they were after the pit.

I startle awake, bleary-headed and confused. Dawn is creeping soft and inevitable across the horizon. After our movie, we both passed out early. My nonsleeping nights finally caught up to me with a vengeance.

I lie silently in bed, thinking about what we learned. Our mother was the daughter of a Slayer. If she hadn't been, she never would have met the Watchers. Never become one. Never met our father. We wouldn't be Watchers. But we also wouldn't even exist.

And this means that my grandmother was a Slayer too. I wish I could talk to her. I wish I could talk to anyone who understands what I'm going through. I wish Cosmina had been nicer. Gods, I'd even take a chat with Buffy right now.

I could always go find Eve Silvera. Or even old Bradford Smythe. He knew my grandmother. He could tell me about her. But I don't want either of them. I want actual family.

I want my dad. Artemis didn't want to read my father's diary, but I *need* to.

I get it from under my bed, grab Bradford's from where it's lying open in the corner, and hurry toward the gym—where I almost run right into Eve Silvera.

"Nina!" She steadies me with her hands on my shoulders. Does she ever sleep? "Where are you off to?"

"Training room?" I don't want to tell her I'm trying to read my dad's diary in peace.

She smiles approvingly. "I didn't find you yesterday to talk after what happened in Dublin, but I thought you might like a day to decompress. None of it demands immediate attention. I'm so sorry you ran into such a mess. I feel like I've failed you, sending you into something without having all the information."

"You couldn't have known! You were supporting me. You believed me about Cosmina." That means a lot. And it also means a lot that she cares about my feelings.

"I will always believe in you. And while I regret my haste in sending you, what you did in Dublin is *incredible*. Especially considering that you've had no training. Your abilities are genuinely astonishing. I guess there is something to the notion of saving the best for last. Apparently even when it comes to Slayers."

It's so much the opposite of my mother's reaction—even Artemis's reaction—that I stand there stunned. Eve not only wants me to be a Slayer; she thinks I'm doing a good job.

She squeezes my shoulder. "Don't worry about Cosmina or Dublin. Bradford Smythe and I are looking into it. Best to keep it quiet, though. Your mother, Wanda, and Ruth don't know, and I would like to keep it that way."

"Right. Of course. Anything I can help with?"

She shakes her head. "You already did your part, and you should be very proud." She beams, then walks away to wherever she was going.

Happier, I settle on a pile of mats in the corner of the gym. I need to research more about the Coldplay demon too, but he's not going anywhere. Cillian has texted me regular updates, so I know he's safe. For now my own questions about being a Slayer feel more pressing.

My father's diary is thick, the pages worn and wrinkled. He wasn't only Buffy's Watcher. He had two other Slayers before her. I was always proud that he got to be Watcher to so many Slayers. But now that I'm a Slayer, I realize that means he had to *bury* two Slayers. Because Slayers don't retire. They die.

I crack the book open to somewhere in the middle. I don't recognize his handwriting, which makes me feel a sharp pang of loss. It's messy, but his thoughts are well organized. This section has notes on training techniques that have had more success than others, as well as an anecdote on his Slayer facing a gang of vampires that had taken over a small town. The Slayer lured them to a cemetery, where my father had set up booby traps to take them out one by one so the Slayer's odds would be better.

A tear splashes down onto the page, making the word it fell on blurry and indistinct. Even though he never told us about this, Artemis and I have used half these booby traps in our own rooms over the years. I know fighting vampires isn't genetic, but between his skills and my grandmother's Slayer status, maybe I really was born for this.

I feel a sudden intense connection to my father. I might not remember him very well, but we've carried on his legacy in more ways than we realized.

And I'm certain that my father would be proud of me being a Slayer. My mother might hate it—might even hate me for it— but my father would be as proud of me as he is of this girl he writes about with professional affection. I wish he were here to train me. He wouldn't have kept my Potential status hidden. He would have prepared me. Would have used our years together to help me become the greatest Slayer ever.

For the first time, I'm genuinely happy about being a Slayer. Not just elated over the physical tricks I can do or high on adrenaline. But truly happy. Because I can see how much my dad cared, how proud he was of this girl, in the way he writes about her.

And I can pretend it's me. I can imagine that he would have extended that same pride and care to my own training. My father loved these girls like they were his own. How much more would he have loved a Slayer who really *was* his own? If he were alive, everything would be different. My mother would still be herself. Artemis would never have had to take care of me, because he would have. And I would have been trained, prepared, truly watched over.

Wiping away my tears, I skip ahead. Half of me hopes there will be entries on his family, even though I know this was a professional journal, not a personal one. And then I stop. I've hit the section where he's preparing to meet a new Slayer.

Buffy.

It's close to the end of the book. Because it's close to the end of everything.

"I'm concerned about the prophecy," he writes. "Helen insists we needn't worry, but these things are always more complicated than they seem on the surface. I told Helen I wasn't going to take the assignment. But this new Slayer is the least-prepared girl I have ever seen. I got the preliminary surveillance. It is, quite frankly, terrifying. I am not one to judge the system, as the ancient power knows more than I do about whose potential will translate into the Slayer most needed for our time, but . . . surely it chose wrong?"

I snort. Then I reread the first part that references my mom. I remember a prophecy about Buffy. It had to do with the Master, the first major vampire threat she faced after moving to Sunnydale. Something about "the Master will rise and the Slayer will die." It came true. She did die. It just didn't stick. Buffy always was bad at following the rules.

But . . . the Watchers didn't *have* that prophecy at the time. Her weirdo vampire-with-a-soul boyfriend gave Rupert Giles the prophecy after my father died. I remember, because there was a whole stink about how a vampire could have access to a prophecy the Watchers didn't. So my father couldn't have known about that one. He's talking about another prophecy.

And if the prophecy was about Buffy, why would he want to turn down being her Watcher? It doesn't make any sense. I wish I could ask my mom about it, but that's not going to happen.

"I have to accept the assignment," my father's words continue. "Buffy needs me. I won't entrust her life and safety to anyone else. Helen will see that the prophecy never comes true. Bradford will help. And my girls will never—"

It has to be a different prophecy. Something more personal, if he's mentioning us. But what? I eagerly look to the next page.

It's gone. It's been sliced out. The next page starts mid-sentence with details about his first disastrous training session with Buffy, and his fears that the ancient vampire Lothos had already begun to hunt for her. No mention of our family.

I close it. I can't read the rest. I can't read how hard he worked to train Buffy, to prepare her, knowing what it results in. My father buried two Slayers. And then we had to bury him, because of Buffy.

I stand and slam my fist into a punching bag. It breaks free of the chain, sliding across the floor and hitting the wall so hard it bursts at the seams.

I hear a couple of slow claps, then, "Wow."

I spin around to find Leo behind me. "I'm sorry! I didn't mean to. I was—" I cut myself off. I'm a badass Slayer who can bust up some punching bags without anyone's permission. I want Leo to get mad at me, to chastise me, so I can yell back at him.

Leo bends down and examines the bag. "These facilities were designed for Watchers. Not Slayers. It's not your fault you're stronger than all of them put together."

Not exactly the fight I was hoping for. I grab a broom from a closet to help clean up. When I turn back, Leo's holding the diaries.

"Those are not mine!" My face grows hot, all the past trauma resurfacing.

Leo blushes. He actually blushes. How dare he. "Of course not. I know that."

"I don't even keep a journal." I snatch my father's diary from him, but he grabs my hand.

"Athena. I'm sorry. About that day in the old training room. I never got a chance to talk to you about it before I left."

"I don't remember," I lie. "Why would you have needed to talk to me?" I tug my hand away and hug my father's journal to my chest.

Leo sighs and sits down on the mats. He glances at the other journal. "Why do you have Bradford Smythe's Watcher diary?"

"He was my grandmother's Watcher."

"What?" His shock is genuine.

"It's pretty huge," I acknowledge. "My mom's mom was a Slayer. She got killed right after my mom was born. Bradford took her in."

"Wow. I had no idea. I thought Helen was a Smythe."

"They tucked her right into the family line. I guess we were always destined to be in the middle of the fight against demons."

He flips through more pages. "'What fates impose, that men must needs abide; It boots not to resist both wind and tide.'"

I peer at the page he stopped on. "It says that?"

Leo laughs. "No, sorry. I was quoting Shakespeare. It's a terrible habit. I read everything of his during the last two years. Not a lot to do during demonic stakeouts with your mother."

It's the first time he's referenced specifics of when he and Eve were off the grid. "I thought your life would have been pretty exciting. Out in the field."

"Would you say Dublin was exciting?"

"No!" I pause. No one else wants to hear how I feel about things. Leo's actually listening. "Yes? Sort of. It was terrifying, and terrible, and also thrilling and amazing and awful and I don't know how it could be all those things at once."

He nods. "What we do. It can be exhilarating. There's a huge rush facing death and winning. Being out there, it was all those things you said. But it was also boring a lot of the time. Buses and airplanes and hotel rooms scarier than anything in that pit with you. Waiting. Watching. Hunting." There's a sad, faraway look on his face. "And it was lonely. After the attack took out Watcher headquarters, I thought everyone else was gone. That I was alone out there."

"But you had your mom."

"Which made me miss all of you even more." He had tried to tell me that before, but I didn't let him. I was too mad remembering my own hurt. Now I think I understand. My mom wants to send me away from the only home and family I've ever known. I don't care how much things change. These people—the Watchers—are my people. At least I didn't have to spend two years thinking *everyone* was dead. I still had Artemis and Rhys. Jade. Imogen and the Littles. Even the Council. I wonder why the Silveras kept going. Why they didn't decide to settle somewhere and have lives.

Imagining Leo out there, lonely and missing us, instead of kicking demon butt and being all handsome and cocky about it, makes me soften even more toward him. I clear my throat. "So what does it mean? Your fancy Shakespeare quote?"

"It's part of why I said you shouldn't train if you didn't want to. Even though, in retrospect, that was never an option." He smiles wryly. "I wanted to at least offer. No one ever offered me another life. But in the end, none of us can escape what we were born to."

That's why they didn't settle. When you know as much as we do, how can you ever decide to just . . . stop? Stop fighting? Stop trying to help? Once you're in, you can't turn your back on it. I wonder if my mom wishes Bradford Smythe had put her up for adoption, given her the gift of a normal life to make up for the violence of her earliest days. She never would have known.

I'm glad that's not what happened. As much as I might question everything else in my life right now, I know how the world really works. I know the monsters that are out there. And I know the people who have devoted their lives to fighting them. Even if

I don't always agree with their methods or choices. Even if I have zero idea what my place is in that fight anymore.

"What about those of us who were born to Watchers *and* Slayers?" I try to grin, but it doesn't quite work. "Which one do we pick? Which one can't we escape?"

"Do you want to escape?" There's no judgment in his tone.

I shake my head. "Not being a Watcher. I never have. This is our legacy, our calling. I always wanted to be a part of it."

"If you could choose not to be a Slayer, would you?"

I almost blurt out yes. It's my first instinct. But I'm still holding my father's journal. What would he have wanted for me? What do *I* want for me? Do I really want to give up what I've become? For some reason the dream-memory of the Slayer who saved her entire village washes over me. She was so certain. So brave and powerful and good. If I could be a Slayer like that, I'd choose to be one, I think. But can I?

Maybe with Leo and Eve on my side, I can. My father would want me to try. And I want me to try too. I won't know how much good I can do until I know what I'm capable of. I turn to Leo to tell him how glad I am he's helping me, but the door bangs open.

"Wheezy!" Honora Wyndam-Pryce declares. "*And* Leo? Why, this is as pretty as a poem."

18

HONORA WEARS GORGEOUS OXBLOOD
leather boots that hit midcalf. Her dress is black, her dark hair
shiny and long in loose waves. She has the most perfect cat-eye
liner I've ever seen in person. It's like she walked straight off a
runway and into my gym. Where I'm still wearing yesterday's
clothes, bedhead, and just-been-crying-about-my-dead-dad eyes.

She takes in what we're holding and her face positively lights
up. "Oh my God. Those aren't—are those Wheezy's books of
poetry?"

I want the earth to open up and swallow me whole. But
thanks a lot, *Buffy*. It doesn't do that anymore.

"Go to hell, Honora." Leo's voice is as sharp as I've ever heard
it. I'm shocked out of my humiliation by the force of his anger.
He isn't looking at me, but he shifts almost imperceptibly closer.

"Can't, darling. Didn't you hear? It's closed for renovations."
She grins at us, twirling as she takes in the room. "Has this place
always been so depressing? Remember when we trained here, Leo?
The parties we'd throw right under their noses. Epic. Harry Sirk

made a mean magical cocktail. You'd literally float the rest of the night." She sighs wistfully. "Too bad he's dead. I miss him."

I stand up, grabbing the journals and holding them to my chest. "Speaking of things we miss, why don't you go back to wherever you've been the last two years, so we can keep missing you?"

Honora puts a hand to her heart. "You wound me. I thought I'd be welcomed back, seeing as how I'm the only one out there actually doing anything. Unlike the Council. How's hiding treating them? Sure are protecting a lot of innocents holed up in the castle here."

"You have no idea, do you?" Leo shakes his head. "Athena is——"

I put a hand on his shoulder, rushing to cut him off. "A medic. I put together a medical center for the castle." I assume she hasn't spoken to her mother yet, and I don't want to tell her I'm a Slayer like some sort of brag. It's *mine*. I'm not about to discuss it with Honora, and I don't care at all about impressing her.

She raises one expertly sculpted eyebrow. She may say she's been out protecting people, but it doesn't look like she's been roughing it. "Good for you." I can't tell if she's sincere. I doubt it. "Leo, when did you get back? We thought you were dead."

"Sorry to disappoint."

"Are you kidding? I don't know why you're both acting like this. I'm so happy to see you." Now she sounds . . . almost definitely sincere? "Our years together were so fun. I've missed you guys."

"I think you remember them really differently than I do." I never liked Honora, even before that awful day. She was always pushing limits, finding little ways to rebel. I hated how disrespectful she was of Watcher society when I would have given anything to be trained like her.

An unexpected memory of Honora jumping, dancing, laughing in the middle of flashing lights is triggered by her smile, though. The concert I had remembered being at with only Artemis and Jade—Honora snuck us in. I had forgotten that part. Or repressed it.

"Listen," she says. "I'm not here for a social call. I passed through Dublin and there's a lot of chatter in the underground parts of the city."

Leo's face betrays nothing of what we did there. "Oh?"

"Some big demon trouble."

Maybe she's onto the gambling ring and whatever else is happening down there. If she knows we were involved, our secret is as dead as a hellhound in a pit fight. She'll tell her mother, who will tell my mother. "What kind of trouble?"

"The bloody, high-body-count, deadly-demon kind of trouble. He left dozens of bodies in his wake. I think he came this direction. I wanted to make sure you're all okay, then see if the Council has heard anything."

So, not the pit. A different threat. Fantastic. I definitely don't already have way too much to worry about.

"What kind of demon?" Leo asks.

"Pylean-human hybrid. Male. Neon-yellow skin, black horns, real nasty piece of work."

I cover my startle with a cough. "Sorry. Wow. What has, uh, he done?"

"Kills other demons. Men. Women. Even a few kids. Pure murderer. Heard anything?"

"No," Leo says. Which is the truth, from him.

I try to square what she's saying with my conversation with the Coldplay demon. My instincts were that he wasn't a threat. And while I'm not totally confident in those Slayer instincts, they've been pretty on point so far. Plus, you can't fake the kind of fear he showed when I threatened to call Sean. I can't imagine a demon on a murderous rampage would be utterly terrified of the man I saw at the pit.

Not wanting her to ask more questions, I scramble to only give her the information her mother will have. "We had a hellhound here the other day, but we think it was a stray." No one has mentioned the second one, which means my mother didn't say anything. Which continues to be troubling. The more I think about it, the more I suspect she's not worried because she knows the hellhounds aren't after us. But how could she know that? If she knew about the demon in the shed, I'd already be toast.

Honora perks, obviously intrigued. "Hellhound? Why was it here?"

I hope I don't look as panicked as I feel. But she can't be right about my demon. Coldplay shirt. Pierced ears. And he didn't even try to break free. If there's one person in the world I'm the least inclined to help, it's Honora. I'm going to solve this demon's mystery myself. If he is all murdery, then I'll deal with it. I'm a Slayer. It's my job.

I shrug. "Like you said, we're hiding. Not a lot of demon chatter in the dorms. Maybe check with the Council?"

Honora squinches her pretty face. "They're not likely to know anything. We're the only ones who do any work around here." She pauses, then smiles sweetly. "Well, *I'm* the only one who does any work."

I bristle. "My mother is constantly out there. And Leo and his mother spent the last three years tracking and killing demons in South America."

"Aww, that's fun! We'll have to trade stories. And Wheezy can tell us the latest techniques in removing splinters and fixing up owies." She tosses her hair over her shoulder. "Just kidding. I do think the medical center is a good idea. Love to see it later. I'm going to get breakfast and talk to the olds. Don't read any good poems without me." She sweeps out.

Leo's hand brushes my own. "Athena," he says, his voice soft.

I'm clenching my fists so hard they're shaking. I don't want to talk about this.

"She has a mean streak, and she was always jealous of you."

I grimace. "Jealous? Why would she be jealous of me? I was nobody. I was the other Jamison-Smythe twin. The one who couldn't do anything."

"Exactly." Leo takes the broom and starts cleaning up the split punching bag we had forgotten about. "Honora didn't want to be a Watcher. But her mother put a lot of pressure on her. Everything she did was measured against her family. She was the one who was going to redeem them. To bring honor back to the Wyndam-Pryces."

"I still don't see how that makes her jealous of me."

"Your mom didn't push you to be in Watcher training or punish you for not being the best."

"Because she was trying to keep me from doing anything that might make me a good Slayer."

"Whatever the reasons, Honora didn't see it that way. She saw a girl who was happy in the middle of all the Watcher misery." He sets the broom down. "I'm not defending her. But she lashed out because she hated that you had things she never would. Even back then, you were . . . different. Special. Everything that had happened to you, everything you had lost, and you still managed to be the brightest part of any room." He smiles full-dimples, and my heart cracks. The fissures undo all the work I've done to shut him out these last three years. Thirteen-year-old me crows triumphantly that he really *did* see me back then. Part of my humiliation—the part that was certain he thought I was stupid—finally dissolves.

I put on my sternest face, ignoring thirteen-year-old me but allowing myself to forgive Leo a little. "Honora's still the worst, though."

Leo laughs. "Oh, absolutely."

I hug the journals tighter to my chest. "So we're totally clear, though, she changed that poem. I would *never* write something dirty about you."

"Never?" he asks, and there's a teasing note to his voice that shocks us both. His face turns as red as mine feels. "Sorry," he stammers.

I can't help the laugh that bursts free. Was Leo . . . flirting with me? Even though he was always nice to me, there was never a hint of flirtation when we were younger. I would have noticed. But we're both older. We've been apart for a long time. And what's in his voice now when he talks to me—it's something that feels a whole lot like how Rhys talks to Cillian.

I clear my throat, not knowing how to react to Leo Silvera

flirting. With me. "Well, I wouldn't have written anything like that when I was thirteen. I barely knew what 'orgasm' meant. Watcher education isn't really big on the whole birds-and-the-bees aspects of human development. Not that I didn't know. Or that I don't know. But I'm going to stop talking right now and go ahead and leave and maybe never come back." I've been backing slowly toward the door since I hit "orgasm" and knew my mouth wasn't going to stop in time to save me.

Leo's smile is blinding, the most genuine expression I've seen on his face since he came back. He lifts a hand to his mouth as though he can't believe it's there either, touching the corner of his lips.

Confused but happy, I head for my room.

Leo's right. I always did have something to be jealous of. I had Artemis, and I still do. And she's definitely the best Watcher in the castle, test be damned. It's time to tell her about the demon in Cillian's shed. As Artemis reminded me last night, we're better when we figure things out together. I might not have my dad, but I have her. I won't neglect that anymore.

But I skid to a stop in my doorway. The door is open, and through it I can see Artemis.

And Honora.

She's sitting on Artemis's bed, and Artemis is beaming. If the age difference that used to separate Leo and me isn't a barrier anymore, it isn't for Honora and Artemis either. And Artemis has *always* crushed on Honora.

I shove the door so it bounces hard against the wall. Artemis jumps, then waves her hands excitedly. "Look who's here!"

"I already saw Nina." Honora smiles at me with all the fake

sweetness of a Diet Coke. She never called me Wheezy around Artemis. And I never told Artemis about the poem incident. I should have. Obviously. I should have told Artemis a lot of things. I was on my way to making this better, but Honora is in our room. How can I bring up the Coldplay demon now?

"I thought you were going to breakfast," I say.

"How could I when I hadn't even visited Artemis yet?" Honora turns back to my sister. "God. I've been gone so long. You're like a totally different person. I was a hag from thirteen until seventeen, but you're *gorgeous*."

Artemis blushes. I want to vomit.

"Seriously," Honora continues, reaching out and playing with a curl that's fallen free from Artemis's ponytail. "Don't tell me you've also gotten faster, smarter, and stronger, too, or I'll be so jealous I'll have to kill you."

I mime puking behind Honora's back. Artemis catches me and glares. "Let's go get breakfast while Nina changes."

I don't want to follow them. But there's no way I'm leaving Honora with full access to the castle *and* my sister. And I've got to sneak back to the shed to determine whether the demon is, in fact, as dangerous as Honora says. But it doesn't feel right.

Do I really trust a demon over a legacy Watcher?

Honora's poetry-performing voice rings through my memories. Yes. Yes, I do trust a neon-yellow demon more than I trust Honora.

At breakfast, Honora monopolizes Artemis's attention with hilarious and daring stories of her demon-hunting exploits. Even Jade is engaged, leaning forward and listening. Rhys pretends like he doesn't care, but the way his eyes widen at the good parts indicates otherwise.

"Can I talk to you?" I ask Artemis.

She nods, but doesn't stop listening to Honora. "Later, okay?"

"Don't you need to talk to the Council, Honora?"

"Bradford Smythe and Ruth Zabuto both sleep until ten or eleven every morning," Artemis says.

Honora steals some fruit off Artemis's plate. "Layabouts. I already tried my mum's door. She didn't even open it. Said she's sick. Everyone here looks a little rough. You should get them vitamins or something, medic. And anyway, they can wait. That's what they *do*. They should be the Waiters Council. Besides, I'm not going to leave Artemis to clean all this by herself. You're the best trainee I've ever seen. I can't believe they didn't make you full Watcher. It's crap."

Artemis shrugs, but I can tell she's pleased. "After breakfast I've got some time to train."

"Can I join you?"

"Aren't you hunting a demon?" I interject.

"No leads," Honora says. If the Coldplay demon were really as nasty a killer as she said, she wouldn't stop for anything. Or at least, if she were a good Watcher, she wouldn't.

"There aren't going to be any leads in our gym."

Artemis scowls at me. I scowl back, then text Cillian. All is quiet in the shed. I could talk to Leo about it. Or anyone, really. But I wanted to talk to Artemis. And I can't very well admit I kept this huge secret with Honora here.

It's barely 8 a.m., but I'm exhausted from the emotional strain. I collapse into bed. My mother is the daughter of a Slayer. She wants to ship me to boarding school. There's some sort of prophecy that my dad was concerned about. The demon I'm hiding in Cillian's shed may or may not be a killer.

And stupid Honora is back.

As soon as Honora is gone, I'll tell Artemis and get her help. I close my eyes, hoping for a few minutes' rest with nothing but blankness on my mind so I can sort through some of this mess.

Instead, I find myself back in Bradford Smythe's room.

19

OH GODS, NOT BRADFORD SMYTHE *sleeping again*.

It's the same. Him tossing and turning. The darkness taking shape on top of him. But the room is a little lighter—like it's not the middle of the night. His curtains are drawn tight, but I can see more in the room. Except the figure on top of him. That remains impenetrable night. Tendrils of darkness trail from it, infecting the room.

Bradford smiles at first, his face tender. Then his expression becomes panicked. Sweat breaks out on his forehead. The figure on top of him arches triumphantly.

Bradford goes completely still.

Wake up, wake up, wake up.

It's dark. I can't open my eyes, can't move. There's a pressure on my chest, a weighted heaviness that feels as dark as the insides of my eyelids.

I want to scream, to cry out for help.

"That's right," the darkness whispers. "You can't do anything."

I feel the presence shift closer, feel its ice-cold breath brush my ear. "You can't save any of them."

I gasp, finally breaking free of the paralysis of the dream. Only to find myself on a rooftop in San Francisco. Buffy sits, small and alone, on the edge looking out over the sunset. I don't have time for this.

If I were really a Slayer, if I were a hunter like Artemis, I would run forward and push her off. Dream or not, I owe her. I owe her for everything messed up and crappy in my life. She defied the Watchers and ruined the order of everything. She let in so much chaos that the First was able to rise and kill almost all my people.

And she got my father killed.

"You didn't deserve him!" I shout, consumed by my anger toward Buffy. "He should have let Lothos kill you! The whole *world* would have been better off!"

I don't know if it's the wind blowing her hair or if her shoulder moves in a shrug. I want to hurt her. I want her to know how it feels to lose everything, how it feels to be powerless, how it feels to—

The edges of the dream pull tight, then snap.

I hit the floor running. Or at least I try to. I'm a little dizzy and winded.

If I visited Buffy in a Slayer dream, then maybe what came before was a Slayer dream too. I've got to check on Bradford Smythe. I almost run into Leo in the hall as he comes toward my room.

"What's wrong?" he asks.

"I think Bradford is in danger!"

He falls immediately into place next to me as I tear through the castle and into the residence wing. I pause outside the old man's door. I'm glad Leo's here. Whatever I walk in on, it's nice to have someone by my side.

I knock. There's no answer. I knock louder. Then I try the doorknob. It's locked. "Bradford! Bradford, let me know you're okay, or I'm breaking down your door!"

"What's going on?" Eve leans into the hallway from her room.

Wanda Wyndam-Pryce's door opens and she peers out blearily, clutching a silk robe around herself. "Keep it down!"

For a few seconds I question myself. Leo's voice is almost a whisper. "Kick it down," he says.

I do.

The wood cracks and splinters with a single kick, the door hanging wildly on one hinge. I push through. My stomach sinks. It's the room from my dream, even though I've never been inside. I rush to Bradford's bedside, take his wrist between my fingers.

No pulse.

Leo throws open the drapes to give me some light. Bradford Smythe's body is already blue and gray, mottled with death. His skin is cold.

I do CPR anyway. I do it as Wanda comes into the room and lets out a wounded cry. I do it as Ruth Zabuto wanders in and comforts Wanda. I do it until a hand comes down on my shoulder.

"It's too late," my mother says. "You couldn't have saved him."

I shake my head, still checking his wrist. "I could have. I knew this was happening. I saw it!"

"What do you mean, you saw it?" Eve asks.

"In a dream! There was something on top of Bradford. It was draining him or something."

"Was he in pain?" my mother asks.

I finally drop his wrist. The only way he's coming back is as something no longer human, and I hope that's not the case. I don't want to have to kill him after failing to save him. "No. He wasn't in pain. He was—well, he wasn't in pain."

"He had a bad heart," Eve says.

"Why would I dream him having a heart attack? That has nothing to do with my Slayer abilities."

Eve's smile is sympathetic but firm. "Nina, sweetheart, you've only been a Slayer for a couple of months. Most of that time you didn't even realize you were one. I don't think your abilities are anything you can understand or trust."

My mouth drops open. I'd expect my mother to say that to me. Not Eve.

Leo steps closer to me. His jaw is twitching, his hands fists. "But she *knew*. How can you discount that?"

My mother checks Bradford's neck, then his chest. Her movements are precise, perfunctory. "There are no marks on him. I'd hoped we would have more time with him. But this is not exactly a surprise." She pulls the blanket up and covers his face.

"Nina, you're so in tune to the health of everyone in the castle," Eve says. "Of course you would notice, maybe on a subconscious level, that Bradford was not well. And it manifested in your dreams. Maybe your heightened Slayer abilities even picked up on his heartbeat irregularities. But there's no sign of a demon attack. We've been here all morning. I can't imagine a demon strolled through the castle, broke into Bradford's locked room, and got away without anyone noticing."

"But—I saw—" I deflate. I know what I saw, what I felt. How do I prove to them that my dream was real if they won't listen to me? And I can't use my dream about Cosmina as proof, because my mother, Wanda, and Ruth don't know about it. Can't know about it.

My mother picks up a photo from Bradford's nightstand. It's a black-and-white photo of a young woman. "Was there anything else in the dream? Did you see a demon?"

"Nothing specific. Just shadows in a vague form. The rest of the dream was Buffy."

My mother takes a sharp breath in. "Buffy? Did you talk to her?"

"Umm, sort of." I yelled at her. That counts.

Wanda lifts her head from where she's crying against Ruth Zabuto's shoulder. "Those aren't prophetic dreams. They're pathetic dreams. Will you *stop* trying to make this about yourself and let us mourn our colleague?"

I look, aghast, to my mother. She shakes her head.

Eve puts a hand on my shoulder and steers me out of the room. "Let us handle this, Nina. This is neither children's nor Slayer's business. I'm sorry."

"I need to speak with you," Leo says to his mother. His voice is tight. He believed me, but it doesn't matter. The Council doesn't. *Eve* doesn't.

"Of course, darling." Eve grabs my hand as I'm about to run away, humiliated and sad and furious. "Find me later," she whispers.

With confusion added to my toxic mix of emotions, I run out of the residence wing and straight out of the castle. I can't go to Artemis with Honora there. Leo and his mother are talking, and I wasn't invited. None of the Council believes me.

But I have another source of information. I jump over the fence and throw open the door to Cillian's shed.

The demon is there, in the exact same spot I left him. He cracks open an eye. "I thought you'd be dead by now. Sean must be off his game."

"Don't be so disappointed." I examine his chains. Everything is in place. I didn't think it was him, but I had to check. "What kills people in their sleep but leaves no marks?"

The cracks in the demon's skin shift with his incredulous expression. "Is that a riddle?"

"This morning my great-un——" I stop as the emotions catch up to me. The reality that the man who raised my mother is really gone. "A man I know woke up dead."

"He's a zombie?"

"That's not what I meant! I mean, he didn't wake up this morning. And I had a dream about it happening. I don't think I'd dream about it if it weren't demonic." Eve's explanation seems like it makes sense, but it doesn't feel right.

The demon looks surprised. "You dreamed it? Are you a seer? And your mojo is still working? Be careful. Those are skills that are worth something on the black market. Another reason you should let me go and avoid attracting Sean's attention."

"Not a seer. I'm——I can't explain it. But do you know any demons that do that? Kill when someone is asleep? Leave no mark?"

"I mean, sure. Dozens. Can you give me more details? And can you give me something to eat, please? You're never happy."

"A man I know just died! You want me to be sunshine and rainbows?"

"Nina!" Cillian leans against the door frame, halfway through brushing his teeth. "Thought I saw you jump the fence. Rhys is coming over soon."

"Oh, thank you." The demon breathes in deeply, sighing out contentment. He sits up straighter. "At least someone in here is happy."

Cillian shrugs defensively at my accusing glare. "Can I help it if I look forward to seeing my boyfriend? We're gonna watch Eurovision."

"What did you think of their decision to have Australia back?" the demon asks. "Because I thought it was bullocks. I don't care how good they were. It's Eurovision, not Anywherevision!"

"It did sort of ruin the whole 'guest event' concept when they kept letting them come back year after year."

"Hello?" I wave in front of Cillian's face. "You do know he's eating your happiness, right?"

"Doesn't feel like anything."

The demon shifts position again with a clanking of chains. "I can't take away his happiness. It's like if you spray perfume and I smell it. Just because I'm inhaling the scent doesn't mean it leaves you."

"Yeah, but smelling someone's perfume is a little different from consuming their emotions."

"Says you, a person who has never consumed emotions." The demon shifts again. "Listen, it's been, what, three, four days? Can I at least get a chair? Or a pillow?"

Cillian nods amiably. "Sure, mate! I mean, demon. I mean—do you have a name?"

"Doug."

Horns. Black teeth. Virulent yellow skin cracked like desert ground.

"Yeah, you look like a Doug," Cillian says, then turns and leaves.

I sigh, leaning against a table. "Details, then. It kills in the victim's sleep. Bradford didn't seem to be upset or in any pain until he just sort of . . . died. I didn't really see the demon. There was more of a sense of it. Darkness. Shadows."

"Interesting." Doug breathes in through his teeth, making a strange whistling noise. "You're sure it's demonic? Not a vision?"

"Both."

"Hmm." He plays with one of his delicate gold hoop earrings. "Why would the demon kill this man, specifically? He the only one there?"

"No, there are a bunch of us."

"If I were a demon who ate people, I wouldn't pick an old man. I'd pick a tender young thing."

"Gross! You're awful!"

"You're the one asking me to figure this out! Stop being so speciesist. I've never killed anyone in my life. I don't even eat *meat*. I exist to make people happy. That's it. That's all I want. To be free and make people happy and also get backstage passes to a Coldplay concert. Think of how much I'd have to eat around Chris Martin. Doesn't he seem like the happiest bloke?"

"Can we focus, please?"

"Fine. Think of why your man would be a target. Why a demon would show up now."

"I mean, you did." I pause, pieces moving slowly into place. "Actually, we've never had a demon problem until you showed up. Is it possible this is connected? To the hellhounds?"

"I've never heard of Sean employing something like what you described. It's not really his style."

"Something else hunting you, then? Or some other group?"

Doug's eyes dart guiltily to the center of the floor. I follow them, but it's just junk. A jumbled pile left from Cillian's dad's box.

"Look at me," I say.

Doug drags his gaze back up to meet mine.

"What aren't you telling me? Somehow you're connected to this."

"I'm not! I've been locked up here!"

I shake my head. "I talked to someone who's looking for you. She told me you killed a bunch of people, and now a man in my castle is dead."

Doug freezes. "She? She who?"

"I'm not telling you until you tell me the truth!"

"Anyone looking for me is someone you need to avoid. You have to trust me."

"You're a *demon*."

"Then for Cillian's sake. I don't want to see him hurt. I'm sorry I hid in his yard and drew all this trouble to him. Get rid of me. Throw me over a cliff into the ocean. But whatever you do, do it soon. Because if she found you, she'll find me, and then we're both in trouble."

"I can handle trouble." It makes me wonder how Honora is involved in this. Am I going to trust a demon over her? I mean, probably. But *should* I? I pace, running my hands through my hair. His concern for Cillian seems genuine. And I honestly can't imagine Doug killing anything or anyone. "Why did you come to Shancoom, then?"

"I was looking for help, okay? I got a name. Someone who has connections. Who makes deals with demons."

"What was the name?"

Doug lets out a puff of air. He's scared. If it's an act, it's a good one. "Smythe."

It hits like a bolt of lightning. Smythe. Bradford Smythe, my great-uncle. Who is dead now. Whoever is hunting Doug must have known that Bradford Smythe was Doug's contact. So the death *is* connected to Doug. He's just not the one responsible for it. "Where did you hear about the Smythes?"

"None of your bloody business."

"It is, because I am one!"

Doug snorts. "You are not."

"I am so!"

"I've heard about the Smythes. You wouldn't even survive infancy in that family. They're born weapons. You're . . ."

"Something fluffy!" Cillian declares, popping in and holding up a dog bed.

Doug nods. "I mean, he said it. Not me. But you're fluffy."

Cillian throws the dog bed at the demon's face. "Quit acting the maggot. She's stronger than you'll ever be."

"Sure." Doug's voice is muffled by the bed. He pulls it off and sets it on the floor, resettling. "Listen. If Honora is here—"

I flinch. Doug sees it, which confirms he got her name right. He trembles, his eyes wide. "Please unchain me. If she's here, we're all in trouble."

"She says she's hunting you because you kill people."

"She's hunting me because she *needs* me!"

"I'm hunting you," Honora says, stepping into view in the yard, Artemis behind her looking shocked and horrified, "because you're a demon, and that's what Watchers do." She looks at me with derision. "At least those of us who know what it means to be a Watcher."

20

"DID YOU *FOLLOW* ME?" I ASK ARTEMIS AS I shift to put myself between Honora and the shed entrance.

"Obviously we were right to." Honora sweeps one perfectly manicured hand toward Doug. "Artemis said you've been disappearing for hours at a time. Thought we ought to see where you've been going."

Artemis ducks her head. "I was worried, Nina." Then she narrows her eyes and stands up straighter. "And I was right. This demon is dangerous! You could have been hurt!"

"If he's so dangerous, why is Honora wasting time lecturing me? If he's racked up the body count you claim, kill him. Right now."

"Hold up," Doug says, trying to stand.

"No. Go on." I gesture toward him. "You can do it from there, Honora. I remember how good you are at throwing knives."

She scoffs, tossing her hair over her shoulder. "You don't have any idea what's going on. It's not that simple. I can't just kill Doug."

"So you know him!" I jab my finger toward her, triumphant.

"Which means you know the dude who's been using Doug for drugs! Wait. Doug was looking for Bradford Smythe for help. Oh my gods. Did you kill Bradford?"

"What is your damage?" Honora physically recoils from the suggestion. "Bradford died of a heart attack! I was with Artemis all morning, and I had nothing against the old man. He was always nice to me. You're the one sneaking around with demons!"

"I didn't say anything about Bradford—" Doug says.

"I'm hardly sneaking around with him!" I gesture to the chains. "I've taken precautions. And they've worked. But if he's so dangerous, again, why aren't you killing him?"

Artemis looks torn. Then she shakes her head. "Honora has way more experience than we do. If she doesn't think we should kill him, there's a reason. Right?" She looks to Honora for confirmation.

"Of course. Doug's blood is toxic. If we spill it, we'll all die."

"Liar!" I hold up my hands. "I bandaged his bleeding face when we found him. And I'm super not dead!"

"You don't know *anything*," Honora hisses. "Now get out of my way." She grabs my arm and tries to shove me to the side.

I don't budge. She pushes harder. I still don't move.

"What the hell?" she says.

Artemis might have told her I've been sneaking out, but apparently she didn't tell Honora the full truth—that I'm a Slayer. And I suspect she didn't keep it secret to protect me. I think she didn't want Honora to know because she wanted all of Honora's attention. But my heart sinks that Artemis didn't think the biggest thing that's ever happened to me was worth mentioning.

I force a grin. "Who doesn't know anything now?"

Honora grabs my shoulders to throw me aside. I push her. She flies out of the shed, landing hard on the ground. She scrambles back, then stands. "Not possible."

I pick the padlock up off the ground and close it in my fist, then drop the ruined mess of metal onto the ground. I'm showing off—I know I am—but I can't help it.

This is *amazing*. If I had known I'd be able to use this against Honora, I would have tried to become a Chosen One years ago. "You might be a Watcher, but I'm a Slayer. So back off and let me deal with Doug on my own."

Honora's face shifts from disbelieving to delighted. It's a terrifying change. She pulls a band off her wrist and ties her hair back in a ponytail. "Well then, at least it'll be a fairer fight when I kick your ass. Get out of my way. I won't warn you again."

Artemis holds up her hands. "This is ridiculous. Nina, you have no idea what you're doing. Give the demon to Honora, and we'll go back to the castle and figure this all out."

I shake my head. "You've never seen what she's really like."

"*You've* always hated her. And now you're using that as an excuse to be an idiot. Honora is an expert. You are not."

Honora tries to slip past me. I block her. She grabs me for balance, then her fist slams into my stomach. We're angled so Artemis doesn't see the hit. Honora dances back away from me.

"Come on, Nina," she sings. "You don't want to do this."

I shake off her blow, raising my own fists. "I really do."

I aim a high kick at her head, but she ducks under my leg, pushing up to throw me off balance. I spin and land awkwardly in a crouch. I dive, rolling under her own vicious kick. I sweep out with my leg. She trips, going down hard. But before I can take advantage, she pushes herself up, flipping back onto her feet in a super cool move I'm instantly jealous of.

"*Guys,*" Artemis chastises. We ignore her.

Honora throws a punch. I catch her hand in mine, easily holding it in place. She grins even bigger. And then she shoves.

I stumble back, shocked. She shouldn't be able to do that. I'm not sure exactly how strong I am, but I *know* I'm stronger than a normal girl. She spins and kicks my stomach. I fly across the yard, slamming into the fence. The post cracks.

"Nina!" Artemis shouts.

This is Honora. The architect of the single most humiliating moment of my life. If I get nothing else out of being a Slayer, I sure as every known hell dimension will get the satisfaction of beating her in a fight.

Honora stalks toward me. I dodge a kick. Her foot smashes into the fence. I stand, uppercutting her with my momentum. I catch her under the chin, hard, and her head snaps back. I have a single moment of adrenaline-soaked triumph before horror overtakes me as I watch her fall, completely limp, to the ground.

What have I done?

Artemis rushes to Honora's side. I kneel next to her, but Artemis shoves me away. "How could you?"

"She started it!"

"She didn't! Even if she had, she's our friend!"

"She hit me first! You didn't see. And she's never been my friend!" I struggle to get myself under control. "Let me check her out. I didn't mean to hit her so hard."

Artemis looks like our mother when she meets my eyes. It

winds me, leaves me struggling to catch my breath. "You *did* mean to. You meant to hit her exactly that hard."

Honora's eyes flutter open. I slump in relief against the fence. Maybe she was faking. I don't even care as long as it means I didn't break her neck or her brain. I might have been okay with breaking her jaw, though.

Gods, what's *wrong* with me? I fix bones. I don't break them.

Artemis's hands dart around Honora's face. "Are you okay? Can you move? Maybe you should lie still for a bit."

Honora smiles, a lazy, dazed expression. "It's not fair," she says to my sister.

"What's not fair?"

"You should have passed the test. You gave it up for *her*. If either of you were going to be a Slayer, it should have been you."

Artemis doesn't look at me. She doesn't have to. We both know she feels the same way. How could she not? But I don't understand what Honora means about the Watcher stuff. I had nothing to do with Artemis failing the test.

Honora accepts Artemis's help up. I stand too, keeping my distance.

"I won't let you take Doug." It comes out as more a mumble than a challenge.

"Too late," Honora snarls.

Cillian is sitting on the floor in the middle of the shed, playing with the empty handcuffs. He looks up, his eyes half shut and glazed. "Man, I feel good. I feel so good. I haven't felt this good since my mom left. I'm not even sad about that. It's cool that she needs magic more than she needs me." He laughs, lying back on the floor. "I feel really good." He picks up the ring from his dad's box of things, sliding it onto his finger and giggling.

I rush into the shed as if Doug might still be in there, hiding. "Where did he go?"

Cillian waves a hand languorously through the air, then pauses, watching his fingers like they're the greatest things ever. "He——" Cillian stops, giggling. "He put his hand over my mouth so I wouldn't shout. Some of his—whatever—got in." Cillian laughs harder, closing his eyes. "Then he asked me to unlock his chains. Such a nice bloke. I'm gonna sleep now." He curls on his side, smiling.

Honora is holding her head, leaning against the fence. "Great job, Wheezy."

My fists compulsively clench at my sides. "*Don't* call me that."

"Or what, you gonna hit me again? Come on. Show me what a big, bad Slayer you are now. Show us the truth: that all those years you pretended to be so sweet and nurturing were really because you needed other people to feel sorry for you so they'd like you."

My fists go limp. Is she right? Was I always a Slayer inside—violent, predatory—and only forced to care about others because I needed them to care about me? Was I only helpful and kind because I was terrified of being left behind again?

"It wasn't like that." I hear how petulant and whiny I sound. She turns me back into my thirteen-year-old self, and I hate it.

"You have no idea what you've done, letting him get away."

"I'd rather him be free than be in your hands! You're not telling us everything."

Honora pops something into her mouth, tipping her head back to swallow it. She's getting steadier by the minute. The force of my hit is the only reason she didn't jump the fence and run after him immediately. I bought him a few precious minutes. And I'm *glad*.

"You're pathetic," she says. "You still think you're the good guys, hiding in that castle, hoarding information and not doing anything with it. Pretending like you still matter."

Artemis flinches at her words. Honora puts a hand on my sister's cheek. "It breaks my heart to see you there. You are so much better than *any* of them, Artemis. And you can do so much more."

She leans forward and brushes her lips against my sister's. Now I'm definitely ready to hit her again. But then she pulls back, runs, and jumps the fence—faster and higher than she should be able to. What is the deal with her?

"Artemis," I say. She doesn't turn around. "You know Honora is mixed up in this."

"All I know is what I saw. You protecting a demon, and fighting Honora to do it."

"That's not what— She's poisoning you against me!"

Artemis waves her hand, huffing. "She's never said anything bad about you. You're the one who hates her."

"Because she's the worst!"

"She's the one person I used to be able to talk to. She's been writing me for the last two years too, checking in. She gets it. She cares. She's the only one who understands what I go through."

Her words slice through me. Wasn't I that one person? Weren't we each other's person? Becoming a Slayer has forced the truth about my relationship with the sister I love more than anyone in the world.

We're not close.

And if things continue how they are, we never will be again.

I think about Buffy, the stories of all her broken relationships with friends and loved ones. Is this part of what being a Slayer is? A loneliness that goes down to the bone?

I swallow back the hurt, trying to figure out what happened between us. "What did Honora mean, that you didn't pass the test because of me?"

Artemis's face closes off as she turns to leave. "I'll see you back at the castle. I have to figure out how to fix your mess."

I sit on the floor of the shed. Cillian snores softly, smiling in his sleep. Should I follow Doug and Honora, make sure she doesn't catch up to him? I'm still convinced that he isn't evil. He ran away only because Honora showed up. He never even tried before. And while we were distracted, he had every chance to hurt Cillian and didn't.

How much of a threat is Honora? She may not be a Slayer, but she's got some kind of extra juice. And she knows so much more than she told us. Everything she said about Doug was a lie.

Plus, I still don't know how any of this ties to Bradford's death.

The only thing that's clear is that I'm in over my head. I need Watchers, even though I don't want to admit how badly I've screwed everything up. Not to mention the fact that I beat up another Watcher to protect a demon.

Oh my gods. I always thought I'd make better choices if I had the kind of power Buffy has. Now? It turns out I am just. Like. Her.

The least Doug could have done was give me a shot of happy too, because I have none of my own.

21

I TRUDGE BACK TO THE CASTLE, DRAG-
ging a still drugged-up Cillian along. For several minutes he
points wordlessly to a particular tree, tears of joy streaming
down his face.

Doug wasn't kidding. He's good stuff.

I keep an eye out for any sign of him or Honora, but I don't
see anything. She'll catch him or she won't. I can't pretend like I
can handle this alone anymore.

When we get to the castle, Rhys is outside practicing crossbow while Jade lounges in the shade with a book. I tug Cillian
to Rhys and get the hard part over with first. "So, long story
short, there was a demon, we were keeping it in Cillian's shed, it
drugged Cillian and got away."

Rhys's finger twitches, and his bolt lands dead center in the
target. Jade looks up, surprised. "Nice shot," she says. Either she
doesn't notice Cillian high out of his mind or doesn't care. She
goes right back to her book.

"Cillian can fill you in when he sobers up." I shove Cillian at his boyfriend. Rhys stares at me, mouth gaping open like a fish's, Cillian in his arms. I head into the castle, Cillian's voice following me as he croons, "And I-I-I will always love you-oo-oo!" at the top of his lungs.

It's time to come clean. But not to my mom or to the rest of the Council. I need actual help. Someone who won't judge me for what I did to Honora. Someone who knows about being a Watcher in the real world. How complicated it can get. How messy.

Someone I hope will still like me after he hears what a tremendous mess I've made of everything.

I pause, about to knock at Leo and Eve's suite. There are loud voices inside. Shouting, maybe? Or just animated conversation? I can't tell. The door flies open and I'm face-to-face with Leo, my fist still raised to knock. His expression is a solid mask, like someone holding everything inside. I take an involuntary step back. But by the time I've done that, he's smiling.

I've seen his real smile. This isn't it. "Athena," he says. "Hey."

"Come in!" Eve Silvera beams. It can't have been yelling I overheard. She looks totally relaxed. She gestures to an elegant tea set, and I take a seat across the table from her. Leo stays standing. I was only planning on going to Leo, but this is probably better. I'm in so deep, I need more than one Silvera to dig me out.

"I'm glad you came by," Eve said. "I need to explain my reaction this morning."

"Huh?"

"In Bradford's room."

"Oh. Right. Yeah." In all the Doug-and-Honora drama, I had actually forgotten for a few precious minutes. Both that Bradford

Smythe is dead and that Eve, my champion, didn't believe me about my dream.

"I'm so sorry I acted that way. I couldn't have your mother suspect that we're training you. The easiest way to put her off our trail is by pretending like we don't trust you as a Slayer. Really, nothing could be further from the truth."

"So you believe me? About my dream?" I look hopefully toward Leo. His jaw is clenched. He nods, once. It hits me how worried I was that he would join his mother's side. His unquestioning support this morning meant so much more to me than I realized.

"Of course!" Eve says. "Now, I'm not discounting my theory that as a Slayer your senses are so fine-tuned that you knew he was sick, and your dream was a way of communicating that to yourself. But I'm also not discounting that it could very well have been something demonic. I'm looking into it, and I'll let you know as soon as I find anything. In the meantime, I don't think any of us are in danger, but if you feel we are, or you dream something similar, come to me immediately."

I nod, relieved. At least Eve believes in me. Leo too, though he's being weird again. He's always like this around his mom. It must have been hard, working with her. As both her son and her subordinate. Like Artemis and our mom.

"Did you need something else, dear?" Eve smiles encouragingly.

Right. The real reason I came. I wish I could leave right now, firmly in Eve's good graces. I fidget with the delicate spoon in front of me. "I, uh, messed up. Like, really bad. Like, the worst way a Watcher can mess up."

Eve puts her hand over mine. "You can't mess up in the worst way a Watcher can, because you're not one. You're a Slayer. So tell us what happened, and we'll help."

It's such a *mom* thing to say. I don't get that often. I actually can't remember the last time I had a mom thing said to me. "Right. Okay. See, there was this demon?" I blurt out the whole story as fast as I can. But I stumble when I get to the part where I'll have to tell her about my mom killing the second hellhound in secret. Eve can tell I'm leaving something out. She raises an eyebrow, and I slouch.

"My mom," I say. "There was another hellhound. It found me in the village, and I wanted to keep the villagers safe, so I led it back here. Which I know was the wrong move!"

"I don't think it was."

"You don't?"

Eve's warm smile confirms her statement. "You were protecting innocents, and you knew there were weapons and other capable people at the castle. It was the right decision. You need to trust your instincts more. You have them for a reason."

A rush of warmth better than the tea fills me. "Well, I didn't kill it. My mom did. But then she didn't tell anyone else about it. Which is weird, right? We went on lockdown for the first one. It was almost like . . ."

"Almost like she expected the second one," Eve fills in for me. Concern creases her brow. "Or at least knew it was hunting something other than us and we weren't in danger. This demon in the shed—whom you suspect was the target—do you know what he was running from?"

I tell her about the demon drug dealing, the marks on Doug's wrists, the connection to the pit-fighting organizers. And then I bite my lip. "But I think it's less about who he was running from than who he was running to. He said he had a contact. Someone who made deals with demons. Smythe. And now Bradford Smythe is dead."

Eve coughs on her sip of tea. "Wait. You think Bradford Smythe is connected?"

"Maybe. It explains why I had that dream, and makes it more likely it was demonic, right?"

Eve leans back, setting down her teacup. "It does indeed." She taps her red fingernails on the saucer, then speaks again. "But did the demon say it was Bradford Smythe specifically?"

"No, he just said Smythe."

"There's another Smythe in the castle."

I lean back, feeling like I've been punched. My mom. *Of course.* What if my mom was his contact? If she knew Doug was coming, she wouldn't be surprised by the hellhounds hunting him. She would have known the hellhounds weren't hunting us specifically. But would she really risk the castle, all of us, for a demon?

But hadn't I sort of done the same thing by keeping him secret?

I rub my forehead. "Well, we can't ask Doug, because Honora followed me to the shed, and we fought."

"You fought Honora?" Leo looks alarmed.

I can't help but smile a little. "You won the bet."

His face cracks into his own smile, but it looks sad. "I knew I would."

"Anyway, Doug got away. I think Honora's connected to the

group that was holding Doug captive. He knew her. She took off when he disappeared. Probably hunting him. But my money's on her never bringing him back here. I think she'd return him to his captors."

"What happened while we were away? How did things spiral this far?" Eve straightens, radiating strength. "Well. It's up to us to fix things. And we will. Because that's what we do. First things first, I'll go speak with your mother."

"Don't do that!" I squeak. "If you ask about any of this, she'll figure out I've been training. And if she knew that, she'd send me away for sure."

Eve shakes her head. "I would never let that happen. She kept your potential hidden from us for all those years; she's not sending you away now that we know what you are. You're not just a Slayer. You're *our* Slayer. Let me handle your mother. We're your Watchers; our job is to support you." She reaches across the table and squeezes my hand. I squeeze back, more grateful and relieved than I can say.

She smiles warmly at Leo. "Why don't you two go train, work out some of Nina's stress. I'll get to work on the demon questions. If Honora is involved in something this big, I'll find answers. I still have a few Watcher tricks up my sleeves."

Leo nods curtly. I follow him out, feeling lighter than I have since the first hellhound attacked. I shouldn't have been trying to do this on my own. I was making a classic Buffy mistake. Not trusting my Watchers. Not using them. How could I have fallen into it so easily? I have Leo, and, even better, I have Eve. She'll take care of things, because that's what Watchers do. That's what mothers do.

As if on cue, my mother bursts out of her room. She startles when she sees us, holding her large tote bag to her chest like she thinks we'll try to take it.

"Nina!" she says. "Leo?"

I want to ask her about Doug. What she knew. But I also want to ask how she is, to try and express how sorry I am about losing Bradford, a man she must have loved dearly even if I never really saw that side of their relationship. But my mother speaks first.

"I'm glad I ran into you. I have an assignment for you."

"What?" My chest flutters with surprise and excitement.

"Not you. Leo."

I deflate, but she doesn't notice or doesn't care.

"There's a Slayer in Dublin. I have reason to believe she's in trouble." My mother reaches into her suit jacket and retrieves a small address book. She flips through it—I see dozens of entries—until she finds the page she's looking for. She *does* still have a list of Slayers that she's keeping to herself. She rips the page free and hands it to Leo.

"Cosmina," Leo says. Then he course corrects. We shouldn't recognize her name, as far as my mother is concerned. "That's the Slayer?"

If my mother knows about Cosmina, does she know what we did? No. There's no way. We'd be in so much trouble if she had any idea.

But why this sudden desire to send Leo to meet Cosmina? Why now, when we've avoided Slayers for two years?

Actually, Eve mentioned something about a Slayer in Costa Rica. That was how they found each other again. But that Slayer was already dead. Maybe my mom *has* been contacting Slayers for a long time and hiding it. But I don't know why she would do that either.

I always thought she hated Slayers. But her mother was one. And I'm one now too. I suspect it's a lot more complicated than I've ever understood.

"Yes," my mother says, answering Leo's question. "Cosmina Enescu. That's her address. I'd like you to go immediately." She's snatching up Leo. He's not hers. He's *mine*. My Watcher. She doesn't get to be part of this.

Besides, how is my mother handing out assignments right now? It's only been hours since Bradford's death. What have they done with the body? Anything? What are they going to do? Shouldn't my mom be dealing with that instead?

"Are you sad?" I blurt.

"What?" She raises her eyebrows.

"About Bradford Smythe! He raised you. And now he's dead."

"He didn't raise me." She stops, something stricken finally breaking through on her face. "The whole community did. It's complicated."

"Why, because he was your mother's Watcher?"

She freezes. Leo stares down at the slip of paper like it's filled with text he's suddenly compelled to read. I can't believe I'm doing this in front of him.

Actually, his presence is why I finally feel able to do this. He makes me stronger. Braver. I refuse to back down or explain myself. "If I don't understand, it's only because you never talk to me. I can't believe you didn't tell me your mother was a Slayer."

Emotions battle across her features, and then finally her tight, distant expression returns. "Because it doesn't matter.

Leo, please let me know as soon as you find Cosmina. Invite her to the castle, if she'll come."

"What?" I shout.

They both turn to me, surprised. Eve opens her door and peers out into the hallway.

"You can't invite her here! We don't know anything about her! You're the one who's always going on about secrecy and how we can't work with Slayers because we can't trust them to keep our secrets safe!"

"Dublin has gotten dangerous, Nina. Would you rather me leave Cosmina vulnerable and alone?"

"Yes!" I stop, take a deep breath. *"No.* But, gods, are you really so desperate to replace me that you'll find the nearest Slayer and bring her in instead?"

"That's not what this is about."

"That's exactly what this is about! Well, guess what, Mom? Producing another Slayer won't change anything. I was already Chosen. Past tense. It's done. You might hate it, you might hate me, but like you said: *It doesn't matter."* I turn on my heel and stomp out of the fancy residence wing.

I almost run into Artemis in the main hall. Her face is flushed, sweat on her forehead. "No sign of the demon. Or Honora."

Rhys walks past us, chipper and oblivious. "Come on," he says. "We're going to be late for class."

Class? It feels almost laughable right now to behave like students when we're already deep into real-world scenarios. "Where's Cillian?" I ask Rhys. "He's okay?"

"High as a kite. I left him in my room to rest. In the meantime, I'm going to class, where you can fill me in on what you and my boyfriend have been up to." He doesn't sound happy with me. I don't blame him. I violated his trust and put Cillian at risk.

"I'm sorry," I mutter.

"Class," Rhys snaps.

It feels tremendously unimportant, but Leo didn't follow me out of the residence wing, so I can't train with him. I could go out and search for Doug, but Artemis is watching me, perched like a hawk ready to swoop in. And I don't want Rhys any madder at me.

"Great." I force the words out. "Let's go to class."

Artemis slips into the library a few minutes after us, not sitting next to me. Her arms are folded, her lips forming a tight, stern line. Rhys is scribbling in a manner that can only be described as aggressive. Poor Imogen stumbles through her lecture on the difficulties of translating runes into verbal language.

I'm churning with anger too. Honora. My mother. Cosmina. Maybe it's selfish of me—definitely it's selfish of me, knowing what I do about Cosmina's life—but I don't want her here. First boarding school, now a new Slayer. My mother is determined to make sure I have no place in the castle.

I flip through my notes but pause when I get to my last entry. It was the prophecy translation assignment. My eyes bug out as I read it.

> *Child of Slayer*
> *Child of Watcher*
> *The two become one*
> *The one becomes two*
> *Girls of fire*

Protector and Hunter
One to mend the world
And one to tear it asunder
When all else ends, when hope perishes alongside wonder,
her darkness shall rise and all shall be devoured.

Suddenly it's personal. "Child of Watcher, Child of Slayer" didn't mean anything before. But now I know the truth of my family history. My father was a child of a Watcher. My mother wasn't.

And my father mentioned a prophecy in his diary that seemed of personal concern to him and my family.

I stand. "Artemis."

Imogen stops midsentence, alarmed by the expression on my face. "Is everything okay?"

"I need to talk to Artemis. Now." I grab my notes and hurry out of the library. Artemis is behind me. I'm relieved. I worried she wouldn't come. When we get back to our room, I slam the door and throw my notes onto the bed. "Look at this prophecy."

Artemis rubs her forehead. "With everything else going on, I hardly think me helping you cheat on translations is a priority."

"No, that's not— The prophecy! It's about a child of a Watcher and a child of a Slayer having two girls who will go on to break the world!" I jab my finger at it. "Gods, Artemis, look at it. It could be—it might be—it could be us. There's no timeline, but we should at least talk about it."

Artemis gives me a flat stare. She's always the first to support me. But she looks like our mother again. "There's a demon loose and you're worried about some musty old prophecy?"

"I found a reference to a prophecy in Dad's diary. I'll bet it's this one."

She looks like I've struck her. "You read it without me."

"You didn't want to read it. I never said I didn't. I came straight here to talk to you after, but you were getting cozy with Honora, and I wasn't about to share personal information with her!"

"This isn't about Honora!"

"It is!"

Artemis kicks over the stack of books I stole from the library for Doug research. "Nothing is about Honora! You need to get over this grudge. People could die because you decided you would rather punch it out with her than listen to someone with way more demon experience than you'll ever have!"

"What's that supposed to mean? Just because I'm not a Watcher-in-training, my instincts don't matter? I'm a Slayer!"

Artemis throws her hands in the air. "Oh, good. Let's bring that up! Because you discovering you're a Slayer—two months *after* the change happened—makes you an expert in everything!"

I flinch at her tone. All my anger dries up, leaving only hurt in its wake. It's not like I didn't know *something* had happened to me. I was afraid to face what it was. "Why are you being like this? I'm asking for your help."

"Of course you are. That's what you do. That's what everyone does." She spits out the words. "We have hundreds—thousands—of prophecies in that library. If this one mattered, someone would have said something. This is the last thing we should be worried about now. You're *trying* to find something else to distract me from the fact that you hid a freaking demon from me."

It hits me hard. She's right. She's absolutely right. This isn't a priority now, but I want it to be. I want anything that brings us together to be a priority. I latched onto this prophecy as soon as I saw it because it was easier to think about than everything else. It was easier than sitting in class, easier than making things up with Rhys. Easier than talking about this growing chasm between my sister and me. "That's not it at all," I lie. I step toward her.

She steps back.

"What about you?" I ask. "What was Honora talking about, saying you gave up your chance at being a full Watcher for me?"

Artemis turns away. "It doesn't matter." She might as well be our mother. This is how we deal with pain, with hard things. We shut down. And we shut each other out. She leaves me alone with a prophecy of doom and a broken heart.

She had studied the words enough that she knew them by heart. But she still found them sometimes. Ran her finger over them.

Her own mother had failed. Spectacularly. And for a while the hunter had thought, perhaps, she wouldn't be needed. After all, if a prophecy ends up being inaccurate, how can it come true? She told herself that, but she didn't quite believe it.

Prophecies are slippery things, after all.

And so she watched, and she waited. There was no rush. The girls grew. One strong and smart and capable, one weak and clever and kind. Maybe the prophecy had never been about them. Maybe all her work, all her sacrifice, had been for nothing.

She was okay with that. Better to be wrong and have sacrificed a few lives than to be wrong and sacrifice the world. She wouldn't have felt guilty if she had succeeded in killing one of the girls. That was why she was the hunter. Because she knew she would do whatever it took to keep the world safe.

For a long time—for years—it looked like she wouldn't have to do anything.

But then the weak became strong. The healer became killer. Which meant the other twin's fate beckoned as well.

Something would have to be done. And soon.

A knock on her door pulled her from her reverie. She pasted the smile on her face. "Just a minute!" The knives she had been stroking were placed gently back in her drawers, alongside a box of ballpoint pens, her favorite lipsticks, and a photo of Artemis and Athena.

22

THERE'S A KNOCK. EVEN THOUGH ARTEMIS wouldn't knock on our own door, I'm still disappointed when I open it and find Eve Silvera.

I must look as miserable as I feel; she radiates sympathy. "May I come in?"

"Of course."

She takes in the room with a smile. "Where's Artemis?"

Tears well up in my eyes and Eve envelops me in a hug. She smells cool and crisp, like an autumn night breeze. "It will work itself out. And I'm here to help with whatever doesn't. This is why Slayers have Watchers. It's too much for any girl to bear alone." She pats my back and I pull away, sniffling but comforted. What would it have been like, to have a mother like Eve?

Eve gets to business. "Leo told me about your mother's request that he go find Cosmina. I'm concerned."

"Me too! I think it's a terrible idea."

"We don't know anything about this girl, except that she was more than willing to leave you to die. We have a responsibility to reach out to Slayers, yes. But this is hasty and ill-advised. I'm still waiting on information from contacts within the city. Between the demon you discovered and whatever mess this Cosmina is embroiled in, I don't see any reason to rush into a relationship with her. I've told Leo as much." She frowns in concern. "I'm leery of the other Council members too. Not just your mother. If you're right about Honora, she's not acting as a Watcher anymore. I don't know how much Wanda knows about it. She could be involved as well. So we can't discuss this with any of them. But I wanted to make sure you agreed with my decision to wait before contacting Cosmina. I may be a Watcher, but you're our Slayer."

I am. *I'm* the castle's Slayer. I know it's just reinforcing my own petty reasons, but I latch onto her justifications. "We need more information about Cosmina. That's how Watchers do things." I may not agree with all the Watcher practices, but I have always agreed with that one.

A twinge of guilt and uncertainty tugs at me. My dreams sent me to Cosmina. And I helped her. But I know she still needs help.

I don't want to give it to her.

"What a stroke of tremendous good fortune, having a Slayer who is also a Watcher." Eve means it as a compliment, but I feel like I'm failing as both. I give her a fake smile. She opens the door to leave. "You tell me if anything comes up in your dreams, and in the meantime, I'll handle Dublin, the demon, Cosmina, and Bradford's death. If there's a connection, I'll find it."

"Let me know if I can do anything?"

"I don't doubt I'll need you very soon." She smiles and leaves.

Still uneasy, I pull on one of Artemis's black leather jackets and head to the gym. Instead of training, I'll ask Leo to scout with me to see if we can turn up Doug's trail. Maybe we'll get lucky and find him. Artemis didn't, but she's not a Slayer. At least then I'll be doing something instead of just waiting. I know Eve is a Watcher, but I can't sit back and let her do *everything*.

Leo's waiting for me. "There you are. Come on." He turns and walks out of the gym.

"Oh, good. I was thinking we'd look for Doug."

"I trust your instincts that he's not dangerous."

"I was actually more worried about what would happen if Honora gets to him first."

"Then we'll know where he is, and we'll deal with her." He says it matter-of-factly. Instead of leading me to the forest, we go to the garage.

"So then where are we going?" I ask as he grabs the keys to the Range Rover.

"To talk to Cosmina."

I freeze with my hand on the door. "Your mom said we shouldn't. She said you talked about it."

"You and I both saw how much trouble Cosmina was in. My mother didn't. What if it were you out there all by yourself?" His concern is so genuine that I feel like the worst person in the world.

I didn't want Cosmina here because of how it would affect me. And because our last encounter made me reasonably reluctant to trust her. But I have so much that she never had. Life is harsh for Slayers out there alone, like Cosmina. It's even harsh for Slayers who aren't alone. Like my grandmother.

Whatever is in me that makes me a Slayer connected us. I

shouldn't deny that. "If I were out there, I'd want our help," I
admit. I've always had Artemis, after all. No matter how things
are between us right now, ever since the fire, she's been there
for me. Leo trusts me. So I'll trust him, too. "Oh, fine. Let's go
rescue Cosmina. Ideally with less carnage this time."

Leo laughs dryly. "We won't bring her back. She'll have to
work hard to gain some trust if she wants it after how she left
you in the pit. But someone needs to check in on her." Then his
face turns thoughtful. Shy, even. Not blank like the mask he
wears around the adults. "I'm glad you're coming. It'll be nice
to talk."

"Yeah." My face betrays me by flushing bright red. "Talking is
good." It is good, with Leo. He actually listens instead of telling
me how to feel. Honora interrupted us this morning. I'd love
to talk more with him about being a Slayer. Or anything else,
really. I've shifted from hating his presence to feeling like he's
someone I can truly depend on. Someone who believes I can do
this, which makes it easier for me to believe it too.

"There's something I need to tell you." He climbs into the
driver's seat. "I haven't been able to figure out how to bring it up,
or when, or even whether I should. But—"

"Where are you going?" Artemis runs up to us from the
direction of the forest, grabbing my door and holding it open.
She was probably scouting for Doug. I hope Honora isn't still out
there, skulking around like a creep.

I hesitate, but only for a second. Artemis and I don't agree
on who to trust. We don't even trust each other the way I once
thought we did. But keeping secrets from her has only made
things worse. "We're going to Dublin to talk with Cosmina.

Mom wanted us to check in on her." I pause. "Well, she wanted Leo to. She definitely wouldn't want me to."

"My mother didn't want either of us to do it." Leo doesn't so much as crack a smile.

"So you're both disobeying your own mothers by doing what the other person's mother asked you to."

I try to sort through the tangle of connections. "Right. Wait, no. Well, yes. Sort of. No one's mother wants me to go. Unless you know something about Wanda Wyndam-Pryce that I don't." Going to talk to a hostile Slayer who almost got me killed the last time I helped her? Wanda would probably approve, now that I think of it.

Artemis raises an eyebrow. Her tone isn't critical. It's almost . . . curious. Like she can't quite understand it, but she maybe gets it. "You're directly defying the Council."

Leo shakes his head. "We're Watchers. Athena's a Slayer. This is our job."

"I'm coming." Artemis climbs into the backseat of the car. So much for talking with Leo. And I'm pretty sure he was on the verge of telling me something big. Personal, even. I *really* want to know what it was. She leans forward. "I can't believe you're doing this, Nina."

I shrug, but Artemis is right. Even when I've disagreed with the Council's tactics and ideologies, I've always done what they told me. But I can't get over what Eve said—that if my mom wasn't worried about the hellhounds, it means she had information we didn't. Which means she's connected to all this somehow. So whatever she doesn't want me to do, I'm going to do.

I hate to go against Eve, but Leo's logic makes sense too. My only real issue with talking to Cosmina is that I don't want to. And good Watchers don't get to make decisions based on their own feelings. Pretty sure Slayers don't either.

Once again we head for Dublin. I stare out the window, hoping that the body count will be lower, if nothing else.

Leo's fingers strangle the steering wheel.

"Maybe we could stop and get food?" I suggest.

"Why would we do that?" From the sound of her voice, Artemis's jaw is clenched. I don't dare look back. When she joined us I hoped it meant all was forgiven. But something still feels broken between us. I want to blame Honora, but I was the one who didn't go to Artemis when I needed help.

Then again, maybe it isn't only Artemis who needs to do the forgiving. Instead of supporting me through this maelstrom of suckage in my life, she's been acting like I'm a problem she needs to solve. *And* she instantly sided with Honora over me. I want to blame Honora, and I still will. But that doesn't mean Artemis is entirely without blame. Things were bad before Honora came back into the picture.

I spend the rest of the drive suffocated by Artemis's steely silence. Leo isn't any better. With Artemis here, he hasn't said a word. I hadn't pegged him for the teenage rebellion type, but this whole trip feels like him being mad at his mom for some reason.

When you're a Watcher because of your family, but the Watchers take precedence over that family, it gets complicated. The three of us—sitting here sulking in a car as we defy our mothers—are evidence of that. Maybe we should ask Cosmina to take us in, instead of the reverse.

After two stops for petrol—this car has issues—it's almost dark when we finally pull to a stop. The neighborhood leaves a lot to be desired, like safety and buildings that won't fall down if someone sneezes next to them.

"Being a Slayer isn't a very lucrative gig." I stare up at the bleak apartments.

I used to resent Slayers, but now that I've felt some of their lives and fought some of their battles in my dreams, I get it. At least a little. It's too much for one girl. Cosmina shouldn't have to do this alone. I hope we can convince her of that.

Leo's a good Watcher. Better than the rest of us, who are so bitter toward Slayers that we didn't put any of them before our own safety. Maybe . . . maybe that's what happened with Buffy all those years ago when she broke with the Council. It was the wrong choice, obviously. But I've seen behind the scenes. We don't always work the way we should, or even could.

Maybe that's why my mother made another unilateral move. She knew the idea of bringing Cosmina in would get deadlocked in the Council, and while they argued and debated, Cosmina would still be out here alone. Not in the castle where she could take my place.

My mother's motivations might have been selfish, but Leo's weren't. He made the right call. He's still that boy showing up in the darkness to help when things are dire. I glance over at him, glad he's on my side. His expression is worried, his shoulders tense.

"We got this," I whisper. His tension eases ever so slightly.

Artemis tries the door to the building, but it's locked. She pulls out a lockpick.

"Allow me!" I say. She moves out of the way, waiting for me to kick it in. I push a random buzzer instead.

"What?" a voice grumbles.

"Let me up," I say. "I've got the stuff."

"About time." There's a buzz and a click, and the door opens.

"What stuff?" Artemis asks.

"I don't know. It looks like the type of place where a lot of people are waiting for stuff. Worked, didn't it?"

She walks past me without responding. Leo nods in approval, but his nervousness has only increased. It radiates off him with the same level of intensity as Artemis's derision.

I follow them up four flights of stairs, half the lights broken and my shoes sticking on substances best left unseen. The building is even colder than it is outside. I shrink into Artemis's leather jacket, wishing I had worn another layer. When we get to the door, I knock. No one answers.

"It's dark," Leo says. "She's probably already out patrolling."

"We can leave a note." Artemis searches her weapons bag.

Leo leans against the wall, settling in. "I want to talk to her in person. Make sure she's okay."

We can't afford to hang around all night. The Doug problem is still waiting for me back at the castle, as well as the mystery of Bradford's death. I want to press my mother for some actual answers. I bet Eve will back me up. Hell, Wanda Wyndam-Pryce will too, if only to catch my mom in wrongdoing again. I don't want to believe it was my mom who's been contacting demons and bringing them to the very castle she spent all this time keeping secret, but it seems more and more likely. That, or it really was Bradford, and he's dead because of it.

Cosmina can't take up too much of our time. She's pretty low priority, all things considered. I knock harder, and the door swings open. It hasn't been latched all the way. Dread pooling deep in my stomach, I force myself to step into the apartment.

Cosmina's home after all.

Sort of.

23

I'M FIXATED ON THE YELLOW DUCKS. NO girl wearing pajamas with yellow ducks on them should be lying dead on the floor.

"Bed's cold," Artemis says. "But it looks like she was in it before this happened. Check the body for marks."

Leo's frozen at my side. We came to help her. We were too late. *I* was too late. My dreams gave her to me, and I failed her. My father died to save a Slayer. I wouldn't even risk losing my spot in the castle for her sake.

"Window's secure, and we're four stories up. They probably got in through the door. Check the body!" Artemis snaps her fingers impatiently.

She's not my Watcher. But she is the only one of us who seems capable of coherent thought. I half expect her to tell me to leave the room, to shield me from this, but she's done doing that, apparently. I kneel next to Cosmina's body. She's lying on her back, staring at the ceiling. According to movies I should close her eyelids, but it feels disrespectful. She met death open-eyed and fighting. Who am I to pretend she's at peace?

"No marks." I check her neck and exposed skin. "Her knuckles look raw, but that might have been from before." She's stiff, too. I haven't studied dead bodies as much as living ones, but I suspect she's been dead for more than a few hours. Possibly a full day.

"Was it your demon?" Artemis asks.

"First of all, he's not *my* demon," I snap. "If anything, he was Honora's. And second of all, Cosmina's been dead awhile, probably since before Doug got free. Maybe it was the fighting pit people." Cosmina knew they were dangerous. They'd already proven as much. Why didn't we force her to come with us then? Protect her?

It would have been against her will, though. I don't know that we could have. She'd been a Slayer a lot longer than me.

And now she's dead.

Artemis steps around a fallen lamp, her boots crunching brightly in the glass. "You don't know Doug's not a killer. And there was definitely a struggle."

"This *wasn't* Doug," I repeat, but I'm distracted.

Cosmina was probably asleep when she was attacked. And there are no marks on her. It's too much like Bradford Smythe. I want Eve's other theory to be true—the one where I dreamed Bradford's death because my super Slayer senses clued me in that he was sick—but the similarities are too much to discount. Which makes two dead bodies. But what do Bradford and Cosmina have in common? Or rather, what *did* they?

"Why do you think Mom decided we needed to help Cosmina right now? And only wanted to send Leo?" I ask. "Doesn't it seem suspicious that Mom wanted to track down Cosmina specifically? The one Slayer we secretly already knew?"

"And who was already dead." Artemis frowns, staring at the body. "Where did Mom get her information?"

"She had a book full of addresses. She must have taken her Slayer database off the computer."

"It *is* weird," Artemis says. I fight back the deeply inappropriate elation I feel that she agrees with me. "And why send Leo? Why didn't she come herself?"

"She could be helping take care of Bradford's body," Leo says. It's generous of him. But it doesn't seem right.

"She was going somewhere. When we ran into her and she told you to do this. Remember? She had a bag. I don't think it was anything to do with Bradford."

"Don't jump to any conclusions," Leo says. "You don't have all the information. I—"

"Looks like I don't need an invitation anymore." A vampire steps across the door's threshold, grinning. Before we can react, she jumps at Leo, going straight for his neck. He ducks under her lunge, twists, and throws her against the wall.

She lands in a heap, then stands, laughing. "Whoops. Should have gone for the scrawny one first." She winks at me.

Artemis pulls out a stake, doing a super-intimidating move where she spins it over the back of her hand and catches it again. I spent a whole summer when I was fourteen trying to learn it. Emphasis on "trying."

"Who sent you?" Artemis demands.

The vampire bares her teeth at us. "No one sent me. I was here to pick up Cosmina."

"Someone sent you to get the body?" I ask, horrified.

"I didn't know she *was* a body. We've been working together to eliminate the zompire problem in the city." She shakes her head. "I can't believe she's dead."

I know she has no soul, but apparently she somehow managed to care about Cosmina. There were cases—rare—of vampires who worked around their demonic natures. Most of them dated Buffy, actually.

The vampire's face goes back to normal. It's a plain face. Unremarkable. Wistful, even, as she stares at Cosmina's body. "We had one nest left to clear, and then we were done. We would have cleaned up all of Dublin." She looks devastated.

I don't really know how to comfort a vampire. I had never considered a scenario in which a vampire would *need* comforting.

"Were you two close?" I try tentatively.

She gives me a withering glare. "Are you touched? She was my *reward*. She didn't know, of course, but when we were done with this nest, I was going to drain her. I've been looking forward to it for months! Someone beat me—and they didn't even take her blood, which makes it all the worse. All cold and clotted now. Sticks in the teeth. What a waste." She pauses, tilting her head to the side for a few moments. She takes a deep breath, then her eyes light up and she smiles sweetly. "Hey, since you're here, maybe you could help me?"

Leo steps between us. Artemis holds up a cross and forces the vampire against the wall. I'm left standing in the middle of the room. They don't need to protect me, but they can't help themselves.

The vamp snarls at Artemis. "You're a little girl with some toys and a few desperate tricks."

Artemis punches her, hard.

"Stop it!" I shout. We already have all the weapons *and* the upper hand. Something about adding extra violence on top makes my stomach turn.

Artemis looks at me with as much derision as the vampire had. "She was going to kill Cosmina. She'd have already killed you if we weren't here. And she's going to tell me what she knows before I stake her."

That's not fair. I wouldn't have been dead if Artemis wasn't here. It's like she wants me to be weak, to prove to both of us that I still need her to protect me. Or that she's still better than me.

The vampire laughs. "Darling, you're not going to kill me. I know where the last zompire nest in Dublin is. If I don't clear them out, they'll spread."

Artemis hits her again, then backs up. "Fine. Do you have any idea who did this?"

The vampire adjusts her shirt, smoothing back her hair. "Word on the street is a couple big demons—real powerful nasties—turned up dead. No marks on them."

"Did they have enemies?" Leo asks.

"They were demons, darling. They have enemies just by existing."

"Any suspects?" Leo seems troubled by the demon deaths. I can't see the connection. But maybe he suspects something I don't.

She laughs. "Why, yes, Officer! We've got the tip lines ringing off the hook! Everyone is real cut up about the deaths."

"Did they die in bed?" I ask.

"How do you imagine demons sleeping? All tucked up in their four-poster queen? I don't know how they died. Just that they were alive, and then they weren't. No struggle, no marks. Could be the same thing, could be unrelated. It's a bloody world out there." Her stomach rumbles and she winks. "Not bloody enough, lately. Anyway, Cosmina also ran into trouble with some vampire heavies for an underworld type. Not sewer underworld. Human underworld. Sean something or other."

Sean. Doug's Sean. Which confirms that the same man who kept Doug captive was also running the demon-dogfighting rings. The one that almost got Cosmina and me killed. If we hadn't been trying to keep our activities secret, we could have acted like real Watchers and investigated them. Maybe Cosmina would still be alive if we had. Instead, we ran back to the castle and pretended like nothing happened. Gods, Honora is right. We really have been hiding.

The vampire shrugs. "That's all I know. We were zompire-cleanup partners. She didn't exactly confide in me. Now, do any of you see her phone?"

Leo looks around the floor. "Do you think she had info on there that might help us?"

"No, I think she had at least a month more paid on her account, which means free phone for me until they shut it off." She grins at me, tapping her nose. "I can smell it on you too. This is a preview of coming attractions for you, little *Slayer*. Ain't it great to be Chose——?"

Artemis slams a stake into the vampire's chest.

"What did you do that for?" I shout, shocked, as the vampire disappears into dust.

If a look could kill, I'd be as dead as the vampire. "You're a Slayer, Nina. Try to remember."

"But the zompire nest!"

"I don't believe for a second she was going to take care of this alleged zompire nest. But I know for certain Dublin is better off with one less vampire. Let's finish up."

Still wigged out by Artemis's violence, but also bothered that it should have been me staking the vamp, I take a soft, well-worn blanket off the end of Cosmina's bed and drape it over her body. Leo stands over her, staring down.

Artemis puts her cross away. She glances under the bed. "The phone really is gone, though. So our killer demon is either a thief or there was something worth having on there. Let's go."

"What about the body?" There's a framed picture lying on the floor. The glass is cracked between two girls. One is a much younger, chubby-cheeked Cosmina. Her hair is dark and pulled back from her unmangled ears. The other looks like a sister. I run my finger along the crack between them.

"What about it?" Artemis steps over the frame. "Come on. We still have a demon to find."

"Shouldn't we look into this Sean guy?"

"Loose demon is a bigger threat than loose human. And I don't agree with you that Doug couldn't have done this. Honora said he was a killer."

"For once, could you please listen to me and trust that—"

Artemis has already left the apartment.

I look to Leo for his opinion, but he's still staring at Cosmina's covered body. I can hear Artemis stomping down the stairs beneath us. But I can't quite force myself to move away from Cosmina. Once we leave, she's alone. Forever. I doubt her parents or her sister know where she is.

Rhys has taken whole courses on how to dispose of demon bodies. But what about the human bodies demons leave in their wake? Bradford will get as traditional a Watcher send-off as we can manage. Gone are the days of funeral pyres on seaside cliffs, but he'll be cremated. The worst fate a Watcher could have is to come back as a vampire. We're never buried. Always burned.

Except my dad. There was no question that his death was permanent.

"That's not going to happen to you." Leo's voice is as hard and cold as the cement floor beneath Cosmina's body. "I promise. Whatever else happens, you're not going to end up like her."

"Don't make promises you can't keep." I take one last look at the ducky pajamas. If Cosmina's phone were still here, I could call the police anonymously. That way I'd know she'd at least be found quickly. But I can't even give that to her.

I pick up the photo and set it reverently on the nightstand next to a white business card. I stare at it in surprise.

Cosmina came through for us, even if we failed her.

We catch up to Artemis at the car. "Hold up," I say. "We aren't going home yet."

"Where are we going, then?" she asks.

"To visit a demon drug dealer, demon dogfight organizer, and probable source of information. You want to find out more about Doug, and I want to make sure Sean didn't kill Cosmina." I hold out Sean's card, listing a business address for a place called Naked Grains. "It's our only lead."

"No, our only lead was the actual demon that you let escape."

"That was Honora's fault!"

Artemis drops the card onto the ground. Her eyes blaze with fury. "Honora was trying to do the right thing—the thing you should have done! I can't believe you're still blaming her."

"Why can't you trust me? She——"

Artemis holds up her hand. "I know about the poetry, Nina. She told me herself. She wanted to apologize to you, but you wouldn't let her. So because of one bad joke, you've held a grudge and decided Honora can't be trusted, and now a demon is loose and a Slayer is dead. So don't ask me to trust your judgment." Artemis gets into the car and slams her door.

"Are you kidding me?" I kick the tire. The whole car shakes. I slink back, abashed. But I can't believe Artemis knew about the poetry and never brought it up. Never asked me for my side. She heard all about how poor *Honora* suffered and left it at that.

Artemis is pretending like Sean isn't our best lead just because she's mad at me. It's absurd and immature. Aren't Watchers the ones who are supposed to be careful and check out every lead and piece of information while Slayers get to be single-minded about a hunt?

Leo picks up the business card Artemis dropped on the sidewalk. "I want to get back to the castle. I need to talk to my mom."

"We have to follow up on Sean, though." I'm miserable that he too doesn't think I'm making the right choice. "He's connected to Doug, and now Cosmina. And if Doug *is* somehow the killer—which I don't think is possible—then it's my fault. I have to know."

Leo considers it, then relents. "Okay. It's on the way."

And with that ringing vote of confidence in my plan, we're off to Naked Grains. I don't even want to know what kind of establishment it is. We'll find out soon enough.

24

"*THIS* IS DEMON DRUG DEALER SEAN'S headquarters?" Artemis asks.

Her scathingly doubtful tone doesn't hurt my heart this time. Based on the name, I had assumed Naked Grains was some sort of strip club. I mean, demon-dogfight-runner-slash-demon-drug-dealer using a strip club as a front made sense to me.

But this?

"Sorry," a woman shouts. We turn around from where we're standing next to the car. "Are you leaving? I want your spot."

"No," Leo answers. "We just got here."

Scowling, she pulls away. The tiny parking lot is full in spite of the late hour. People are streaming into the store and leaving with bulging bags of produce. There's an added urgency since it's almost closing time. Everything is bleached of color under the yellow parking lot lights, rendering the scene surreal.

"Have you tried their new kale smoothie? Savagely good," a girl says, walking arm in arm with her girlfriend toward the sliding glass doors of the trendiest health food store I have ever seen in my life. It looks like it belongs in Southern California, not Dublin. Even the buildings nearest it seem to lean away as though to say, *We aren't with him.*

"This can't be the right place." Artemis scowls at the entrance.

"We won't even blend in," I whisper. "We're not nearly cool enough."

Leo has a pensive but dubious expression. "We could shave half your head."

I squeak and reflexively cover my hair with my hands.

He cracks a smile. "I would never."

"Let's get this over with." Artemis grabs a basket from a stack by the doors and holds it like a shield. The store greets us with the heady scent of citrus, underlaid with rich, bitter coffee, a hint of fresh bread, and the overall sensation that we're healthier just for breathing it all in.

"I hate these stores," Artemis says.

"Not exactly demonic, though." Leo's not as dismissive as Artemis, but it's obvious he wants to get back to the castle. He sped the whole way here, and he has one eye on the door.

We walk the perimeter. It isn't huge, but after two years in Shancoom, where the post office doubles as the town shop and has three whole rows, it's overwhelming. There's a bakery on-site and an entire section for buffet-style food. Most of the people are there, loading up for a late dinner. My mouth waters. Being a good Watcher-slash-Slayer leaves so little time for eating.

"I don't see anything alarming," Artemis says. "Maybe Sean works here on the side."

"But isn't this whole place kind of weird? It doesn't belong." I found this lead, and I desperately want it to pan out. I have to prove to Artemis I can do something right. I have to get her back on my side.

Besides, when I'm right, she'll know Honora was wrong.

We walk up an aisle that's entirely coffee beans. When did coffee start coming in so many varieties? Is there really a difference between coffee beans grown in Kenya versus Guatemala? If so, what?

We turn into the next aisle—loose tea—and Artemis stops so fast we almost bump into her. "Look at the salesclerk," she mutters.

The rest of the clerks are all twentysomethings with effortlessly beautiful hair and elegant tattoos. But this guy is *hulking*. Buzzed head, aggressively tattooed, the Naked Grains apron straining around his bulging neck muscles. He stands, feet apart, arms folded.

Leo leans forward to inspect a label. "Wearing a gun on his hip," he whispers. Sure enough, there's a bulge covered by the apron that's decidedly gun-shaped. He's a security guard disguised as a clerk.

Guarding . . . tea?

We meander. There are a few varieties of tea I recognize— English Breakfast, which I like. Earl Grey, which tastes like old ladies' underpants soaked in perfume. Chamomile and ten different types of green. But then there are bins with weird names and descriptions of the effects. Those don't have any prices listed.

"Excuse me." Leo steps in front of the fake clerk with an air of vague annoyance. "There are no prices. How much is the 'Dreams of My Enemy's Weakness' tea? Is it caffeinated, or is it like Sleepytime?"

The guard raises one scarred eyebrow. "That's available by special order only."

I cluck my tongue. "Bummer. What about . . ." I peer around the guard to an empty container. "What about 'Happiness in a Cup'? That sounds yummy. Ooh, guaranteed to cure depression and ease anxiety! Maybe I'll slip it in my mom's teacup the next time I want to ask for more allowance. Is it like Saint-John's-wort?"

"It has similar effects to psychotropic drugs," the guard says, his expression as friendly as a machine gun. "All organic, of course. It's a natural mood enhancer."

"I think I heard about that from a friend!" I look heavily at Artemis and Leo. "You remember. My friend I met at Cillian's. When will it be restocked?"

"The supplier's having technical difficulties. You can sign up for our mailing list." He reaches into his pocket and pulls out a piece of paper. I take it with a smile. It has a website listed under the Naked Grains logo. Along the bottom is some weird triangley symbol, like a logo.

"Thanks! Do you have any—" I try to think of the most absurd food product imaginable. "Probiotic chocolate?"

"Aisle four."

"Fantastic!" I hurry out of the guard's aisle and go several down before stopping to huddle with Artemis and Leo. "An armed guard for tea?"

"All the tea with no prices had a special symbol on the bottom of the label," Leo says. I hold up the mailing list slip. He nods. "That's it. The interlocking triangles."

"There might be something here after all." Artemis studies

the back of the store. I use every ounce of Slayer strength I possess not to shout *I TOLD YOU SO*.

There's an employees-only door along the back wall. It's closing after someone, and I see a flash of gray leather. I recognize that outfit. "She was at the pit!"

Artemis cracks her knuckles. "We need a distraction. Nina, go pull over a shelf. Make a mess. A big one."

My irritation flares. Why does Artemis get to call the shots? She's not the Slayer *or* my Watcher. But this isn't the time or place to fight about this. I go to the coffee aisle. Glancing to either side to make sure no one will get hurt, I reach between two coffee bins, grab the metal shelving support, and tug.

The shelves groan and tip at a dangerous angle. I dart to the next aisle and am rewarded with the sound of plastic crashing and thousands of beans of coffee—expensive, expensive coffee— spilling onto the floor. I guess I'll never know the difference between Kenyan beans and Guatemalan beans. And neither will anyone trying to clean them up.

Artemis and Leo are waiting, staring at a display of organic salt conveniently located next to the staff door. Several employees run out. Artemis hooks her foot to catch the door before it closes.

The room is about what I'd expect from an employee room. Two tables, some chairs, a vending machine filled with more preservatives and fake cheese powder than the rest of the store combined. But against the back wall is a metal door, heavily reinforced, with a keypad lock.

"Bingo," Artemis says. "Nina, you know the code."

"I do?"

"Your fist."

I glare at her, but at the same time, it doesn't escape me that she's starting to accept I have these powers. Maybe asking me to use them is her way of finally acknowledging this isn't going away.

I punch through the keypad and pull out all the wires. There's a clicking noise, and Artemis opens the door. We creep down a winding metal staircase, then through another fortified door to a massive basement space. It arches overhead like at one point it had been a cellar. Or a sewer. It has to run beneath the entire block.

And it's filled with cage after cage of demons.

"Split up." Artemis turns but pauses. "Be careful. Promise?"

"Promise," I say. "You too."

She disappears, sprinting down the length of the wall toward the back.

Leo and I ease cautiously down the nearest row. I'm glad he didn't leave my side. The cages are almost all filled. It's much more orderly than the derelict warehouse that held the other cages. That seemed like a temporary setup. This is very permanent.

Seeing demons in tiny cages, curled up sleeping or slouched and staring dead-eyed at me, is unnerving. I know, rationally, that if I ran into them on the street, I'd be terrified. But here, like this, they're not the drawings and dire warnings I've studied. They're . . . *beings*. None of them react to us. None of them make a sound. Either they're drugged or they're used to visitors. Or they've been caged so long, they don't care about anything anymore.

There's a demon with only the thinnest layer of skin. I can

see its muscles, veins, tendons, all showing through the translu-cent outer layer. I tug on Leo's arm. "Is that—"

"An unpellis demon."

"The one that jumps out of its skin! No way!"

"I've heard the skin can be used to seal wounds and heal scars."

"Eew." I can't imagine wanting to use a demon's discarded skin as my own. But also . . . if it's in a cage, and it looks like it's recently been de-skinned . . . how often has that happened?

The demon blinks at me, and it looks less horrifying and more unimaginably weary. Its eyes are set far back on either side of its head, like a rabbit's. Which, according to biology, hints that this isn't a predatory species. Unlike humans. I want to set it free. Which surprises me, because I'd almost gotten used to my instincts to punch first, ask questions later. Either my Slayerness is broken or this demon is so pathetic even a Chosen One can't feel like it deserves any more pain.

Leo moves on, but I pause again in front of a pale demon, humanoid in form but with no mouth. It stares at me with mournful eyes. Across the aisle is an identical demon. It lifts its hand, reaching out to me. It needs my help. I lift my own hand, and—

"Wouldn't touch them," says a cheerful voice that I last heard announcing odds on my death. "Unless you fancy telepathy so powerful you'll go mad within two days. Good in small doses, though, innit? Provided you also purchase the antidote." The man—Sean, I assume—is in another sleek, expensive-looking suit, his hair pulled back into a ponytail.

He waggles a radio at us. "Security's on hold, but I'd rather not call them. I suppose you two are the source of my cleanup on aisle four?"

"Surprise?" I'm glad he isn't armed.

"Not really. I've been expecting you after your performance the other night. Is Cosmina here too?"

"Nooo." I draw the word out, watching him. There's no indication he knows she's dead, but that doesn't mean he wasn't behind it. He could have a great poker face beneath his excellent exfoliation and artful stubble. Leo, master of his own poker face, is silent and still. But I know he's ready to spring into action the second Sean does anything threatening. Leo neither provokes reactions nor reveals anything. Ever. No wonder he stayed alive so long. He has a way of blending into the background until he needs to act. Gods, he's an amazing Watcher.

"Come into my office," Sean says. "You could have asked for me, you know. You wasted a lot of coffee."

I feel sheepish now that he's being so reasonable. "Can you sort it and, uh, wash it? Put it back?"

He laughs. "I'll refill the bins with the same cheap, manky coffee beans they held before. It's all the same, innit? These stooks'll buy anything if you put a fancy label on it. Especially if the label says 'Organic.' Technically everything is organic."

"Charming business ethics," Leo mutters.

Sean leads us to a portion of the giant cellar in the opposite direction Artemis had run. Unlike the rest of the stone-and-brick space, his office is boxed in and finished. It's brightly lit, all clean modern lines, with a fish tank that takes up an entire wall.

"No way!" I lean close to the tank. What some might take for an eel turns in a lazy circle to reveal a human eye watching us all with disturbing awareness. "That's a remora demon, isn't it?"

"You know your stuff." Sean sits at his desk, leaning back.

I point to it, looking at Leo, more excited than I should be. "In the open air, they grow to fit whatever container they're in. Water pressure keeps them from expanding in aquariums, though. Otherwise they just keep going. And they eat lead and turn it into gold! It was actually a Watcher way back in the Middle Ages who used one to turn lead into gold to fund our whole operation. It started all the rumors that caused alchemists to try and re-create turning lead into gold. But they never could, because hello, demon. They're super rare!"

"And picky eaters." Sean frowns. "I'm lucky to get a nugget a month from the damn thing. Hasn't even paid itself off yet. Now. To the point. What do you want? I'd apologize for the other night, but to be fair, you were the one who jumped in the pit. And you killed all my best hellhounds *and* several of my highest betters. So you really ought to apologize to me."

"I didn't kill anything except the hellhounds and the zompires!" I say defensively. "Serves you right, throwing a Slayer in the pit!"

"She was in on it."

"She was not!"

"Okay, maybe not *in* on it. She's done jobs for me, here and there. But she got rid of a zompire nest I had quarantined and marked for the fights, and then she ran afoul of one of my vampire allies. She knows how things go—she cost me money, so I used her to make more. If she has a problem with it, she can come talk to me herself. I would have cut her in on the profits if she had won fairly. She's even fought willingly a few times before."

She participated? Willingly? Then why did I have the dream about her in trouble? Maybe because that was her first unwilling event. Or maybe because I was supposed to bring her back with us. To save her from what was coming after the fights. I slump in one of the chairs facing Sean. It's a beautiful chair, all clean lines and utterly rigid bottomly discomfort. No matter how I shift, I'm sure my entire butt will be asleep within seconds. "I'm actually not here about Cosmina. I'm here about Doug."

Sean sits up straight, intense greed lighting his face. "You know where Doug is?"

"I did. He, uh, got away."

"Dammit. I sent two of my best-trained hellhounds after him."

"Those were yours? They attacked my friends and me!"

Sean holds out his hands in an *oops* sort of gesture. "Hazard of the trade. I make certain they're well fed before they go out, but some of their instincts can't be avoided. They were only trained not to rip apart their actual target. If something else gets in the way, well. It can end poorly. If it makes you feel any better, they're an endangered species now."

"Good riddance." I might have some weird compassion for the caged demons and for Doug, but not hellhounds. "Your hellhounds aside, we've got two dead bodies we need to figure out. And the last one led us here."

Sean looks genuinely surprised, peering past me. "You have a zombie? How much do you want for it?"

I've *got* to start being more specific. "No, I mean, clues at the scene led us here. And you're connected to everything that's happened. You and Doug."

"Could Doug have killed anyone?" Leo asks.

Sean scratches at his artful stubble, frowning at Leo. I half suspect Sean forgot he was here. "Nah. He only eats happiness."

"Maybe your hospitality pushed him too far." Leo cocks an eyebrow. He didn't sit and is standing ready and alert in the center of the room.

"Wouldn't be unprecedented, but it's unlikely. Doug is just . . . Doug. I can't see him killing anyone, and I've known him for years."

I have the sudden urge to raise my fists in triumph. Score one for the Slayer instincts.

"My guess is it was another demon entirely. Tell me where you're located and I'll pop up and take care of the problem," Sean continues.

I glare at him. "And profit from it."

"Naturally." He smiles. "Who are your dead people? Any connection to Doug?"

"One of our Wa—one of my relatives."

"A Watcher, huh?" Sean grins at my cringing reaction. "You mentioned them earlier too. Best be careful with those secrets, love. Wouldn't want the wrong type to know that there's still a group of Watchers, alive and well. Wasn't just followers of the First who had it out for you. But I'm safe as churches with that secret. How did this bloke die?"

"In his sleep. No marks. The other death was similar."

"Another Watcher?"

"No. Cosmina." I watch for his reaction.

He leans back again, letting out a long exhaled curse. "That's disappointing, innit? I don't have any other Slayers. There's good money there. Used to be *fantastic* money, but then the market got flooded with them. Still, people will pay a lot for a Slayer."

"You'd *sell* a Slayer?" I'm ready to punch things now. I actually believe that he didn't know she's dead. His disappointment is too callous to be faked. No one could pretend to be this awful.

"Not sell, *employ*. Like with Cosmina. I do all sorts of things in this brave new world, and Slayers are useful. And okay, I might also sell if the conditions were right. What can I say, I'm a businessman."

"Tell us about it," Leo says dryly.

Sean takes his request at face value. Most of his accent fades, as though he's giving a practiced pitch. "The black market for demon products has always existed. I dabbled. It was tough work. Most of my competitors depended on magic. They went under when magic died, may it rest in peace." He solemnly traces a pentagram onto his chest, then grins. "But I was always old-fashioned. I preferred hunting down my demons to summoning them, preferred relying on human means to trap the supernatural. My competitors are out of business. Meanwhile, all these demons with no hell dimensions to slip back to are wandering around, trapped on earth. Alone and vulnerable. My empire is booming. I even have a new investor."

"Are you the one killing demons, then?" I ask. When he frowns in confusion, I add, "We heard from a vampire that demons are turning up dead in the area."

"I'll look into it. No money for me in dead demons. Well, except the ones with good skin or valuable bones. But I'm not killing demons left and right. Bad for business, innit? You have to think long-term. Keeping them alive means you can generate continual income."

I know my entire family exists because of the need to fight demons, but Sean is . . . gross. There's a difference between protecting people from demons and profiting off them. "Income like you generated with Doug?"

"Like Doug! Exactly. I built everything on him. Started on the streets, dealing my own brand of happy pills. Worked my way up from there. And now? Sky's the limit. I have to avoid any governmental attention, but my newest investor has connections. I'm talking with pharmaceutical companies. Think about it. There are seven species of self-healing demons in this basement alone. If we can isolate that, do genetic research on them, imagine what we could do. We could cure cancer. We could reverse aging. I'm turning profits, sure. But I'm also doing good! That night in the pit—those zompires were ready to infect this whole city. Now they're gone. Everything is for the benefit of humanity, innit."

"Wasn't much humanity for the werewolves, or any humanity out there in those cages."

Sean waves his hand dismissively. "Half those demons would kill you the instant they got out."

"And the other half?"

"You don't understand."

I do. I really do. A demon forced my father to kill himself. Another killed Cosmina and probably killed Bradford Smythe.

And Sean's right too. Demons are a threat. Am I such a broken Slayer that I can't kill demons *and* I can't stand to see them caged? How can I reconcile my natural instincts to take care of things, to heal things, with what my calling actually is? Maybe Honora's right, and I was only ever compensating for the things I couldn't do. Am I still doing that, pretending like I care about living creatures when really I'm just a sucky Slayer and I don't want to admit it to myself?

I hope not. But with so many lives at stake, I can't afford to be wrong.

Leo has drifted over to the aquarium. He turns from the remora demon. "How did you get involved with demons in the first place?"

Sean undoes a flask, taking a drink. He holds it out to me. I recoil, and he shrugs, putting it back. "Same reason I do anything. Pretty girl. And there she is."

The girl in the leather walks into the office. I turn around and we both freeze, stunned.

"Honora?" I ask.

"Wheezy." She pulls out a gun and points it at my head.

25

"WHY DO YOU HAVE A GUN?" I SHOULD
have known Honora would be here. Of *course* she's here. She's
working hand in hand with Sean. I can't believe she'd tell
someone like him about the Watchers. After everyone we've
lost.

Honora rolls her eyes. "I have a gun, idiot, because I'm not
going to carry around a miniature crossbow. We don't all pretend like being a Watcher still means anything. This is *my* city. I
don't have to play by any rules at all." She lowers the gun slightly,
shaking her head meaningfully at Leo, who had started moving
to get around her. "You should try it sometime, Leo."

Sean clears his throat. "Honora, love, you realize that I'm
directly behind her, so there's a high likelihood that you'll shoot
me as well?"

"This bitch is the reason we lost Doug."

"Don't you dare call my sister a bitch." Artemis appears
in the doorway behind Honora, her face a mask of fury. She's
here! And she finally knows I'm right. She kicks Honora's hand,

knocking the gun free. It clatters menacingly to the floor. "You *lied* to me. You used me to find that demon. He didn't really kill anyone, did he?"

"There are two of them?" Sean looks both alarmed and bemused as he stares at Artemis and then me.

"I don't want to fight you, Artemis. I like you." Honora holds her arms out to display her innocence. I stand, ready. Leo is perfectly still, waiting to see if he needs to pounce. Honora ignores both of us, focusing on Artemis. "Listen to what we have to say. I think you'll understand."

Then, to my shock, she throws a punch. Artemis ducks it. Honora laughs. They spin in a flurry of kicks and blocks, punches and dodges.

Honora is holding back, though. I can tell. She used so much more force on me this morning. If she were really fighting, Artemis wouldn't be conscious. I think Artemis knows it too. She dodges another punch and—smiles? She's smiling? Gods, they're *flirting*. Honora was pointing a gun at me not two minutes ago! I look at Leo, aghast. He shrugs.

Catching herself smiling, Artemis scowls, kicking at Honora's side. "How could you work for him?"

"Please." Honora dodges the kick, then spins around behind Artemis, pinning her arm to her back. She rests her cheek against Artemis's neck. "They don't deserve you. They have you serving them *meals*, Artemis. Look at you. You're a goddess."

"And you're working with a drug dealer!" Artemis spins away, chest heaving, fists up.

Leo clears his throat. He has a slender but heavy-looking metal rod in his hand. It must have been up his sleeve. I feel a surge of triumphant glee. Honora thought he was unarmed. I doubt Leo's ever unarmed. "Let's all calm down, or I'll shatter this glass and release the remora demon."

Sean stands in alarm. "Are you touched? Without water pressure, they grow to the size of their container! It'll fill the office and kill us all!"

Leo smiles. It's weirdly adorable, given the situation. I catch a flutter in my stomach and squash it. He gestures with the rod. "We've got two Watchers and a Slayer on our team. I like my odds. Do you like yours?"

"Honora!" Sean snaps. "Please!"

Honora steps back from Artemis. "Sean, remember how I told you about the woman who hated my mum, so she made sure I got sent away on assignment to the crappiest places imaginable? Meet her daughters."

"I thought you wanted to leave," Artemis says. "You could have come back." She looks more upset by this than she did by the fight with Honora. But they were never really fighting. They might as well have been dancing for all either of them intended any damage.

"I did want to leave! You should too."

Sean clears his throat. "Are you sure you wouldn't rather work this out somewhere else?"

Honora has a knife in her hand now. She picks at her fingernails with it. "It's okay, really. I got assigned deep cover in a demon-worshipping cult, and then acolytes of the First Evil blew up the Council. So your mum hating mine actually saved my life."

"Honora, I——" Artemis starts, staring down at the floor.

In a flash, Honora darts to me and holds the knife under my chin, spinning so that I'm between her and my companions. "Go on," she says to Leo. "Try to free the remora. Artemis won't let you. She won't let anything happen to endanger poor little Nina. Nina's the reason Artemis stayed with the Watchers, played their servant when she deserves so much more. 'Nina needs me,'" Honora says in a perfect imitation of my sister. "And now you're a Slayer?" Her knifepoint digs into my chin. "Tell me how it makes any sense that you're a Slayer and Artemis isn't. What kind of fate would choose you over her?" She pauses, and her next words are so soft I wonder if she meant them to be out loud. "I wouldn't."

Her words cut better than her knife could. Artemis won't meet my eyes, confirming what Honora says. I did hold her back. And it's obvious even Artemis feels like, of the two of us, she should have been the Chosen One.

But she's not. I am.

I grab Honora's hand and twist until she drops the knife.

Honora's eyes go wide with fear and pain. I remember all the taunts, the nickname, the way she humiliated me. I twist harder.

"You're hurting me," she whimpers.

I don't buy it. I maintain pressure but don't increase. She rolls her eyes, annoyed, and swings her free fist at my face. I lean back, dodging the blow, then push. She flies across the office and slams into a wall, sliding down in a heap to the floor. Fortunately, it was *away* from the remora tank, not into it.

"She—" She laughs, gasping in pain. "She broke my ribs." She pulls something out of her jacket and swallows it. Her eyes close, and she takes a deep breath. Then she stands, shaking out her arms as if she's totally fine. "Let's go again, Slayer."

What the hell kind of drug is she taking?

Artemis steps between us. "Please, Honora." Her voice is quiet. Pleading. Intimate.

Honora tears her eyes away from mine. She looks at my sister, and something softens. "I wouldn't have hurt her. Not really." Then she shrugs, walking to the open chair and sitting in it. She puts her boots up on Sean's desk. "You're still letting her control your life."

"Well, this has all been very interesting." Sean pokes at Honora's boots. She doesn't move them off. "On the bright side, our search for a replacement Slayer is over before it started, innit. I have a lot of work for you if you're interested."

Leo has Honora's knife, picked up during the distraction. The gun is gone too. He got both weapons when we were all looking elsewhere. "Does he know anything that will help us? Because I don't like the things he knows now."

Sean holds up his hands all defenselessly. His smile slides into place like the remora demon slides through the water. "We're on the same side. You want to protect people from demons. I keep demons where they won't hurt anyone. Our jobs are six of one, half a dozen of the other."

"We are *not* the same," I snap.

"You came to me, remember? You *want* me as an ally. We all want Doug caught."

I shake my head. "You want Doug caught. I just want him to get into a Coldplay concert."

Sean smooths his suit. "Well, we can agree that we all want whatever it was that killed Cosmina stopped. Caught. Killed, if necessary. Besides, I know more about this new world of hell-less demons than anyone else. I can give you access to things the Watchers never will. Information. Powers."

Artemis draws an involuntary gasp. Honora tips her head back, giving my sister an upside-down wink. "We can hook you up," she sings.

Sean's smile gets slicker, sharper. "That's right. There might not be magic in the world, but I've got the best of what's left. You missed my big pitch, Artemis. You'd be amazed what I can do with a dash of demon and a pinch of medical science. We can change the world."

A demon outside the office moans in pain, the sound haunting and lonely. "I don't really like your style," I say. Sean looks hurt, his fingers drifting to his ponytail. I roll my eyes. "Not really a fan of that, either, but I meant this whole demon-captivity thing you've got going on."

"You kill them. How is what I do worse?"

"I don't know. It just is." I rub my face, remembering Cosmina. Remembering how brutal she was, how determined to work alone. And how alone she was at the end. We're supposed to kill demons. She was good at it. And now she's dead.

How has Buffy survived this long?

Sean stands. "All I want is Doug back. We'll do a trade. You bring me my happy demon, I'll figure out who killed Cosmina and your Watcher fellow. We'll all come out ahead." He sweeps his arm toward the door. "Forgive me if I don't escort you out. And please, next time you drop by, call. No destruction necessary."

"You know where to find me," Honora says. I bristle, thinking it's a threat. But she's not looking at me. She's looking at Artemis, and there's no threat in her eyes.

There's only promise.

Sean's true to his word. No one stops us as we leave. I try not to look at the pathetic demons as we pass them, but they're seared onto my brain.

Back in the car, Leo guides us smoothly to the road that will take us to Shancoom. "So," I say, because no one else is, "I was right."

"Can you not," Artemis says.

"Why not?"

"Just let me think!"

"Think out loud. Honora has new employment. No wonder Sean has done so well! He has a Watcher on his side. How could she take the generations of knowledge and training she's been entrusted with and use them to help someone like him?"

"Nina," Artemis snaps.

"Too many bodies led us to Sean and whatever he's running here. We have to tell the Council about Honora."

"Why?" Artemis asks.

"Umm, because she's working with the demon underworld? And she's also got some kind of superstrength that's not normal."

"Look, I get it, she's doing some messed-up stuff. You were right. Fine. But you had no problem keeping secrets before. I want to give her a chance to explain herself."

I twist in the passenger seat so I'm facing her. "Did you miss the part where she could have done that, but instead she held a knife under my chin?"

"Everyone was being confrontational!" Artemis pauses, taking a deep breath. "She shouldn't have done that. I know. I really do, Nina. Honora can be impulsive and defensive. You don't know what she went through growing up. There's a reason she doesn't trust the Watchers. Why she would choose to work for someone else."

"Even after everything you saw tonight—everything Honora did and has done—you're *still* taking her side?"

"I'm not taking her side! I'm trying to tell you why you need to stop judging her until you have all the information."

"Then by all means, give it to me!"

Leo pulls into a petrol station. "I'm, uh, going to fill up." He gets out and closes his door.

Artemis stares out the window. "She used to show up to training with her wrists covered in welts. When she didn't perform as well as her mother thought she should, she'd be whipped. Did you know that?"

"I—no."

"No, you didn't. You have no idea what Honora went through. What her mother was like. So if Honora wants to use what she learned to try and have some sort of life, I guess I don't blame her. She deserves some happiness."

"Does she? Does having a mean mom justify what she's doing? She betrayed the Watchers by—"

"They betrayed her by not taking care of her when her mother so obviously wasn't! God, you talk like they're holy. You're the one who's always questioning the Watchers' traditions, telling me over and over that we can do better. But when it comes down to it, you're totally fine with the Watchers staying the way we are. We find a friend in trouble, and you want to turn it right over to them. Let them discuss her. Censure her. Maybe even lock her up. Did you know that's what the bottom floor of the castle is? It's not ruins. It's *cells*."

I take the information like a blow to the stomach. They told me the bottom floor was off-limits because it wasn't safe. Not because it was a prison. "I—I didn't know."

"No, because you've never seen it. You never have to see anything you don't want to. You don't see that the Watchers have become completely *useless*—a sad, broken society desperately trying to hang on to the glory days that will never come again."

"If you felt this way, why didn't you talk to me? I thought you liked being part of it. You were so good at it."

Artemis finally sits back, letting out a long breath. "How could I tell you I wasn't happy, when I had what you wanted? I knew you'd trade places with me in a heartbeat. You worship the Watchers."

"I don't worship them."

"You do."

"It's important to me. There's a difference. It's our family heritage. In his diary, Dad was—"

"Dad's dead. That's our legacy. Dad's dead, and Mom lied to both of us our whole lives. About everything." She brings her hands to her face and covers her eyes. "I felt so bad that she chose me first in the fire. I wanted you to know that someone would always choose you first, always protect you. I wanted to be a damn Watcher so I could make the whole world safer for you. All these years, Mom could have mentioned that you'd be a Slayer one day and I'd be absolutely pointless." Her shoulders shake, and I don't know whether she's crying or laughing bitterly.

Would she really have left if it wasn't for me? Does she want to now?

"I'll always need you," I whisper. "You're my sister."

"It's not the same, though. We can't pretend it ever will be again."

She's right. As much as I don't want her to be, she is. Everything is different. "I won't say anything about Honora," I offer as a bridge over the chasm between us. "You can decide what to do about that."

"Thank you," she whispers, but she doesn't look at me.

Leo gets back in, silent with his own internal strife. He starts the car, and we're sealed in the hum of the engine and the road beneath the tires. No one talks.

I remember the split between the two girls in Cosmina's photo. Slayers are supposed to be alone, Cosmina had said at the pit. Was that my destiny too?

26

LEO SLAMS THE CAR INTO PARK AS WE stop in the castle garage.

Something else has been bugging me, and I have to get it out. "Leo, we need to talk about the possibility that my mom was setting you up."

"What?" Leo and Artemis exclaim at the same time.

I've had the whole miserable car ride to think about it. My mom with an out-of-the-blue demand that Leo—and Leo alone—go see a Slayer. When she's never made any effort to bring a Slayer in. And no matter what that vampire said, she showed up right after we got there. When Leo was supposed to be there by himself. We can't know that it wasn't a setup.

"I don't want it to be true," I say. "But think about it." I lay out my reasoning.

"That's barely coincidence." Artemis opens her door.

"Hear me out! There's something else." She pauses, and I cringe, realizing it's yet another secret I kept from her. "There was another hellhound. It found me in Shancoom when I was checking on Cillian. I lured it here. Mom killed it. But she didn't put the castle on lockdown or even tell anyone. Which means she must have been expecting it in some way or was at least confident that it wasn't after us. So she had to have known it was after something else. And Doug said he had a contact he was supposed to meet. A Smythe."

"You think Mom is setting up meetings with demons." I can't tell from Artemis's voice how she feels about my theory.

"I don't know. Maybe?"

"But why would she want me dead?" Leo asks.

"Maybe she figured out you were training me? She really doesn't want me to be a Slayer."

"Bad enough to try to kill Leo?" Artemis sounds dubious. I don't blame her. It's extreme.

But . . . is it? "She hid me. She never told us about my Potential status. Or about her mom. And . . . she left me. The day of the fire."

"You can't honestly think Mom wanted you to die!"

The silence fills the car until it's palpable. I don't think that. Not really. But I know she wanted Artemis alive more than she wanted me alive.

"All I know," I finally say, "is that Bradford Smythe revealed my Potential status, confirming I'm a Slayer. And now he's dead. Cosmina knew I was a Slayer, and now she's dead. And Leo's been training me, and he could have been killed tonight."

Leo looks mildly offended. "By *one* vampire?"

"Regardless, our mom has a lot of secrets. And I don't think we can trust her. With anything."

"I don't buy it," Artemis says.

"Well, my other theory is it was all Honora. You wanna discuss that one?"

She folds her arms, answering with her silence.

"We should keep all this between the three of us," Leo says. "Even if we aren't certain who we can trust, we know we can trust each other."

I look at Artemis. She doesn't meet my gaze.

Leo continues. "No mention of anything to your mom. Or to mine."

"But—" I start. He looks over at me, his brow furrowed. I trust his mom. And I need her advice. I wanted to ask her about my mom and about my conflicted demon feelings and even about that dumb prophecy and whether I should worry about it. She'll be able to tell me if it's something the Watchers are concerned about.

"No," Leo says. "They're both on the Council. They talk. We don't tell them about Cosmina or Honora or Sean. Not until we know more."

"What do we know, even?" Artemis asks. "Really. What have we learned?"

I lean against the dashboard. "That it's not Doug."

"Which narrows it down to one of the other thousands of demons roaming the earth."

Leo's eyes are cold and dark. "All we know is that the attacks have happened while they were sleeping."

Artemis undoes her severe ponytail, shaking out her hair. "Assuming Bradford didn't die of a heart attack. He was old."

"If Slayer dreams warned me about people dying of old age, I'd have to break into every retirement community in the area trying to save them. It was demonic."

Artemis lets out a long breath, but she nods. She's mad at me, but she's not unreasonable.

Leo opens his door. "We can't be sure of anything. Which means the castle isn't safe. Neither of you should sleep alone tonight." Then he's out of the car and striding toward the castle. I want it to be lit up like a beacon against the darkness, but the few lights in the windows only serve to emphasize how empty it is.

Was it only a few years ago that it was bursting with life? Bustling with Council members and aspiring Watchers and all the people behind the scenes who made our work possible?

But—it wouldn't have been. Not really. Because even before the Council was blown up, there weren't that many of us in my generation. We've been slowly bleeding out. Buffy's rejection sent the organization spiraling, scrambling for a new place in the world.

I'd have thought that a sudden influx of Slayers would have made Watchers relevant again, but I can't help feeling like all it did was make us even more archaic. Even more useless. Maybe Artemis was right.

Ugh. But that would mean Honora was right too.

I shudder, trying to get the bad taste of even *thinking* that Honora's right off my brain and tongue. The Watchers hid in order to survive. I have to trust that the Council has a plan.

The Council, though . . . Ruth Zabuto, who can't get over the loss of magic. Wanda Wyndam-Pryce, who is even worse than I had always thought. My mother, who hates Slayers and is definitely hiding more than we ever realized. And Eve Silvera. One for four I trust, then.

"I'm sleeping in Jade's room," Artemis says.

"Why?" I ask, hurt.

"It's not—I need some time to think. That's all. You should spend the night in Rhys's or with Imogen." She walks away. She's taking Leo's warning seriously. And leaving me on my own. All these years of being together, of taking care of each other. Well. Of her taking care of me. I clearly haven't done a very good job of taking care of her. How much has she shouldered all this time? I couldn't train with her, but I could have helped more. Taken more of the duties. But she never told me, never talked to me about how she was feeling.

Angry and hurt and confused, not to mention buzzing with excess I-want-to-beat-up-Honora energy, I turn and run into the forest. It's asleep, all the insect hum and normal forest sounds muted and hushed so I feel like an intruder.

I push myself, trying to find my limits. I want to know the borders of my body, the edges of my powers. I need to. Because if I can define them, then I can understand them, and I can figure out who I'm supposed to be now.

I dodge branches, jump over logs, twist and turn through the depths of the trees. The castle is in a section of forest miles wide, untouched for centuries because the ground isn't good for planting. It's wild in a way that makes me feel small. For two years we'd been perfectly hidden here. I can't escape the idea that the thing that is different—that drew hellhounds and demons and chaos and death to our seclusion—is *me*. Because nothing else has changed in the two years we've been here.

As a Slayer, death is my gift. Is it also my curse? By being built for it, do I attract it?

I veer toward an old, abandoned cemetery. No one has been

buried there for almost a century. I found it not long after we arrived here. It's been my little secret ever since. There's something peaceful about it, the names and dates faded with time and the elements. I guess, in a way, it's like Artemis's secret passages. Made for something else, but serving as a refuge for me.

I'm lost in my thoughts until I'm close enough to see there's a light. There should not be a light. I skid to a halt, then tiptoe closer. There's a cheery fire in a pit. Sitting by the fire is Doug the demon. He's bobbing his head in time to music playing from headphones, and there's a book in his hands. I peer at it.

Nicholas Sparks. Doug really *might* be evil, then.

A twig snapping nearby warns me that someone else is approaching. I duck behind a tree, watching. Not knowing who I expect to show up. Honora? Sean? Another demon? Don't they know this is my cemetery?

Nothing prepares me for the shock of who puts a hand on Doug's shoulder before sitting across from him.

My mother.

It's confirmed, then. Smythe, not as in Bradford Smythe. As in Jamison-Smythe. She *is* Doug's contact. She's the reason he ran here, the reason hellhounds attacked, the reason Honora came back into our lives to screw everything up.

Doug takes off his headphones. "Hey, Helen. Thanks for the stuff." He gestures to a sleeping bag set up among the gravestones, his book, and an empty tote sack. The tote she had been carrying earlier in the hall.

"How's your face?" my mother asks.

"Better. A lot better. Nina's not half bad at fixing things."

I tamp down my pride at his words. My mother has the small

book that she took Cosmina's address out of. Doug sets down his novel and leans close to her, looking over a page. He points to part of it. "He's a good bloke. Messy. But should make a good ally. This is like a who's who of the demons of Dublin. You found them all."

"I'm good at my job."

"What about Slayers? They could be a problem."

"I know of at least a dozen we can get easy access to." She points to another section of the book. "I can handle them."

"What about Nina?" Doug asks. I freeze. "She's not being exactly low profile. Far as I could figure, she's told Cillian everything. Who else does she talk to?"

My mother shakes her head, her mouth a thin, sharp line. "I should have sent her away years ago, but I always hoped it wouldn't come to this. I've worked for so long to avoid this mess. It was selfish of me to keep her."

"Prophecies are tricky things."

"So are daughters. But I'll take care of it."

I back up, horrified. My mother has a book full of demons and Slayers. She's consulting with a demon on them. She has a plan for "handling" the Slayers, and one for taking care of me, whatever that means.

Doug mentioned a prophecy. I don't have to wonder which one he was talking about. It has to be the same one I translated, the same one referenced in my father's diary.

The prophecy *is* about me. About us.

My mother knows—and Doug the neon-yellow demon knows. I turn and run for the castle. Maybe her leaving me behind in the fire was about more than me being a Slayer. Maybe the prophecy is so bad, she risked my life to save Artemis. She would have known, as soon as I was identified as a Potential, that *I'm* the world breaker. I have demonic power in me, after all. And in spite of all her efforts, she couldn't keep it from coming out.

I finally get why my mother has pushed me to the side all my life. She doesn't just hate the Slayer in me. She's *afraid* of me.

My eyes burning and streaming with tears, I rush through the castle, straight to our room to get the prophecy and bring it to Artemis. We're two parts of one person, two parts of one foretold doom, and I can't do this alone.

I almost trip over the body in the hall outside my door.

"It's me!" Leo says, sitting up. I cover my mouth to muffle the scream that almost escaped. "What is it? What's wrong?"

I take in a shaky breath. I don't know where to begin, and I'm afraid that once I do, I'll lose my grip completely. "I'm okay," I lie. "Just tired. But what are you doing on the floor outside my room? I thought you were a dead body. And I am all dead-bodied out for the night. I don't have another dead-body opening in my schedule for at least a week."

It's dim, the only light a bulb at the other end of the hall. But I can *feel* Leo smiling. I can hear it in his voice.

"I'll do my best to clear your schedule of dead bodies, then. I'm sorry. I thought you were inside, asleep."

"Weirdo." I reach past him to open the door. But I'm secretly touched that Leo was worried enough to come guard me.

"Where's Artemis?" He peers inside as I flip the light on.

"Sleeping in Jade's room tonight. She's still pissed at me."

Leo hovers in the doorway. Seeing his hands jammed into his loose sweatpants pockets and his mouth twisted to the side is kind of adorable. He's embarrassed and feeling awkward. I'm so fricking glad it's not me for once that I'm instantly at ease and no longer feeling so desperate to get to Artemis right away. She didn't want to talk about the prophecy before. I don't know if that has changed. And I can't handle another rejection if she refuses.

Doug's camping and still being hunted. He's not going anywhere. Neither is my mom. I'll figure this out on my own. "Oh, come in," I say. "It's silly for you to be out on the floor. Besides, I'm a Slayer, remember? I don't need a bodyguard."

"And I'm your Watcher. It's my job to protect you."

"It's your job to train and guide me. The protecting is my job."

"Agree to disagree." Leo finally steps into my room. His eyes take it all in, and I look at it as though for the first time. Artemis's side of the room is tidy, weights stacked neatly next to demonic texts she's been studying. A row of weapons hangs from a shelf above her bed.

My side of the room . . . less tidy. I have a bookshelf double-stacked and crammed with everything imaginable. CPR instruction manuals, anatomy books, first-year medical student texts I begged Cillian to buy me off eBay, my Redheads of Literature shelf. There's the stack of the demon books I was looking through to find information on Doug. And there's a huge pile of notebooks.

Ah, there's the awkwardness I had been missing! I'm sure that Leo is eyeing the notebooks. Or am I just paranoid? "They're notes. Not poetry! Anatomy. Health stuff. I watch a lot of medical tutorials and write down what I think will be useful. I also keep logs of stuff. So mostly it's records of the Littles having a fever or a stomach bug. But Imogen takes good care of them, so even that's not a lot."

Leo nods. Then he looks up at the ceiling and his eyes widen. "Are those fan blades actual blades?"

I rub the back of my neck. He's perceptive. "Oh. Right. Um. You know we lost our dad, and then there was the fire. After all that, I started having bad nightmares and was scared to go to sleep at night. So Artemis and I decided to set booby traps. Squirt guns with holy water hidden everywhere. Stakes. Actually, in the kitchen, every wooden stirring spoon still has a sharpened end. Anyway, as we got older, they got more elaborate. The fan was our project when we moved here and both needed a distraction from what happened with the Council going boom and all." I go to the spot right under the fan. "See here? This board is loose. On a fulcrum. There's a spring on the other side. The idea is you lure the vampire or whatever to this spot, then stomp on the board. Ta-da! Instant decapitation."

Leo is still staring up at the fan. "I was always afraid ceiling fans would come loose and kill me. How can you sleep under this thing?"

"We don't turn it on." I point to the fireplace. "We never use that, either. Not huge fans of fires. But there's a pressurized gas canister there." I point to what looks like a normal gas feed for the fire. "Jade helped us rig it up. If you flip this switch right inside the mantel, it's a flamethrower. But again, stationary. The vampire would have to be standing right here. We weren't really big on practicality. It was mostly to keep ourselves busy, to pretend like we had some control."

"You wanted to feel safe."

I sit on Artemis's bed, sad and exhausted. "Yeah. Artemis was always good at keeping me busy. *And* at making me feel safe." But she's not here. Maybe it's better that he's here. He's easier to talk to than Artemis lately. "So, I just saw my mother out in the woods with Doug."

"*What?* Did she catch him?"

"They were having a meeting. I went for a run, and there they were. My mom had her address book, which apparently also contains a who's who of demons in Dublin. And a lot of other Slayers. I don't know what they're planning, or why. But I think it has to do with me and a prophecy. So I'm freaking out. A little bit."

Leo nods, but he speaks slowly, like he's holding something back. "Nothing is ever black and white. Not prophecies, and certainly not people. We don't know what your mom is doing, but Doug didn't kill Cosmina or Bradford. If there is a prophecy, it's kept for this long. It'll keep for a few more days. So we keep our cards close to our chests. We don't talk to anyone else about this until we figure it out. In the meantime, you should get some sleep."

As soon as he says it, I realize how bone-deep tired I am. "You too." I feel his presence in my room acutely. It's not a huge room to begin with, but he takes up far more space in it than just his body can account for. "You can, uh, use my bed. If you don't want to sleep in the hall."

"I'd like to read, if that's okay?"

"Of course." I lie back on Artemis's bed. Leo pulls a book from my shelf—it's called *Joseph Lister and the Story of Antiseptics.* "That's good bedtime reading. Lister was the man who revolutionized surgery by introducing antiseptic procedures."

"There's a museum of surgery in Edinburgh that highlights

his achievements." Leo sits down with the book and opens it up. "We should go. Though it will break your no-dead-bodies rule."

"I'd break that rule for you." I turn away so he can't see my blush. I can't be as hopeless as I was three years ago. I peek over at him after a few minutes. He reads with his eyebrows drawn ever-so-slightly together, giving him a look of deep concern. I force my eyes closed. But there's no way I'm falling asleep with Leo right there.

I roll onto my side, hitting the notes I left all over Artemis's bed. Any thoughts of museum field trips fall away. I look at the prophecy with new eyes, no longer suspecting it might be about us—knowing it is, or at least that my parents thought so. And my mother still does.

Child of Slayer
Child of Watcher
My parents.
The two become one

Eew. Arcturius liked a good euphemism, and I can't believe I'm reading a sentence about my parents getting it on written centuries ago.

The one becomes two
Identical twins.
Girls of fire
Our hair *is* quite red.
Protector and Hunter
One to mend the world
And one to tear it asunder

A few weeks ago, I wouldn't have known which was which. But it's obvious now. Artemis is the protector. She always has been. She's protected me not only from harm but from her own sadness. It hurts to even think about it.

And the hunter? What else is a Slayer?

My stomach turns with fear and dread. I've seen too much evidence of prophecies coming true not to take it seriously. Not only am I a Slayer but there's a good chance I'm going to tear the world apart. Guess I have more in common with Buffy than ever.

Arcturius's last note is one final swift kick to the ribs.

When all else ends, when hope perishes alongside wonder,
her darkness shall rise and all shall be devoured.

Wonder is already dead. Buffy broke it. There's no time stamp on the prophecy, but the Seed of Wonder being broken means there's a ticking clock for the ending. For when Artemis is going to mend the world.

And I'm going to break it.

27

"PROPHECIES ARE HARD TO INTERPRET."
Leo makes me jump for the second time.

I gather the notes and slam them into a notebook. "It—it's not what it looks like," I stammer.

"Prophecies never are."

"No, I mean—I don't know what I mean. Gods, I don't know anything right now." I scoot so I'm sitting against the wall. Leo surprises me by doing the same, sitting right next to me. He's taller than me. Enough so that I could lean my head on his shoulder and it'd be the perfect fit.

"Let me help?"

I pick at Artemis's threadbare quilt. It takes on a different meaning, as does her half of the closet. Does she even like the color black? I never asked. I assumed she was happy with her life because it seemed so impressive. And because she never said otherwise. I was quick to speak up about what bugged me or what I felt I was missing. But how often did I ask Artemis what *she* wanted from her life?

I am a terrible sister.

I know how awful it was to be left behind. But it must have been excruciating for her to watch me disappear in the smoke. She should never have felt guilty over something she couldn't control. She should never have considered it her burden to help me, to be the best, to do everything right. To atone for being the one who was chosen.

I clear my throat. Leo's patiently waiting for me to talk to him. And I need someone to talk to. "So, you know I have my father's Watcher diary. And he mentioned a prophecy. Then I realized I had translated this one. And . . . it seems like it's about us. 'When hope perishes alongside wonder'—that's probably the Seed of Wonder. It's dead. Which means we're on that timeline."

Leo takes the prophecy translation, rereading. "Your mom isn't the only child of a Slayer. It's unusual, sure, because—" He cuts himself off. The reason hangs in the air between us. Because they don't live that long. He pushes forward, ignoring the unsaid. "Other Slayers have had children. Even around the same age as your mom. There's Robin Wood. His mother's Watcher was Crowley."

"I don't remember any Crowleys."

"My mom said he was nice."

So much past tense with Watchers. Someday soon everything having to do with the Watchers will be past tense. "But did this Robin have twins with a Watcher?"

"Not yet." Leo tries to sound hopeful, then shrugs. "Okay, and not likely to happen given our dramatic reduction in ranks. Still. This probably has nothing to do with you."

"My parents obviously thought it did."

Leo's voice is as dark as the night pressing eagerly outside my window. "Our parents always think they know more about us than we do. They make decisions for us before we even realize we're being controlled."

"But look at everything bad that's been happening. We've lived here for two years in perfect secrecy. No one found us. No violence. No attacks. Then we figure out I'm a Slayer and boom—Demons! Death! Destruction!"

"You could just as easily say all this happened because my mom and I came back."

I roll my eyes. "Sure. Except the first hellhound attack was before you got here."

He pauses, his lips tight. Then he moves on. "But the hellhound attack didn't come *after* you realized you were a Slayer. You realized you were a Slayer *because* the hellhound came. And you can't discount Honora. She's not connected to your mother, and she's involved in at least part of this. There could be totally different things going on. It doesn't all have to be connected."

I bonk my head back against the wall. "That doesn't make me feel better! It just means we'd have even more mysteries to solve. Gods, I thought my life was complicated when all I worried about was getting supplies for my medical center and trying to convince the Council we could focus less on combat training and more on mediation."

"Your life *was* complicated then too. This wasn't an easy way to grow up. So many secrets. Both those we keep as Watchers and those being Watchers forces us to keep."

I can't believe my mom thought she could send me to boarding school. All those normal teens, with no idea what the world is really like. Leo understands my life in a way none of them ever could. And he's right about how we grew up. I wasn't wrong when I was thirteen. He really did see me. He still does.

I want to take his hand, but nerves hold me back. "This could be why my mother is so opposed to me being a Slayer, though. She knows the prophecy. And she's worried that, now that I'm a Slayer, it's one step closer to coming true."

Leo shifts so he's looking right at me. His eyes are so dark they're almost black. I can tell he hasn't been sleeping well, but exhaustion accentuates his cheekbones, and the dark stubble at his jawline is oddly vulnerable.

"Athena," he says, "I know darkness. I know the hunger that drives chaos. And you have none of that in you. Slayer or not, you are and have always been good." He pauses, searching my face, and for one brief aching moment I think he's going to kiss me.

Then he smiles, and that mask he wears so well slides back into place. He disappears into it. He's retreating from me into what must have become a defense mechanism all that time he spent alone with his mother, believing his only friends were gone, afraid to care about anyone. So I'm shocked when he leans forward and brushes his cool, soft lips against my forehead.

"Get some sleep, Slayer. I'm your Watcher. I'll research, and I'll watch, and we'll figure it out in the morning." He slides off the bed and back onto the floor. He takes the stack of books I borrowed from Rhys, setting them down on top of the prophecy

book. I lie on my side, this time not turning my back to him. My
eyelids gradually lose the fight against sleep.

When I close them, I still see him.

I dream of the fire.

But this time I'm not alone. As I watch my mother carrying
Artemis out, walking straight through the fire, untouched, I feel
the presence of hundreds of other minds.

"Oh God," a voice says, "this is the third time I've been
dragged into this one. No one else dreams like you. So either
bring supplies for s'mores, or keep your trauma on lockdown."

I turn to see a gorgeous brunette with pouty lips, big brown
eyes, and a wry expression. She's sitting in the middle of the fire.
"Listen, kid, whatever happened, you're five by five now. Try to
let it go."

"But—" I start, choking and coughing on the smoke. I'm not
actually breathing in smoke, though. Not anymore.

The brunette winks at me. "Come on. I'm a pro at this. I
once spent a whole year sleeping. But there was only one other
Slayer to connect with back then. And I don't like peeking in
on B." She holds out her hand. I take it. She tugs, and—

I've never been to a party like this before. I don't think
there ever *has* been a party like this. The lights flash, the music
pounds, and all around me are girls dancing with ferocious
abandon.

"That's more like it!" The brunette winks at me again. "Live
a little. You're out of the frying pan *and* out of the fire. You're a
Slayer. Enjoy it!" She dances away into the crowd.

I'm left alone, but I'm not. I breathe in the energy around

me, the pulsing life of so many incredible, strong, *angry* girls. There's a fine line between a party and a riot, and we're stomping up and down it. I throw my head back, close my eyes, feel the beat down to my very soul, telling me to let go.

But I'm scared. I don't want to let go. What might happen if I do? Will I become a true Slayer? A hunter?

Will I break the world?

I draw back, and the room around me twists in a bright swirl of lights, disappearing.

I'm on the rooftop. Alone. Apparently this is where Slayers go when they're sad and pathetic. Buffy waits, sitting on the edge, looking out over the sleeping city. "I never wanted this!" I shout.

She turns so I see her profile. "Me neither."

"I'm going to break the world, and it's all your fault!"

She lifts an eyebrow. "How is that my fault?"

"If I wasn't a Slayer, I definitely couldn't break the world."

"Well, if you break the world, I'll stop you."

"I dare you to try!" I shake my head, confused by my own reaction. I don't *want* to break the world. I would hope someone could stop me if it came to that. Why am I thinking this? Feeling this? Rage funnels into me, a vortex of thousands of years of pain and anger and power, but there's nowhere else to push it. I'm the end. It pools in me, dammed. I close my eyes. I want to push her off. I want to—

A soft glow from a bedside clock shows 3:25. It casts muted green light onto a rumpled bed.

I don't have a clock with a green display.

That's not Artemis's bed. It's Cillian's. He turns his head from side to side, whimpering, as though trying to wake himself.

The darkness forms, taking shape on top of him.

I sit straight up, my heart racing. The clock on our nightstand—the numbers red, not green—reads 3:24.

"Cillian!" I fall out of Artemis's bed. Leo is gone. Cillian is in mortal danger. I don't doubt it's a demon now, so I don't trust myself to fight it off. I won't risk Cillian's life on my skills.

"Artemis!" I shout, hopping down the hall as I pull on my shoes and throw on her leather jacket. I bang on Jade's door. "Artemis, bring weapons!"

Artemis peers out, bleary-eyed.

"What's going on?" Rhys comes out of his room, two doors down from Jade's. He has a pillow mark on his cheek, and his glasses are askew.

"Cillian's in danger!"

Rhys doesn't hesitate. He runs back into his room and comes out with a sword, two stakes, and a knife. I take a stake and shove it in the waistband of my jeans. I know this thing isn't a vampire, but stakes feel right in my hands in a way other weapons don't.

"Let's go." He sprints down the hall. Artemis doesn't even put on shoes. She just runs.

"I'll get a car and follow," Jade says, for once tuned in to what's happening. I race for the castle exit.

"I can't wait for you two," I say, passing Artemis and Rhys.

"You don't have to." He points to the shed where we still keep a few four-wheelers. It's locked. I kick it. The door flies off the hinges, revealing hulking objects in the dark.

I run ahead. I can hear as the engines start and begin following me.

"What are we facing?" Artemis screams over the roar of the engines as she pushes her four-wheeler hard to keep pace with me.

"I don't know!" I dodge a branch and jump over a fallen tree. Artemis and Rhys have to stay on the trail; I run alongside it through the more difficult terrain. "I had a dream! The same one I had about Bradford Smythe."

Rhys guns his four-wheeler, going faster. I match pace. Please, I think, please *please* let this be the most embarrassing night ever. Please let this be another example of how I don't know how to be a Slayer, how my dreams are the result of my stressed-out mind falling asleep to thoughts of demonic conspiracies and doomsday prophecies. Please let Cillian be awake in bed watching Eurovision.

When we get to his house, the front door is ajar. That line of darkness cuts me like a knife.

"Cillian!" I shout. Rhys and Artemis jump off their four-wheelers, weapons brandished. I race up the stairs to Cillian's room. "Cillian!" I slam through his door, stumbling in the dark. He's on his bed. Alone.

And not breathing.

"No!" I rush to his side, feeling for a pulse. There isn't one. But his skin is still warm. I take a deep breath, reminding myself of everything I've learned. Everything I've trained for. I carefully move him to the floor. And then I start CPR.

"Nina?" Rhys whimpers.

"Movement!" Artemis shouts from downstairs. "Window!" There's a crashing noise.

I have a choice in that moment. The Slayer part of me is already tensed to sprint down the stairs. To give chase. To catch and kill this demon so that it can never hurt anyone again. And I know I can do it if I leave right now.

But Cillian would pay the price. And I can't leave him. Not if there's a chance I can still save him. Mustering my will, I push aside all my Slayer instincts, quiet the fierce rush in my blood, and put my lips on Cillian's. My lungs breathe for both of us. I hold back as much of my strength as I can to push gently on his ribs, reminding his heart—his wonderful heart—what it's supposed to do.

"Please," I whisper, forcing air into his lungs.

The silence in the room is deafening.

And then, *finally*, Cillian's breath answers. He coughs violently, putting a hand to his chest.

"What—*oh*, my ribs."

"Cillian!" I throw my arms around him, and he cries out in pain. "I'm so sorry!" I sit back, giving him space. "Your heart stopped. I had to do CPR."

Rhys kneels next to us, taking Cillian's hand in his own. "You were dead," he whispers.

"No wonder I'm racked. It's exhausting being dead." Cillian closes his eyes and squeezes Rhys's hand. "I really like being alive." He coughs again, then cringes. "I think my ribs are broken."

"That's common after CPR." I stare guiltily at the carpet. "It wasn't because I'm strong. I was careful."

A hand takes mine. Rhys pulls me in for a hug. He's trembling. "Thank you."

"I— Artemis!" I race down the stairs. The back window is

shattered. I go through the door, running out into the yard.

Artemis jumps back down from the fence, sword hanging at her side. "I lost it," she says.

"So there *was* a demon." I don't mean to be relieved—it's terrible news—but it means my instincts, again, were right.

"Yeah. And we might have caught it if I hadn't had to do it alone."

I wince at the harshness in her voice. "Cillian was *dead*, Artemis. He was dead. And if I hadn't hung back, he would have stayed that way."

She drops the sword at my feet. "It wasn't the right decision. Now that demon is out there, and obviously it knows about us. Knows about you."

"How can you even say that saving Cillian wasn't the right call?"

"Because you're not a Watcher. You're not a nurse or a medic. You're a *Slayer*. And if you don't figure out how to make hard choices, you'll fail just like I did. Only all my failure did was screw up my whole life. Your failure? Means a demon is now running free. Your failures mean people die."

I shake my head, confused and hurt. "What do you mean, just like you failed?"

Artemis folds her arms. "The Watcher test. The reason why I'm the castle errand girl instead of a full Watcher-in-training, like I should have been."

"You never told me about it."

"Because I didn't want you to know!" Artemis paces, prowling in a tight circle around the sword on the ground. "They put us under a spell. But it felt real. I was absolutely sure it was all

happening. And I had a choice. The choice was to save the world—
or to save you. And I chose you." She stops. Her shoulders, always
so straight, slump. "I chose you, because how could I not? I saw
your face when Mom took me instead of you. I could never bear to
see that again. And how could they make me a Watcher knowing
that, in the face of the hardest, most impossible choice, where only
one option is right, I'd choose the selfish one?"

I'm so touched that she chose me and so horrified that she
had to. And so angry that they put her through that, that choosing her family meant she lost the future she should have had.

I reach out to her. "Artemis, I—"

She shrugs my hand away and wipes under her eyes. I'm
glad it's dark. I've never seen her cry, and I know she wouldn't
want me to. "I can't protect you anymore. You don't need me to.
And after everything I did, everything I gave to the Watchers, I
haven't been good enough, ever. I'm not a Watcher, and I'm not
a Slayer. I'm too selfish."

"It wasn't selfish of you, Artemis. You love me. I love you.
I'd choose you too."

"Don't you get it? You can't! If you choose people you love over
everything else, more people will die. And you probably will too.
You have to be a better Slayer! You have to be the best one!"

"You didn't even want me to be a Slayer!"

Artemis shakes her head. "You can't give it up, though. And
I can't stop whatever's going to come for you. I'm not strong
enough. I chose you over the world and I'm terrified that I'm
still going to have to watch you die. Slayers *die*. Nina, I'm going
to lose you."

She leans against the fence, sobbing. I run to her and put my arms around her. "You're not. You're not going to lose me." All her anger, all her bossiness, her weird shifts between pretending I'm not a Slayer and demanding I be one. It's because she's been absolutely terrified this whole time. I don't know what to say.

"Promise me," she says, still shaking. "I don't care about the world. Just promise me that if it's between saving anyone else and saving *yourself*, you'll save yourself. Please."

"Artemis, I—"

"Promise me!" she shouts, no longer crying.

"I promise," I whisper.

She nods, wiping under her eyes. "Good. Okay. I'm going back to the castle to make sure everyone there is safe." She picks up her sword. Then she runs, jumps the fence, and disappears into the night.

Stunned, I wander back into the house. Rhys has moved Cillian down to the couch.

"How are you?" I ask.

"Sore. But alive." He smiles at me, his eyes low and heavy with sleepiness. There's a tightness around them that's new, though, and it breaks my heart.

"Do you want to talk about it?"

"I really don't." He never talks to me about the real things, the scary things. I hope he talks to Rhys about them. We all need someone to tell the real things to. Artemis was my person.

And no one was hers. Except maybe Honora.

"Any sign of the demon?" Rhys asks.

"No."

"Why would it go after Cillian, though? When there's a whole village here? Was it Doug?"

"No. I don't think so."

Cillian nods in agreement. "It didn't feel like him. His effect was far more pleasant. But I was never conscious for this, really. There was a dream I couldn't wake up from. Heavy weight on my chest. Also I'm pretty sure the demon was, umm, interested in getting up close and personal with me in a romantic sense."

"What?" Rhys and I both exclaim in unison.

"Nothing actually physical took place! There was just a . . . vibe to the whole thing. I would have told the demon that it was not my type, but I was frozen. Really not my idea of a good time."

I grimace. "I had forgotten that part of the first dream. Old Smythe seemed pretty into it."

"Forgot, or deliberately repressed?" Cillian asks.

"Definitely the second."

"Succubus," Rhys says, snapping.

"Seriously sucky," Cillian agrees.

"No, I mean 'succubus.' Attacks during sleep. Sucks out energy. Incubus-type demons too. It fits. I'll do some research." He looks at Cillian, worried. Research means going back to the castle.

"I'll do the research," I say. Rhys smiles in relief and gratitude. I turn back to Cillian. "So we know that you're a target. We need to figure out why." If it wasn't Doug, what other demon would have it out for Cillian? His only connection to the castle and Cosmina is——me. Oh gods. Did the demon go after Cillian because he's my friend? Or because he knows I'm a Slayer? Is this my fault?

Cillian shakes his head. "Maybe I'm just irresistible to everyone, human and demon alike."

"Regardless, we aren't leaving you alone. I'd say take him back to the castle, but the demon has already struck there."

Rhys sits on the armchair in the corner. He has a wickedly sharp dagger in his hands. "If this thing only attacks when people are sleeping, that makes me think it's not so strong." His smile is as menacing as the blade. Sometimes I forget that Rhys had to pass a *lot* of tests to get Watcher status—not all of them purely brain powered. "I'm not going anywhere. And the demon is welcome to try again."

Cillian's expression is sloppy with exhaustion but happier than I have maybe felt in my entire life. This is my fault. I'm the one who got Cillian involved, who brought him in on our secrets. And if my suspicion is correct, I'm the reason he was targeted.

"Okay." I kiss Cillian on the forehead. "You rest. You could not be in better hands." I walk out into the night.

Artemis is right. It's time to make the hard decisions. It's time to be a Slayer. But in order to do that, I need all the information. And some of that information won't be found in the library.

It's time to confront my mother.

28

I CHECK MY MOTHER'S ROOM FIRST. IT'S 4 a.m. I hoped that she would be here. That she'd be waiting, brimming with perfect explanations that would make everything okay.

Her room is empty.

I find Artemis in the gym. She's hitting a replacement punching bag with all the considerable force her body can handle.

"Hey," I say.

"Hey," she says back. "Did a sweep. Nothing unusual. I considered lockdown, but I can't see how it would do any good if the demon already struck in the castle once without us knowing."

"Okay," I say. "Listen. I saw Mom in the woods with Doug earlier. I have to talk with her. She knows something, I'm sure of it. Maybe she even knows what demon has done this, and why. Maybe—maybe she brought it here."

"Why would she do that?" Artemis isn't challenging me. She's asking, genuinely puzzled.

I know why. I think. If our Mom passed the same test Artemis failed, it meant she *was* willing to do whatever it took to save the world. So whatever she's involved in, she thinks it's in defense of the whole world. Probably because of the prophecy.

Because of me.

I know what choice Artemis will make. She'll choose me. She's already proved it. Maybe that's why our mother wanted to separate us. Why she wants to send me away but not Artemis. Why she saved Artemis first, and only then came back for me.

If it's true, and someday I'm going to destroy the world, I hope Artemis doesn't choose me. I hope she chooses the world. I hope, most of all, that someday Artemis has a life where she can choose herself first.

"I don't know why she'd do it," I lie. "But she's mixed up in it somehow. I'm not solid on the details. I'm going to get them, though."

"Great." Artemis hits the bag again. "How?"

"I'll bring her back here. To Eve. I don't think Ruth Zabuto or Wanda Wyndam-Pryce is in on anything, but Eve's our best bet. Hopefully it's all a big misunderstanding."

"A misunderstanding that left a Watcher and a Slayer dead, and almost killed an innocent. Right." Artemis delivers a brutal blow to the punching bag. Then another. And another. My knuckles ache in sympathy. "If Mom brought the demon here, this is on her."

"It wasn't your fault," I say.

"What wasn't my fault?"

"It wasn't your fault she saved you first. You don't have to feel guilty, and you don't have to sacrifice anything else to protect me. I'll take care of this. I owe you."

She pauses, her arms around the punching bag. Now it looks like it's holding her up. But still she doesn't say anything. I wish she would, but this isn't about me.

"So. I'm going after Mom. Will you find Eve and let her know we need to talk?"

Artemis nods, mute.

I walk back out of the castle, dragging my feet, feeling a hundred years older. I don't really think my mom is capable of having people killed. But I do know she's capable of hiding the truth and lying to those she's supposed to love. I hope this is a mistake. And I hope we can still fix it, at least in part.

Though it's still dark, I don't have a hard time finding my way back to the cemetery. The campfire winks through the trees as I get closer, much smaller than it was before. I don't disguise my footsteps. I want them to hear me coming.

But when I get to the camp, nothing is as I was expecting. A few sticks have been kicked free and are smoldering and sparking. I stomp them out, my heart racing. I have a stake in my hand. I don't remember grabbing it, but it feels essential.

The whole site is in disarray. The tent is askew. Doug's novel is lying forlorn on the ground, the ink-and-paper tragic romance abandoned. His beloved Coldplay shirt is torn and crumpled next to it. And Doug is nowhere to be found. I stumble over an unexpected depression in the ground. I bend close, the firelight revealing deep tire treads. Someone was here.

I take three steps to check out the rest of the campsite, and then I trip over something much bigger than tire tracks.

A body.

I land hard, smashing my knee into a rock. Then I pull my

legs away. I don't want to see. I don't want to know.

The body stirs, groaning. I let out a gasp of relief. I crawl to my mother's side and turn her over. There's a trickle of blood where someone hit her on the head. Her eyes flutter open, searching wildly before settling on me.

"Nina?"

"What happened? Why did Doug do this?"

My mother tenses. "Doug? Where's Doug?"

"I don't know! He's gone."

She sits up, swaying dangerously before reclaiming her sense of balance. "They took him."

"Someone took Doug?"

She scowls impatiently. "Yes. They attacked me and took Doug. What did you think happened?"

"I thought Doug attacked you!"

"Doug wouldn't hurt me. He wouldn't hurt anyone." She stands, unsteady. I offer her a hand, which she takes. And then I remember I came here to confront her. This doesn't change anything.

"You need to answer my questions."

"We don't have time for that. It was Honora and that worm Sean."

"You know about Honora and Sean?"

"Of course I do. It's my job to know things."

I shake my head. "This isn't about Doug. Or it is. I don't know! But you need to tell me the truth: Did you bring another demon to Shancoom? Besides Doug? One attacked Cillian."

"A demon attacked Cillian?"

"Yes! And Cosmina was dead when we went to go see her."

This time my mother sways and stumbles, sitting hard on one of the moss-covered stone memorial benches. "She's dead?"

"You didn't know, then." My body goes limp with relief, and I sink onto the bench beside her.

She shakes her head. Her face is pale, and I don't think it's because of the head wound. "Oh, that poor child. I should have contacted her sooner."

"Tell me what's going on!"

My mother's face snaps back into its usual form. Firm. Distant. "This isn't about you."

Her words sting. She acts like I'm being selfish or immature. But I know what I heard before when I was spying. I know about the prophecy. "It's entirely about me!"

"Innocent lives are in the balance. I can't let them have Doug again."

"Why are you even helping him?"

"Why did *you*?"

I pause, caught. "Because he seemed like he needed it."

She meets my eyes—something she has almost never done in all these years. "You were right. And he needs help now more than ever. If I don't get to him fast, they'll move him to another facility, and I'll never find him again."

I hold her gaze, drinking in her words: *You were right.* But is she manipulating me? How can I trust anything? "Tell me what happened to the others, then. What killed Cosmina and Bradford? What attacked Cillian? Because you and Doug are the common threads."

Anger flashes across her face, quickly swept away by something that looks like . . . hurt? "You think I would harm your friend Cillian? Bradford? That poor lost girl Cosmina? Why would I do that?"

"Because you hate Slayers!"

She reels back like I've slapped her. "I don't hate Slayers."

"Of course you do. Buffy got Dad killed. Your mother was a Slayer, and she left you alone. And you did everything in your power to keep me from being a Slayer. You don't want me to be one."

"Why would I *ever* want that for you?" She reaches out her hand as though she would take mine in hers. But I pull my hand back and grip my stake, afraid to let her. If I do, I might break. I might accept whatever she gives me because of how badly I want to. Her hand hovers, alone.

"Your father didn't want to take the assignment with Buffy. I told him to. Because she was so young. Just a girl. I knew some-day that could be you, and I would want the very best Watcher to take care of you. To protect you." She breaks off, swallowing.

I open my mouth to reply, to tell her she could have pro-tected me by preparing me. But my mother holds up her hand.

"Wait, I have to say this. You have to know. I don't hate Buffy. I never did. And I'm sorry if you thought that your being a Slayer made me hate you. I'm sorry I never learned how to talk to you. Motherhood was not a skill the Watchers prioritized. I tried. I tried so hard." Her voice cracks, and for a moment dream mom, the snickerdoodle mom, almost comes through. But then her voice hardens again. "When it became clear I couldn't keep you safe, I did the same thing my own mother did. I gave you to the Watchers. I tried to keep you shielded, keep you sheltered." A pause. "I'm sorry. It was the wrong choice. For both you and Artemis." She stands. She seems stronger already.

"And the fire? At our house?" I ask, campfire smoke making my eyes water and my throat tighten. "Why did you leave me behind?" That question has never been asked, but now that it's out there, a charge passes between us.

There's a smile sadder than any tears on her face. "You were a Potential. I knew you could survive longer. The magic wasn't powerful enough for me to shield more than one of you at a time. I took Artemis first because it was the only way to save you both."

Her words hit me like an anvil to the chest.

I was the strong one. That was why she left me behind. Not because she hated me or because she loved Artemis more. Because it was the only way for Artemis to live. I never knew it, she never knew it, but *I* was protecting *her*.

"You should have told us," I whisper.

"I couldn't. Not without telling you why you were stronger. I'm sorry, I'm so sorry you thought—but it doesn't matter now. I have to go, because I can't stay here and let another innocent be destroyed on my watch. I've done too much of that in my lifetime." She turns and hurries into the darkness. I wait, stunned, until I hear an engine start up far in the distance. The roar slowly fades away.

And then she's gone.

The walk back to the castle is far longer this time. Everything I thought I knew has once again evaporated. Would a woman who risks her life to go save a demon from torture and captivity do anything that would threaten a castle full of people she cares about?

Who is my mother?

Artemis will be waiting inside with Eve. I want to tell Artemis it wasn't her fault that Mom picked her first. She doesn't have to feel guilty anymore, ever. I don't want to tell her that Honora attacked our mom and took Doug. Or maybe I do. I can't decide which.

However, Honora and Sean's presence in the forest is deeply suspect. It places them here around when Cillian was being attacked. Sean had a vendetta against Cosmina, and she died. Cillian kept Doug hidden from Sean, and he was attacked. Maybe Sean thought Bradford was the one who was trying to help Doug. And Bradford died the morning Honora came back.

Artemis isn't going to like it, but we have to look into it. With all the demons Sean has at his disposal, surely a succubus type isn't out of the question. I promised Rhys I'd research, but a trip to Dublin is a better strategy. This time I won't leave without answers.

Leo is waiting for me on the edge of the castle grounds. His voice is bright against the darkness. "I was looking for you."

"Oh gods, I have so much to fill you in on."

Leo takes my elbow, spinning me back toward the forest and the path to Shancoom. "Great! We're going this way." He carries me along like a leaf caught in a current, his fingers a gentle guiding pressure.

"Is your mom already out here looking for mine? Because I was wrong. About everything. We need to get to Dublin."

"There's a lot we need to talk about. This way."

"No, I need a car."

He tugs my elbow, then stops when I don't respond. "Athena. It will keep. The world isn't going to end. Let's just walk for a bit. Please?"

The predawn sky is slowly bruising with the promise of the sun. I can't quite make out Leo's expression, but his voice sounds strained. My phone buzzes with a text from Cillian. "Weird," I say, shoving my cell back in my pocket.

"What?"

"Cillian wants me to come over and watch Eurovision. Odd request when he was technically dead a couple hours ago." I pause. "Oh, you don't know about that. A demon attacked him. I think it's the same one who got Bradford and Cosmina. Our working theory is succubus. Do you think the text is a code? He needs help but can't say? No, he would never use Eurovision lightly." My phone buzzes again.

Everything is fine. Bunk off and come over right now. Rhys wants you to too.

Kind of busy, I text back.

Stop being busy. Or be busy here.

I'm with Leo.

Perfect! Bring him.

Cillian has Rhys to watch over him. They don't need me. And Leo's not quite right—the world *might* end. It tries to with aggravating frequency. One of these days, I could be the girl behind it.

Leo keeps looking over his shoulder like he's expecting someone else. "We'll go to Cillian's, then. Check up on him. We can talk there."

"No, Rhys is there, so Cillian's safe. We have bigger problems. Sean and Honora attacked my mom and took Doug back to Dublin. My mom's going after them. I am too. You can tell the Council. What's left of it, anyway." I turn toward the castle again.

"No!" Leo dances around me, blocking me. "Let's go talk with Rhys and Cillian." He glances over his shoulder again.

"Is someone else coming?"

"Nope. Let's go."

"Why aren't you listening to me?" It stings. Leo is the one person who has listened to me this whole time, without fail. "Sean and Honora were here when Cillian was attacked. Bradford died the morning Honora showed up and was distracting us. Cosmina messed up Sean's pit fight. I have to confront them."

"No." Leo is vehement. "It's not your problem."

Now he sounds like Artemis! I glare. "Umm, it definitely is. It's my responsibility to protect the Watchers."

"It's not your responsibility, though." Leo huffs in frustration. "They don't need you."

I step back, folding my arms. The sting of his words has turned to a deep cut.

He hurries on. "Besides, you have your whole life ahead of you. It's hard to see, because you've been in between for so long. I understand . . ." He tips his head back. "God, I understand what it is to be two things at once, and at the same time not quite either." He reaches out and takes my hands, fixing his eyes on mine. "You're trying so hard to prove you have a place here. But you don't need to. Please. Let me clean all this up for you. Let me redeem myself that way. I swore I'd protect you."

His cool fingers slip between my own and he takes a sharp breath. His dark eyes clear of their distraction. They burn now, like coals breathed back to life. And then, before I realize what's happening, he kisses me.

It's like the first shock of diving into a cool pool on a summer day—bracing and delicious. He lingers, his lips over my bottom lip. "Run away," he whispers. "Right now."

I pull back, startled. I daydreamed this exact scenario more times than I could count back when I was thirteen. And if I'm being honest, maybe a few times since Leo returned. I laugh, but when he opens his eyes, he's not laughing.

"Get Cillian and Rhys. Jump in Cillian's car and go. Don't ever look back."

"And do what?"

"Anything!"

Why does everyone want me to leave? The thrill of the kiss has gone right back to pain at his words. "This is my home, Leo. Besides, are you going to run with me?"

"I can't," he says. "I have to—"

"Exactly. We all have things we have to do. I'm part of this too."

"But you *shouldn't* be."

I flinch. Even my Watcher thinks I can't handle being a Slayer. I thought he was the one person who really saw me. Maybe he is. And this is his conclusion: that I should leave it to the people who are capable. The ones who matter.

I untangle my fingers from his.

Dawn is here. That liminal space between night and day has broken, and with it, my reignited dream of being with Leo. The black of the trees overhead is slowly fading to reveal orange and brown. Soon the forest will wake up in a crisp salute to the changing seasons. The trees are gnarled and ancient, growing close together over the carpet of ferns.

Easy to get lost in here. And easy to hide. I'm done hiding.

Leo sighs, his face falling. He pulls out a phone. "Change of plans," he says into it. "Meet me on the south end of Shancoom." I edge around him, but he sticks out his arm, holding up a finger for the universal *wait a sec* symbol. "Yeah. I'm bringing her." He pockets his phone, then gives me a tight smile. "I need you to come with me."

I take a step back.

He takes a step forward. "I'll explain when we get there. But we need to go. Now."

I take another step back. My mind spins, turning to things I don't want to consider. "Where were you this morning? You said you were going to stay in my room. And then you were gone."

"Another thing I'll explain. Trust me." He holds out his hand.

I want to take it. More than anything. I want to kiss him again, to get lost in it. To luxuriate in the miracle of Leo Silvera wanting me. I want to walk through the woods holding hands, go hang out with Rhys and Cillian, turn this whole mess over to Wanda and Ruth and Eve.

But I can't. I have to be a Slayer. I can't take things to the Council, can't wait for the bureaucracy to slowly churn to life and examine what's happening. I have to *act*.

I finally agree with Buffy for giving up on us. We're a mess. We can't even take care of our own ranks, much less anyone else. I judged her because I could only see my side of it.

It's different when you're the one with the power. The choices are so much harder and so much more important. What would Buffy do? She'd charge in and figure this all out with fists and sheer force of will. If people didn't believe in her, she would *make* them. And she wouldn't stop until she beat back anyone who threatened the ones she loved.

Buffy isn't here right now. But I am. I'm the last Slayer.

Watchers had it wrong all along. They thought Slayers needed to be told what to do. To be kept out of trouble. But *trouble* is exactly where we belong. I reach out for that pool of anger. The channel of fury that ends in me. It's a destructive force, but it's also a powerful tool. I'll use it to get to the bottom of this. To save the people *I* love.

I think of the Slayer who sacrificed herself for her village.

My grandmother, who died but saved her baby.

Buffy, who died to save the world——*twice!*——and was so stubborn she came back to save it yet again. I don't think she was selfish or impulsive. I think she was doing the best she could in the middle of complete and utter chaos. Watchers try to control, try to predict. But in the end, we Slayers have to learn that all you can do is react and hope you win.

I've been racked with turmoil this whole time about what it means to be a Slayer. But one thing is clear to me now, without question——I *want* this. I can do this. I'm proud of what I am.

And I'm ready.

"Sorry, Leo. I have to finish this." I angle around him toward home.

"Goddammit," he mutters. Then he grabs me, spins me upward, and throws me over his shoulder as he starts running through the woods.

29

"WHAT ARE YOU *DOING?*" I BOUNCE WITH each jarring step Leo takes.

"Please keep your voice down. I don't want to attract attention."

"Well, I do!" My mind bounces as much as my body. Leo wasn't in my room this morning when Cillian was attacked. Leo himself pointed out that everything started going haywire when he and his mom got back. Was he teasing me? Telling me the truth knowing I wouldn't see it? Maybe the source of all this chaos and death is much closer to me. In this case, so close my chin is slamming against his lower back with every step.

Leo jumps over a fallen log. I use the momentum to swing up and grab hold of a branch. I hold on with all my strength, his forward motion ripping me out of his grasp. I scramble up the tree to where he can't reach me. I look down, expecting rage, and see only panic.

"Please!" he says. "We don't have much time!"

"No!" I climb higher.

"I promise I'll explain, but we *have* to hurry." He runs his hands through his hair, practically pulling it out.

I eye the next tree. I can make it. I jump, swinging on a branch and launching myself through the air. I slam into the trunk but hold on. A shower of red leaves and debris rains down beneath me.

Leo's desperation turns to determination. He lowers his head and runs straight at my tree, barreling into it. It rips free from the ground with tearing roots and a tremendous crash. I'm trapped in a jumble of branches, the scent of soil and sap overwhelming.

I fight my way free. I'm strong, but I don't think I could take down one of these old giants in a single blow. If my strength is superhuman, Leo's is . . . inhuman.

All those hours I spent spying on him training with Rhys. His movements were always so careful. So precise. I thought it was because he was good, but what if it was because he was hiding how much *more* he was?

Leo has me blocked in by the tree. "I really am sorry. But you're coming with me."

How is this happening? Leo is a lifelong Watcher, from a Watcher mother. And his father—

His father died before Leo was born. I've never actually heard anything about him. Dead fathers aren't remarkable in our community, but I suspect Leo's father was extremely remarkable in the worst possible ways.

"Let's stop saying sorry so much," I say. "But I *am* sorry for this." I push up off the tree, jumping in the air and kicking him in the chest with both feet.

It's like hitting a mountain. I bounce off, landing hard on the ground.

"Ow," I whimper.

Leo picks me up. He sets me on my feet, keeping his hands on my shoulders. "Any injuries?"

"What *are* you?" I know with a despairing and fearful certainty that my kick would have sent any *human* flying. "How are you still standing?"

His smile is as sad and empty as a good-bye. "I defy gravity. Rhys will explain. We have to—"

I twist out of his hands and dart past him. One of my ankles is sore from the impact with his chest, but I race as fast as I can. I know where I'm going. I've been there enough times in the last few hours to have the path memorized. I still have my stake, but I can't imagine plunging it into Leo's chest.

Buffy once had to slide a sword into her boyfriend's heart. *Oh, Buffy. You are so much stronger than I am.* But I have an idea.

I slide to a stop in Doug's campsite, snagging the torn Coldplay T-shirt just as Leo grabs me.

He swings me up and around his shoulders so I'm facing the same direction he is, my body bent around his upper back. I'm locked in place by one arm around my knees and his other one bracing my neck. He looks down at my face.

And I shove Doug's damp-with-psychotropic-demon-ooze shirt right in his mouth.

Leo staggers back. He shakes his head, then drops me to pull the shirt free. "What did you—" The tension in his body melts away. His expression turns sweet and open with bliss. It shows *exactly* how careful his expressions have always been. Even when he was smiling at me with what I thought was sincerity, he held back. I had been viewing Leo through a carefully constructed screen.

Now?

"You're so pretty." He reaches down and grabs my hands to help me stand. Then he gently brushes the hair from my face, letting his fingers linger there. "When I came back and saw you again for the first time, it was like—it was like magic. All the magic that was gone went right into you."

It's even worse than if he hit me. It *hurts*. "Would have loved this information *before* you tried to kidnap me."

"Oh, right." Leo tries to frown. His face wars with itself before resettling in his dimpled smile. I didn't know his dimples even went that deep. Another detail I would have loved before suspecting him of being evil. "Rhys's waiting for us. We should go. It'll be fun. I'll go with you. I should run away too. I don't want to be me anymore." He beams, holding up a strand of my hair to a ray of sunshine breaking through the thick trees. "I can't believe a color like this exists on people. It feels like magic. Everything about you feels like magic. You're too good to be a Watcher. They hurt people. You don't hurt anyone." He strokes my hair. "Magic."

I steer Leo to the bench and push him down to sit. "Explain yourself."

He laughs. "It doesn't matter. None of it matters. The only thing that matters is us. Let's be happy." He stands up and tries to kiss me.

I put my hand on his chest and gently push him back to sitting. "No, sir. Not just because I think you're not human and maybe, possibly a murderer as well. Oh gods, please don't be a murderer. But also because you're super high, and it would be like taking advantage. Why were you kidnapping me? And what are you?"

Leo *giggles*. It's adorable and awful and useless. Just my luck, the demon drugging didn't loosen Leo's tongue, only his happiness.

I try changing tactics. "Rhys and Cillian are safe, right? You didn't hurt them after I left?"

"I would never. I don't hurt anyone. Even when I'm hungry."

"What? You *eat* people?"

"It's not like that. Besides, I like Rhys and Cillian. They're nice. But not as nice as you."

Please let him be drugged enough to be telling the truth. I already feel sick, gutted by the fact that he's been lying to me our whole lives. I can't believe I picked a worse crush than Artemis. Wait—did I pick a worse crush than *Buffy*?

I have to get away from him. I don't think I can restrain him, though. I'll go for speed and hope the Doug drugging doesn't wear off fast. "Hey, you know what would make me super happy? Sit right here."

He grabs my hands, his smile painfully intense. "You deserve so much better than me. But I'm still glad I came back. Even with all the harm I've done. Is that selfish?" His face briefly clouds. Then he's distracted by my hands. "Look at your fingers. They're perfect. I'll make sure you never have to punch anything again."

I withdraw my hand and pat Leo on the head. "Wait here. I'll be right back!"

He nods, his hands encircling my waist. "Hurry, okay? There's something we need to do. I'm trying to remember. . . ."

"I'll hurry!" I twist free and walk away, periodically turning to wave at Leo so he won't get alarmed and snap out of it. A bird lands nearby, distracting him.

I change direction, sprinting out of Leo's sight line.

Hot tears fill my eyes. The boy I let myself trust and fall for again is possibly a demon. I don't know where my mother and her demon conspiring and Slayer tracking fit into all of this or if she's in trouble. I still have to chase down Honora and Sean. And I've got to tell the castle that Leo Silvera has gone bad.

It's even worse than the last time my crush on him crushed me. Because this time, I'm certain he actually cares about me. And it doesn't change anything. It only makes me an absolute idiot for not suspecting him sooner.

I throw open our bedroom door. "Artemis! It wasn't Doug or Mom. And we've got another problem because— Oh, hello, Mrs. Silvera, what are you doing here?"

Artemis gapes at me as I give Eve my best *I didn't just leave your probably demonic son high in the middle of the woods* smile. Until I know what Leo's secrets are, I'm not giving his mother information. I hate that suspicion has clouded the trust I have in Eve. For some reason it's worse than suspecting my mom was up to no good. Maybe because Eve has never failed me.

She sits on my bed and crosses her legs, resting her hands primly on her knee. "Artemis had some very disturbing news about your mother. I'm concerned."

"I don't think my mom has done anything wrong." I give Artemis a heavy look, but she frowns at me. Of all the times for us to be out of sync, this is quite possibly the worst.

Eve nods. "Helen has done so much for the Council. I would never rush to judgment. But if it's true she's working with a demon, I *am* worried that she's introduced danger to us—and especially you. Do you know where your mother's book is? The one with the information on Slayers and demons? We have to make certain none of the other Slayers she knows about have been hurt or killed. And I can't do that unless I can find them."

"Yeah. We should schedule a Council meeting." A Council meeting will take forever. It'll give me time to talk to Artemis alone and to get to Dublin. I'll have Artemis take Jade, Imogen, and the Littles out of here. Rhys and Cillian will have to hide too, since Leo knows where they are and we can't trust him anymore.

I desperately hope Leo isn't behind the attacks. Some of the information lines up but not all of it. I can't think of when he could have gone to Dublin and killed Cosmina. And he seemed genuinely surprised and upset by her death. Rhys and Cillian are still fine. It doesn't make sense for Leo to attack Cillian in the first place.

But I can't know anything for certain, so I'll treat everyone except my friends as a threat.

Eve stands, studying my bookshelf. Maybe she has no idea about Leo. It certainly isn't unusual among Watchers to have no clue what their kids are doing or even what their kids are.

"*Artemis.*" I very deliberately turn on the ceiling fan. I look up at it then back down at her, hoping she'll get my meaning that there's a threat. That we need to be careful.

She frowns. And then finally she understands. Her features shift to weary annoyance. "Is that what you were doing in the woods, then? Hiding Mom's address book?"

I sigh dramatically. "Yes. Fine. I didn't want to turn it over to the Council until I knew more, so I took it when she wasn't looking. Then I went to confront her. But she's not there anymore. She went to find Doug."

Eve straightens, turning around. Her red lipstick looks like a wound as she purses her lips. "Nina, dear, I can tell when people are lying to me. So either you are lying about what you did with the book or you are lying about what your mother has been up to. Let's go get Wanda and——"

"No!" Not her too. She's been out to get our family forever. She might even have been working with Honora. Wanda Wyndam-Pryce in the castle, Honora outside of it. I need them to meet with each other, not with me. I have to get my friends out. "I really don't think my mom has hurt anyone. And she's off looking for Doug now anyway, so there's no rush. Call a Council meeting."

"Who is Doug?" Eve asks.

"He's the demon. The one I had in Cillian's shed, remember? It's not a big deal. I'll explain to the Council when you're all gathered."

"I think it *is* a big deal." Eve folds her arms, her expression stern. "I think it's a very big deal when a Watcher uses our resources to actively conspire and consort with demons. And it hasn't escaped my notice that when we met your mother, the Slayer we were looking for was already dead. Now Cosmina turns up dead as well. Tell me where your mother's book is so we can confirm the other Slayers are unharmed. Then we'll decide how to handle your mother's extracurricular activities."

Artemis looks torn. "Maybe you *should* give it to them. That way we can prove Mom isn't hurting anyone."

I've *got* to get Eve out of here so I can leave. Maybe if she knows I can't get the book, she'll give up that line of reasoning. "I'd really like that. But I lied. I don't have the book. Mom took it with her. She's trying to protect Doug."

Eve sighs, rubbing her forehead. "So she's out protecting a demon, which means she's not here. And she's obviously hit some sort of crisis point. I wouldn't put it past her to snatch you and run again. I can't lose you." She shakes her head. "I'm afraid we're out of time."

"What do you mean, we're out of time?"

Eve lowers her hand, smiling. "Sorry. I meant you're out of time."

Suddenly the lights go out. But not in the room.

In *Eve*.

Every shadow swirls, gathering on her. Her edges blur, her form becoming like something half remembered from a nightmare.

From a nightmare I've already had.

"Oh my gods," I whisper.

Eve smiles. "Quite the opposite."

30

EVE WHIPS OUT A SHADOWY LEG. ARTEMIS screams as she falls. I jump at Eve but she moves as fast as a memory, sliding out of my reach before I can grab her.

"I need her to be asleep." Eve's voice is like an icy breeze on the back of my neck. "But unconscious will work too."

I lunge for Artemis. Eve gets there first. Artemis goes limp and silent, hanging like a rag doll from Eve's hands. I try to come at her from the side, but Eve mirrors me, keeping the wall at her back and Artemis in front of her.

"Careful now." Eve squeezes, and points of blood break through Artemis's shirt from where Eve's fingernails have extended into black claws. "Just a little pressure and I'll puncture straight through to all the fragile, precious things that separate the living from the dead. And if you take too long to decide, I'll rip away her life force and break her neck too, so your CPR will be worthless."

I trusted Eve. I thought she was helping me. And this whole time, she's been using me. Of course she said she'd find out what happened to Bradford. She already knew.

I can't let her kill Artemis. Not for anything. "What do I have to decide? What do you want?"

"Your power."

It takes me a moment to comprehend what she's saying. "My power?"

"The channel that opened up and connected you to a well of power women have drawn on for thousands of years. I was so surprised and delighted you were a Slayer, right here for the taking. Leo made me promise I wouldn't hurt you. But I've tasted you while you were sleeping."

"What?"

"Didn't you notice? I tasted you all. Everyone shambling around the castle, pale and tired and quick to anger. But you! Are you really so strong you didn't even notice I'd sampled?"

The morning Bradford died. When I got out of bed I was dizzy. Weak. It passed quickly, so I ignored it. But it had been Eve. I shudder.

She smiles, two black lines parting to reveal white teeth. "You're more powerful than any of us could imagine. You're the last one, after all." She laughs, a sound that whispers like dry leaves around the room, creeping from under the bed and behind the closet door, surrounding me. I know it's morning outside, but I feel as choked by darkness as though it were midnight.

"It was you I saw. In the secret passages that night."

"Yes. Convenient for sneaking from bedroom to bedroom, eating."

Eve's been *snacking* on us while we slept. "What about Cosmina?" I'm not trying to stall—I believe her when she says she'll kill Artemis. I just need to understand.

"I wanted to try it on her first. But that's the problem with Slayers. They're too strong. She fought back. Woke up halfway through, and the connection was broken. She still lost her Slayer power—and the shock of it killed her—but I didn't get it either."

"Bradford Smythe?"

"He really did have a bad heart. I've been nonlethal with everyone here. His misfortune that he couldn't handle all of this." She waggles her hips suggestively, the shadows shifting from side to side and trailing off her like smoke. "Twenty years, right under their noses, and they never noticed. Not how I had changed, and not what Leo was. And not when I invited Leo's father to join us for particularly nice meals. For all their watching, they see *nothing*."

"And Cillian?"

"You're stalling." She sings it, her shadows pulsing.

"I'm not stalling! It makes no sense! Why did you try to kill Cillian?"

"So you would understand what was at stake. So you would know loss."

I laugh. I can't help it. It's hollow and dark, like her soul. "Haven't you been paying attention? I've always known loss, moron."

She squeezes Artemis. I hold up my hands. "Okay! Sorry. So if I don't let you kill me, you'll kill Artemis."

"I don't want to kill you. I honestly think you can survive it. It's in both our best interests if you do. That way I have time to get all that juicy power without you dying on me, and you have a shot at surviving the removal process. That's why I wanted you trained. Wanted to push you to be at your strongest. And why I have to do this now, before your mother can come back and hide you. I had hoped to wait, gather more energy first, but the timetable has been moved up by so many outside forces interfering. And by my son." She sighs.

Leo. My Watcher. The only person who always had my back. He had been fattening me up for the slaughter.

"Oh, sweetheart." Eve's voice, which I had found so motherly and comforting before, is like claws skittering across a stone floor. "Leo doesn't want this. But he needs me. He can't live without the energy I take. So in a way you'll be saving him too." She tightens her grasp. Artemis groans but doesn't wake up. "That's the choice. Give me your power, whole and intact, willingly. Don't fight it. Save Artemis and your mother and your fellow pathetic Watchers and your little village friend. Even save Leo. Choose to give it up. Choose to stop being Chosen."

I clench my hands into fists. "I'm strong enough to kill you."

"You keep your power, you could kill me. But . . . *can* you? Look at your room. Look at your bookshelves. You want to fix things. You want to heal, to save. Do you really think you can look me in my human eyes—the mother you wished you had, don't deny it—and end me? I don't think you can. And you can't do it before I snuff out your sister. So you'd be choosing to kill her in order to kill me." The shadows lift, then fall, darkness seeping from her more steadily now. Artemis looks pale.

"Stop! You're already draining her!"

"You're out of time."

I know Eve will use my power for something awful. She's already a murderer. And for her to work this hard, for this long, she has to have some bigger goal in mind. Something that requires more juice than normal people can provide. Maybe even some-thing so bad there's a prophecy all about us. I thought I'd break the world myself, but what if it's my *power* that makes it happen?

The irony of all this is so devastating it's almost funny. I'm finally facing the Watcher's test. The same one Artemis took. The one she failed, because of me. I know what the Watchers would have me choose: the world. Let my sister die so I can stop the demon's plan. And I know what Artemis would want me to choose: Let her die so that I can be strong enough to save myself.

But Artemis is my world. She always has been. Looks like nei-ther of us was really cut out to be a Watcher in the end.

Numbly, I nod. "What do I have to do?"

"Go to sleep." Eve drops Artemis and slams a book into my head.

31

"SHH," EVE CROONS, STROKING MY FACE so that the darkness swirls off her and around my eyes.

The rage of a thousand beating hearts pulses through my veins. Abandonment. Betrayal. Disappointment. Confusion. All funneled into a white-hot tunnel of hatred swirling around the woman on the edge of the roof.

She took my father. Ruined my mother. Turned her back on the generations of my people who tried to help her. Made me a Slayer. Put a target on me and everyone I love.

And there she is.

Alone.

Maybe I should hate her. But I don't.

She stuck a sword into the man she loved, sending him to hell in order to save the world. She dove into a dimensional portal, closing it—and dying—so her sister wouldn't have to. She destroyed the Sunnydale Hellmouth. She defeated the First Evil. She gave up being an actual goddess so she could save our sad, broken little world. Her life has been an endless series of impossible decisions that she's had to make, because if not her, then who?

And she's still just a person. Just a young woman. Trying to do her best with an incredible burden of power and responsibility.

Understanding cuts through me, separating me from the rage and letting me step to the side of it. I can still feel it. Can rejoin if I want to. But instead I focus. I take shape, form, reclaiming myself from the communal Slayer subconscious. Then I walk across the roof and sit down next to Buffy.

"Hey," I say.

She looks over, surprised. "Hey?"

"This is nice." I gesture to the dreamscape, a San Francisco exaggerated and sharpened.

"Yeah. I guess." She looks back out over it. If she can control her dreams like I can, then this is a choice. Every time I've seen her, she's been here. Not at the Slayer rave. Not visiting her own past trauma. But waiting. Available. Almost like she's always here in case someone needs to talk.

Someone like me.

"I just wanted to say—" I take a deep breath. There are so many things I had imagined saying to her over the years. So many awful things, designed to hurt her. I let them all fall away. "I just wanted to say, I forgive you."

She frowns. "Confusing much?"

"My name is Athena Jamison-Smythe." She startles in recognition at my surname, and tears well in her somber green eyes. I push on. "I forgive you, Buffy Summers, for being Chosen. And I forgive you for every choice you've made since then."

She stares at me for a moment, and then her mouth quirks up. "This is really weird," she says, but she leans her head on my shoulder. The dreams of other Slayers pulse behind us. She must feel them every night as she sleeps. A thousand girls like us, the only ones who understand what it is to be a Slayer, and she's apart from even that. Buffy Summers, destroyer of worlds, ruiner of lives, and the loneliest girl on the planet.

"My dad would be proud of you," I say.

"Would he really?"

"I have no idea. I don't really remember him. It seemed like a nice thing to say, though."

She laughs. "It *was* nice. Thank you." We watch as the sun rises over San Francisco. The air shimmers like water, and a sea monster elegantly wraps itself around the Golden Gate Bridge. It reminds me of something I can't put my finger on.

"Can I give you some advice?" Buffy asks.

"Please do."

"Oh." Her eyebrows rise in surprise. "Wow. I kind of thought you would say no. Everyone else in the big dreamy blob of rage hates me." She jerks her head back to the Slayer energy behind us. "Except the First Slayer. Have you met her yet?"

I shake my head.

"Well, there's a super-special grunty judgment treat you have to look forward to. But that's a tangent." She turns toward me. I had always thought she looked sad in photos. But now I see that it's the shape of her eyes. Maybe her genes had known what her life would hold, and they prepared her face for it. Then she narrows those eyes and all sadness is replaced with a strength and determination that instantly makes *me* feel stronger. I understand why

a thousand Slayers followed her into battle. I understand why my
father recognized potential in a tiny blond teenager. And for the
first time, I begin to understand what I can be, maybe, someday.

Buffy speaks. "We were Chosen for something we wouldn't
have picked for ourselves. But you were Chosen because of who
you are. So don't let being a Slayer define you. *You* define being
a Slayer."

I define being a Slayer.

I define being a Slayer.

I've been so consumed with fear that embracing the Slayer
inside me would mean the end of the person I was—the girl who
wanted to make the world better by healing, not hurting.

I don't have to choose one or the other. If I want to, I can be
both. And maybe be stronger for it. All the fear that being *me*
made me a bad Slayer evaporates.

Tears burn. But unlike the burning of the rage, this feels
cleansing. I nod, mute with gratitude. Then I finally find my
voice. "Thank you. And I am sure of one thing. My dad would be
glad you're still alive and fighting. I am too."

Buffy snorts. "Well, that's good. I'm glad I'm still alive too. I
tried the whole death thing. It's fine for a while, but I'm kind of
over it in a long-term sense." Then her face softens, and when she
reaches over to hug me, I hug her back.

When we pull apart, Buffy's face relaxes into a peaceful
smile.

"This dream has been a lot better than most of my nights,"
she says. "You would not believe how often Kennedy shows up.
I know it's petty, but she's so *annoying*. Anything else I can help
with while you're here?"

"*Oh*, actually." Everything rushes back. "There's this demon thing? She's a succubus? And if I'm thinking correctly—which I'm not sure I am, because that giant sea serpent on the Golden Gate Bridge is waving at me—the succubus is going to try to pull out my essence or my power or whatever, and it might kill me, and it will definitely make her stronger, so I don't know if I should let her, but if I don't she'll kill my sister, and also I kissed her son and sort of have feelings for him, but if she's a succubus and her husband is something demony too, then Leo is definitely not human, and—"

"Oh my god. Let me give you my number." She writes something on her hand. We both squint at it. The numbers are all jumbled. It's a dream, after all. I never could read in dreams. But in the middle of them is the triple triangle symbol I saw on Sean's tea labels. "Weird," she says. "What does that mean?"

"It's—"

A ringing noise shatters the stillness of the dawn. Buffy grimaces. "Time to wake up," she says. "Evil to fight. Coffee to pour. It was nice to meet you, Athena Jamison-Smythe. Good luck with the succubus. And remember, whatever you do, don't—"

The dream pulls away. I can stay asleep. Or I can wake up and fight.

I define being a Slayer.

I get to choose.

Artemis chose me over her own future. And I know what she would tell me to do. Maybe this is part of the prophecy. I don't care. I refuse to believe that I have to choose death to save people. If I can be a hunter *and* a healer, a Watcher *and* a Slayer, it proves that life isn't binary. There's always another way out there, and no matter what, I'm going to find it. If I'm a Slayer, my choice is to use everything I've been given to protect those I love *and* to protect those I'll never even know.

At that thought, I relax.

Eve can take what she wants from me now. And then, powers or no powers, I will make her regret it.

I feel Eve, hands on my chest, somehow sinking past the skin and bones and muscle. Past the organs, to something that hadn't always been there. I know the contours of the power as she touches it. It's the first time I've truly understood it, bright and burning, flooding my body.

In that moment, I know what I'm losing.

I take one last deep breath, holding on to the feeling of life. Of a connection to other girls across the globe, each with her own messy life and her own tremendous potential. Of power— power so deep and dark I could dive into it and never find its limits.

Eve tugs, the light fighting to stay. It curls, clinging to me, burning me in protest. My Slayer instincts roar up, demanding I fight. But I don't resist. I hold Artemis's face in my mind.

And I let it all go.

32

"NINA! NINA, WAKE UP! PLEASE WAKE UP!"

Everything hurts. I don't want to wake up. But Artemis is scared. I peel my eyes open, then cough. I cough so long and hard I can't draw a breath. When I'm about to pass out again, I manage to stop long enough to breathe.

I'm . . . weak. So weak. What had been my normal before stands in such stark contrast to being a Slayer that I honestly don't know how I ever moved. How I survived feeling like this for so many years.

I gasp, finally getting enough air that lights aren't dancing in my vision. Artemis helps me sit up. She's on the floor next to me, her knee at an angle a knee is not supposed to be. My back is against my nightstand.

"Where is she?" I croak, eyes darting in panic around the room, searching every shadow.

"She demanded to know where Mom went. She wants Mom's book so she can get to other Slayers in case she needs more power." Artemis grimaces, holding her knee. "Eve said she'd kill

Imogen and the Littles, so I told her about Naked Grains. I'm sorry."

"Did it work? Did she get my power?" I know the answer. I feel it in every inch of my body, but still I ask.

Artemis's hand trembles as she smooths back my hair. "It worked. She mentioned something about her husband again. He was trapped in a hell dimension when the portals closed. Nina, I think—I think she's going to use your power to open up a hellmouth."

I stand, swaying woozily. Everything feels trembly and disconnected, like I haven't eaten in three days. I fight back nausea, and I fight back a deep sorrow, a piercing sense of loss for something I was only beginning to truly accept. But Slayer or no Slayer, people are in danger. "If she gets to Naked Grains—"

"Mom," Artemis says.

"And Honora," I add, my voice soft. Because as much as I hate her, I don't want her to die. And I really don't want Artemis to go through that. Plus, once Eve gets what she wants there, there's no telling who else she might hurt or kill. And we for sure do not want a hellmouth under her control.

"What do we do?" Artemis is looking to me for help. For guidance. And for the first time in years, I'm going to be the strong one for her.

I grab two stakes and use them to splint her knee. She hisses in pain, but then she stands, able to put a little weight on it. "Meet me at the garage," I say. I take a small notebook from my collection and shove it into my pocket, then run into the hall—which makes my head spin. I slump against the wall until I can move again. And then I speed walk instead of run to Imogen's door.

"What is it?" She's still in pajamas, a bag of Cheetos in her hands, the three Littles lounging on their stomachs around a television.

"Do you trust me?" I ask. Imogen nods, her eyes narrowing as she sees how serious I am. "Okay, so Eve is a demon, she stole my Slayer power, she's gonna open a hellmouth if we don't stop her, and if she comes back here, no one is safe."

Imogen blinks once. Twice. Then she drops the Cheetos and claps her hands. "Hey, kiddos! It's a field trip day!"

The Littles jump up, squealing.

"We'll go to Cillian's," I say. "Rhys is there. Cillian can take you all somewhere safe. Somewhere we don't know about." In case Eve gets to us. Better that no one can betray where the Littles are.

"Can you drive?" Imogen grabs a duffel bag from a trunk by the door.

"Stake me." I slap my forehead. I never learned, and neither did Rhys. Artemis can, but with her knee injured, I don't know if she'll be able to.

"Jade!" Imogen shouts as the Littles scramble to put on their shoes. George Smythe, my favorite with his mop top of curls and enormous eyes, is pulling on rain boots over footie pajamas.

Jade stumbles out of her room. "I *just* got back to sleep. I'd like to note that no one bothered telling me Cillian was fine! I burst into his house ready to fight, but you and Artemis had already left. Then Rhys cussed me out for waking Cillian up!"

"Demons!" I shout. "Immediate threat!"

"Fine." Jade glares sullenly at me.

"I'm driving," Imogen says. "Jade, you'll be in charge of the

Littles. If we aren't back by the end of the day, we aren't coming back. Nina will text Cillian if we survive. There's fifty thousand American dollars in this bag. If we die, take them far away and live a happy life."

Jade looks briefly alarmed, then she takes the duffel Imogen hands her. "Cool. All right."

I smile falsely at little Thea Zabuto throwing herself against my legs. "Jade, please go tell Ruth and Wanda that Eve's a demon and we're going to fight her. They can do whatever they want. Then meet us at the cars." I allow Jade a second for that to wash over her, then I push her down the hall and help Imogen usher the three Littles into the back of the Range Rover.

The last Little has been lifted into the backseat when Artemis and Jade both make it over to us.

"Old Crone Zabuto said she'll die protecting the library. Wanda demanded the money so she could 'safeguard' it." Jade smiles wickedly. "I gave her a swift kick in the arse instead. And then an extra one for good measure. So I kind of hope you guys lose, because I think I won't be welcome here anymore." She climbs in the back. The Littles crawl over the seats, thrilled to be leaving the castle. I know we should have car seats or something for them, but that's the least of our worries right now.

George beams at me. "This is the best day ever!"

"Right," I say. "The best." Also maybe the last.

Imogen drives as fast as is safe. Probably a little faster. We squeal to a stop in front of Cillian's. Jade herds the Littles into Cillian's car, shouting to Rhys and Cillian what the situation is. I watch as Cillian and Rhys embrace fiercely. Rhys whispers something in his boyfriend's ear. Then Rhys climbs into our car as

Cillian climbs into his, and after one final look between us, we drive in opposite directions.

I have to focus on what we're going to do, because even the idea of facing off against Eve is less horrible than thinking about what I've lost. What I let her take away from me. So I take stock of our arsenal.

Imogen—untrained, a glorified nanny.

Rhys—a budding Watcher more suited to research than fighting.

Artemis—injured and barely able to walk.

And me—not a Watcher. And now not a Slayer.

Off to save a world threatened by the very power I'd been given to protect it.

33

"SO, UH, WHERE'S LEO?" RHYS ASKS AFTER a few minutes of tense car silence.

"Leo's part demon." I stare out the window. Every passing tree marks a second lost, a minute lost, maybe the chance to save my mother and also quite possibly the world . . . lost.

"I know. He told me."

Leo said something about asking Rhys, that he'd explain things. But I didn't believe him. "He did?"

"That's why we tried to make you come over. We needed to get you out of the castle without Leo's mom knowing. If she knew, she would have come after you. He wanted you safe."

I'm leaning halfway between the driver and passenger seats, lunging for Rhys. "When did he tell you this?"

Rhys holds up his hands. "Whoa, don't kill the very helpful and much beloved messenger. He showed up right after you left this morning. Told us that his mother was a succubus, turned into one by his father. Who's an incubus. And not the band, which would be a much preferable option at this point. Leo knows his mom isn't great, but he says she's always been nonlethal before now. And he kind of needs her to survive. She can pull energy from anything, but he can only get it from her. After they lost access to his dad, she's gone off the deep end. He was trying to make sure she was okay, but she was sneaking around killing things. Anyway, Leo's what's known as a cambion. They have varying powers, depending on the combination, but one thing is always the same: gravity recognizes that they come from somewhere else and tries to pull them back down. That's why the car guzzled so much gas when he was in it."

"And why I couldn't knock him over."

"Yeah."

"He told you this himself?"

"Brought me a page of a book on cambions. He ripped the page right out, which was difficult for me to forgive. But he wanted to help you, even though he's part demon. And by the way, what is it with you girls and demons? Buffy and the soul vamps, you and a cambion. Is it a Slayer thing?" His smile fades as he sees the stricken look on my face. As he remembers that I'm not a Slayer anymore. Not really.

So Leo wasn't one thing or the other. No wonder we had been drawn to each other. I was not quite a Watcher but not quite a civilian. And even when I was a Slayer, I had too much Watcher in me. Too much of an instinct to protect instead of slay. Never all one thing, and therefore having no place to belong.

I didn't realize I could be both until it was too late.

"Anyway," Rhys rushes on, "Leo and his mom came back to the castle to get information to try and break through to his father. He thought it would help his mom get back to normal. But then when Eve found out you were a Slayer, she decided to stay. Leo made her promise she wouldn't touch you. When she killed Cosmina, though, Leo knew he had to get you out. He was tracking his mom earlier this morning, but he lost her. That's when she attacked Cillian, to distract you and keep you away from Leo."

"So he really was trying to protect me?"

"Yeah." Rhys shrugs apologetically. "Where is he?"

"I left him in the woods."

Rhys's eyes widen. "Did you kill him?"

"*Gods*, no. I just got him super high with Doug's dirty old shirt." I lift a hand to rub my aching forehead. My fingers tremble. I can barely keep my head up. "Then his mom attacked me. And she won." I turn back to the window. So Leo was trying to help me after all. But he still lied to me. And he knew all along what was going on. He let me run in circles, suspecting my own mother when his was the evil one. My heart hurts almost as much as the rest of my body.

Artemis reaches between the seats, takes my hand in hers, and squeezes. I don't regret sacrificing my power to save her. But I can feel the loss everywhere, and it's so hard not to sink down and cry.

"What's the plan now?" Rhys asks.

I wait, but no one answers. He's talking to me. Artemis too is waiting for my plan. They finally trust my instincts, now that I have no power to back them up. Fantastic. Still, I'm a Jamison-Smythe. I'm not totally defenseless. And I'm going to fight with everything I have left. "Eve's a demon. We're Watchers. We'll do what Watchers do best."

"Research?" Rhys says.

"Babysit?" Imogen offers with a wry eyebrow.

"Spar," Artemis says bleakly, gesturing to her knee.

"No. We kill the demon. Save the world. Protect the Slayers, even if they don't know we're doing it. Even if they don't care. Eve's not touching any more of us." I pause. "Them, I mean."

The rest of the ride is silent.

Imogen makes it to Naked Grains in record time. I hope we've beaten Eve, until I see a familiar matching Range Rover parked next to the motorcycle my mother must have ridden here.

They're both inside.

We hurry through the parking lot, vacant this long before the store opens. The front door has been smashed in. Glass glitters in the morning light as we step gingerly over it. The rest of the store is untouched. Waiting.

I take them through the tea aisle. "Hold up," Imogen says, studying the labels. She grabs a fistful of "Dreams of My Enemy's Weakness" and shoves it in her pocket, then another fistful of something called "Sleep like Death." That, she keeps clutched in her hand.

We continue on. The employee room door handle has been shot off. I push it open. No one is inside. The door to downstairs is open as well.

We creep down the spiral staircase and into the big room of demons. They're agitated. Some are moaning, some growling, some pacing back and forth in the tiny confines of their cages.

I hear a voice, too far to make out the words. But close enough to know the tone. "Eve's here," I whisper. "And we don't have any weapons."

"Actually." Rhys stares in wonder throughout the room. He

gestures to the rows and rows of cages. "We do. Imogen, come
with me. Let's figure out how to open these up."

"All of them?" She leans close to the nearest cage. A snakelike
demon slithers to the bars, sticking out a purple tongue.

Rhys tugs her backward. "That one eats bone marrow. Children's bone marrow. It will stay in its cage. But some of these are
relatively benign breeds. I suspect they'll help us in exchange for
their freedom." Rhys beams at me, pushing his glasses into place.
"I told you my demon encyclopedia was going to come in handy
someday."

"I never doubted you."

"What are you doing here?" Sean stalks up to us. "Did you do
that damage upstairs?"

I shake my head. "No, that would be the succubus here to end
the world. Or it might have been my mom. I'm not actually sure
who broke the doors."

"We need to release some of the demons," Rhys says.

"Like hell you do!" Sean glares. "I was generous last time.
You'll not find me so kind this—"

I punch him in the face.

"Ouch," I hiss, mindful we need to keep our voices down.
"That really hurt!"

"It hurt him more." Artemis gestures to Sean, slumped
unconscious on the floor. She sounds . . . *impressed*. I try not to
let it go to my head.

Rhys reaches into Sean's slick suit jacket, pulling out a master
key. "Bingo. Come on, Imogen. I'll tell you which ones we need."
They hurry off in the opposite direction of the voices. Artemis
and I head toward Eve.

We're nearly to Sean's office when Honora slides backward along the floor, slamming into a cage and slumping brokenly to the ground.

"No!" Artemis limps to her.

"Nina, Artemis! Run!" Our mother gestures with her gun back toward where we came from. A shadowy form grabs her by the waist and throws her against the wall. The form sharpens, and suddenly Eve is standing in front of us.

"Did you not understand my generosity in leaving you alive?" she asks me, incredulous. "I did it for Leo's sake. I do *try* to be a good mother. But you're making it difficult."

Honora presses something into Artemis's palm. Artemis pops it in her mouth and stands, cracking her neck and flexing her fingers. She rips off the splint, taking a stake in either hand. Then she launches herself at Eve. She's a flurry of fists and kicks. Eve shifts and moves like smoke, but Artemis moves just as fast. Not knowing what Artemis took worries me, but right now we need every advantage.

I hurry to our mother. She presses the address book into my hands. "We'll keep her busy. Get out of here."

Artemis flies across the room, slamming into Honora, who does her best to catch her. There's a gash across Artemis's side; her shirt is already slick with blood. More is pooling out on the floor.

"Artemis!" I scream.

"Enough," Eve snaps, her voice distorted. If she was shadows before, now she is night. She is dreams and nightmares and darkness personified. My power is like a cloak on her shoulders, pulsing and seething.

Without another word, Eve punches a hole right through reality.

34

ONE OF US WOULD MEND THE WORLD, and one of us would break it.

I kneel on the floor next to my mother, watching the hole Eve made in the world using my power. It starts small, but the air blurs around it, cracking and shimmering. And behind the hole, nothing. No, not nothing. Like the magical purple flames from my nightmares, only worse. I can't make my eyes look at it. They refuse. The darkness *burns* within the hole. It's hungry.

And something is moving there. A hand reaches through, grasping Eve's. If Eve is shadows, this hand is tar. She didn't start out as a demon. Whatever Leo's father is, he definitely did.

She croons with delight. "Only a little longer, my love." She releases the hand, then grabs either side of the hole and pulls. It tears slowly in protest as our world resists giving way to hell. But it's losing the battle.

"*Why?*" I ask.

She laughs. "This is the only way in or out of the world now. Everything that comes through will have to go through me.

Nothing will happen unless I let it. I'll be the ultimate Watcher."
She tugs again, straining, and the hellmouth opens a little more.
The waiting darkness writhes in anticipation.

I expect heat, but biting cold radiates from the hole.

"It won't be a large hellmouth." Eve switches sides, trying to
get a better grip. "Nothing like Sunnydale, or even Cleveland.
But it will be *our* hellmouth. The Dublin Hellmouth. And we'll
take a tithe of power from every demon who crosses. My son and
I will never be hungry again."

"Why do you need the other Slayers, then?" I ask.

"You're the best thing I've ever had." She smiles, teeth showing white through the shadows of her face. "I'm going to drain
every Slayer, and then this world will truly know power. It will
know safety and protection. Because I *will* protect it." She pushes,
and the hole widens. "For a price."

A figure barrels into Eve, knocking her away. The hellmouth is almost big enough for a person to slip through. The air
around it crackles, brittle and freezing. The tar hand reaches
through, grasping at the air, pulling at the edges. But it can't
rip the hellmouth larger. Only Eve is strong enough to do that.
Because of me.

Eve screams in rage and frustration. I see who knocked her
to the floor, who is keeping her down.

Leo hits his mother's clawed hands away as they rake against
his chest, then pushes his own hand against her ribs, holding
her on the ground. She bucks, trying to throw him off, but I
know from experience that Leo can't be budged. A shriek echoes
through the space. The shadows shift, swirl. Leo begins to glow
like a black light.

"Nina," Honora says, panicked. She's holding her own shirt against Artemis's side. "She's bleeding too much."

I rush over to them. There's nothing I can do down here. The cut is too deep, too long. "Can you carry her?"

"I don't think so. I'm out of my pills." Tears stream down Honora's face as she looks at Artemis, now alarmingly pale.

"Allow me." A pair of toxic-yellow hands reaches down and gently lifts my sister. Doug cradles her to his sticky chest. "Come on, little Slayer. Let's run."

I look back at the hole in the world. I let this happen. And I have to fix it. "Take her out of here."

Doug hesitates, then hurries away. Honora, unable to stand, crawls after them. My mother pushes herself up. She looks at the new hellmouth, and she breaks. Her face, always so strong and remote, cracks like the barrier between our world and this hell dimension.

I've seen this terror on her once before. When she had to choose which daughter to save first. But this is worse, because she knows what I do: If this hellmouth is left open, none of us are safe.

"What do we do?" She looks to me for answers for the first time in my life.

But I don't know.

I stare numbly past her into Sean's office, so incongruously modern and clean, no indication that hell is quite literally outside its doorway. I wish Buffy were here. I wish I could talk to her again. I wish I were back on that rooftop, staring at the sea serpent, chatting with the Slayer who changed everything.

You define being the Slayer, she said. I may not be a Slayer any-more, but I still get to make the choice of how I live. So what are the choices here?

Stay, and definitely die.

Run, and probably die.

Find the third choice.

A shimmer glinting from one of the walls in Sean's office catches my eye. And just like that, I know. I know what to do.

Eve screams. I spin around to see her on top of Leo, smash-ing his head against the floor. "How dare you! Give it back!"

Another demon streaks across the floor and slams into her. Rhys and Imogen have done their job. Eve rolls, grappling with it. I dart to Leo, wanting to help him, to check his pulse. Instead, I reach into his sleeve and pull out the metal rod I know he keeps there.

I rush back to my mother's side. "Hide," I whisper. She looks at me in confusion and fear. "Trust me. Please. Go hide."

And to my relief and surprise, she trusts me. "You're strong enough for this. You always have been." She goes down a few cages and ducks behind one.

The attacking demon yelps once in pain, then lopes away as quickly as it came. Eve crawls back to Leo, shaking him. "I'll take it all back, you little monster!" Leo's head bounces, no tension in his neck. Either he's unconscious, or he's . . .

"Okay, Mom!" I shout. "I'll burn the book in here!" I hurry into Sean's office and start digging through his desk drawer as though I'm looking for something.

I feel the darkness in the doorway before I see it. Eve stands there trembling. She looks diminished by whatever Leo did to her. "Give it to me," she snarls.

I clutch the notebook to my chest. I don't have to pretend to be shaking in fear. It's not an act. I back up against the glass of the aquarium. "I won't let you hurt another Slayer."

"All that power was wasted on you," Eve spits out. "It has always been wasted. Given to foolish little girls who don't know what to do. You should thank me for taking it. And you should do it quickly, on your knees, while giving me that book, if you want to live to see another day. You're not a Slayer. You're not even a Watcher. You're nothing. There is *nothing* special about you. Now give me the book."

She steps toward me. I smile. It's enough to make her hesitate.

"I may not have taken the Watcher tests, but I was always a Watcher. A Watcher studies. A Watcher waits. And I learned from my dad that a Watcher does whatever it takes to protect their Slayer. I *am* a Watcher. All the Slayers are mine." I think of them, their fury, their fear, their joy. I think of Cosmina. I think of Buffy, sitting on that rooftop, the strongest and the loneliest of us all. Waiting. And watching. Perhaps she learned more from us than we gave her credit for. And I've learned from her too. "You might have taken my strength, but I'm still a Slayer." I pause, and Eve blinks, confused. "First rule in the Slayer handbook? When in doubt, hit something."

I drop the book, then slam the metal rod I took from Leo into the remora demon's aquarium. Eve lunges for the book. I twist around her, diving for the door. The tank glass cracks, spiderwebbing.

And then it shatters.

The remora demon spills out, writhing as it hits the air, finally freed from the confines of the water. Without that pressure around it, a remora demon will grow to fill whatever space it's in.

An office.

A cellar.

Or a tiny new hellmouth.

Eve screams, trapped beneath it. I hear a crunching noise, but before I can look for her, rubbery skin pushes against me, expanding so rapidly it shoves me out the door. If I hadn't put myself there, I would have been smashed to death against the wall. I fly into the main room, falling on all fours. The remora's one eye, a pleasant hazel, regards me impassively as it finishes filling the office and begins tumbling out through the door. At this rate, it will fill the cellar within minutes.

I'm almost positive the cellar is strong enough to contain the remora from growing out into our world. Gods, I hope so. The far end past Leo has a giant metal door. I've never been on the other side of the space, but all I can do now is hope it's blocked off too. Otherwise I traded an opening to hell for a demon that will eventually grow to take over all of Ireland.

"Rhys!" I shout. "Time's up! Get everyone out!"

"On it!" he calls back.

The remora demon's side bubbles free from the office, bumping up against the hellmouth. The demon arm desperately clutching at our world is smashed against the edge, then sliced clean off. There's a roar of pain and rage, and then the hellmouth is covered, filled. The remora demon will never stop growing in that direction.

I did it. I sealed it. Nothing can get out now. And if I don't hurry, I'm not getting out either.

I rush to Leo, grab his arms, and tug. And tug. And tug.

He doesn't move so much as an inch.

I couldn't move him when I was at full Slayer strength. And now I have nothing left. I doubt I'll be able to run out of here myself. All my years of studying, of trying to become someone who could save people, and I'm still too weak to do any good.

Leo lied to me, kept secrets from me. And he also saw me for who I really was, all these years, long before I ever did. Today he made the Watcher choice. He sacrificed himself to save the world.

I collapse next to him, emptied out. The mossy green slick of the remora demon inches closer to us. Someone takes one of Leo's arms and pulls. My mother. With a strangled cry, I push myself up again and join her, renewing my efforts. But it's no use. We can't move him.

"We have to go," she says.

"I can't leave him!"

"I'm sorry. I'm so sorry. But I will never leave you behind again." My mother picks me up. I'm too weak to fight her. She races past the edge of the remora demon. The walls around us groan under the pressure. I watch over her shoulder as Leo is cut off from view by the expanding demon.

She carries me like a child, and I watch Leo.

Left behind.

I could still fight her, I know. I could crawl back so that Leo won't be crushed alone. But it won't save him, and it will kill me.

Being chosen is easy.

Making choices will break your heart.

35

MY MOTHER SLAMS THE METAL DOOR TO the cellar and locks it. It holds. She stumbles on the stairs, dropping me. I crawl up them and hurry numbly through the employee break room, past the rows of coffee shaking with the tremors, and into the parking lot. The ground rumbles but doesn't cave in. I pray my decision was right, that the cellar space is enough to contain the remora. That it will grow only to that space, and then expand forever into the Dublin Hellmouth, not into Dublin itself.

The ground stops shaking. Silence settles over the parking lot. After a moment, the ragged group of survivors—me included—lets out a huge sigh.

I did it. I didn't let Artemis die, and I didn't let Eve win. I found another way, even without Slayer powers.

I stumble over to Honora. She's holding Artemis, tenderly stroking her hair. The skinless demon has pulled off its own arm skin like a sleeve and is carefully pressing it against Artemis's side. Already it's sealing off the gash, stopping the bleeding. I take Artemis's wrist. Her pulse is faint, but it's there. My mother crouches next to them, tending to Honora, who has ignored her own wounds.

"Thank you," I whisper to Honora. Then I turn to the skin- less demon. "And thank you." I think it smiles.

I survey the parking lot. Sean is locked in his car, talking angrily on his cell phone, dried blood crusted around his nose. He's eyeing the parking lot warily, a gun in his free hand. But he isn't moving to attack any of us. Not an immediate priority for me, then.

Doug is helping Rhys calm down two extremely short, extremely purple demons. When they won't stop screaming, Doug puts his hands over their mouths. They sit, grinning. There are several other demons, but a few are already slinking away.

Imogen is on the hood of our car, a faraway look on her face. She glances down at me and her eyes narrow. "I thought you were going to die." Then she smiles. It looks almost deranged. I proba- bly look the same way.

The handful of demons that haven't left mill about, free from cages but still trapped on an earth that has no place for them.

"What now?" Rhys once again turns to me for answers.

I look at my fellow Watchers. We're as lost as these demons. As directionless. I remember Cosmina. Leo. It hurts, so much. If we had given them a place, if we had let them be themselves without fear, without judgment, maybe they'd both still be here with us. Maybe Cosmina would have trusted us. Maybe Leo would have been able to tell us the truth before it was too late. I can't really blame him for hiding his demonic heritage in the middle of a group dedicated to destroying his kind.

But Leo *was* good. He tried to help me. And in the end, he saved us all by giving me time to defeat Eve.

I look at Doug—who only wants to make people happy, and also get backstage passes to Coldplay. I look at the poor skinless demon. Even Honora. All without a place to be. Imogen, Rhys, Artemis. None of us asked to be here. None of us chose to be Watchers. Not my mom, whose life was stolen from the moment she was born. Not Artemis, who always should have been more.

And none of these creatures chose to be here. I don't doubt they all would have preferred to be somewhere else. Somewhere safe. Somewhere they weren't *other*, weren't hunted, weren't used.

And suddenly, I know a place they can go.

I pull the book—the real book, not the fake notebook I brought with me as a decoy—out of my shirt. It's filled with other demons like Doug. It's filled with Slayers, out there all alone. Targets because of a power they never asked for. I hold the book close to my heart, and I remember what we've lost. I remember my vow to be the Watcher for every Slayer.

"Now," I say, smiling at Rhys. "Now we change what it means to be Watchers. We protect the vulnerable. Whoever they are." I take off my coat and put it over the skinless demon's shoulders. It snuggles in, and this time I'm certain it's smiling.

"I will not have demons infesting my castle!" Wanda Wyndam-Pryce shrieks, slamming her fist down on the table. We're in the Council room. It used to intimidate and awe me. Now all I see is an empty, useless room with a too-big table and only one person sitting there. Honestly, I'm a little embarrassed for her.

"This is an outrage! You will remove them immediately."

I smile. "I'm sorry. You don't have the authority to demand that."

"I'm on the Council!"

"You've been voted out." Rhys takes off his glasses and polishes them.

Wanda glares down her long nose at him. "By whom?"

"By the next generation of Watchers." Jade pops her gum. She puts her feet up on the table, crossing them at the ankles. "We're in charge now."

Ruth Zabuto, knitting in the corner, giggles. "This should be fun." Her wrinkled face is mischievously gleeful. I told her she could keep her library. She didn't much care what we did after that.

I escort a huffing and indignant Wanda to the gate. We've already packed one of the cars with all her things. She snatches the keys from me, pausing only to give a withering glare to the skinless demon playing a game of tag with two of the Littles. Rhys joins Cillian, who's attaching a rope swing in the deep shade of an oak tree. The tiny purple demons, whose names I don't have the right mandibles to pronounce, critique their every choice.

"Disgusting," Wanda spits. Then she climbs in the car and takes generations of Watcher tradition with her.

"Good riddance." Jade wanders off to join Doug in setting up a game of croquet. She's taken to him nicely. I suspect it's because he's quite liberal with doling out his happiness boosts.

Back in the great hall entry, Imogen is lying on the floor, coloring next to little George. She looks up at me and smiles, her sleeves pushed up, revealing pen doodles all along her forearms. She was amazing during our time of need. We won't neglect her like the Council did. We all know that our parents don't determine who we are.

I bend down to ruffle George's hair, then keep going to the residence wing. My mom is confined to bed for a while yet. Eve broke three of her ribs, puncturing a lung. And she still managed to carry me out to safety.

She tries to sit up when I come into her room.

"Hey, relax." I pull up a chair and sit next to her bed.

"How did Wanda take it?"

"About as well as you'd expect. I'm glad she doesn't have magic anymore. I think we'd all be cursed if she did."

A grin works at the corner of her lips. "I wish I could have seen it." A puff of air escapes her, and then she closes her eyes. Her eyelids are thin, almost translucent. They make her look fragile. "You should take Doug with you when you contact more Slayers or demons. He's a good go-between. If things get tense . . ."

"He happies them right up." I take out the book and stare at the entries. Tonight I'll open it to the Slayer section. I can't reach them in my dreams anymore, but I can find them in person. And even though I'm not strong, I have something to offer them. To offer the world. The world I'm no longer capable of breaking. So that's a relief, at least. We're free from all the history of the Watchers, including the dumb prophecy. If I had to lose my Slayer powers in order for the apocalypse to be averted, it's an acceptable sacrifice. After all, I didn't have to die. I got off way easier than Buffy.

Weirdly, I miss her. I wish I *could* have gotten her number in that dream.

"This is so much more than I was planning to do," my mother says. "Are you sure you're up for it?"

"Actually, yeah, I am. It's important. It's more than important: It's *right*. We're going to take anyone who needs a place to live, free from fear. Slayers. Demons. Those that don't fit anywhere else. No requirements or expectations, except that everyone protects each other. We're calling it Sanctuary." I pause, blushing. "Is that too pretentious?"

My mother smiles. "I think it's perfect. And I'm proud of you."

A while ago, I would have given anything to hear her say that. But after everything I've been through, I find I don't need to hear it anymore.

It's still nice, though.

Rhys knocks on the door. "You better come out here," he says. I rush outside, worried that something has gone wrong. Instead, I find Artemis, her side healing up nicely, holding a motorcycle helmet. Honora, clad once again in her gray leather, is waiting with a motorcycle idling.

"Where are you going?" I say, running up to them. I'm not as fast as I was. I never will be again. I wish I didn't have the comparison, but someday I'll get used to being un-Slayer me again.

Artemis sets down the helmet and finger combs my hair back from my face, then pulls a band off her wrist and ties it back in a ponytail. "There." She steps back to admire her work. "Much better."

She's not going for a joyride with Honora. The plea bursts from me. "I want you to stay."

Artemis looks as lost as I used to feel. "I wanted to be a

Watcher so badly. But I wasn't. And if we're being honest, they weren't Watchers either. Not really. I don't think any of us have been for a long time. I'm tired of watching, of waiting. Of biding our time until the world is about to end again and we have to figure out how to stop it. And I'm not going to sit here while you try to make some demon utopia. We know what goes bump in the night. We know what darkness is out there." She shrugs, zipping up her jacket. "I'm going to figure out what I can do about it."

"Artemis, I get it. I want . . ." With no words left, I throw my arms around her. I know I could make her stay if I really wanted to. But while I want her to stay, I don't need her to stay. And what she wants—what she needs—has to come first.

She hugs me back. "Thank you for saving me. But it was the wrong choice. You should have kept your power. You got it for a reason." She laughs, but it's brittle, empty. "We still don't know what reason that was. And we never will. But I *didn't* get it for a reason. And I want to know why." She steps away from me. "Take care of yourself, Nina."

"We could use your help here. Honora's, too, even."

Artemis smiles at my blatant lie. "You don't need my help. Not anymore. I don't think you ever did. I just needed someone to need me." She throws her arms around me again and squeezes me in a hug so tight I can't breathe. I don't want it to end.

"I love you," she whispers.

"Remember," I whisper back, "no matter where you go, you'll always have a home here."

She releases me and climbs onto the motorcycle, putting her arms around Honora's waist. Honora lifts her hand up like she's going to wave, but as soon as Artemis buries her head in Honora's shoulder, Honora lifts her middle finger to me instead. Then she guns the motorcycle.

I stand at the edge of the grounds, watching them get smaller. And I stay there watching long after they've disappeared and twilight has fallen. I will never not miss Artemis. I hate that she chose Honora. But I'd hate myself more if I made her stay when I've held her back for all these years. She needs to figure out who she is without having to take care of me. Without having to live a calling she never asked for. Without having to compensate for the fact that our mother saved her first.

It's okay. It will be okay. I turn around to face my own new life.

I was born to be a Watcher. I was Chosen to be a Slayer. Now I'm neither.

But that doesn't mean I can't be a protector.

I crack my knuckles. It's time to get to work.

Her work had almost been done for her. Artemis and Athena came so close to dying, only to escape, yet again.

If you wanted something done right, you did it yourself.

Facing the near death of Artemis and the de-Slayering of Athena had, however, left her with questions. There was a clarity that came with thinking it was finally finished. Thinking that Athena would die in the cellar and the prophecy would never be able to come true. Instead of relief, the hunter had felt . . . disappointment.

After all these years, all her sacrifice, she discovered she was no longer interested in preventing the prophecy from coming true. It had been her mother's calling, forced on her. She didn't choose it. If the rest of them could shrug off the weight of Watcher tradition, she could shrug off the weight of prophecy prevention.

What had this sucky world ever done for her, anyway? Everyone who had tasked her with guarding the prophecy, with hunting the girls, was dead. That's what they got. That was their reward.

Not for her anymore. She wasn't giving up, though. She had always needed a cause. She was lying in wait for a different outcome now. They thought the prophecy had come and passed. That it was that easy. A pokey, aborted hellmouth wasn't enough to get Arcturius's attention all those centuries ago. Even if it had been opened all the way, it wasn't an apocalyptic event. Just another demonic nuisance.

No, the prophecy still loomed. And she was going to do everything in her power to make certain that it came true. If one of the twins was going to break the world apart, she would be at her side.

If only she could be certain which girl, exactly, was the apocalypse and which was the protector. Twins! Always so tricky to tell apart.

It didn't matter either way. She would help the destroyer or destroy the protector. Both options led to the same outcome: ending the world that had failed them all so miserably. It was time. Arcturius had seen it—it was the last thing he'd seen—and who was she to argue?

"Boom," she whispered, scoring the word onto her arm.

"Imogen, I finished my drawing!" little George said.

"Oh, it's brilliant! Well done. Should we go give it to Nina now?"

George waited for her to put her cardigan on, then took her hand, and they walked down the hall together.

EPILOGUE

I CAN'T MOVE.

But it's not the terrifying, can't-breathe-can't-move-can't-scream kind. It's the warm, hazy, everything-relaxed-and-perfectly-comfortable kind. I hang in the limbo between sleeping and waking, knowing soon my alarm will ring. Hoping this space will last a little longer.

And then I realize I'm not alone.

Leo kneels down so he's in my line of sight. Even though the room is dark and his eyes are darker, I see them with perfect clarity. They really do have a hint of color in them. Violet.

Not being able to move also means not being able to talk. I try dragging my tongue across my mouth, try forcing my vocal cords to respond.

"Shh. Don't wake up." He smiles, his expression painfully tender. Those dimples that had held all my romantic hopes and had haunted my dreams were there, perfect, alive. "I know you tried to save me. That was more than I deserved. And I can never make it up to you, can never apologize enough for what she did to you. What I helped her do. Someday, maybe, I can explain. But no explanation excuses it. Nothing was worth hurting you." Then his smile brightens, with a hint of mischief. "In the meantime, I have a present that I hope makes up for some of it and that will help make sure nothing can hurt you ever again."

He leans forward, closing the distance between us. Darkness cloaks him, transforming him. But his darkness is less nightmare and more the velvet secret of night. A caress of cool air and a prickling of goose bumps. His lips touch mine, and finally I can move. I press mine against his, so happy, so confused.

And then everything is lit in brilliant white as I'm flooded with something that is both familiar and oddly new. If the feeling of it as it left my body was brightest sunshine, this feels more like . . . lightning. Power and brilliance with a sense of chaotic destruction that hadn't been there before. But I can't stop, can't ask him what it is. As the light becomes so bright I know I'll wake up, Leo brushes my cheek with one more kiss. "Good-bye, Athena Jamison-Smythe. The last Slayer."

I wake up with the taste of dream Leo still on my lips. Gasping, I reach out for my alarm clock.

It crumples in my hand.

Leo's words ring in my mind. *The last Slayer.*

Again.

ACKNOWLEDGMENTS

When I was a teenager, a blond cheerleader taught me that our struggles navigating friendships and love deserve just as much attention as our battles with monsters. It changed my life and shaped me as a storyteller. So, to *Buffy the Vampire Slayer*—the creators of the show, the writers, the actors, and everyone who made the series that made me who I am as a writer—thank you. You changed the world. A lot.

On the bookish end of things, special thanks to Liesa Abrams at Simon Pulse. Was it fate that when we met I was wearing my Sunnydale High T-shirt? Or just really good odds, because of course I was. Thank you for bringing this project to me and for seeing our girl Nina through many drafts, crafting and shaping her into what she needed to be. You're my very own Watcher. And to my Scoobies, Sarah McCabe and Jessica Smith—your feedback and guidance were invaluable. I just wish we could include the margin GIF reactions in the final version of the book.

To my agent, Michelle Wolfson, thank you for always fighting at my side and for being our test reader. But now that you've read it without any bias, it's time to watch the series. I'll wait.

My family is very patient when I channel my inner angst with regularity. From the support of my husband, the constant status checks of my two older children, and the never-not-adorable question of "Are you watching *Buffy the Bampire Slayer?*" from my four-year-old, nothing I do would have heart or joy without them in my life.

Stephanie Perkins freaked out with me to an appropriate level and then helped me get down to work carving out my own small corner of the Buffyverse. And nothing I write is accomplished without the support of Natalie Whipple. Thank you both, as always, for your friendship. I'd face down any apocalypse with you two by my side. (And let's be honest, being my critique partners probably feels a bit apocalypsey most of the time.)

To the team at Simon Pulse who helped at every stage— Stephanie Evans, copyedits warrior; Talexi, art wizard; Sarah Creech, cover mastermind; along with Katherine Devendorf, Caitlin Sweeny, Nicole Russo, Mara Anastas, and Chriscynethia Floyd—I'm so grateful to fight the forces of darkness (and formatting and marketing, etc.) with all of you.

To every other writer who died when they found out there was going to be a Buffy spin-off series and I had already claimed it: I'm genuinely sorry. I'm not even being sarcastic. The Buffy fandom is made up of the greatest people on earth, and I love sharing that love with all of you.

And finally, thank you to everyone who has freaked out with me online and off, who has squeed with me over this, who has talked episodes and ships, who has pestered me for details I wasn't allowed to give. The Buffyverse is so lucky to have you, and so am I.

NINA'S STORY
CONTINUES IN . . .

The world is quiet now.

It used to be so loud. So much chatter, beating, drumming, buzzing buzzing buzzing. The buzzing of it all. It used to keep him awake at night, inescapable, like mites crawling through his veins. Sometimes he would scratch at his arms until they bled, but even the bleeding never dampened the buzzing.

Until it stopped. All the lines to and from the world, all the hungry beings clawing and sucking and pawing at it, everything cut off.

But not him. He is still here. And with everything quiet, he can finally focus. He's powerless, which is unfortunate but temporary. Everything here is temporary. He will not be.

He strokes his arms, smooth and unscarred, so deceptively human-looking. But he is no human. And this world, this quiet world, this cut-off and free-floating world, this magic-less and empty world, this unprotected and uncontested world, this waiting world—

He will be its god, and everyone will buzz with him beneath their veins, they will breathe and bleed and live and die for him, and it will be good.

Amen.

1

THE DEMON APPEARS OUT OF NOWHERE.
Claws and fangs fill my sight, and every instinct screams *kill*.
My blood sings with it, my fists clench, my vision narrows. The
vulnerable points on the demon's body practically flash like
neon signs.

"Foul!" Rhys shouts. "No teleportation, Tsip! You know
that." Even while playing, Rhys can't help but be a Watcher,
shouting out both advice and corrections. He's not wearing his
glasses, which makes his face look vague and undefined. Cillian
passes him, mussing Rhy's carefully parted hair into wild curls
and laughing at Rhys's frustration.

I take a deep breath, trying to clear my head of the impulse
to kill this demon I invited into our home and swore to protect.
"It's just soccer," I whisper. "It doesn't matter. I don't even like
soccer."

"Football, bloody American," Cillian sings, neatly stealing
the ball from me. His shorts are far shorter than the January
afternoon should permit, but he seems impervious to cold.

Unlike those of us who are translucently pale at this point in winter, his skin is rich and lovely. He passes to Tsip. Tsip is a vaguely opalescent pink, shimmering in the sunlight. She paints her claws fun colors when we do manicure nights, and I try desperately not to miss Artemis.

I stay rooted to the ground where I'm standing. Tsip caught me off guard, but that shouldn't matter. I like her. And the fact that I went from trying to score a goal to plotting a dozen ways to kill my opponent in a single heartbeat is frankly terrifying. I can't get my heart under control, can't shake the adrenaline screaming through my veins.

"Gotta take over for the Littles. I'm out." I wave and jog from the field. No one pays me much attention. Jade is lying on the ground in front of the goal, the worst goalkeeper ever. Rhys and Cillian are bodychecking each other in increasingly flirty ways. Tsip keeps shimmering and then resolidifying as she remembers the no-teleportation rule. They're all happy to keep going without me, unaware of my internal freak-out.

I've deliberately kept them unaware. Things here are going so well. I'm in charge. I can't be the problem. So none of them know how I can't sleep at night, how my anger is hair-trigger fast, how when I do manage to sleep, my dreams are . . .

Well. Bad.

They don't need to know and I don't let them. Except for Doug, his bright yellow skin almost nineties Day-Glo levels in the thin winter sun. Annoying emotion-sniffing demon. He watches me from our goal, his nostrils flared. I can't lie to him the way I can to everyone else. I shake my head preemptively. I don't want to talk about it. Not with him. Not with anyone. There's only one person I want to talk to about it, but Leo Silvera's not exactly available.

I do a quick sweep of the perimeter of the castle. *Leo loved me.* Check the woods. *Leo betrayed me.* Check the locks on the outbuildings. *Leo saved me.* Pause and just listen and look, feeling for anything pushing against my instincts. *I let Leo die.*

I keep walking. Leo loved me, betrayed us, saved us, and then died, and I can't be sad without being mad or mad without feeling guilty or guilty without feeling exhausted.

Past the meadow, the tiny purple demons are taking turns pushing each other on the tree swing. That, or they're trying to push each other off. It's hard to tell with them. With nothing else needing my attention outside, I end up at the front stairs to the castle.

"Hey, Jessi." I wave halfheartedly to our resident vengeance demon. She's leading the Littles through an elaborate game of hopscotch. George Smythe, bundled up and barely able to see under a floppy knit hat, is shouting each letter as he lands on it. "*G!*"

"What?" Jessi snaps at me.

"*E!*"

"I can take over for you." I find the Littles soothing. They might be three incredibly hyper children constantly needing snacks, entertainment, and education, but at least none of them ever randomly triggers a *kill* reflex in me.

"*A!*"

"No," Jessi says, her voice as sweet as summer fruit. "*G-E-* what-comes-next . . .*"

"*O!*" George course corrects, wobbling on one short leg before jumping to the required *O*.

"Good! Oh, you're so clever. Priya, how are your letters coming?" Priya, a tiny moppet with shiny black hair, is crouched over her own chalk work, which looks more like Klingon than any alphabet I'm familiar with. "Very good, darling! You're really working hard. Hold the chalk with one hand, like we talked about. Thea, love, fingers out of noses, please—that's a dear."

And to think, we once considered these children the entire future of the Watchers. I watch as Thea spins until she falls flat on her bottom. Actually, the future of the Watchers is pretty accurately captured here. I pat Jessi on the arm. "So, you can take the afternoon off."

Everything sweet in Jessi's voice turns to ice. "I said no. I don't trust you with these three precious wonders. We have an entire day's curriculum to get through, and we haven't even done story time yet or finished our art projects. Are you going to do any of that with them?"

"I—I could?"

"You were going to turn on a cartoon and read while their fertile minds were filled with weeds."

Jessi doesn't have her powers anymore, but I'm pretty certain if she did, I would have been vengeance-demoned right into something oozing and seeping. She's already turned away from me and back to her three charges. Her whole face is full of gentle warmth and absolute love.

"R!" George declares, hopping emphatically down on it. Jessi claps like he's cured the common cold.

Thoroughly dismissed, I skulk up the stairs and into the castle. Jessi could at least pretend to be nice. She's got a lot of enemies out there—vengeance is a nasty cycle—and without her powers she's vulnerable. We took her in despite her obvious hatred for everyone over the age of ten. There was some debate, given her history, but my mom argued in her favor. It's a little easier to forgive a vengeance demon who made it her immortal life's work to avenge children than a vengeance demon who specialized in, say, fantasy league sports rivalries.

But Jessi's dismissal leaves me with nothing to do. I used to have my medical center and my studies, all my little Watcher duties. Even with so few of us, the castle ran as near to Watcher traditions as we could manage. Which in retrospect was absurd, since we didn't have a Slayer and weren't actually doing anything Watchers should.

But now everything has changed. We lost Watchers—Wanda Wyndam-Pryce, sulking off into the sunset, good riddance. Bradford Smythe, murdered. Eve Silvera, secretly a succubus demon and murderer, smushed thanks to my actions. Artemis, off to find herself with her awful girlfriend, the thought of whom makes my jaw ache as I grind my teeth. And Leo, who didn't warn us what his mother was (and what he was) but fought her to give us enough time to stop her from opening a new hellmouth.

And now we have a Slayer, again some more, thanks to Leo somehow returning the powers his mother stole from me. I don't know how he did it, and it hurts too much to think about, like everything else. I spend so much of my days trying not to think, and it's harder than it should be. I used to believe that all Slayers did was act without thinking. I was wrong, but I wish it were true. There's so little acting and so much thinking these days.

It's good. It's all good. It's good, I remind myself, over and over like a chant. Sanctuary, what we decided to turn our castle into, is just starting out, but it's exactly what we dreamed it could be. We've taken in demons who had nowhere else to go. We're keeping them safe, and ourselves safe, and we'll keep looking for those who could benefit from the generations of knowledge and abilities we have. We're protecting, not attacking or destroying.

Between our new demonic additions and existing Watchers, everyone has tasks and times to do them. It's more work than anyone anticipated, keeping everyone taken care of and fed, making sure the castle runs like it should. But so far everyone is happy. Everyone is safe.

I sink down against the wall, feeling the cold of the stone radiating outward. The unpellis demon, all four gentle eyes soft and brown and hopeful, snuggles up to my side like a dog. It's more animal than human in nature, nonverbal, and still recovering from its frequent de-skinning treatment in Sean's demon-drug manufacturing scheme. I saved Pelly from that cellar.

I didn't save everyone, though.

I wrap my arms around Pelly and close my eyes. Everything is exactly what we dreamed it could be. Except I feel Leo's loss everywhere, and I miss my twin, Artemis, with a constant, physical ache.

And, worst of all, with enough time after Tsip surprised me to calm down and remind my body there's no danger . . .

I still feel like killing something.

2

I'M ON THE FLOOR WITH PELLY WHEN Imogen finds me. With Artemis gone and Jessi taking over the care of the Littles, Imogen has shifted to the kitchen. Food quality in the castle has improved tenfold. It feels like everyone has settled into roles that truly suit them. Except me. I don't know what I want.

"You look like you could use a cookie," she says, hands on her hips. She's wearing cheerful pink lipstick and has her hair in two low pigtails. She's been in a really good mood ever since we stopped the apocalypse prophecy when I blocked Eve Silvera's new hellmouth. Preventing an apocalypse cost me my Slayer powers (briefly) and Leo Silvera (permanently). In my darkest moments, when I wake up from a nightmare alone in my room without even my sister to comfort me, I'm not sure it was a good trade. Would a new hellmouth have been that big of a deal? We've dealt with them since the beginning of time. Surely we could have handled a new one.

But I know that's selfish. Arcturius the Farsighted had a

whole prophecy devoted to Artemis and me, all about breaking and healing the world. I made the right call. It just cost so much. It took away his warm eyes and long-fingered hands and swift, sure movements. His soft lips. The most dazzlingly elusive smile. And the one person who ever really saw me.

The two people, actually. Leo died, and Artemis left. And I'm here on the floor snuggling a demon. I wish Arcturius had seen this, too. They never talk about how hard the part *after* the hard part is.

I look up at Imogen. "I could use a cookie, yeah. Actually, cookies. Plural."

"Cookies should never be singular." Imogen holds out a hand to help me stand. My phone rings. The caller ID is the number we designated for demon scouting trips. Today, and most days, my mother is on the other end of the line.

When we first started meeting with demons for potential acceptance into Sanctuary, I was always with her. But a month ago, there was an . . . incident. I hadn't slept at all that night, and I was already on edge, so when I turned around and saw the dead black eyes of a shark staring at me, I punched first and asked questions after. Turns out it was a demon with a shark head try-ing to escape some bad debts. My mother assured me he wasn't a good fit for Sanctuary anyway, but the fact that I attacked him didn't exactly do our reputation any favors. Word of mouth (or whatever the demon species equivalent of a mouth is) matters in finding demons who need our help. So I basically blew it.

I still feel bad about it. I like sharks! On television. Under-water. Where I am not. I can't even think about the incident without feeling roiling guilt. When did I become a punch-first-ask-questions-later Slayer? And it made me a liability instead of an asset. My mother tried to make it sound like she needed me at the castle for scheduling reasons, but we both know it was to protect me. Or to protect the demons. I don't know which is worse.

Working together is already awkward enough. She's trying to be my mom again, but she doesn't really know how to, so it comes across like those aggressively friendly employees at grocery stores who constantly ask how you are and if you need help and if you're finding everything okay, and all you can do is smile and answer back in the same bright voice when really you *know* where the cereal is, thank you very much. And there's the added pressure of feeling like I have to reward all her efforts, even when I don't want to. I appreciate it, I really do, but I wish I had Artemis to share the burden of Mom Version Four, or at least to complain to. She'd get it. No one else does.

I answer the call. "Mom? Everything okay?"

There's a popping noise in the background that sounds distinctly like a gun. I keep the phone to my ear and sprint outside.

"Hello, Nina. I didn't want to interrupt your work today, but we've been pinned down and I didn't bring the firepower necessary to get out." By her tone, she might as well be calling to ask if we need more milk. My mother is baffling and also slightly terrifying.

"Is it Sean?" I don't mean to sound so excited, but it's almost a relief. I've been waiting for demon drug dealer Sean to make a play for Doug again. Doug's happy-time skin secretions were

Sean's biggest moneymaker. And with ex-Watcher and worst person ever Honora among his former and possibly current allies, Sean knows more than enough about our operations to be very dangerous to us. Plus, I sort of destroyed his entire operation by unleashing a remora demon to crush everything. I can't imagine he thinks fondly of any of us.

Today's demon outing was a first meeting with a family of werewolves. Werewolves are low-risk, so my mother went alone. Normally, she takes Tsip, Jade, or Rhys. But we should have known better. Nothing in our world is ever truly low-risk. I wave frantically to Rhys, Cillian, and Doug. Jade doesn't even look up. She's probably blissed out on Doug right now. Useless. My sober friends jog up to me as I open the garage.

"No," my mother says. "This isn't Sean's MO. It appears to be some aggressive freelancers. I believe there are two in sniper positions. I'm using my ammunition sparingly to avoid running out, but it won't be much longer before they feel confident launching a full attack."

"We're on our way! When you run out of ammunition, hide. Don't engage. And don't risk yourself, okay?" It sounds horrible to say, but I don't want my mother to die protecting strangers. Not when I've just started to get her back after years of being strangers to each other. I want her to annoy me for decades to come.

"Thank you. See you soon. And, Nina?" Her voice gets softer, more tentative. For the first time, she sounds a little worried. "Be careful. You're not bulletproof."

The silence hangs between us. I struggle to fill it, to close that gap. Because this mom who is open about caring about me?

It's new, and, like being a Slayer, or my anger or my guilt or my grief, I still don't know how to react. So instead of telling her to be careful too, I default to something less emotionally fraught. As soon as I start joking, I know it's the wrong choice, but it just keeps going, and I can't stop it.

"Yeah, we should totally take that up with our ancient ancestors who created the Slayer line. Bulletproof would have been useful to add alongside prophetic dreams, superstrength, and killer instincts. Though I guess bullets would have been an unfamiliar concept on account of this all happened thousands of years ago."

"Oh, for goodness' sake, be *careful*, Nina."

I take a deep breath. I wanted my mother to be mine for so long. Now I have to be strong enough to let her be, to trust that this won't go away. "I will be. Promise. You too." I hang up. Cillian, Rhys, and Doug are all waiting for instructions. Tsip has wandered over too.

"Can you teleport me?" I ask her.

"Yes!" The fangs jutting from her lower jaw are showcased in an enthusiastic smile. "But I can only teleport short distances. And you have to be able to reconstitute yourself after being disintegrated on a molecular level while shifting through the void beyond reality. It hurts quite a bit, but you get used to it."

"I'll drive then, yeah?" Cillian grabs the keys and starts the car.

Doug looks scared but determined. "Sean?" The fact that he's willing to come and face the man who held him captive for years speaks volumes about him.

I put my hand on his arm and shake my head. "Mercenaries.

With guns. I don't think you're going to be any use. Wake Jade up and make sure you're all on alert while I'm gone, okay?"

Doug nods, holding a hand up in farewell. Tsip waves energetically as we pull away.

"The void beyond reality?" Cillian navigates the forest dirt road far faster than is safe. "Demons. Total nutters, the lot of them."

"I like Doug." Rhys checks his crossbow.

I bounce impatiently in the back. "Everyone likes Doug. He's biologically impossible to dislike." We always pick a destination with several roads in and out so we can't be traced, so the warehouse is thirty minutes away. Thirty minutes is thirty minutes too far, though.

"What are we going into here?" Cillian drives at double the speed limit. I'm grateful, and I wish he would go even faster. But we don't have our get-out-of-tickets-free Doug in the car with us, so we're risking a police encounter as it is.

"Mercenaries. Two snipers. They have my mom pinned down in the warehouse."

"Plan?"

"The plan is Cillian stops before we get there and stays in the car."

"Hey now, I can—"

I cut him off. "I can only focus on saving so many people at a time. I can't worry about you, too." It comes out harsher than I intend it, but it's true. Cillian is one of my favorite people in the world, and he almost died last fall because of it. His dark brown eyes meet mine in the rearview mirror. He nods.

Rhys turns back toward me. He forgot his glasses. His crossbow is going to be pretty useless if he can't see to use it. I want to make him stay in the car with Cillian. But he's a Watcher. This is his job too.

No. It's only my job. I'm the Slayer. "Rhys, you'll take the alleys to cut around to the back of the warehouse. Get a high vantage point and make certain there aren't any more waiting there for an ambush. I'll find the snipers and take them out."

I'm confident I can get it done before Rhys ever gets to his position. I can keep them all safe. I can keep everyone safe.

The image of Leo, unconscious on the floor, disappearing behind the ever-expanding remora demon to meet the same crushed-to-death fate as his mother flashes in my mind, contradicting me with brutal accuracy.

I can, though. I have to. I'm never losing anyone again.

Cillian slows down on the outskirts of the old fishing district where the warehouse is. I open my door and jump, hitting the ground running.

The sound of a bullet pinging off metal is all the direction I need. I don't worry about cover. I run as fast as I can, and, gods, it's fast. My red-gold hair streams behind me, my emerald-green trench coat flapping in the wind like a cape. Another shot rings out. There's a fire-escape ladder fifteen feet up on the side of a brick building. I leap, catch the bottom rung, and climb up, feeling a flash of surprise that I made that jump. I'm pretty sure I couldn't have made it when I first became a Slayer. And I haven't exactly been training—going to the castle's gym brings too many painful memories of Leo. But there's no time to wonder at my skills.

The roof is flat, rusted corrugated metal. At the far end of it, a figure is crouched, holding a rifle. A mercenary. Firing a rifle at my mother and a *family*.

"Hey!" I shout. Anger burns in me with the same devouring intensity as the black-purple flames that nearly killed me as a child. I can feel them inside, eating away everything else, purifying me, leaving only rage. The mercenary stands and swings the rifle in my direction in the same amount of time it takes me to sprint across the roof and slam into him.

I watch in slow motion as he flies backward into thin air.

RIVETED

BY *simon* teen ♥

BELIEVE IN YOUR SHELF

Visit RivetedLit.com & connect with us on social to:

DISCOVER NEW YA READS

READ BOOKS FOR FREE

DISCUSS YOUR FAVORITES

SHARE YOUR IDEAS

ENTER SWEEPSTAKES FOR THE CHANCE TO WIN BOOKS

Follow @SimonTeen on

to stay up to date with all things Riveted!

HIGH SCHOOL IS HELL

Buffy
THE VAMPIRE SLAYER ™

AN ALL-NEW SERIES FROM
WRITER
**JORDIE
BELLAIRE**
(REDLANDS)
AND
ARTIST
**DAN
MORA**
*(SABAN'S GO GO
POWER RANGERS)*

WITH STORY CONSULTANT
JOSS
WHEDON

IN STORES
JANUARY
ISBN: 9781684153572
WWW.**BOOM-STUDIOS.CC**

BOOM!
STUDIOS
DISCOVER YOURS

BUFFY THE VAMPIRE SLAYER ™ & © 2019 Twentieth Century Fox Film Corporation. All rights reserved.